BY MARIE RUTKOSKI

THE KRONOS CHRONICLES

The Cabinet of Wonders

The Celestial Globe

The Jewel of the Kalderash

The Shadow Society

THE WINNER'S TRILOGY

The Winner's Curse

The Winner's Crime

The Winner's Kiss

THE WINNER'S KISS

THE WINNER'S TRILOGY: BOOK THREE

A NOVEL BY

MARIE RUTKOSKI

FARRAR STRAUS GIROUX   NEW YORK

SQUARE
FISH

An imprint of Macmillan Publishing Group, LLC
175 Fifth Avenue
New York, NY 10010
fiercereads.com

Square Fish and the Square Fish logo are trademarks of Macmillan and are
used by Farrar Straus Giroux under license from Macmillan.

Our books may be purchased in bulk for promotional, educational, or business use.
Please contact your local bookseller or the Macmillan Corporate and Premium
Sales Department at (800) 221-7945 ext. 5442 or by e-mail at
MacmillanSpecialMarkets@macmillan.com.

Library of Congress Control Number: 2015037277

ISBN 978-1-250-10443-4 (paperback)   ISBN 978-0-374-38474-6 (ebook)

Originally published in the United States by Farrar Straus Giroux
First Square Fish Edition: 2017
Book designed by Elizabeth H. Clark
Square Fish logo designed by Filomena Tuosto

1 3 5 7 9 10 8 6 4 2

AR: 4.7 / LEXILE: HL590L

For Sarah Mesle

THE FROZEN WASTES

TUNDRA
(TATH)

SULFUR MINES

WORK CAMP

VALORIA

CAPITAL
(VAL)

CITY
(LAHIRE)

HERRAN

THE EMPTY
ISLANDS

ITHRYA
ISLAND

SOUTHERN ISLES
(CAYN SARATU)

THE WINNER'S KISS

HE TOLD HIMSELF A STORY.

Not at first.

At first, there wasn't time for thoughts that came in the shape of words. His head was blessedly empty of stories then. War was coming. It was upon him. Arin had been born in the year of the god of death, and he was finally glad of it. He surrendered himself to his god, who smiled and came close. *Stories will get you killed,* he murmured in Arin's ear. *Now, you just listen. Listen to me.*

Arin did.

His ship had sped across the sea from the capital. Now it nosed in among the fleet of eastern ships docked in his city's bay, nimble sloops of war, flying their queen's colors of blue and green. The sloops were Arin's, at least for now. The Dacran queen's gift to her new allies. The ships were not as many as Arin would have liked. Not as heavy with cannon as he would have liked.

But:

Listen.

Arin told his ship's captain to sidle up along the largest of the Dacran sloops. After giving his captain orders to dock and find Arin's cousin in the city, Arin boarded the sloop. He approached the commander of the eastern fleet: Xash, a lean man with an unusually high-bridged nose and brown skin gleaming in the late spring sun.

Arin looked into Xash's eyes—black, always narrowed, and lined with the yellow paint that indicated his status as naval commander. It was as if Xash already knew what Arin would say. The easterner smiled slightly.

"They're coming," Arin said.

He explained how the Valorian emperor had arranged for the water supply to Herran's city to be slowly poisoned. The emperor must have sent someone months ago into the mountains near the aqueduct's source. Even from the deck of Xash's ship, Arin could see the arched trail of the Valorian-built aqueduct. It was faint in the distance, snaking down from the mountains, carrying something that had weakened the Herrani, making them sleep and shake.

"I was seen in the capital," Arin told Xash. "A Valorian ship chased mine almost to the Empty Islands. We must assume that the emperor knows that I know."

"What happened to the ship?"

"It turned back. For reinforcements, probably—and the emperor's orders." Arin spoke this man's language in a clipped tone, his accent heavy, the syllables quick and hard. The language was new to him. "He'll strike now."

"What makes you so sure there's poison in the city's aqueducts? Where did you get this information?"

Arin hesitated, unsure of the Dacran words for what

he wanted to say. "The Moth," he answered in his own language.

Xash narrowed his eyes even more.

"A spy," Arin said in Dacran, finally finding the right word. He spun the gold ring on his smallest finger and thought of Tensen, his spymaster, and how the Valorian ship that had followed him could be a sign that Tensen had been arrested even as Arin had left the imperial palace. The old man had insisted on staying behind. He could have been caught. Tortured. Forced to speak. Arin imagined what the Valorians would have done . . .

No. The god of death set a cold hand on Arin's thoughts and curled tight around them. *You're not listening, Arin. Listen.*

"I need paper," Arin said out loud. "I need ink."

Arin drew his country for Xash. He sketched Herran's peninsula swiftly, his pen sweeping the curves. He hatched the islands scattered south of the peninsula's tip, peppering the sea between Herran and Valoria. He tapped Ithrya, a large, rocky island that created a thin strait between them and the peninsula's tip. "The spring currents in the strait are strong. Difficult to sail against. But if a Valorian fleet's coming, this is the route they'll take."

"They'll take a strait that's hard to navigate?" Xash was skeptical. "They could sail around the three islands and turn north to hug the peninsula all the way up to your city."

"Too slow. Merchants love that strait. This time of year, the currents are strongest, and push ships from Valoria right up to Herran's doorstep. Shoots them fast through the strait. The emperor expects to attack a weakened city. He doesn't expect resistance. He'll see no reason to wait for what he wants." Arin touched east of Ithrya Island and the peninsula's end. "We can hide here, half the fleet just east of the peninsula, half on the eastern side of the island. When the Valorian fleet comes through, they'll come through fast. We'll flank them and attack from either side. They won't be able to retreat, no matter what the winds. If they try to sail back into the strait, the currents will spit them out."

"You've said nothing of numbers. We're not a large fleet. Flanking the Valorians means splitting our fleet in half. Have you ever been in a sea battle?"

"Yes."

"I hope you don't mean that one in this bay the night of the Firstwinter Rebellion."

Arin was silent.

"That was in a *bay*," Xash sneered. "A pretty little cradle with gentle winds for rocking babies to sleep. It's easy to maneuver *here*. We are talking about a battle on the open sea. *You* are talking about weakening our fleet by cutting it in half."

"I don't think the Valorian fleet will be large."

"You don't *think*."

"It doesn't need to be, not to attack a city whose population has been drugged into lethargy. A city," Arin said pointedly, "that the emperor believes has no allies."

"I like a surprise attack. I like the thought of pinning the Valorians between us. But your plan only works if the emperor hasn't sent a fleet that vastly outnumbers us, and can easily sink each of our flanks. It only works if the emperor truly doesn't know that Dacra"—Xash's voice betrayed his disapproval—"has allied with you. The Valorian emperor would love to crush such an alliance with an overwhelming show of naval force. If he knows *we're* here, he might very well send the entire Valorian fleet."

"Then a battle along the strait is better. Unless you'd rather they attack us here in the bay."

"*I* rule this fleet. *I* have the experience. You're barely more than a boy. A *foreign* boy."

When Arin spoke again, it wasn't with his own words. His god told him what to say. "When your queen assigned you to sail your fleet to Herran, whom did she name with the ultimate command of it? You or me?"

Xash's face went hard with fury. Arin's god grinned inside him.

"We set sail now," Arin said.

The waters east of Ithrya Island were a sheer green. But Arin, from where his ship lay in wait for the Valorian fleet, could see how the currents pushing out of the strait made a broad, almost purple rope in the sea.

He felt like that: like a dark, curling force was working through him. It flooded to the tips of his fingers and warmed him. It spread his ribs wide with each breath.

When the first Valorian ship flew out of the strait, Arin was filled with a malicious joy.

And it was easy. The Valorians hadn't expected them, clearly had no idea of the alliance. The size of the enemy fleet matched theirs. The slenderness of the strait made the Valorian ships sail out into Herran's sea by twos. Easy to pick off. The eastern fleet drove at them from either side.

Cannonballs punched the hulls. The gundecks fogged the air with black smoke. It smelled like a million burnt matches.

Arin boarded his first Valorian ship. He seemed to watch all this as if from outside himself: the way his sword cut a Valorian sailor apart, and then another, and on until his blade was oiled red. Blood sprayed him across the mouth. Arin didn't taste it. Didn't feel the way his dagger hand plunged into someone's gut. Didn't wince when an enemy sword crossed his guard and sliced his bicep.

Arin's god slapped him across the face.

Pay attention, death demanded.

Arin did, and after that, no one could touch him.

When it was done, and Valorian wrecks were taking on water and the rest of the enemy ships had been seized, Arin could see straight again. He blinked against the lowering sun, its light an orange syrup that glazed the fallen bodies and gave the blood an odd color.

Arin stood on the deck of a captured Valorian ship. His breath heaved and hurt in his chest. Sweat dripped into his eyes.

The enemy captain was dragged before Xash.

"No," Arin said. "Bring him to me."

Xash's eyes were bright with anger. But the Dacrans did what Arin asked, and Xash let them.

"Write a message to your emperor," Arin said to the Valorian captain. "Tell him what he's lost. Tell him he'll pay if he tries again. Use your personal seal. Send the message and I'll let you live."

"How noble," Xash said, contemptuous.

The Valorian said nothing. He was white-lipped. Yet again Arin marveled at how the Valorian reputation for bravery and honor so often fell short of the truth.

The man wrote his message.

Are you really a boy, like Xash says? the god asked Arin. *You've been mine for twenty years. I raised you.*

The Valorian signed the scrap of paper.

Cared for you.

The message was rolled, sealed, and pushed into a tiny leather tube.

Watched over you when you thought you were alone.

The captain tied the tube to a hawk's leg. The bird was too large to be a kestrel. It didn't have a kestrel's markings. It cocked its head, turning its glass-bead eyes on Arin.

No, not a boy. A man made in my image . . . one who knows he can't afford to be seen as weak.

The hawk launched into the sky.

You're mine, Arin. You know what you must do.

Arin cut the Valorian's throat.

It was when Arin was sailing home into his city's bay, his hair hard with dried blood, his clothes stiff with it, that the story slipped inside him. It lay on his tongue and melted like a bitter candy.

This is the story Arin told.

Once there was a boy who knew how to cower. One

night, the gods could see him locked alone inside his rooms, shaking, near vomiting with fear. He heard what was happening elsewhere in the house. Screams. Things breaking. Harsh orders, the actual words muffled yet still clearly understood by the boy, who retched in his corner.

His mother was somewhere beyond that locked door. His father. His sister. He should go to them. He said so to his pointed knees, tucked up beneath his nightshirt as he huddled on the floor. He whispered the words, voice warbling out of control. *Go to them. They need you.* But he couldn't move. He stayed where he was.

The door thumped. It shuddered on its hinges.

With a splintering crack, the door gave way. A foreign soldier pushed inside. The soldier's skin and hair were fair, his eyes dark. He grabbed the boy by his bony wrist.

The boy tugged madly back, but it was ridiculous, he knew how pathetic his effort was. He squawked and flailed. The soldier laughed. He shook the boy. Not very hard, more as if trying to wake the child up. *Come along nicely,* the soldier said in a language that the boy had studied yet never expected to use. *And you won't get hurt.*

Not getting hurt was very important. The mere promise of it made the child go limp with ugly relief. He followed the soldier.

He was led to the atrium. Everyone was there, the servants, too. His parents didn't see him arrive. He was so quiet. Later, he couldn't say how things would have been different if it hadn't been his sister, standing at the far side of the room, who noticed him first. He wasn't sure how he could have changed what happened after. All he knew was that at the most important moment, he had done nothing.

He'd heard there were women in the Valorian army, but the soldiers in his house that night were men. Soldiers stood on either side of his sister. She was tall, imperious. Her loose hair fell around her shoulders like a black cape. As Anireh's gaze fell upon him and her gray eyes flashed, the boy realized that he'd never before believed that she loved him. Now he knew she did.

She said something low to the Valorians. The boy heard the tone of it, musical in its mockery.

What did you say? a soldier demanded.

She said it again. The soldier seized her, and the boy understood with a sick horror that this was his fault. It was, somehow, all his fault.

They were taking his sister away. Soldiers were taking her toward a cloakroom used in winter when his family had evening guests. He'd hidden in there before. It was close and dark and airless.

This was the point in the story when Arin wished he could reach through time and put his hands over the boy's small ears. He wanted to deafen the sounds. *Close your eyes,* he wanted to tell that child. The echo of an old panic fluttered in Arin's chest. It was crucial that he imagine how he would stop the boy from witnessing what happened next.

Why did Arin do this to himself? It made him ache, this effort to try to change his memory of that night. It was compulsive. Sometimes he thought it hurt more than the actual truth. Yet even now, more than ten years after the Valorian invasion, Arin couldn't help thinking with desperate fervor about what he should have done differently.

What if he'd called out?

Or begged the soldiers to let his sister go?

What if he'd run to his parents, who were still unaware of his presence in the room, and stopped his father from snatching a Valorian dagger from its sheath?

Or his mother. Surely he could have saved his mother. It wasn't her nature to fight. She wouldn't have done it if she'd known he was there. He'd stared as she lunged at the soldier holding his sister. Soldiers cut his father down. The cloakroom door shut behind Anireh. A dagger sliced his mother's throat. There was a bright plume of blood.

Arin's ears were roaring. His eyes were dry rocks.

After the soldiers had yanked him shrieking off his mother's body, he was led with the servants into the city. The royal palace burned on its hill. He saw the corpses of the royal family hanging in the market, including the prince that Anireh was supposed to marry. It was possible that his sister was still alive, wasn't it? But two days later Arin would see her body in the street.

Even though it didn't seem like anything worse could happen, Arin swallowed his sobs, was silent in his terror. He did as he was told. *Come along nicely,* the soldier had said.

He saw an armored man stalking among his troops. Later, Arin would learn that the general had been young at the time of the invasion. But that night the man had seemed ancient, enormous: a flesh-and-metal monster.

Arin imagined how, if he could, he would kneel before the boy he had been. He'd cradle himself to his chest, let

the child bury his wet face against his shoulder. *Shh,* Arin
would tell him. *You will be lonely, but you'll become strong.*
One day, you will have your revenge.

What had happened with Kestrel was not the worst thing.
It did not compare.

Arin thought about this as his ship, with the rest of his
victorious fleet, dropped anchor in Herran's moonlit bay. He
ran a thumb along the scar that cut down through his left
brow and into the hollow of his cheek. Rubbed at the line
of raised flesh. A recent habit.

No, it didn't hurt anymore to think about Kestrel. He'd
been a fool, but he'd had to forgive himself for worse. Sister,
father, mother. As for Kestrel . . . Arin had some clarity on
who he was: the sort of person who trusted too blindly, who
put his heart where it didn't belong.

She might even be married to the Valorian prince by
now. She was playing her games at court. No doubt winning.
Maybe her father would write to her from the front and ask
for more of the same excellent military advice she had given
him when she'd condemned hundreds of people in the eastern plains to starvation.

Arin used to clutch his head in disgusted wonder at
how fascinated he'd once been by the daughter of the
Valorian general. He used to sting at her rejection. Now,
though, the thought of Kestrel gave him a cold relief. Ice
on a bruise.

Gratitude. Because she meant nothing to him. Wasn't
that a gods-given gift, to remember her and feel nothing?

Or if he felt something, it was really no more than the way it was to touch his scar and marvel at its long ridge, the nerve-dead skin. Arin knew that some things hurt forever, but Kestrel wasn't one of them. She was a wound that had finally healed clean.

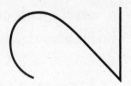

SHE HAD NO ONE TO BLAME BUT HERSELF.

As the wagon trundled north, Kestrel stared at the changing landscape through the barred window. She watched mountains give way to flat lands with patches of dull, reddish grass. Long-legged white birds picked their way through shallow pools. Once, she saw a fox with a white chick dangling from its teeth and Kestrel's empty stomach clenched with longing. She would have gladly eaten that baby bird. She would have eaten the fox. Sometimes she wished she could eat herself. She'd swallow everything—her soiled blue dress, the shackles on her wrists, her puffy face. If she could eat herself up, there'd be no trace left of her or the mistakes she had made.

Awkwardly, she lifted her bound hands and knuckled her dry eyes. She thought that maybe she was too dehydrated to cry. Her throat hurt. She couldn't remember when the guards driving the wagon had last given her water.

They were deep into the tundra now. It was late spring—or no, Firstsummer must have already come. The tundra, frozen for most of the year, had come alive. There were clouds of mosquitoes. They bit every bare inch of Kestrel's skin.

It was easier to think about mosquitoes. Easier to look at the low, sloping volcanoes on the horizon. Their tops had blown off long ago. The wagon angled toward them.

Easier, too, to see lakes of astonishingly bright green-blue water.

Harder to know that their color was due to sulfide in the water, which meant they were nearing the sulfur mines.

Harder to know that her father had sent her here. Hard, horrible, the way he had looked at her, disowned her, accused her of treason. She'd been guilty. She had done everything that he believed of her, and now she had no father.

Grief swelled in her throat. She tried to swallow it down. She had a list of things to do—what were they? Study the sky. Pretend you're one of those birds. Lean your forehead against the wagon's wall and breathe. Don't remember.

But she never could forget for long. Inevitably, she remembered her last night in the imperial palace. She remembered her letter confessing everything to Arin. *I am the Moth. I am your country's spy,* she'd written. *I have wanted to tell you this for so long.* She'd scrawled the emperor's secret plans. It didn't matter that this was treason. It didn't matter that she was supposed to marry the emperor's son on First-summer's day, or that her father was the emperor's most trusted friend. Kestrel ignored that she'd been born Valorian. She'd written what she felt. *I love you. I miss you. I would do anything for you.*

But Arin had never read those words. Her father had. And her world came apart at the seams.

Once there was a girl who was too sure of herself. Not everyone would call her beautiful, but they admitted that she had a certain grace that intimidated more often than it charmed. She was not, society agreed, someone you wanted to cross. *She keeps her heart in a porcelain box,* people whispered, and they were right.

She didn't like to open the box. The sight of her heart was unsettling. It always looked both smaller and bigger than she expected. It thumped against the white porcelain. A fleshy red knot.

Sometimes, though, she'd put her palm on the box's lid, and then the steady pulse was a welcome music.

One night, someone else heard its melody. A boy, hungry and far from home. He was—if you must know—a thief. He crept up the walls of the girl's palace. He wriggled strong fingers into a window's slim opening. He pulled it open wide enough to fit himself and pushed inside.

While the lady slept—yes, he saw her in bed, and looked quickly away—he stole the box without realizing what the box held. He knew only that he wanted it. His nature was full of want, he was always longing after something, and the longings he understood were so painful that he did not care to examine the ones that he didn't understand.

Any member of the lady's society could have told him that his theft was a bad idea. They'd seen what happened to her enemies. One way or another, she always gave them their due.

But he wouldn't have listened to their advice. He took his prize and left.

It was almost like magic, her skill. Her father (*a god*, people whispered, but his daughter, who loved him, knew him to be wholly mortal) had taught her well. When a gust of wind from the gaping window woke her, she caught the thief's scent. He'd left it on the casement, on her dressing table, even on one of her bed curtains, drawn ever so slightly aside.

She hunted him.

She saw his path up the palace wall, the broken twigs of fox-ivy he'd used to clamber up, then down. In some places the ivy branches were as thick as her wrist. She saw where it had held his weight, and where it hadn't and he'd almost fallen. She went outside and tracked his footprints back to his lair.

You could say that the thief knew the moment she crossed his threshold what he held in his tightening fist. You could say that he should have known well before then. The heart shuddered in its cool white box. It hammered inside his hand. It occurred to him that the porcelain—milky, silken, so fine that it made him angry—might very well shatter. He'd end up with a handful of bloody shards. Yet he didn't relinquish what he held. You could imagine how he felt when she stood in his broken doorway, set her feet on his earthen floor, lit up the room like a terrible flame. You could. But this isn't his story.

The lady saw the thief.

She saw how little he had.

She saw his iron-colored eyes. Sooty lashes, black brows, darker than his dark hair. A grim mouth.

Now, if the lady had been honest, she would have admitted that earlier that evening as she'd lain in bed, she'd woken for the length of three heartbeats (she had counted them as they rang loud in her quiet room). She'd seen his hand on her white-covered heart. She had closed her eyes again. The sleep that had reclaimed her had been sweet.

But honesty requires courage. As she cornered the thief in his lair, she found that she wasn't so sure of herself. She was sure of only one thing. It made her fall back a little. She lifted her chin.

Her heart had an unsteady rhythm they both could hear when she told the thief that he might keep what he had stolen.

Kestrel woke. She'd fallen asleep. The floor of the moving wagon creaked beneath her cheek. She hid her face in her hands. She was glad that her dream had ended where it did. She wouldn't have wanted to see the rest, the part where the girl's father discovered that she'd given her heart to a lowly thief, and wished her dead, and cast her out.

The wagon stopped. Its door rattled. Someone set a key into its lock. It grated. Door hinges squealed and hands reached inside. The two guards hauled her out, their grips firm and wary, as if she might fight them.

They had reason to worry. Once, Kestrel had knocked one of the men unconscious by striking his temple with the manacles on her wrists. The second guard caught her before she could run. The last time they'd opened her door, she'd flung the contents of the waste bucket in their faces and pushed past them. She'd sprinted, blind in the sudden daylight. She was weak. Her bad knee gave out and she hit the dirt. After that, the guards stopped opening the door at all, which meant no food or water.

If they had decided to take her outside now, it was because they had arrived at their destination. For once, Kestrel didn't struggle. Her dream had numbed her. She needed to see the place where her father had condemned her to live.

The work camp was enclosed by a black iron fence the height of three men. Dead volcanoes loomed behind the two blocky stone buildings. The tundra stretched to the east and west: tattered blankets of yellow moss and red grass. It was chilly. The air was thin. Everything smelled rotten.

This far north, twilight had a greenish cast. A line of prisoners filed into the camp through an open narrow gate. Their backs were to Kestrel, but she caught a glimpse of one woman's face in the pale green light. The expression frightened Kestrel. It was utterly blank. Although Kestrel had been following her guards quietly, those empty, glassy eyes made her dig in her heels. The guards' hands tightened. "Keep moving," one of them said, but the prisoner's eyes—all of the prisoners' eyes—were shiny mirrors, and Kestrel, although she'd known her destination in the north and had known that she, too, was a prisoner, only now fully realized that she was going to transform into one of these empty-faced people.

"Don't be difficult," said a guard.

She went boneless. She sagged in their grip. Then, as they bent and swore and tried to drag her upright, she abruptly straightened and rammed her head back into one man's face, threw the other off balance.

It was the least successful of her escape attempts. Stupid, to try anything just outside a camp that held scores of Valorian prison guards. But even as several of them swarmed out to help subdue her, she couldn't think how she could have done anything else.

Nobody hurt her. This was very Valorian. Kestrel was here to work for the empire. Damaged bodies don't work well.

After she'd been dragged inside the camp, she was shoved across the muddy yard and right up to a woman who looked Kestrel over with amused, almost friendly scorn. "Pretty princess," she said, "what did *you* do to end up here?"

Though now dirty and disheveled, Kestrel's hair had been braided with aristocratic flair the day she'd been caught. She remembered slipping into the soft blue dress and seeing the spill of it across her lap when she'd sat at the piano on her last night in the imperial palace—when was this? Nearly a week must have passed, she thought. Had it been that long a time since she'd written that reckless, wretched letter? That *short* a time? How had she fallen so far so fast?

Kestrel plunged again into that icy well of fear. She was drowning in it. She couldn't even react when the woman drew the dagger from her hip.

"Hold still," the woman said. With a few rapid slashes, she cut Kestrel's skirts straight down between the legs. From her belt, the woman unhooked a loop of thin rope that hung next to a coiled whip. She cut the rope into several short lengths that she used to tie the slashed fabric to Kestrel's legs, fashioning something like trousers. "Can't have you tripping over yourself in the mines, can we?"

Kestrel touched a knot at her thigh. Her breath evened. She felt a little better.

"Hungry, princess?"

"Yes."

Kestrel snatched what was offered. The food vanished down her throat before she even registered what it was. She gulped the water.

"Easy," said the woman. "You'll get sick."

Kestrel didn't listen. Her manacles jangled as she tipped the canteen to drain the last drop.

"I don't think you need these." The woman unlocked the manacles. The weight dropped from Kestrel's wrists. Each wrist, now bare, bore a raised welt. Her hands felt disturbingly light, like they might float away. They didn't look like they belonged to her. Grimy. Nails jagged. A nasty, infected graze over two knuckles. Had she really once played music with those hands?

Her skin prickled. Her stomach cramped—she *had* eaten and drunk too quickly. Kestrel tucked her hands under crossed arms and hugged them to her.

"You'll be fine," the woman said soothingly. "I hear that you've been somewhat of a troublemaker, but I'm sure you'll settle down in no time. We're fair here. Do as you're told and you'll be treated well enough."

"Why . . ." Kestrel's tongue felt thick. "Why did you call me princess? Do you know who I am?"

The woman clucked. "Child, I don't care who you are. Soon enough, neither will you."

Kestrel's scalp was crawling. She had the odd and yet vivid idea that tiny beetles were marching in her veins. She looked down at her hand, half expecting to see moving bumps beneath the skin. She swallowed. She wasn't frightened anymore. She was . . . what was she? Her thoughts streamed by in a blur: a magician's trick with colored rags, a long line of them pulled out of the mouth, hand over hand . . .

"What did you put in the food?" she managed to say. "The water?"

"Something to help."

"You drugged me." Kestrel's pulse was so fast she couldn't feel each heartbeat. They blurred into a solid vibration. The prison yard seemed to shrink. She stared at the woman and tried to focus on her features—the broad mouth, the silvered braids, a slight tilt to the eyes, the two vertical wrinkles between her brows. But the woman's smile was far away. Her features grew vague, unfinished. They pulled and drifted apart until Kestrel became convinced that if she reached out, her fingers would go right through the woman, whose smile broadened.

"There," the woman said. "Much better."

Kestrel didn't know how she'd gotten inside the cell. She was consumed by an urge to move. Before she realized it, she was pacing the short space, hands opening and closing. She couldn't stop. Her pulse thrummed in her ears: loud and high and soaring.

The drug wore off. She was spent. She sort of remembered that she'd paced for what might have been hours, but now that she was aware of the size of her cell—her wardrobes in the imperial palace had been larger—the memory didn't seem possible. But her feet ached, and she saw that she'd worn down the thin soles of her elegant shoes.

Her heart felt like lead. She was cold. She sat in a heap on the dirt floor, looking at bright mold on the stone walls: a host of tiny green starfish. She touched the knots on the ropes that tied the cut-up dress to her legs. The gesture made her feel more like herself.

Most of the escape attempts on the road north to the tundra had probably been doomed to fail. Still, Kestrel couldn't help hoping that her first effort might ultimately be the best. As desperate, perhaps, as the others, but maybe more likely to work. On her first morning in the wagon, the guards had stopped to water the horses. Kestrel had heard the voice of a Herrani. She'd whispered to him, pushing a dead masker moth through the bars of her window. She could still feel the moth between her fingertips, its furred wings. Part of her hadn't wanted to let it go. Part of her thought that if she kept the moth, she might somehow reverse her mistakes. She would have said different things to Arin as he stood in her music room. It had been only the day before. She'd sat at the piano, smoothing hands over her blue skirts, feeding him lies.

Kestrel held the papery moth. Then she dropped it into the Herrani's waiting hand. *Give this to your governor,* she said. *Tell Arin that I—*

She hadn't managed more. The guards had seen her reaching out to the Herrani through the bars. They'd let the Herrani go after a rough search seemed to prove that Kestrel had not, in fact, given him anything. Had the moth dropped to the ground? Had it simply been too camouflaged for the guards to notice it? Kestrel hadn't quite been able to see through the window.

But if that Herrani man went to Arin and reported what had happened, wouldn't Arin be able to understand what she'd done and where she'd been exiled? She listed the pieces of the story in her mind. A moth: the symbol of Arin's anonymous spy. A prison wagon headed north. Even if that Herrani man along the road didn't know who Kestrel was, he'd still be able to describe her to Arin, wouldn't he? At the very least he could report that a Valorian woman had given him a moth. Arin would figure things out. He was quick, cunning.

And blind.

I would do anything for you, she'd written in the letter her father had found. But that part, despite feeling true when she'd scrawled it on the page, had been a lie. Kestrel had refused Arin. She hadn't been honest with him, not even when he'd begged. She'd pretended she was empty and careless and cruel.

He'd believed it. She couldn't believe that he believed it. Sometimes, she hated him for that.

She squashed her sneaking hope that Arin might discover what had happened and come to her rescue. That was a terrible plan. It wasn't a plan at all. She could do better than that.

All the food was drugged. The water, too. On her first morning in the camp, Kestrel ate in the yard with the other prisoners, who were slack-faced and didn't speak, even though she'd tried to talk with them. As she filed out of the camp with them in an orderly line, Kestrel felt the drug hit her heart. Her blood roared.

They entered the mining area at the base of the volcanoes. Kestrel couldn't remember having walked the path to arrive here. She also didn't care that she didn't remember. This distant awareness of not caring brought a bump of pleasure.

It was a relief to work. The urge to move, to *do*, rode high. Someone—a guard?—gave her a double basket. She eagerly began to fill it, prying crumbly yellow blocks of sulfur from the ground. She saw tunnels that led below a volcano. The prisoners who went there carried pickaxes. Kestrel was made to work out in the open. She gathered—the realizatíon was plucked like a stone from the rushing river of the drug—that she was too new to be trusted with an ax.

All the guards carried looped whips attached to their belts, but Kestrel didn't see them being used. The guards—they could not be Valoria's best and brightest, if commissioned to serve in the worst corner of the empire—were content to keep a lazy eye on the prisoners, who obeyed directions easily. The guards talked among themselves, complaining about the smell.

The boiled egg odor was very strong here. She noticed this without being bothered by it or by the sweat that stained her dress even as she shivered hard (was it very cold, or was this just the nature of the drug?). She loaded each of the two baskets attached by a flexible pole that she heaved up onto her shoulders. The weight felt good; it was so *good* to dig and lift and carry and dump and do it all over again.

At some point she staggered under the baskets. She was given water. Her marvelous strength returned.

By twilight, she was hollowed out. Her good sense returned. She refused the food served when the prisoners had filed through the black iron gate and into the yard.

"This food is different," said the silver-braided guard from yesterday, whom Kestrel understood to be in charge of the female prisoners. "Last night I gave you a taste of how nice it'd be to work, but from now on you'll get a dose of something different at night."

"I don't want it."

"Princess, no one cares what you want."

"I can work without it."

"No," the woman said gently, "you can't."

Kestrel backed away from the long table with its bowls of soup.

"Eat, or I'll force it down you."

The guard had told the truth. The food contained a different drug, one with a metallic scent like silver. It made everything slow and dark as Kestrel was led into her prison block and to her cell.

"Why doesn't the empire drug all its slaves?" Kestrel mumbled before she was locked up.

The woman laughed, the sound murky, underwater. "You'd be surprised how many tasks require a mind."

Kestrel felt foggy.

"New prisoners are my favorites. We haven't had one like you in a long time. New ones are always entertaining, at least while they last."

Kestrel thought she heard the key turn. She dropped into sleep.

She tried to eat and drink as little as she could get away with. She remembered the guard's words . . . until, in fact, she no longer remembered them and avoided full meals simply out of the awareness that the drugged food changed her and she didn't like it. She'd tip her bowl of soup out onto the muddy prison yard when no one was looking. She crumbled bread and let it fall from her hands.

Still, she was hungry. She was thirsty. Sometimes, she ignored her nagging worry and filled her belly.

I would do anything for you. The words echoed in her mind. Often, she couldn't quite sort out who'd said them. She thought she might have said them to her father.

Then she'd feel suddenly ill, nauseated with an emotion she would have recognized as shame if she'd had a clearer head. No, she hadn't said that to her father. She had betrayed him. Or had *he* betrayed *her*?

It was confusing. She was certain only of the sense of betrayal, thick and hot in her chest.

Kestrel had moments of clarity before the morning drug shot her up, or before the twilight drug dragged her down. In those moments, when she could smell the sulfur on her and feel its dust in her eyelashes, saw the yellow stuff beneath her fingernails and powdering her skin like pollen, she'd envision those words, written in ink on paper. *I would do anything for you.* She knew exactly who had written them and why. She became aware that she had been pretending to herself when she'd believed her words had been untrue, or that any of the limits she'd set between her and Arin mattered, because in the end she was here and he was free. She *had* done everything she could. And he didn't even know.

The guards still didn't trust Kestrel with a pickax. She was starting to worry that they never would. A small ax was a real weapon. With it, she might be able to escape. In her clearer hours, on the days when she ate and drank less, Kestrel was desperate to lay her hands on one of those axes. Her nerves screamed for it. At the same time, she was afraid that by the time a guard gave her one and sent her down into the tunnels, it would be too late. She'd be like all the other prisoners: wordless, eyes wide, minds gone. If Kestrel was sent into the mines underground, she couldn't be sure that she wouldn't lose her sense of self along the way.

One night, she managed to avoid consuming anything before being locked in her cell. She regretted it. She shook with hunger and fatigue, yet nothing could make her sleep. She felt the dirt floor beneath the holes in her shoes. The air was chilly and damp. She missed the velvet warmth of her nighttime drug. It always swaddled her thickly. It smothered her to sleep. She'd grown to like that.

Kestrel knew that she was forgetting things. It was horribly unsettling, like walking down a staircase in the dark, hand on the rail, and then the rail vanished and she held nothing but air. Try as she might, Kestrel couldn't remember the name of her horse in Herran. She knew that she had loved Enai, her Herrani nurse, and that Enai had died, but Kestrel couldn't remember *how* she'd died. When Kestrel had first come to the camp, she'd had the idea of searching the prisoners for the face of someone she knew (a disgraced senator, wrongfully convicted of selling black powder to the east, had been sent here last autumn), but she found that she didn't recognize anyone and wasn't sure if that was because she knew no one here, or if she *did* and had simply forgotten his features.

Kestrel coughed. The sound rattled in her lungs.

That night, Kestrel pushed away thoughts of Arin and her father. She tried to remember Verex instead. When she'd first met the prince she'd agreed to marry, she'd thought him weak. Petty, childish. She'd been wrong.

He hadn't loved her. She hadn't loved him. Yet they'd cared for each other, and Kestrel remembered how he'd set a soft black puppy into her hands. No one had given her such a gift. He'd made her laugh. That, too, was a gift.

Verex was probably in the southern isles now, pretending to be on a romantic excursion with her.

Maybe you think that I can't make you vanish, that the court will ask too many questions the emperor had said as the captain of his guard had held Kestrel and the sour scent of terror rose off her skin. Her father had watched from the other side of the room. *This is the tale I'll tell. The prince and his bride were so consumed by love that they married in secret and slipped away to the southern isles.*

Verex would obey the emperor. He knew what happened to people who didn't.

The emperor had whispered, *After some time—a month? two?—news will come that you've sickened. A rare disease that even my physician can't cure. As far as the empire is concerned, you'll be dead. You'll be mourned.*

Her father's face hadn't changed. Something fractured inside Kestrel to remember this.

She looked out the bars of her cell but saw only the dark

hallway. She wished she could see the sky. She hugged her arms to her.

If she'd been smart, she would have married Verex. Or she would have married no one and joined the military like her father had always wanted. Kestrel tipped her head back against the stone wall with its cushion of mold. Her body shuddered. She knew that this wasn't just from cold or hunger. It was withdrawal. She craved her nighttime drug.

But it wasn't simply withdrawal, either, that racked her limbs. It was grief. It was the horror of someone who'd been dealt a winning hand, had bet her life on the game, and then proceeded (deliberately?) to lose.

The next night, Kestrel ate and drank everything she was given.

"Good girl," said the silver-haired guard. "Don't think I don't know what you've been up to. I've seen you spill your soup and pretend to drink from a cup. This way"—the woman pointed at Kestrel's empty bowl—"is better, isn't it?"

"Yes," Kestrel said, and was tempted to believe it.

She woke to see, in the weak dawn light that filtered from the corridor through the bars to her cell, that she had been drawing in the dirt floor. She jerked upright.

One vertical line, four wings. A moth.

She had no memory of doing this. This was bad. Worse: maybe soon she might not even understand what such a drawing meant. She traced the moth. She must've sketched it last night with her fingers. Now they were trembling. Crumbs of dirt shifted beneath her touch.

This is me, she reminded herself. *I am the Moth.*

She'd betrayed her country because she'd believed it was the right thing to do. Yet would she have done this, if not for Arin?

He knew none of it. Had never asked for it. Kestrel had made her own choices. It was unfair to blame him.

But she wanted to.

It occurred to Kestrel that her moods weren't her own.

She wondered if she'd feel so desolate and alone if she weren't constantly drugged. In the morning at the mines, when she was a tireless giant and prying sulfur blocks from the ground was an obsession pushed into her by the drug, she forgot how she felt. The worries about whether what she felt was real were far away.

Yet at night before sleep, she knew that her darker emotions, the ones that curled inside her heart and ate away at it, were the only ones she could trust were true.

One day, something was different. The air—hazy and chilled, as usual—seemed to buzz with tension.

It came from the guards. Kestrel listened to them as she filled her baskets.

Someone was coming. There was to be an inspection.

Kestrel's fast heart picked up even more speed. She discovered that she had not, in fact, lost hope that Arin had received her moth. She hadn't stopped believing that he would come. Hope exploded inside her. It ran through her veins like liquid sunlight.

It wasn't him.

If Kestrel had been herself, she would have known from the moment she'd heard about an inspection that it couldn't be Arin, pretending to have come in some official imperial capacity to inspect the work camp.

What an idiotic, painful idea.

Arin was visibly Herrani—dark-haired, gray-eyed—and scarred in a way that announced his identity to anyone who cared to know it. *If* he'd received her message, and *if* he'd understood it, and *if* he came (she was beginning to despise herself for even contemplating such implausible *ifs*), every Valorian guard in the camp would arrest him, or worse.

The inspection was just an inspection. From the prison yard that evening, Kestrel saw the elderly man who wore a jacket with a senator's knot tied at the shoulder. He chatted with the guards. Kestrel winnowed through the prisoners, who milled aimlessly in the yard after a full day's work, the morning drug still jangling inside their veins as it did in hers. Kestrel tried to get close to the senator. Maybe she could get word to her father. If he knew how she suffered, how she was losing pieces of herself, he would change his mind. He would intervene.

The senator's eyes snapped to Kestrel. She stood only a few feet away. "Guard," he said to the woman who'd cut Kestrel's skirts on the first day. "Keep your prisoners in line."

The woman laid a heavy hand on Kestrel's shoulder. The weight settled, gripping hard.

"Time for dinner," the guard said.

Kestrel thought of the drug in the soup and longed for it. She let herself be led away.

Her father knew full well what the prison camp was like. He was General Trajan, the highest-ranking Valorian save the emperor and his son. He knew about his country's assets and weaknesses—and the camp was a huge asset. Its sulfur was used to make black powder.

Even if the general didn't know the details of how the camp was run, what did it matter? He'd given her letter to the emperor. She'd heard his heart thump calmly as she'd wept against his chest. It had beaten like a perfectly wound clock.

Someone was stabbing her. Kestrel opened her eyes. She saw nothing but the low black ceiling of her cell.

Another prod against her ribs, harder.

A stick?

Kestrel climbed out of gooey sleep. Slowly—it hurt to move, she was a tangle of bones and bruises and blue rags—she pulled herself up into a sitting position.

"Good," came a voice from the hallway, clearly relieved. "We don't have much time."

Kestrel shifted toward the bars. There was no torchlight in the hallway, but it never got fully dark this far north, even in the dead of night. She could make out the senator, who pulled his cane back through the bars.

"My father sent you." Joy rushed through her, popping and sparkling all over her skin. She could taste her tears. They ran freely down her face.

The senator gave her a nervous smile. "No, Prince Verex did." He held out something small.

Kestrel kept crying, differently now.

"Shh. I can't be caught helping you. You know what would happen to me if I were caught." In his hand was a key. She took it. "This is for the gate."

"Let me out, take me with you, please."

"I can't." His whisper was anxious. "I don't have the key to your cell. And you must wait until at least several days after I've left. Your escape can't be tied to me. Do you understand? You'd ruin me."

Kestrel nodded. She'd agree to anything he said, if only he wouldn't leave her.

He was already backing away from her cell. "Promise."

She wanted to scream at him to stop, she wanted to grab him through the bars and make him stay, make him get her out *now*. But she heard herself say, "I promise," and then he was gone.

She sat for a long time looking at the key on her palm. She thought about Verex. Her fingers curled around the key. She dug a hole in the dirt and buried it.

Curling up with her hands beneath her cheek, she rested her head right above the buried key. She tucked her knees in close and toyed with the knots that bound her cut dress to her legs. Kestrel's mind, though still sticky and slow, began to work. She didn't sleep. She began to plan—a *real* plan, this time—and as she arranged the different possibilities there was a part of her that reached for Verex in her mind. She embraced her friend. She thanked him. She dropped her head to his shoulder, breathing deeply. She was strong now, she told him. She could do this. She could do it because she knew that she hadn't been forgotten.

The senator left. There were several lean, thirsty days. Once Kestrel caught the guard in charge of the women prisoners watching as she spilled her drugged water to the dirt, but the guard just gave her the sort of look a mother gives a misbehaving child. Nothing was said.

It worried Kestrel to grow weaker than she already was. She wasn't sure how she'd survive the tundra in her condition. But she needed to keep her wits about her. She was lucky it was summer. The tundra was brimming with fresh water. It was full of life. She could raid birds' nests. Eat moss. She could avoid the wolves. She could do anything, as long as she got out of here.

Her body didn't like being weaned off the drugs. She shook. Worse, she craved the nighttime drug. In the morning, it wasn't so hard to pretend to eat and drink, but at twilight she wanted to gulp everything down. Even the thought of it made her throat dry with desire.

She waited as long as she could for the senator's sake. One warm night in her cell, she untied two lengths of rope from around her legs. She adjusted her makeshift trousers, which were held together with the remaining knots the guard had tied on Kestrel's first day in the camp. The trousers looked more or less the same as they had before.

Kestrel knotted her two pieces of rope together. She tied them with the strongest knot her father had taught her to make. She tugged at the new length—about as long as four of her hands, from fingertips to wrist. It held. She curled it up and shoved it down her dress.

Tomorrow would be the day.

Kestrel made her move after the prisoners returned from the mines.

In the fuzzy, greenish twilight, Kestrel pretended to take her meal. Her heartbeat still held a trace of the morning drug; it tripped over itself. Then it seemed to steady, pulse strong. Kestrel should have been nervous, but she wasn't. She was sure. This would work. She knew that it would.

The silver-braided guard led Kestrel and the other female prisoners into their block of cells. They turned down Kestrel's hallway. Unseen, Kestrel slipped the knotted rope from her dress. She made a fist around it and let that fist rest against her thigh in the shadows. The guard imprisoned women one by one. Then, her back turned, she stood before Kestrel's cell and unlocked it.

Kestrel came up behind her, rope stretched taut between her hands. The rope went down over the woman's head and tightened around her throat.

The woman thrashed. Kestrel had the wild thought of having caught an enormous fish. She clung hard, ignoring the wheezing. Even though she was rammed back against a wall, she didn't let go. She tightened the rope until the woman slumped and collapsed.

Kestrel ran into her cell and feverishly dug up the key to the gate. When she came back into the hallway and saw the woman on the floor, the cell door key having fallen from her hand, she registered the other prisoners, standing where they had been, their faces blank but their bodies uncertain, fingers twitching at their sides. They were aware enough to know that this was not how evenings went. None of the women, though, seemed to know what to do about it.

"Come with me," Kestrel said to them, though this offer was foolish enough to border on suicidal. How would she get them to the gate without being noticed? She couldn't save the entire camp. How would they survive on the tundra, and not be caught? But . . . "Come with me," she said again. She moved back down the hallway, toward the exit. She beckoned them after her. They stood still. When Kestrel took a woman's hand, it was snatched back.

Finally, Kestrel picked up the cell door key that had fallen to the ground and pressed it into a prisoner's hand. The fingers stayed loose. The key dropped.

Frustration surged through Kestrel—and relief, and shame at her relief. She wanted to apologize. Yet she wanted most of all to live, and she knew—the knowledge was sudden, lancing, sharp—that if she didn't leave *now*, she would die here.

Kestrel clutched the gate key. "I'll leave the gate open," she promised.

No one replied.

She turned and ran.

It wasn't dark enough. She cursed the greenish sky. Someone was going to spy her shadow, creeping along the outside wall of her prison block.

But no one did. The windows of the guards' barracks burned brightly. She heard laughter. She saw one lone guard by the gate. The young man was leaning lazily against the bars.

Still crouched in the shadow of the prison barracks, Kestrel shifted the heavy key in her palm, its jagged teeth pointing out.

The guard at the gate shifted. She thought she saw him close his eyes as he sighed and settled into a more comfortable position.

Swiftly, her tattered shoes silent over the ground, Kestrel sped toward him. She swung her fist with the key at his head.

He lay in a heap at her feet, his temple bleeding. Kestrel fumbled with the key, her breath loud, gasping. It wasn't until she moved to set the key into the gate that she thought of the possibility that it was the wrong key, that she had been tricked, or Verex had, or the senator.

Horror spiked through her. But the key went in smoothly and it turned, making no more sound than a knife in butter.

A giddy rush. Her heart soaring in her chest. Her ribs spread wide with relief. A laughing breath.

She pushed the gate open. She slipped out onto the tundra, stealthy at first, then running as fast as a deer.

She was free.

Her foot plunged into a puddle. The ground was soggy, the vegetation short and shrubby. Little cover. Nowhere to hide. She was too exposed. Her breath rasped. Her heart faltered. Her legs were hot and thick and slow.

Then: horses.

A sob of fear burst past her lips. She heard them behind her. Fanned out wide. Galloping. A hunt.

A shout. She'd been seen.

Little rabbit, little fox.

Run.

She fled. She couldn't really see where she was going, couldn't look back. Gasps tore at her throat. She stumbled, nearly fell, forced herself forward. She heard the horses stop and that was worse, because the guards must be dismounting now, they were close, and she didn't want to know this. It could not be over.

But someone caught her from behind. Pitched her down. She screamed against the wet earth.

She was dragged back inside the prison gate. She refused to walk. They pulled her through the mud and then finally carried her.

As on her first day in the camp, she was brought before the silver-braided woman. A thin purple welt cut across the woman's throat. Kestrel should have killed her. She should have locked all the women prisoners in their cells. Her escape had been too quickly discovered. She hadn't had enough of a head start. Yet another mistake.

"I told you that if you behaved, no one would hurt you," the woman said. She unhooked the whip from her belt.

"No." Kestrel shrank. "Please. I won't do it again."

"I know you won't." The woman shook the looped whip. It snapped out loose at her thigh.

"That makes no sense." Kestrel's voice got threaded and high. "I won't be able to work if you do that."

"Not at first. But afterward I think you'll work much better."

"No. Please. Why punish me if I won't remember it? I won't, I'll be just like the other prisoners, I'll forget it, I'll forget everything."

"You'll remember long enough."

Kestrel twisted wildly, but hands were already opening the back of her dress, she was being turned around, pushed up against the gate, tied to the bars. The wind whispered across her bare back.

I have been whipped before, she heard the memory of Arin's voice. *Did you think I couldn't bear the punishment for being caught?*

Kestrel strained against her bonds, terrified.

"Princess," said the guard behind her.

Kestrel's muscles went tight. Her shoulders hunched. She couldn't breathe.

"Every new prisoner shines with a little light," the guard said. "Your light happens to shine brighter. It's best for everyone if it goes out."

Kestrel pressed her forehead against the bars. She stared

at the tundra. Her breath was coming again now. Hard and fast.

There was a sharp, whistling sound like a bird taking off.

The whip came down. It carved into her. Something wet ran down her ribs.

She wasn't brave. She could hear herself as it continued. She wasn't anything she recognized.

It used to be that Kestrel would treasure the memory of Arin singing to her. She'd worry that she'd somehow forget it. The sliding low notes. The sweet intervals, or the way he'd sustain a long line, and how she loved the sound of him taking a breath as much as she did the way he could hold a musical phrase aloft until it ended exactly where it should.

But after the guards untied her from the gate, when her back was on fire and she couldn't walk and her bones were a trembling liquid, she looked at the cup in the woman's hand. Kestrel reached for it. She begged to drink.

The cup was set to her lips. She caught the silvery scent of the nighttime drug. The thought of becoming just like the other prisoners no longer seemed so bad.

It would be a blessing to forget.

After all, what was there to remember?

Someone she never could have had. Friends dead or gone. A father who did not love her.

The cup tipped. Water ran over her tongue, cool and delicious. She forgot the pain, forgot where she was, forgot who she'd been, forgot that she had ever been afraid of forgetting.

ARIN ADDED THE CAPTURED VALORIAN VESSELS
to his fleet.

Some of the Dacran sailors who had been sent to scour
the aqueducts found the source of the poison that had been
flowing into the city's water supply. It was a large vat lodged
in a mountain tunnel that connected the water's path to ar-
cades that came down the mountainside in a series of tiered
arches. The vat was cleverly designed; it leaked a thick,
brownish liquid in a dose measured by internal weights and
counterweights.

When Arin saw it, brought forth from one of the old
mountain trenches that had been used ten years ago by Herrani slaves to construct the tunnel, he had wanted to pitch
the vat off the cliff and watch it shatter on the rocks below.
Instead, he helped carry it carefully down the mountain and
stored it in the city's arsenal to be used against the Valorians
in case of a siege.

Everyone in the city drank rainwater collected in barrels
or brought in from the countryside. They all went a little

thirsty until Arin, having waited a few days for the aqueduct to flush itself clean, drank some of its water and felt no different than he had before.

"Do you really think it could work?" Sarsine asked. Arin's cousin lay in her bed in his family home, still pallid. Her movements were slow and she slept most of the day, but her eyes had grown brighter in the past few days.

"It *does* work." Arin described the different parts of the miniature cannon he had designed in the Dacran castle forge. "It's what made the eastern queen agree to ally with us," he added, though with an uncomfortable sense that this perhaps had not been the whole explanation for the queen's decision. "This weapon might give us the edge we need against the empire, but we must make more. Sarsine, I need you." He brushed lank hair from her forehead and looked into the face that reminded him of his father, for whom she'd been named—an unfashionable, solid-sounding name she'd hated as a girl. He cupped her cheek. "I can't do this alone."

She reached for his hand and held it. She no longer looked so weak. Sarsine smiled. "You're *not* alone," she told him.

Eastern reinforcements came by ship roughly a week after the sea battle, and Arin was hugely relieved to see the new sloops drop anchor in his harbor. The Valorian counterattack would come soon—possibly somewhere along the western coast, he suspected.

One of the new arrivals in the harbor created quite a commotion. A cage was lowered from the largest sloop into a launch and rowed slowly to the piers. As the launch approached, Arin saw that the Dacrans at the oars were stiff and silent, edged as far away as possible from the cage. One figure, though, leaned against the bars, crooning to the pacing animal inside. Arin immediately recognized the young man. He felt a surge of gladness. He hadn't expected Roshar to come.

The eastern prince looked up to see Arin standing on the pier. A grin split his face. Arin used to think that Roshar had a skull's face; the nose and ears had been cut off. But Roshar looked so ferociously alive, his black eyes shining and lined with green paint, his teeth white and even, that although Arin remembered what he'd thought when he'd had his first shocking glimpse of Roshar's mutilations, that memory felt distant now.

Roshar, ignoring the startled cries of his crewman, leaped from the launch onto the pier. The launch rocked in the water. The small tiger growled.

Arms folded across his chest, Arin walked to the end of the pier. "Did you have to bring the tiger?"

"I kept him hungry during the journey here, just for you," Roshar said. "Go give him a nice snuggle, won't you? He's come all this way to see you. The least you could do is give him one of your arms to eat. Too much? What about a hand? At least some fingers. Arin, where's your hospitality?"

Arin, laughing, embraced his friend.

He choked on his first lungful of smoke. "This is vile."

"I told you you'd like it." Roshar bit the stem of his pipe, lighting the tobacco. He shook the match out. For a few moments, he smoked in silent contentment. Both the silence and the contentment were, in Arin's experience, rare for the prince. "Try it again," Roshar said, "or I'll think you're rude."

Arin, ignoring him, went to open a window. Sweet warm air washed into his father's study.

"Arin," Roshar complained. "Shut the window. I'm cold. Why is your country so damned *cold*?"

"It's summer." The first day of the season, which Valorians celebrated as Firstsummer, had already passed.

Roshar shuddered. "I want to go home."

"What *are* you doing here?"

"Admit it. You missed me."

Arin looked at him. Softly, he said, "I did."

The prince squinted at him through a cloud of smoke. "You seem better."

Arin frowned, leaning against the casement. "I wasn't aware that I seemed all that bad."

Roshar snorted. "As one of Dacra's royal line and educated in the finest points of grace and discretion, I shall pass over any description of exactly how you were when you set your no-good, illegal foot in my city." Roshar eyed him closely, then his gaze wandered to the sword that Arin had unbuckled and slung by its belt over the back of a chair when they'd entered the study. "What happened to your dagger?"

"Gone." Arin had dropped Kestrel's dagger into the sea.

Roshar toyed with his pipe. "As for why I'm here, the queen thought that you could use someone with authority."

"I've been managing fine."

"So I understand. Xash is impressed. Also, he hates you. But your delightful little power struggle is moot now that I'm here and outrank you both. Don't I?"

Slowly, Arin said, "Of course."

Roshar smiled. "The queen sends her greetings."

Arin was silent.

"Hoping for something a little more friendly? Well"—Roshar's voice went sly—"*you* know how she is, don't you?"

Arin flushed. "I think we should discuss possible scenarios for a Valorian attack."

"Boring."

"We don't have time for—"

"Oh! Oh! The Valorians are battering down the door *right now*. We have to *do something*."

"You can go home now."

Roshar settled comfortably into his chair. "Speaking of Valorians, I hear that Lady Kestrel and Prince Verex married in secret. Yes, word has it that they were so consumed with passionate love that they disappointed hundreds of wedding guests with a private ceremony right after the lady's birthday at the end of spring. The amorous couple simply couldn't wait."

Arin doubted that "passionate love" had much to do with it. He shook his head. "She wants the empire. She gets what she wants."

"They're on a lovers' holiday in the southern isles."

Arin shrugged. His shoulders felt tight. Roshar didn't appear to notice. "You *are* better," said the prince.

"Can we talk about the war now?"

"Whatever you want, little Herrani."

Arin unrolled a map and spread it across his father's desk. They studied the western coastline, the cliffs and rocky shores that would offer the Valorians an opportunity for a surprise attack, and the beach, known as Lerralen, that led to flat land running right into the southern Herrani estates.

When daylight had darkened and Roshar's eyes grew slowly heavier, Arin realized that the prince's gleeful needling had hidden a genuine fatigue from his journey. Arin told him he should rest.

"Choose whatever suite suits you best," Arin said. "But please: keep that tiger in his cage."

"Arin's a kitten," Roshar protested. Purely for the purpose of annoying Arin, it seemed, Roshar had named the tiger after him. "He's sweet-tempered and polite and very good-looking . . . unlike some people I could mention."

"You're wrong," Roshar said.

They were leaning over a map in Arin's library. Arin kept his fingers stubbornly pressed down on the cliffs along his country's western shore.

"Wrong," Roshar insisted.

Arin shook his head. "You're underestimating the Valorian general."

"He's not going to send soldiers up *cliffs*. He doesn't need to. He's got the numbers. He can land his ships on that beach and take the countryside with sheer force. He doesn't have to be clever."

Arin remembered Kestrel. "I think he enjoys being clever. I think he might be undercut by his own cunning, if we can catch him at it."

"Those cliffs are monstrously high."

"His Rangers are capable of it. If they scale the cliffs and come south while we're dealing with the Valorians that have landed on the beach, they'll flank us and squeeze us between them."

Roshar made a dismissive noise.

Frustrated, Arin said, "Are you so proud that you think no one can outmaneuver you?"

"Are you so ready to make the general into some almighty being capable of anything just because he had your family slaughtered?"

Anger knocked the wind out of Arin. There was a hard silence.

Roshar rubbed his eyes, smearing the green paint that lined them. He sighed. "I didn't mean—"

"Arin." It was Sarsine. She was standing in the library doorway.

"Not now," he told her.

"Someone's here to see you."

"Not now."

"He says it's important."

"What is important?"

"His message."

"Which is?"

"He won't tell me. He wants to tell you himself."

"I'm busy."

"No, no," said Roshar. "Go ahead, talk to him. We're done anyway. I'll inform the battalion leaders of my battle plan, and—"

"Wait. Sarsine, who *is* this person?"

"A Herrani groom who took care of horses at a way station in Valoria along the road that goes north to the tundra."

"Does his message have anything to do with a Valorian military operation?"

"I asked him. He says no."

"Does he have information on the general, his troops, or the emperor?"

"No, nothing like that. But—"

Arin turned away. "Later."

She took a breath as if to argue, then seemed to change her mind. "I'll put him in your old rooms. He's traveled far to see you."

"Well," Roshar said cheerfully, rolling up the map he and Arin had argued over. "Everything's settled, then. What's that beach called? Lerralen? We'll set out for it tomorrow at dawn."

Arin couldn't sleep. He threw his windows open. He heard an owl hunting in the summer dark.

It was, of course, safer to send the majority of the eastern forces to the beach at Lerralen, with no soldiers held back to guard the cliffs. The beach was an ideal place for the Valorian army to land. The beach and its surrounding terrain were relatively flat and wide open—good for an invasion. The Dacrans, who didn't know the land they were defending, wouldn't have any height on the Valorians, and that would make repelling the invaders harder . . . which General Trajan would like. Roshar was probably right.

Probably.

Arin had no power to overrule him anyway. Few of his people were in any condition to fight. He had no troops to command. He was lucky to have the eastern queen's help.

Yes, lucky.

The queen, however, was no fool. She must have heard of Xash's resentment at being ignored by Arin in the planning of a key battle.

Arin was glad Roshar was here, but it was nonetheless clear that he had been sent to put Arin in his place.

Arin braced an arm against the casement, resting his forehead against his wrist. The night curled around him. He'd lit no lamp. He wondered if one of the reasons Valorians trained to get by on little sleep was so that they could feel the way he did right now: like there was no difference between him and the darkness. He heard the sough of trees. He thought of the general landing on Herran's shore. The muscles in his arm hardened. He'd never sleep now. He kept seeing the cliffs. They rose, white and sparkling, in his mind.

Kestrel wouldn't be able to resist those cliffs.

If she were mustering an invasion, she'd like the looks of the beach at Lerralen, but she'd love the cliffs. The cunning of it would be its own attraction. And the results . . . if even a small force got up those cliffs and came south to meet the Valorians already massed on the beach, Herran's defenses would be easily broken. The Valorians would take the countryside and work their way to the city, whose bay was now too well defended to take by sea.

If Kestrel were the general, that's what she'd do.

If Arin were Kestrel, that's what he'd do.

Arin found that his loose hand had become a fist.

He remembered the golden, oiled line that had marked Kestrel's brow as the sign of an engaged woman, and how much he'd hated it. One evening in the palace, Arin had slowly nudged Kestrel up against the wintered windows of a closed balcony door. He'd felt her slender length against him. He'd kissed her mark. Later, he tasted the cosmetic oil on his lips. It had been bitter. He'd touched his tongue to it again.

Arin had had to struggle so hard for clarity. The things he had believed! He thought about the night the spell had finally broken. He'd sailed from the east. He'd risked everything to creep into the palace. He saw her again: the dismay on her face, the cold irritation, the way she'd rubbed her hands against the skirts of her blue silk dress, the sleeves belled and fastened tight at the wrist. That deep blue poured around her as she'd sat at the piano and tried to ignore him and played a laughing little melody. When he refused to leave, she'd turned cruel.

It wasn't entirely true that Arin felt nothing when he thought of Kestrel. He felt shame. He shuddered to think of his godsforsaken questions. He couldn't believe he'd asked them.

What did you do for that treaty?

It gave me my country's freedom. It saved my life. What did you do to make the emperor sign it?

Did you ... are you ... marrying the prince because of me? Was it ... part of some kind of deal you made with the emperor?

He still heard her cutting replies.

He thanked the god of chance he'd stopped short of asking whether she was Tensen's Moth—yet another of the fantasies he'd entertained about her in his compulsion to transform her into the person he longed for her to be. This, despite Tensen's loyalty to him, his honesty. Tensen had already told him the identity of his anonymous spy: Risha, the eastern princess held hostage in the imperial court.

Arin straightened. His shoulders ached. He'd been standing in one position for too long. He sat on the wide windowsill, spine against the frame. He was aware of feeling both inside and outside. He let himself enjoy the balance of it. It cleared his head.

What happened with Kestrel hadn't been for nothing. He'd gotten a feel for the way her mind worked. He'd caught her weakness for a sly move. He'd seen just how much she was her father's daughter.

Arin wondered how many people he'd need to handle Valorian Rangers coming up the western cliffs.

He wondered if he, too, was tempted by cunning. Maybe he was drawn as well to the biggest gamble.

The first morning bird sang.

The Herrani god of games had once been mortal. Arin knew the tale. She'd gambled her way into immortality, then wreaked merry havoc. The gods were not pleased. They began to lose treasured possessions—a pair of gloves that let the wearer touch colors and sounds, a ring that contained a whole other world within its circle, the god of night's favorite cat. When she won the sun, everyone lost their patience. The god of war was sent to deal with her. But nothing is ever simple between the gods, and the stories of the gods of war and games were many . . . and took certain sensual twists and turns that Arin hadn't been allowed to hear as a child.

Arin shut the window. He took his sword, which had been his father's and forged with beautifully tempered steel. For almost ten years after the invasion the sword had hung on a wall in this house like a corpse on display. It felt good against his palm, and for a moment it felt as if he weren't holding the sword but his father's hand. Then the hilt became steel again.

He made his way (quickly, it was almost dawn) to his stables. He saddled Javelin—Kestrel's horse, Arin's now. The animal was strong and smart and fast.

Arin rode the stallion out into the gray morning. He thought that a commander of any army had better pray to both the gods of war and games. No battle is won without a good gamble.

As the ground sped beneath Javelin's hooves, Arin had a fleeting thought of the messenger who'd come to see him.

Later, he decided, and spurred his horse.

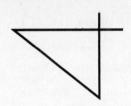

ARIN SLUNK FORWARD ON HIS BELLY AND inched over the patchy grass. The wind shrilled in his ears. It whipped dirt into his eyes. He blinked it away, eyes streaming, and crept to the edge of the cliff. He heard soil crumble beneath his weight. It sifted down the cliffs.

Arin's pulse thumped hard. He imagined the lip of the cliff giving way. He'd plummet fast.

Quickly, as he'd already done several times that day, Arin dug his elbows into the earth and pulled himself just far enough to look down the cliff. The sea was dizzyingly far below. It foamed white against the rocks.

There were no ships.

No Valorians climbing up the cliffs.

Nothing.

Arin pushed himself away from the edge, rolled onto his back, looked up at the pale sky, and then at the waiting Herrani.

He met their eyes. He shook his head.

Arin had ridden to Etrea, a country estate he'd helped liberate during the Firstwinter Rebellion. The people there were too far from the city and mountains to rely on aqueducts for water; they had wells. They were healthy. Maybe they weren't born fighters, but Arin would take what he could get. He'd ridden through the village and begged for help. About twenty men and women followed him to the cliffs.

The bare cliffs.

The quiet ones.

Arin looked out again over the empty water and imagined what Roshar must have thought as he'd looked for Arin in the morning light and made his way to the beach without him.

Arin wondered if his disobedience—or would Roshar see it as cowardice?—had cost him the alliance he'd worked so hard to forge.

But on the second day, Arin saw them.

At first, he wasn't sure it was really happening. He hadn't seen the arrival of any ships—they must have dropped anchor out of sight, behind the southern edge of the cliffs that bulged out into the water at their base. Arin hadn't seen the small launches row up to the foot of the cliffs. He only realized what they were (they looked like dark rocks below in the sea) when he saw tiny black figures against the shining white rock.

Arin peered again through his spyglass. The sun beat

against his shoulders. He tasted sweat. His stomach tightened against the stiff grass beneath him.

Valorian Rangers were climbing up the cliffs in pairs. One held the rope at the bottom. The other, tied to the rope, moved up, setting pitons and strange pieces of gear into the rocks. The climbers clipped the rope to the gear (each looked somewhat like a horse's stirrup) so that the rope passed through freely. Then the climbers scaled the cliff as their partners below fed out slack on the ropes.

There weren't many. A hundred, by Arin's count.

He watched the climbers reach the end of their ropes. They used their gear to anchor themselves to the cliff wall. Then they pulled up the rope, taking in the slack as their partners below began to climb the same path. When they met at the anchor, they repeated the whole process of climbing up as far as the rope's length would let them.

For a moment, Arin let himself imagine how they must feel. The wind screaming. Their skin dusted, lips chapped. Their fingers trembling over the rock until they found a hold. Relief when the grip was good. A jolt of fear when their toes slipped on glassy rock. Their feet cut away. They hung, arms blazing in pain. The rope held. Their feet found purchase and dug into the cliff. Hands bloody, mouths dry, they kept climbing.

Arin pushed back from the cliff. He stopped thinking about what the Rangers felt. They had come to steal his country and kill his people. He didn't need his god to tell him what to do.

He had his small group of armed Herrani fall back and

crouch behind nearby bushes that were stunted and twisted by high winds.

Arin waited until the first set of climbers had hauled themselves up over the cliff's lip. They staked themselves to the ground, then began pulling up the rope as their partners below made the final ascent.

Once the Rangers were nailed to the ground and their hands were full, the Herrani emerged from the bushes.

Arin was the first to fall upon them, to show the other Herrani what to do.

A Ranger turned, brown eyes wide. He was still staked to the ground. Arin's sword sliced the long, gathered rope in the Valorian's hands. It zipped away, spun down over the cliff. A scream floated up from below.

Arin cut the Ranger's anchor and set the point of his sword to the Ranger's sweat-shiny throat. "The blade, or the rocks below?" Arin asked in Valorian. The words sounded airless, scratched raw by the wind.

The whites of the Valorian's eyes showed clear around.

After one loud heartbeat, Arin realized the Ranger was too afraid to answer. Arin made the choice for him, and stabbed.

"I'm not talking with you," Roshar declared as he dropped the flap of the tent's opening in Arin's face. Arin pushed through anyway.

"You're bleeding on my floor," the prince said. "That stain will be impossible to get out."

Arin glanced down. The tent's "floor" was sand. Blood was trickling from his side, darkening the sand in coin-size drops. A Valorian dagger had worked its way past Arin's hardened leather armor, got in right at the ribs where the armor buckled. It had happened on the beach, after Arin had dealt with the Rangers and rode to meet the eastern army.

"You were at the back, I suppose," Roshar said, "away from all the fun. That's what you get for being late." Roshar pulled his sweat-drenched tunic away from his skin. "Fugh. I stink."

"Roshar—"

"Will you shut up? I said I'm not talking with you. You can't do anything right, can you?"

"But the general—"

"Yes, retreated. Yes, without his precious Rangers. I heard what you did. Tossed them from the cliff, eh? Very sporting of you. But you were late to *my* battle when *I* needed you and *I* told you and whose land is this anyway that I just fought to keep?"

"I know. I'm sorry."

The prince snorted.

Arin, unsure what to say, fumbled with his armor buckles. The cut along his ribs stung.

"I see that no one's helped you out of your armor yet. Poor baby. Now, *me*"—Roshar gestured at himself, dressed only in tunic and trousers, arms bare and muscular and smeared with someone else's blood—"I got out of armor as soon as the Valorians cast off from the beach, because *I* am a prince, and *I* told someone to take it off me, and people do as *I* say."

Arin said, "That's what you want from me?"

Roshar lowered his arms.

"Do you really want me to do everything you say?"

No answer.

"Doesn't it matter that I was right about the cliffs?"

Roshar winced. "Honestly, that makes it worse."

"I'm not going to obey you. You're my friend, not my master."

Roshar looked away, his mutilated nose blunting his profile. He studied the tent's blank canvas wall, which glowed in the sun. Roshar sighed, tugging on one cropped ear. Then he turned back and faced Arin squarely. His mouth was a long, tired line. "Here." He jerked at Arin's armor and began unbuckling it. "Stop bleeding. Oh, just look at you. Arin, you're a mess."

"I didn't need you anyway," Roshar told him as they rode back to the city, having left behind several battalions to keep the beach secure. "I happen to be very good at war. It's because I'm so handsome. Like one of your gods. People see me and their minds go blank. I run my sword right through them."

Arin *tchick*ed at Javelin, urging him ahead of Roshar's horse.

Roshar caught up. Like most easterners, he rode without reins, guiding his horse solely through knees, heels, and the shifting of his weight. This left him free to gesture expansively as he talked. "Are you listening?" He leaned to poke Arin in the shoulder. "I'm not sure you appreciate the magnitude of having a god in your midst."

"Can I pray for you to go away?"

Roshar grinned. "We took a few Valorians prisoner."

"Why?"

"For information, obviously. Not much has come out of Valoria lately. Our spies have been quiet. Yours?"

Arin hadn't heard anything from Tensen or his Moth. He shook his head.

"Well." Roshar rubbed his palms together. "Let's see what a little questioning reveals. I'm sure the prisoners will be happy to talk."

Arin shot him a sidelong look.

"Arin, you injure me. Torture is the furthest thing from my mind, I assure you. People love talking to me. I promise I'll ask my questions very, very nicely."

Arin held his breath underwater until his lungs ached, then broke the surface of the bath. His bathing room echoed with the sound of splashed water. Dirty lather lapped around his knees. He touched his side, and his fingers came away pink. The cut along his ribs was bleeding again. It was too shallow to stitch.

He found himself wondering how many scars the general had. Arin's lungs burned as if he was still holding his breath, which made him realize that he was, and that it hurt to feel such hatred and know that no scar could be enough, that the general could suffer no pain that would ever make Arin feel better.

The general and his daughter didn't look alike. Arin remembered how he'd hated to notice this during his first months as Kestrel's slave. He'd wanted to see the traces of that man in her, and it had unnerved him that he couldn't. There was something similar about the eyes . . . but hers were a much paler brown. Arin wasn't even sure he could call them brown. Honey wasn't brown. And the shape. Different, too. Slightly tipped up at the corners. Arin remembered making such comparisons, and how his desire to see something in her that he could hate shifted into self-disgust at far too much attention paid. Then, slowly, a curiosity to find her so different. And then came another emotion, one both softer and harder . . .

Arin got out of the bath. He got dressed, and got out of his rooms.

Sarsine stopped him on the stairway that ran down from the west wing. He smiled. "You look better."

She crossed her arms. "It's been a week."

His brow crinkled. "Since what?"

"Since that messenger came."

"Oh. I forgot."

"You've been busy." Her tone was dangerously even.

"I'll talk with him now."

"You've been busy," she repeated, "*throwing people off cliffs*."

"That's an exaggeration."

"So it's not true?"

"What do you want from me, Sarsine?"

"You blamed Kestrel for changing, but you've changed, too."

His voice was hard. "This is not the same."

"Isn't it?"

He turned his back on her. He jogged down the stairs, the tempo of his boots beating fast and sure.

"I tried to get here as soon as I could," said the messenger. He was a short man, all knobby wrists and elbows and knees. An oddly tiny nose. There were bags under his eyes. The irises were greenish, which reminded Arin of Tensen.

They sat in the receiving room of Arin's childhood suite. He didn't like being there. He looked at his childhood instruments, still hung on the wall. He remembered Kestrel touching them, her fingers plucking a string. He saw the birthmark on her right hand, in the middle of the soft web between forefinger and thumb. It had been like a little black star.

Arin should take those instruments down. He should get rid of them.

"It happened about a month ago," the messenger said.

Arin's attention snapped back to him.

"Someone gave me something." The man knotted his hands together. "She told me to give it to you, but I don't have it anymore."

"What was it?"

"A masker moth."

"What?" Arin's voice was sharp.

"One of those Valorian moths. The kind that change color. A prisoner gave it to me."

Arin's heart picked up speed. "*Who* gave it to you?"

"A Herrani woman."

"That's not possible." Tensen had told Arin that the Moth, his valued spy in the capital, was Risha. No one could mistake Risha for a Herrani. Like all easterners, her skin was brown, a much darker shade than even Arin's, which was tanned from years in the sun.

"I know what I saw," the messenger said.

"Tell me everything."

"I take care of horses along the road that runs north of the Valorian capital. A prison wagon stopped. They go by sometimes. I was watering the horses while the guards were stretching their legs. The woman called to me. She was reaching through the bars, and asked me to give you the moth, but the guards saw. That's why I don't have the moth anymore. It got crushed. The guards were rough with me. Her, too."

"What happened?"

"I don't know. I couldn't see. Anyway, they drove off."

"That's it?"

The man shifted uncomfortably at Arin's tone. "Should I not have come?"

"No, yes." Arin briefly squeezed his eyes shut. His pulse was going too fast. "You were right to come."

"I'm sorry I lost the moth."

"I don't care about that. Just . . . she spoke to you in Herrani?"

"Yes."

"You're sure?"

The messenger gave him an odd look. "I can recognize my own language. She was mother-taught, like you and me."

I don't speak Herrani, he remembered Risha saying. She'd also never said that she was the spy. Arin had taken Tensen's word for it. "You said you couldn't see. *What* couldn't you see?"

"I couldn't see into the wagon. Its walls were solid. The doors, too. I saw her at the window."

"Describe her."

"I can't."

Arin tried very hard to speak evenly. "What do you mean, you can't? You saw her. You said so."

"Well, yes, but"—the man was clearly frustrated, too—"I saw only her hand."

"What color was her skin? Like mine? Yours?"

"More or less. Less, I guess. Kind of pale. The color of a house slave's."

Not Dacran. "There must be something else you can tell me." It felt increasingly difficult for Arin to sit still. "What happened to the prisoner?"

The man rubbed his weathered neck, avoiding Arin's gaze. "The guards hit me. My head was ringing. I couldn't hear what they did inside the wagon. I don't know what they said. But her voice sounded horrible."

"And then?"

"The wagon drove north, toward the tundra."

Dangerously, Roshar said, "You believed my little sister was spying for Herran and you didn't see fit to mention it?"

"I'm mentioning it now."

"Arin, sometimes I really don't like you."

"It wasn't my secret to share. Tensen said that his informant insisted on keeping her identity anonymous. I pressed him, he gave me a name. I admired her. Everyone in this city would be dead if she hadn't told Tensen about the poison in the aqueducts. If she wanted to be anonymous, I had to honor that."

"You had to honor saving your own skin, you mean. The queen and I might have felt a little differently about you if we'd known you were using our sister for information she could have been killed for obtaining."

"It *wasn't* your sister."

"That's not the point!"

"I know, but what would you have done in my place?"

Roshar stared moodily into the library fireplace. No fire had been lit there for months, but the smell of cinders remained. He played with his ring, a thick band that looked as though set with a dull black stone. It was unusual for an easterner to wear a ring; they liked to keep their hands free of any ornamentation. This ring, Arin knew, had a particular purpose: what appeared to be a stone was in fact a vial that contained a numbing serum. He'd never asked, but he suspected that the serum could also kill. Roshar wiggled the ring. "Arin," he said quietly, "you're really pushing things."

"I know," Arin said again. "I'm sorry."

"So. Your Moth is not my sister."

"Yes."

"She's Herrani."

"Yes."

"A dead Herrani."

Arin shook his head. "She was sent to the tundra's prison camp."

"As good as dead," Roshar amended.

"It's a work camp. You can't make a dead body work. This was only a month ago. She could be alive."

Roshar swiftly met Arin's eyes. "No. Oh no. Don't even think what I think you're thinking."

"I could lead a small force north—"

"Stop right there."

"She could have valuable information."

"Not worth it."

"She doesn't deserve to be there."

"She knew what she was getting into. All our spies know the risk." Gently, Roshar added, "You can't save everyone."

Arin let out a slow breath. He pressed palms to his eyes. His hands were cold. Kestrel's hands were always cold, at first, to the touch. He used to like to feel how they would slowly warm . . .

Arin pulled himself up short. He was suspicious of the way his mind worked, how it leaped for no reason to Kestrel, how this reminded him of so many times before, the way his thoughts would turn to her and bank home, like he was a hunting bird and she was the spinning lure.

"I'm not going to tell you what to do," Roshar said. "We've had enough of that. I'm simply going to ask you—*you*, who I will admit have some preternatural gift for strategy—if you think it's smart to send soldiers north, away from the war *here*, to attempt to rescue one woman from prison when you don't know how many lives this rescue would cost, or even the identity of the person you're looking for. Well, Arin? Is it smart?"

"No."

"Are you going to do it anyway?"

"No," Arin said reluctantly. "I won't." And he meant it.

ARIN'S HAND TWITCHED AGAINST THE PILLOW. His legs twisted the sheets.

He opened his eyes. The moon was large and yellow in the window. He wondered how the moon would look from the rooftop gardens, and he suddenly was in the gardens— both of them at the same time, even though the eastern garden and the western one were separated by a locked door. The smooth stones were cold under his bare feet. He was somewhere between sleeping and waking. Then he forgot this realization and was fully inside the dream without knowing that he was.

He heard someone's footfalls on the other side of the garden wall. But *he* was on both sides, in both gardens: his and Kestrel's. He was alone. He was still. He was not making that sound.

Again, he heard the gravel scatter. But no one else was there.

The night sky unfolded. Someone was snipping its threads. It came down on him in panels of silk. The blue of it covered his eyes, filled his mouth. His ribs spread wide. He was drowning. He was trying to drink the cloth. His throat yearned for it even as his lungs collapsed.

He startled awake. The sheets were damp. His breath came short.

The dream deteriorated. He had only images of blue silk. On his eyes. In his mouth, too.

He sat up straight. His bed was washed in moonlight.

His mind flickered with the memory of the last time he'd seen Kestrel. The spill of her blue dress over the piano bench.

He made himself go back to sleep.

In the morning, he vaguely knew that he'd had a nightmare. Then he frowned, uncertain that "nightmare" was the right word. He tried to remember it. He had flashes: the sensation of drowning, the sense that he had *wanted* to drown. Something blue.

Arin suddenly remembered enough to wish that he hadn't. He shoved the dream from his mind. As is the way with fragile thoughts, the cobwebby threads spun away. They became nothing . . . or almost nothing. They became a feeling he could no longer explain as he cupped water from the basin to his mouth. The feeling drifted, not a thought or a memory anymore, just a flutter of unease.

He went to Sarsine's room for breakfast. The suite had been hers as a girl, decorated according to the orders of Arin's sister, whose own suite was closed off, curtains drawn.

Sarsine set her cup in its saucer. "What's wrong?"

"Nothing." He'd come to talk, but found that he didn't know what to say and didn't really want to say anything after all.

"You have shadows under your eyes. The god of sleep does not love you."

Arin shrugged. He peeled a summer fruit, the little knife moving quickly in his hand. The fruit's violet flesh dented and dripped. It smelled fragrant, dusky, sweet. Familiar. A perfume. On the skin, right at the base of her throat.

He dropped the fruit to his plate, no longer hungry.

Sarsine took it from him and ate, sucking her thumb to get the juice. "Aren't you pleased that some of us are well enough to harvest fruit?"

He focused his attention. "Yes, but . . ."

"Not well enough to fight."

"I don't want you to fight."

"Not *me*, perhaps." She drank her tea.

"Could you oversee a project?"

She raised her black brows.

He pulled folded pages from the inside pocket of his light jacket. They described in detail how he'd made the miniature cannon: the process for making the molds for the barrel and ball, the dimensions, the way to fit the barrel into a leather stock.

Sarsine examined the pages. "How many do you want?"

"As many as you can have made."

He went quiet. She let him be. He ate a bit of bread, then caught himself staring at Tensen's ring on his smallest finger. He wondered why his spymaster had lied to him.

Tensen had promised the Moth her anonymity. That had been clear from the first. Then Tensen had seemed to backtrack on that promise—or to let it fall under the weight of his greater promise of loyalty to Arin. Tensen had named Risha as his clever spy.

Why would a Herrani woman be so insistent on her anonymity?

A servant, likely, in the imperial palace. Scared to be discovered. The emperor was a vengeful man.

Arin touched his scar. His fingers were sticky.

Could the Moth have been Deliah? But the Herrani dressmaker, who had sewn Arin's face, had given him information directly. He didn't understand why she would do that *and* go through an elaborate charade of being Tensen's secret spy.

As if guessing the course of his thoughts, Sarsine said, "What about the messenger?"

"I spoke with him. Told him he could go home."

"Arin. The borders are closed. He trekked through the mountains from Valoria. You can't send him back. He has no home."

Arin winced. "I wasn't thinking."

"That only happens to you when your heart gets in the way."

He felt again that flutter of unease. He tried to remember the dream he had made himself forget. He stood, eager to get away from his cousin, who knew him too well—even though that was, he realized, why he had come. "The messenger can stay in my old rooms, then."

Sarsine said, "I'll let him know, if he hasn't already left."

Roshar was in the kitchen yard with his tiger, who'd just killed a chicken. The flagstones were strewn with bloody feathers. The tiger, though still small, had large paws. It lay in the yard, panting in the sun, paws over its prize, muzzle pink and wet.

The prince eyed Arin.

"Was that a laying hen?" Arin asked.

"I have news for you. Not about chickens."

"The Valorian prisoners?"

Roshar sat at the edge of the well, his expression hard to read.

Arin's heart dropped. "What kind of news?"

"Would you like the bad news first, or the news I'm not sure whether you will take as good or bad?"

"Bad news."

"Your spymaster's dead."

"Tensen?" Arin had expected this, yet the stab of sorrow went as deep as if he'd been wholly unprepared.

"The dressmaker, too. The general killed Tensen—or at least, that's what they say. Unclear about the dressmaker."

Arin's stomach was hollow. He remembered looking up at Deliah through the veil of his own blood and thinking, for a moment, that she looked like his mother.

"Do you want the other news?" Roshar tentatively asked.

No. Arin was suddenly sure that he did not want to hear it, would not be able to bear it. He felt a sinking dread.

"Your . . ." Roshar stumbled.

A chicken feather lifted in a sudden breeze and eddied along the base of the well.

"Arin, Kestrel's dead."

His ears were ringing. He felt as if he'd fallen into the well. He heard Roshar's voice from far away. The words tumbled down to him. "It was recent," Roshar said. "A disease. While she was away from the capital, traveling with the prince. The whole empire is in mourning."

"That's not true."

Roshar said something. Arin couldn't hear him. He was at the bottom of the well. The water closed over his head, cold and black.

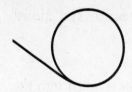

"I'M FINE."

"Arin, I know you're not."

Sarsine had been waiting for him by Javelin's empty stall when Arin returned with the lathered horse. Arin felt a jagged, sharp sort of feeling. Rusted in parts, menacingly shiny in others. If it had been a real thing lying in the dirt, anyone would have known better than to touch it.

He had gone for a ride. He'd left his house so there would be no question of visiting or avoiding parts of it that reminded him of her. He'd pushed Javelin hard. But when he had finally slowed the stallion and paced him under the green canopy of the city's horse paths, he'd wiped the sweat from his face and remembered whose horse was beneath him. He saw that he had no choices. He saw that even avoidance was a reminder.

His hands held the reins too short. An emotion claimed him, merciless and familiar. His heart shrank. It felt small and hard and full, like a nut he could crack in his fist.

His face was still wet. He'd ridden too far. He turned Javelin back home.

When he saw Sarsine waiting in the open, shaded stables on a three-legged stool, he had ignored her and let Javelin drink from the trough in the yard. He had stripped the horse of his saddle. Lifted off the reins. Fetched a bucket of water, which he had slowly poured over the horse, who snorted and lowered his head. Arin scraped water from the coat, then wiped him down with a cloth. He checked the hooves, digging out mud and pebbles with a pick, using his fingers to get gently into the grooves on either side of the hoof's frog.

Finally Arin saw that his silence wouldn't be enough to make his cousin go away. He brought the horse into the stables. He said he was fine, she said he wasn't. He wiped down Javelin's tack and hung it up and tried silence again, this time because he was sure that if he spoke he'd say something he'd regret.

She said, "Why do you think it's wrong to mourn her?"

"Sarsine." His voice was tight. "If you love me, you'll leave."

"Answer me first."

The words shot out of him. "Because she wasn't who I thought she was. You can't mourn someone you didn't know."

"I saw how you were with each other. Why would you think you didn't know her?"

"Because she's a *liar*. She has her games, her clever tricks. Everyone falls into her trap. I did, too . . ." He trailed off, listening to his own words. He began to brush Javelin's brown coat, leaning in hard. "She's not dead."

"She's not?" Sarsine sounded worried.

He watched the horse's muscles twitch and leap under the brush. "No."

"Arin, I know how this feels. You know that I do. Like it's impossible, like some mistake has been made and if you could only correct it—"

"That's not it. I'm saying that the whole story sounds false."

"I don't understand."

The brush was moving rapidly. "The secret marriage, to start with. The Firstsummer wedding was valuable to the emperor. All that goodwill. The excitement to witness the emperor's dynasty growing. The bride. She was a prize, do you know that? That wedding wasn't about the emperor's son marrying Kestrel. It was about the emperor marrying the military. The emperor would never forgo that wedding. If they married in secret, then why didn't the emperor force them to marry again for everyone to see? It doesn't make sense."

"You don't want it to make sense."

"A *disease* killed her? I never saw her sick the entire time I worked in her villa. She was only bedridden once, and that's because—" Arin stopped, remembering how she'd limped. She'd been injured in a duel that she had fought for him.

He lowered the brush.

He'd been here before. He used to do this all the time: invent stories about Kestrel that fit with her bandaged knee, the way she'd kissed him, the night she'd unlocked the door that separated her rooftop garden from his. From a window in his suite, he'd seen the door open. He had waited, pulse rising. Moments like that, right before she had shut the door again, haunted him in the capital, made him imagine things about her. Lovely, tempting scenarios. He remembered how he'd even wondered if she could be Tensen's Moth.

"Firstsummer was about a month ago," he heard himself saying.

Javelin huffed and stamped. He curved his neck to whuffle Arin's chest.

Sarsine started to speak.

"Please leave," Arin said. "I answered your question. I want to be alone. I need to think," he added, though he wasn't even sure what he was thinking.

When she'd gone, Arin threaded fingers through the horse's mane. Kestrel loved Javelin. She'd left him behind anyway.

Arin remembered seeing her hand in Javelin's mane, curling into the coarse strands. This made him remember the almost freakish length between her littlest finger and thumb as her hand spanned piano keys. The black star of the birthmark. He saw her again in the imperial palace. Her music room. He'd seen that room only once. About a month ago, right before Firstsummer. Her blue sleeves were fastened at the wrist.

Something tugged inside him. A flutter of unease.

Do you sing?

Those had been her first words to him, the day she had bought him.

A band of nausea circled Arin's throat, just as it had when she had asked him that question, in part for the same reason.

She'd had no trace of an accent. She had spoken in perfect, natural, mother-taught Herrani.

"I told you everything I know," said the messenger. Arin had gone to his childhood suite, feeling an anxiety verging on panic at the thought of not finding the man there, of having to track him down, of time lost . . . but the man had opened the outermost door almost immediately after Arin's pounding knock.

"I didn't ask you the right questions," Arin said. "I want to start again. You said that the prisoner reached through the bars of the wagon to give you the moth."

"Yes."

"And you couldn't really see her."

"That's right."

"But you said she was Herrani. Why would you say that if you couldn't *see* her?"

"Because she spoke in Herrani."

"Perfectly."

"Yes."

"No accent."

"No."

"Describe the hand."

"I'm not sure . . ."

"Start with the skin. You said it was paler than yours, than mine."

"Yes, like a house slave's."

Which wasn't very different from a Valorian's. "Could you see her wrist, her arm?"

"The wrist, yes, now that you mention it. She was in chains. I saw the manacle."

"Did you see the sleeve of a dress?"

"Maybe. Blue?"

Dread churned inside Arin. "You think or you know?"

"I don't know. Things happened too fast."

"Please. This is important."

"I don't want to say something I'm not sure is true."

"All right, all right. Was this her right hand or her left?"

"I don't know."

"Can you tell me *anything* about it? Did she wear a seal ring?"

"Not that I saw, but—"

"Yes?"

"She had a birthmark. On the hand, near the thumb. It looked like a little black star."

"Arin." Roshar briefly squeezed his eyes shut, then regarded him with the slightly repelled, slightly fascinated look reserved for aberrations of nature, such as animals born with two heads. "This sounds—"

"I don't care how it sounds."

"You've thought this kind of thing about her before."

"I should have trusted myself. She lied. I believed her. I shouldn't have."

"Arin, she's dead."

"Show me the body."

"I'm worried about you. I'm serious."

"I don't need soldiers. I'll go to the tundra alone."

"That's not what I meant."

"I know. But I'm going."

"You can't leave in the middle of a war to chase a ghost."

"I'll be back."

"The tundra is Valorian territory. Do you understand what they'll do to you if you're caught? You can't hide who you are. That scar—"

"You don't need me. You said it yourself."

"I was joking!"

Arin gave Roshar a copy of the same plans for the miniature cannon he'd given to Sarsine. "I've asked my cousin to oversee production on this. The Herrani aren't well enough to fight, but it doesn't require much physical strength to make these. And you can assign the construction of different parts of the mechanism to different people. Even the elderly can make the ammunition. If you start now, you'll have a small arsenal of these weapons by the time I'm back."

"You're giving this to me?"

"I should have given it to you before."

"This is the sort of thing people do before they kill themselves."

Arin shook his head. "Suicide is an undignified way to die."

Roshar drew himself up to his full height. He folded his arms, rippling fingers along the biceps. "I could keep you here by force. In my country, we have laws about making sure crazy people don't hurt themselves."

Arin said, "There *is* something you can do for me."

"I dread to ask."

"Can I borrow your ring?"

THE TUNDRA AIR WAS WHITE WITH MIST.
Through his spyglass as he crouched behind a stunted bush,
boots seeping into cold mud, Arin saw the dark line of prisoners emerge from behind rocks at the base of the volcanoes. He
scanned each prisoner that passed within view. He couldn't
see her face. The mist was too thick. They filed through
the work camp's open gate. It shut behind them.

He waited for nightfall. The temperature plummeted. A
wolf howled in the distance.

Ilyan, the messenger, had warned him about the wolves.
He'd shown Arin a way into the tundra that kept them out
of sight of the Valorian road to the work camp. They'd slept
by day and traveled by night. Ilyan was waiting for Arin
where they'd stopped to unload their gear and rest the
three horses near a shallow lake. Arin remembered the way
Javelin's head had lifted to see him go.

Arin went quiet inside. He stared at the shut gate. He
was filled with a tense, solid stillness, the kind that wouldn't
let him think about anything other than what he needed to

do. It stopped the emotions that had claimed him ever since Roshar's news. It spread like a cold mist over the tarry grief, the elated hope. It kept at bay the feeling that had gutted him, had made it impossible to breathe: remorse.

Another wolf called. It was now as dark as it was going to get.

He left his cover and made for the volcanoes.

At the base of a volcano, whose top disappeared into the greenish half dark, Arin scrubbed loose sulfur into his hair. He rubbed the yellow, crumbly, stinking stuff into his face, smudging it along the line of his scar. He caked his hands with it. He rubbed it over Roshar's ring.

Arin's plain clothes were streaked with mud from days of travel. If he could have seen himself, he would have seen a blur of yellow and brown. A man of uncertain age and origin, unless someone looked closely.

He prayed that no one would. He went down into the mines. His heartbeat seemed to echo in the tunnel like a drum.

He waited for morning.

At dawn, when the prisoners came down into the tunnel with pickaxes, Arin stepped out of the shadows to mingle with them, become one of them. Furtively, he searched their faces. When he didn't see her, he grew terrified that he was too late. *A month*. He hated himself for it. As he went deeper into the mines he couldn't bear his thoughts: that she was sick, hurt. That she'd been transferred to some other kind of prison. Maybe he was wasting yet more time here while she suffered elsewhere.

He couldn't let himself think the worst thought.

Kestrel was strong. She could survive this. She could survive anything. But when he saw the slack faces of the other prisoners—their blank stares, their shuffling gait—he wasn't so sure. Fear slid down his spine.

There were two Valorian guards down in the mines with him, but they paid little attention. They didn't notice when Arin took a pickax right out of a prisoner's hands. The guards broke their conversation with each other only when the empty-handed prisoner, wandering like a sleepwalker, tried to dig sulfur out of the rocky walls with his fingers, which bled, nails broken. Out of the corner of his eye, Arin watched the man's mechanical determination. Arin kept his head down, his shoulders slumped, and his face as blank as the guards neared the prisoner and conferred. Then they shrugged. They found the man a pickax.

Arin worked. He thought of Kestrel doing this. He drove his ax into the wall, swallowed the bile in his throat. He could not get sick, could not draw attention to himself. But the nausea didn't leave him.

Hours might have gone by like this. He couldn't count time passing. The grayish light that filtered down from the tunnel's mouth hadn't changed.

But the prisoners did. They went suddenly still. Arin snatched his ax back in midswing. He, too, made himself into a statue. He wondered what they were waiting for.

It was water. The guards distributed it. The prisoners' bodies went taut, and they eagerly drank.

Arin imitated them. He swallowed the water.

Moments later, his pulse shot up to the sky.

He felt too big for his body. He knew, as if from a distance, that he'd been tampered with. The water.

He struck the rock with an energy resembling delight. This wasn't right. He told himself that this wasn't right, that this wasn't what he really felt. Yet he lovingly filled his double basket with sulfur.

He was going to fail. He'd had a plan, he had come here with a plan . . . sweat soaked his shirt, the pieces of the plan scattered, and he became certain only of his failure.

Because of you.

Arin's hands slowed. He heard Kestrel's voice again, felt the sway of a carriage. Firstwinter. If he put his palm to the carriage window, he'd melt its feathered frost.

Because of you, Kestrel had said. Her mouth had opened beneath his.

The knowledge of what Arin was here to do drove into him and turned like a screw.

He became himself again. He wouldn't fail her, not again.

The drug faded. It was still there—it grasshoppered in his blood—but his body was almost quiet now. Tired. His bones felt loose in their sockets. The guards led him to the surface, where other yellow-coated prisoners waited, too many to count at a glance, enough that they could have overwhelmed the guards even without weapons. And they *did* have weapons. Axes, some of them. Other prisoners could have grabbed the rocks at their feet.

Arin understood obedience. After the Valorian invasion, it had been easy for him to obey. He saw what happened to people who didn't. He'd been a frightened child. Then he grew and changed, resisted. He got what came next. Blood in the mouth. Elsewhere. Sometimes it felt like it was everywhere, in his eyes, too, changing his vision. It coated his thoughts. The taste of things. Once, to prove a point: a horse halter was tightened over his head, an iron bit set between his teeth.

After ten years of slavery, Arin knew obedience in its many forms. The fear of pain, the gritty promise to one-self of vengeance. Hopelessness. A grinding monotony broken just often enough by the strap or fist. The way punishment made his master more his master, and him less himself. He'd been prone to defiance, no matter how stupid it was, because he could insist, at least in that moment, on the integrity of his will: unalterable by anyone. But then pain did alter it. Humiliation did. Obedience became a version of despair.

But he'd never seen the kind of obedience he witnessed when the guards herded the prisoners into a line. They were cows. They weren't even like people *pretending* to be animals, which he had seen and had done. There was no question of resistance here on the tundra, no glimmer of hatred.

Arin couldn't imagine Kestrel obeying like this. He couldn't imagine her obeying at all.

He strained to see her through the ragged line of prisoners. Was she at the front of the line? Was she so changed that he couldn't recognize her?

Was she there at all?

A guard reached for Arin's pickax. Arin's hands jerked back. He wanted to swing the ax and nail it into the guard's throat.

The guard peered at him. Arin forced his fingers to relax. He let the ax go.

He lined up like everyone else and was led to the camp.

He avoided the food and water served in the yard. He was slowly dribbling soup over his bowl's lip and down into the mud when he saw her. Her back was to him. Her hair was matted. She was so thin that he had to swallow hard. For a moment he believed that he was wrong, that this could not be her. But it was.

She was being led to a cell block with the other women. *Look back. Please.* She didn't, and then he was being led in the opposite direction, his heart shaking inside him, yet he had to do what he was told.

Until, that was, the moment he was inside the men's cell block.

He came up behind the nearest guard, wrenched the Valorian's head at an awful angle, and snapped his neck.

There were other guards. They came at him. He stung them with Roshar's ring and they slumped, unconscious, to the ground. Arin found keys on a fallen guard. He locked up the male prisoners. He stuffed as many as he could into as few cells as possible to save time.

The women's cell block was quiet. Most of the prisoners were already in their cells: shadows on the ground.

At the end of the hall, a Valorian woman with silver braids saw him. She drew her dagger. Opened her mouth to shout. He rushed at her, dodged the dagger, clamped a hand down on her face, and stung her with the ring. Then the keys were in his grip and Arin was going cell by cell. He called Kestrel's name in a hoarse whisper. There was no answer. A feeling frothed out of him, an acid mix of dread and hope and desperation.

Then he stopped. He saw her sleeping on the dirt. Again, her back was to him, but he knew the curve of her spine and the spike of her shoulder and the way her ribs rose and fell. He fumbled with the keys.

He kept saying her name. He was begging her to wake up. The same words spilled out of him over and over. He wasn't even sure what he was saying anymore as he came into her cell and touched her cheek and, when she still didn't wake, shifted her body up. Her head tipped back. She slept. Some part of Arin warned that he was going to have to slap her, that she *must* wake up, and then another part recoiled at the thought. He wouldn't, he never would, he would kill the person who would.

"Kestrel?" He couldn't even shake her frail shoulders. "Kestrel?"

Her eyes cracked open. He caught his breath. She came awake more fully, and saw him.

He hadn't allowed himself, before, to consider the possibility that she'd be like the other prisoners, that her mind would be gone, that there'd be no life in her eyes and her face would be drained of everything that made her who she was.

She wasn't like that. She wasn't, and as Arin watched her blink and take him in, and saw the mind behind her gaze, he was grateful. The gratitude came hot and flowing: a prayer of thanks to his gods. He cupped her face between his hands—too rough.

Or he believed he must have been too rough, because she recoiled. He was afraid he'd hurt her. But she narrowed her eyes in the wan light, studying him. He saw her confusion, couldn't translate it.

She whispered, "Who are you?"

Arin didn't understand until she asked her question again.

Understanding arrowed into him.

She had no memory of him. She truly had no idea who he was.

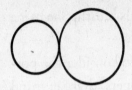

THEY STUMBLED OVER THE TUNDRA. HE SAW how unnaturally drowsy she was. Her ankles sometimes folded beneath her, as if her body was made of stuffed cloth and she was forcing it to move out of sheer will.

"Lean on me," he said. She did, but he could tell that she didn't like it.

"Just a bit farther," he said.

Eventually, he carried her. In the green-cast dark, she slept against his chest.

Arin's legs were slick with mud when he reached the shores of the lake where he'd left Ilyan and the horses. Arin saw what was left of the camp. His knees nearly buckled. He swore.

Kestrel woke. He set her gently down. Then he crouched, burying his face in his hands.

Ilyan's half-eaten corpse had been dragged from the tent. The horses were gone.

Wolves. Arin remembered hearing them howl the night before. His palms slid from his face. He tried not to think about the terror and pain of Ilyan's death, and how this, too, was his fault. He tried not to think about how long it would take without horses to cover the tundra and the mountains that led into Herran. Kestrel's condition . . .

He glanced at her. The poverty of her frame. The wariness with which she regarded him, the way she was doing so even now.

"They might have survived," he said, meaning the horses. He was speaking quickly. "They'd have run. They'd stay together."

She looked like she might ask something, then her face hardened in suspicion and Arin was certain that the only reason she had come with him was because he was a better option than a prison cell.

He turned. There was no high ground from which to see. The tundra night was light enough to see Kestrel's face, but too murky to spot three horses wandering—how far away?

Much too far.

If they were there at all.

"Javelin!" he called. The horses were good, but only one of them was intelligent enough to come when called—*if* Javelin could. Arin didn't know. He'd never heard of a horse doing that, not from out of sight, not without the bribe of a treat.

Arin thought they were far enough from the camp, and he'd left most of the guards unconscious—maybe dead. He hadn't taken any care with how deeply he'd driven the ring's stinger. Still, he and Kestrel might have been followed. Shouting wasn't smart.

Arin looked at her. She was fighting sleep.

He called again. "Javelin!"

He made himself hoarse. He walked as far away from Kestrel as he dared, shouting for the horse. Finally, he came back to her and knelt in the mud where she sat. "Call him," Arin said. "He'll come if you call."

"*Who* will come?"

He realized that nothing he'd said provided any context to understand who and what Javelin was if someone didn't already know. He realized that he'd been hoping that she hadn't meant it, in the prison, when she'd asked who Arin was and looked at him like he was a dangerous stranger. Part of him had believed that she was pretending not to know him in order to wound him, because he deserved it, and it was clear how much she should hate him now.

"Kestrel," he said softly, and could tell from her expression that she accepted her name but didn't trust it. "Javelin is your horse. You love him. He loves you. If you call, he will come for you. We need him. Please try."

She did. Nothing happened, and the look she gave him—as if he was tricking her, making some mockery she couldn't fathom—made his throat close. "Please," he said. "Again."

She hesitated, then did as he asked, though eyeing him the entire time the way you would a predatory creature.

When Arin heard the thud of hooves in mud, he sagged in relief.

Javelin led the other two. One of the mares was limping.

Arin would set a sacrifice to the god of the lost. He swore that he would. Then he looked again at Kestrel, who rose unsteadily to her feet, and he knew he would have to sacrifice to all of his gods.

Kestrel went to her horse. Arin couldn't see her face, which rested against the animal's neck. He didn't see her moment of recognition. But he saw her chest heave. Javelin lipped her hair. She leaned against the horse as she had not leaned against Arin—fully, tenderly. Trusting.

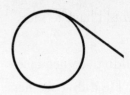

HE UNNERVED HER.

She was grateful to him and didn't argue when he said that they should ride Javelin together and lead the two mares. She saw his worried look. How it assessed her. She knew as well as he did that she was likely to fall asleep in the saddle. Javelin was sturdy enough to bear them both, at least for a while. The plan made sense. But she resented it.

It was the way she felt, tucked up against the stranger's chest, cradled by either arm. It was the way her body seemed to know him.

Her head swayed. She let herself rest against him.

It wasn't right that her body should know this person when her mind didn't. Hazily, she realized that he could tell her any lie he wanted.

Her memory was a mouth with the teeth torn out. She kept reaching in, probing the holes, pulling back. It hurt.

Yes, any lie.

He had saved her, but she didn't know what he wanted from her—or what he might say to get it.

His heart beat against her spine. It lulled her even as she knew that it shouldn't. She slept.

In the morning, she got a better look at him. Her mind was clearer, she thought, than it had been in some time. He was building a fire. He slowed, though, when he caught the way her gaze inspected him. He went still.

He was dirty all over. She had the fleeting thought that she'd seen him both dirty and clean before. Her gaze traced the long scar, quite visible now that the sulfur had rubbed away. A sort of half recognition shimmered inside her. But the scar wasn't what made him memorable.

His gray eyes flashed to hers.

She should remember him. She went over the lines of his face again. Distrust coiled within her. It didn't seem possible that she would have seen a person like this and not remember him.

Something was wrong with the awkward claim he'd made after their escape that they were friends. If the tentative way he'd said it hadn't alerted her to its not being wholly true, the way he'd just let her evaluate him and now waited, breath held, for some judgment, suggested his nervousness. If they were really friends, she wouldn't make him nervous. She felt herself harden.

Now he looked hurt, and like he was trying to hide it, as if he'd guessed her thoughts.

This, too, she didn't like: how easily he read her.

They rode separately. She was on Javelin. He rode a mare. The next time they stopped to rest the horses, she came closer to the fire, even though this meant coming closer to him. She was achingly cold.

He offered her bread and dried meat. He apologized for it. "I know you're used to better."

Which was a stupid thing to say, given that he'd just rescued her from a prison.

"I'm sorry," he said. "That was a stupid thing to say."

When she took the canteen, she couldn't stop herself from doing what she'd done in the morning, which was to sniff the water.

"It's not drugged," he told her.

"I know," she replied, and thought from the way his face changed that he'd seen her disappointment.

He kept apologizing. He kept trying to tell her something that she wouldn't let him finish, and when she cut him off he didn't look remotely like the person who had pulled her across the prison yard and attacked anyone who stood in their way, using that odd, heavy ring on his finger, and then disarming a fallen guard, wielding the stolen dagger as his own, burying it in the next guard's belly.

"Please let me explain," he said as they rode.

Fear flickered in her lungs. Her mind felt sore. Though it was dizzying to not know so much, a shrinking thing inside her warned that it'd be much worse to remember. "Leave me alone."

"Don't you want to know what happened? Why you were there?"

She saw his naked misery. She suspected that any explanation he could provide was more for his sake than hers.

She wanted to shove him off his horse. Make him feel how it was to fall. *She* was falling, she was plunging through the black nothingness of *why* and *how*, she was terrified of what she had forgotten. She blamed him for not seeing her fear even as she was determined to hide it. "All right," she said. "Go ahead. Tell me why."

For all his earlier persistence, he now didn't seem to know where to begin. "You were a spy. You were caught."

"*Your* spy?"

"Not exactly."

"Close enough. So that's why you came for me. That's why you want me to remember. That's what you want from me: information."

"No. Kestrel, we—"

"If we're friends, how did we meet?"

His mare tossed her head. He was drawing the reins too tight. "In the market."

"That's *where*, not *how*."

He swallowed. "You—"

But she glimpsed the market, the dusty heat of it. She heard a crowd roar and remembered seeing his unscarred face looking at her, his features taut with hatred.

"Where are you taking me?" she whispered.

Now he saw the fear. She saw him see it. He stopped his horse. Her horse stopped, too. He reached to touch her. She flinched away. "Kestrel." There it was again: his inexplicable hurt. "I'm taking you home."

"You know what I think? I think that you could be taking me anywhere. I think that you *do* want something from me. I think that you are a liar."

She spurred Javelin ahead.

He let her go. He knew that she needed him to survive on the tundra. She couldn't go far.

She glanced down at the horse moving beneath her. Javelin. This horse was hers. His name felt right. Little else did.

The pink sun lowered in the sky. Mosquitoes rose from the mud. As she rode alongside him, her horse seemed to grow larger and higher. She wasn't doing well.

He asked if she was hurt. After she said that she wasn't, he asked again. "Maybe your memory . . ." he trailed off, and she couldn't stand how *hopeful* he looked, as if some head injury was the desired cause of everything. His searching gaze made her want to snarl like an animal.

By sunset, her body had become almost uncontrollable. The need had been building all day, shuddering inside her. Her stomach cramped. She had the faint certainty that she must have been trained to ride well or she would have already dropped off her horse.

He saw it. He kept slowing the pace even though she could tell that he wanted to push farther. "What's wrong?" he asked.

She didn't want to admit that she craved a drug that she'd been forced to take. He guessed it anyway. He nodded, and said, "They gave it to me, too, yesterday." Then she really hated him, for guessing, and for thinking he understood the clawing desire for something he'd only tasted once.

She kept going until she couldn't see straight and her stomach was wobbling, heaving. Finally, he grabbed her horse's bridle and dragged them both to a stop.

She was sick all over the tundra's moss and bracken. He held her hair away from her face. Some part of her that apparently cared didn't know how he could stand to touch her. He wasn't clean, but she was beyond filthy.

He gave her water. She swished it, spat it out, drank, then eyed the canteen in her shaking fingers. She appreciated that he'd come well supplied—for three people, even—but he kept producing things she needed, and packing them away when she didn't, and building fires and leading the way and doing *everything*, that she almost wished he wouldn't.

"Why don't you hold on to that." He nodded at the canteen.

Her fingers tightened around it. "Don't condescend to me."

He touched his scar. "I didn't mean to."

She got back on her horse. "Let's go," she told him.

Nightfall presented a new set of issues.

"There's only one tent." He cleared his throat. "But there

are three bedrolls." He waited—to see, she thought, if she'd insist that he sleep outside, but she felt that that would be admitting too much, even as she refused to consider exactly what she would be admitting. So she gave him a curt nod.

He didn't build a fire, which made her think he was still worried they might be seen. "We should be traveling by night," she said, "and sleeping by day."

He shook his head. He didn't look at her.

"I'm wide awake," she insisted.

"You should try to sleep. Things should be normal for you."

This, if the pattern of the day was any proof, should have made her wild with irritation. But his expression as he unloaded the folded tent was slow and heavy. His hands were busy. His eyes, though, were quiet. Silver in the dark. Shining. Like water.

"All right." She huddled, arms tight around her knees. She tried to stop her bones from rattling. She didn't want to be sick again. She turned so that she wouldn't see him, and listened to the sounds of him setting up the tent.

Even in the tent, with the heat of him barely an arm's length away, she was desperately cold. She longed for her nighttime drug. She could taste its metallic flavor on her tongue.

He'd already given her all the spare clothes he had. That first night, after the horses came, he'd opened a pack near the body of his friend and pulled out a coat. He'd stuffed her limp arms into it. She had recognized that it was his by the way that it smelled. Her own clothes seemed to have been cut from a sack: dun-colored, long sleeves, trousers. She hadn't been wearing this her whole time in the prison. She'd remembered this as he'd bundled her and she'd drowsed in the gorgeous haze of her nighttime drug. She remembered when her clothes had changed and why. She could still feel the buttons of her dress popping open along her back. A rash of cold and terror as the air hit her skin. The pain. But the drug was soft and she was sleeping then and what did clothes matter, anyway?

Now she was nowhere near sleep. She was a curled worm under a mound of cloth. He'd tucked the second bedroll over her, then got out of his and gave her that, too. There was nothing left for him to give her.

His voice came through the dark, hesitant. "Kestrel . . ."

"I wouldn't be cold if I were asleep," she said through jittering teeth. "I need to sleep."

A pause. "I know you do."

"Give me something to sleep."

"I don't have anything like that."

"Yes, you do."

A longer pause this time. "I don't."

"You have that ring."

"No."

"Use it."

"No."

"I want you to."

"I don't really know how to use it. It could kill you."

"I don't care."

He was angry. "I do."

She knew why his eyes had been too bright earlier. Her own were stinging.

He shifted. She kept her back to him as she felt him move closer. The warmth of him slowly fitted along her spine. It was like sinking into a bath. His words brushed the back of her neck: "Just to keep you warm," he said, a question in his tone.

"You say that we're friends."

"Yes."

"Have we done this before?"

Another pause. "No."

Her shaking quieted to a shiver. She found that she'd moved even closer to him, had sealed herself against him. His heart beat fast against her back. He held her, and the weight of his arm made her feel more solid, more real, less ready to shatter into mirrorlike pieces. She calmed, relaxing into his warmth.

She still didn't sleep. Neither did he. She could feel his wakefulness. She thought, fleetingly, that it was like him not to fall asleep before she did. She didn't know how she could believe this to be true. It was hard to reconcile with the one memory she had of him: his face in the market, across a distance. An enemy's mouth, enemy's eyes.

But he was here, he had saved her, and he'd asked nothing of her except to remember, and had stopped asking even for that. She knew his scent. Knew that she liked it. His hand reached to touch the pulse in her neck. He kept his fingers there, slightly too firm to be gentle, as if he doubted she was alive.

Had they really never shared a bed? No. She would remember that. Wouldn't she?

There was a musical cry far off, out on the tundra.

Wolves. They sounded lonely. Beautiful, though, as they called to each other.

In the morning, she discovered that she had, at some point, fallen asleep. It was brutal to be awake. He wasn't in the tent.

A feeling jolted her heart. The movement she made then must have been loud. "I'm here," he called from outside the tent, and she emerged to see him in front of the fire that she should have smelled and interpreted as meaning he must be there or nearby—or she would have, if she hadn't been so afraid that he had left her.

She walked to the fire, still stumbling on her feet. She had the frustrated idea that she'd never been especially graceful in her body, but that she'd at least been *competent*. Before.

She sat across from him. The pale fire leaped between them. Snapped.

He was no longer wearing the heavy ring. She wondered what he'd done with it, then decided that she wouldn't ask as long as he said nothing about the night before.

They sat and ate in silence.

He kept looking at the injured mare, the one they didn't ride. She caught him doing it, and knew that he didn't want her to see him doing it.

When they stopped later in the day to rest, she held his gaze just as it was about to flick back to the mare. "Don't," she said.

"I don't want to."

"How would you, even?"

He shrugged, and she became conscious of the dagger at his hip, the one he'd taken off a prison guard. She recognized the dagger as the sort of thing that should belong to her and not to him. She had a sudden, intense feeling of difference. She realized that they'd been speaking in his language, not hers.

She imagined him taking the knife and cutting into the horse's throat. There was no other way to do it. A massive gush of blood. Thrashing body. The slide of hooves.

"She's slowing us down."

"I said *no*."

Finally, he nodded.

That felt familiar: his obedience. She had commanded him before. But she also thought that he had never obeyed her this way, and that even when he'd appeared to, he *hadn't*, really.

Definitely not friends. Something else.

That night was like the one before. He held her. She warmed. Her limbs softened. It seemed to be the only thing that could possibly make her sleep.

He said, "You bought me."

"What?"

He had murmured the words against the nape of her

neck. His voice came again, stronger this time. "You asked how we met. It was in the market. I was for sale. You bought me."

Instinct told her to turn in his arms and search his face, to see what expression it showed.

She didn't trust her instincts. She stayed very still. "Why would I do that?"

"I don't know."

"Do I still own you?"

The wind pushed against the tent's canvas.

"Yes."

Her reply was blunt. "No one would believe the things you say. Do you think having no memory makes me a fool?"

"No."

"You say that I was your spy, which means that I worked for you. You say that I own you, which means that you work for me. You say that we are *friends*. Masters and slaves are not friends. And then there is *this*—" she broke off, unwilling to go any further. She was too aware of his heat next to her. "You say impossible things. I don't believe you."

His ribs expanded: hard wings against her back. "If you let me explain—"

"Stop talking. Stop talking. I don't want to hear your voice."

He fell silent. She lay rigid against him, wishing that she could make herself pull away.

At an uncertain hour of the night, she felt him draw breath. He was going to try again to explain, she thought. She went stony with panic. Again, she had that sense of falling, hurtling toward what she didn't remember. The skull-crushing impact.

She didn't want him to speak, she was suddenly not even sure he *meant* to speak. It occurred to her, strangely, that he might sing.

"Don't." Her command was sharp.

He didn't.

Later, she woke because she was shaking again. He was gone.

It was still nighttime. He should not be gone.

She pushed out of the tent and saw him standing beneath an imaginary sky. Above the darkness, beyond the needlepoint stars, were swirls of green and pink edged with violet. She was sure she'd never seen anything like it.

He turned to meet her gaze, which had lowered from the sky to him. She didn't understand how he wasn't freezing. Then she saw the way his shoulders hunched and realized that he was. He looked back up at the night's gauzy colors.

"What is that?" she asked.

"The gods."

"They don't exist." She wasn't sure how she knew that, but she knew that she believed it.

"They do. They've come to punish me."

"It was you," she said, giving voice to her lurking suspicion, and knowing, as his face twisted, that she was right. "You're the reason I was in that prison."

He met her eyes. "Yes."

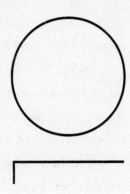

ARIN WASN'T SURE HOW THEY MADE IT HOME.

Kestrel had worsened. She was sick during the day. At night her body became a silently keening thing. He would hold her, worried that it was wrong of him, even (sometimes, especially) when she seemed to welcome it. Then it was as if a wave washed through her and pushed her out into sleep. He felt her go, and became wrenchingly grateful, while knowing that whatever comfort he could offer was something she didn't actually want.

She refused to let him help her inside his house. The glowing summer day did little to warm her. She huddled inside his dirty coat, and their progress up the path to the house was slow enough that by the time they reached the main entrance, the entire household had gathered to see them. Kestrel kept her eyes on her unsteady feet, but Arin knew that she was aware of the crowd; her mouth had set into a grim line.

Roshar came to them first, boots crunching on the gravel.

He was uncharacteristically silent. Appalled, when he wasn't someone given to being appalled by the appearance of others.

"I want Sarsine," Arin told him, but Sarsine was already there. Kestrel eyed her: a moment's worth of hesitation. Then she accepted Sarsine's arm, and Arin had to hide the sting of what could be nothing other than hurt jealousy, after which he had to hide his shame at such a petty feeling. He trailed after them, hands upsettingly empty. He wasn't ready to be useless. He had at least been useful on the tundra.

Arin followed them up the stairs to the east wing, where Sarsine opened the door to the suite where Kestrel had once stayed. When they entered, Arin searched Kestrel's face for some sign of recognition. She kept her gaze averted from his in a way that showed that she knew she was being scrutinized, and why.

Sarsine settled Kestrel onto the nearest soft chair and knelt before her, removing the battered shoes that were barely recognizable as having once been a lady's slippers.

Her expression flickering, Kestrel studied Sarsine's dark, bent head. Kestrel's voice, which she'd used less and less in the past few days, was hoarse. "Are you my maid?"

His cousin flinched. He saw Kestrel realize that she'd said something wrong. Sarsine looked to him. He leaned and whispered in her ear.

Sarsine set the shoes down in a neat pair. "Yes," she finally said. "I will be for now, if you like." She rose and began to peel the coat off Kestrel.

Something that Arin had tried to wind tightly inside him during the days on the tundra began to unwind. He wasn't sure what was going to happen when it came undone. He would have said—if he could have said anything at all—that what he felt was like the desolate trembling that seized Kestrel's body at night.

Sarsine caught his eye. Lifted her brows. She had paused in the removal of Kestrel's clothes. Her message was clear.

He nodded. He should leave, of course he should, yet he couldn't make himself move.

"Arin." Sarsine was stern now.

He turned, but hadn't gotten far when he heard Sarsine's sucked breath. He glanced back.

His eyes went wide. He was next to them before he was aware of having taken a step. His hand snatched the loose cloth of Kestrel's shirt at the shoulder. He saw it: the red welt that slashed down her shoulder blade. She jerked away from his grasp. The cloth tore. Not much. Enough.

"Arin!" Sarsine.

He saw more, he saw how the lashes looked like his own, how they had sliced her skin and went out of his sight under the cloth. He knew it was all over her back. "I asked you." His voice was wretched. "I asked you if you were hurt."

"I'm not. It's healed."

"But you were."

"I didn't remember."

He didn't believe her. "How could this happen to you? How could you not tell me?" He had pulled her to her feet. He was holding her by the upper arms. There was no flesh there. His thumbs met bone. He was not himself. This was not his world. There was no version of his world where this could be real.

"You're frightening her," Sarsine said.

Not fear. Kestrel's face was a blazing challenge: chin lifted, shoulders tight, shirt loose at the neck. One of the lashes had curled up over her collarbone. She tugged free.

His throat was tight. "You should have told me."

"I don't have to tell you anything."

"Kestrel, you . . . did something for me. For this country. Don't you remember? Can't you try? Or let me tell you, please—"

Her flat palm cracked across his face.

It sucked the air out of him. His cheek burned. She'd caught him across the mouth, too. Her eyes were liquid and golden and lost and angry. He was too ashamed of himself to speak.

Gently, Sarsine said, "I know you want to help."

"Of course I do," he whispered.

"Then you need to leave."

It wasn't until he was alone in the hallway, sagged against the wall, that he touched where she had hit him. His fingers came away wet. He stared at the tears. They shone on his fingertips like blood.

"WILL SHE DIE?"

Sarsine shut the door to Kestrel's suite behind her with more force than necessary. Hands planted on her hips, she stared down at Arin where he sat in the hallway, back to the wall opposite Kestrel's door. His joints were stiff. He didn't know how long he'd been sitting there.

"Gods, Arin. Pull yourself together. No, she won't die."

"The lashes. There could be an infection. A fever."

"There isn't."

"It happened to me."

"She's not you."

"She can't keep anything down. It's gotten worse."

"She was drugged twice a day, every day for about a month. Some of what she's going through is because her body wants the drugs it can't have."

He caught the plural form. "More than one kind?" Though he'd already suspected this from his own experience with the exhilarating power of the drug he'd been given in the mines, and the way Kestrel longed for something to make her sleep. Had begged for it, sometimes.

"Yes."

"She told you this." Hurt pinched his heart. He looked away from his cousin so that she wouldn't see how it felt that Kestrel had so easily told her what he'd been forced to guess. He was in the tent again, on the tundra, listening to the wind buckle the canvas. The chill oozing up from the ground, Kestrel in his arms, his pulse wild, the awful shudder of her limbs, the curve of her neck in the dim green dark. The relief to hear, finally, her breath slow and quiet. The way his own breath stayed uneven for a long time after that.

He said, "How did you get her to fall asleep?"

"She's not asleep."

"What?"

"She's calm enough for now."

"You left her alone, *awake*?" He remembered how she'd stood in a small boat high over black water on the night of the Firstwinter Rebellion, ready to jump. He heard her asking for Roshar's numbing ring. "You can't. Go back. Sarsine, you can't leave her alone."

His cousin's hands slid down from her hips. Her stance loosened, her expression growing soft and tired. "Kestrel's too strong to do what you're thinking."

"Look at her." Arin spoke as if Kestrel were in the hallway with them. *Look at what I've done,* he almost said, then bit back the words. Sarsine would only say that none of this was his fault.

He knew the truth.

Sarsine sat on the floor across from him, knees drawn

up underneath her muslin skirts. "I *have* looked at her. I've bathed and dressed her and put her to bed, and she's malnourished and sick, but she's *alive*. She's fought hard to live. If you don't think she's strong, you're mistaken."

"I'll stay with her."

Sarsine slowly shook her head. "She doesn't want you."

"I don't care."

"She won't hurt herself."

"You don't know that."

"Arin, I'll care for her, of course, but we can't be with her every moment of the day."

"I damned well can."

"She would hate it. She doesn't even know who she is anymore. How can she find out if she's never alone with herself?"

Arin tunneled his fingers through his dirty hair and pressed the heels of his hands into his closed eyes until they flashed white under the lids. "I know who she is." Proud girl. Hard, noble heart. And a liar, a liar. "I should have known." Every moment with her in the capital rushed through him, freezing his veins. He'd swallowed her lies. The way she'd mocked him. Set him aside, made him insignificant. It had been easy to believe. It had made sense.

He cursed himself. He saw the opportunities he'd had, over many months before her arrest, to seize the truth of things. But none of what he'd seen or suspected in the capital had made sense. It had been senseless, so apparently wrong, the way he'd seen her eyes slim with longing when he'd found her by a canal. The waters had swelled below. She'd worn a maid's dress. Senseless: that she would gamble her safety to help someone else's people. Senseless: that she'd smuggle information to Arin's spymaster. A traitor to her country. The Valorian punishment for treason was death.

And Arin had accused her of selfishness. In the capital, he'd thought words like *power hungry*, and *shallow*, and *cruel*. He'd said as much to her face. He'd blamed her for the deaths of the eastern plainspeople.

Her stricken expression, clear in the rushlights of that filthy tavern. The white line of her mouth.

He had ignored it. Misread it.

He'd missed everything that had mattered.

Sarsine grabbed his wrists and tugged the hands from his eyes. He looked at her, but didn't see her. He saw Kestrel's wasted face. He saw himself as a child, the night of the invasion, soldiers in his home, how he had done nothing.

Later, he'd told Sarsine when the messenger had come to see him.

No, I won't, he'd promised Roshar when the prince had listed reasons not to rescue the nameless spy from the tundra's prison.

"I was wrong," Arin said. "I should have—"

"Your *should haves* are gone. They belong to the god of the lost. What I want to know is what you are going to do *now*."

He had long avoided the general's estate.

Sarsine's words ringing through his head, Arin rode Javelin through the unlocked gate.

A yellow-throated thrush called from a low bough. The uncut grass of the meadow reached up to the horse's hocks. Arin walked Javelin through the green hiss of it, away from the villa, which he wasn't yet ready to see, and up a hill, through a grove daubed with small, ripening oranges. They'd be hard and dry if he plucked and peeled them. Not ready yet. But their scent made him want them now.

He made a clicking sound with his teeth and tongue, nudged the horse with his heels. Javelin flicked an ear and picked up the pace, gusting a short breath through his nostrils, pleased to go more quickly.

Arin kept clear of the larger outbuildings. The thatched cottage that had belonged to Kestrel's nurse, just west of the overgrown garden. The empty stables. The empty slaves' quarters. The windowless barnlike shape of it, the paint white and flaking in the sun. Arin kept Javelin on his determined path, but turned a little in the saddle for a backward glance at the last building, his sword shifting against his hip as he did so.

He reached the forge and swung off the saddle, dropped his boots to the ground. He loosened the stallion's girth and let him go. The grass was high and good. A horse's heaven.

Arin's boots were loud on the flagstones. There were smithies in the city he could have used, but this one— perversely—felt like his. Things were as Arin had left them last winter. Inside, tools hung where they should. The anvil had a skin of dust. The hearth was long dead. The coal scuttle full.

He built a fire in the forge, worked the bellows, and watched flames snap to life. When it was going strong, he left the fire to burn. He'd be back. The fire would have to burn a while for what he wanted. In the meantime—he forced himself to think it—he should go see the house.

The general's villa—Kestrel's—had stood empty since Arin had killed Cheat last winter. As the leader of the Herrani rebellion, Cheat had claimed the house as his and lived there because it was the best, and because it was the general's. Maybe even because it was Kestrel's. Arin didn't know when Cheat's malevolent fascination with her had begun. Arin swallowed hard to remember it.

His hand was tight on the sword's hilt. He looked at his clenched knuckles, looked again at his father's sword, pulling out an inch of it to see the gleam of finely tempered steel in the sun. Then he dropped it back home into the scabbard and he went inside the house.

Past the portico, the entryway's fountain was silent and scummed over. Bugs walked the water's green surface. Painted gods stared down at Arin from the walls. Other creatures, too: fawns, a leaping stag, birds. He caught a glimpse of one frescoed bird arrested in midflight and remembered seeing it for the first time over Kestrel's shoulder, on the day that she'd bought him.

Inside, the house was mostly bare. He'd thought it would be, but had never thought that it would look like *this*.

After Arin had signed the imperial treaty that seemed to promise Herran freedom, the Valorian colonists surrendered their homes in this territory. Ships came to empty the houses of Valorian possessions. There were disputes over whose was what. Arin had waded in, brokered the negotiations, but had ignored Kestrel's house. The Herrani family who'd owned it was long dead. When a Valorian ship entered the harbor to empty the general's villa, Arin pretended that the ship and house didn't exist. He'd assumed that everything had been taken. He was almost right.

He hadn't been here since the Firstwinter Rebellion. He hadn't wanted to be drawn to Kestrel's rooms, or to see the kitchens where his people had been forced to work, or to find the place where the steward accused him of touching something he shouldn't have. A flogging had followed, set far back on the grounds so that no one in the house would be bothered by unpleasant sounds. Arin hadn't wanted to remember the music room ringing with Kestrel's playing, or to see the library where he'd once shut himself inside with her. He'd wanted nothing of this place at all. Even when he'd come with men and a cart and draft horses to bring the piano to his house, Arin hadn't gone inside. He'd waited outside, rigging a system of pulleys he used to help haul the instrument up and onto the cart after it had been wheeled out the wide doors of the music room.

So he wasn't prepared for the filth he saw and smelled.

Cheat had been vengeful. The corners reeked of piss. There were stains on the walls, the windows. Several panes were shattered.

Arin's feet carried him swiftly to the music room. Things were odd there: leaves of sheet music scattered on the floor, some of it burned, but only a little, as if Cheat had started and then had had a better idea, probably the same idea that had kept him from ruining the piano. Maybe Cheat hadn't been sure whether to force Kestrel to do what he wanted, or bribe her . . .

Arin's stomach seized. His lungs blazed. He flung open a window.

He stared into the garden, remembering this view. He'd watched flowers dip and float in a breeze while Kestrel played a melody written for the flute. His mother used to sing along to it, in the evenings, for guests.

He wondered if this was what it meant to have been born in the year of the god of death: to see everything defiled.

But the air cleared his head. He made his way to the kitchens. There he started yet another fire, this time to boil water. He found a harsh-smelling block of lye. Rags. Buckets. Orange-scented wood oil. Vinegar for the windows and walls. Arin began to clean the house from top to bottom.

As he wrung out a cloth, he felt his god sneer. *Cleaning? Ah, Arin. This is not why I made you. This is not our agreement.*

Arin had no sense of having agreed to anything, only of having been claimed, and liking it.

He couldn't dishonor his god. But he also couldn't dishonor himself. He pushed the voice from his head and kept at his task.

When he returned to the forge, the fire was long dead. He restarted it and stoked the flames. Then he set his father's sword into the fire, heated it to the point of flexibility, and held it against the anvil. He chopped the blade. His mind was quiet as he trimmed it down and something new formed beneath his hands. Folded steel, layer upon layer. Forge-welded. Shorter, thinner. Strong and sprung. He reformed the hilt. Shaped and ground the blade. He did all that he could to make Kestrel's dagger his finest work.

SHE SWAM OUT OF THE MURK.

She was sore—shoulders and ribs and stomach especially. But the spasms that had racked her body were gone. Everything was impossibly soft. The feather bed. Her thin shift. Clean skin. The tender give of the pillow beneath her cheek. She blinked, heard the short sweep of her eyelashes against the pillow's fabric. Her hair lay loose, smooth. It had been disgusting when she'd arrived here. She remembered Sarsine working oiled fingers through it. "Cut it off," Kestrel had said. She'd felt disjointed and eerie as the words left her dry lips, like she wasn't really speaking but echoing something she'd already said.

"Oh no," Sarsine had replied. "Not this time."

Cut it off. Yes. There had been another time. Then, there'd been a tangle of myriad little braids beneath her fingers, and she'd hated the feel of them . . . because of the ghost of an unexpected pleasure . . . yet what kind of pleasure, and why it had vanished, her mind refused to say.

You might regret cutting your hair, a society lady like you, Sarsine had said in this other, earlier time.

Please. I can't bear it.

Sarsine unsnarled the dense clumps left by the prison camp. The movement of fingers in Kestrel's hair made her dizzy. She'd gagged, and was sick all over again.

Now, puzzling through this, Kestrel touched a ribbon of hair on the pillow. She'd lost track of its color in the prison.

Familiar. Dark blonde. A little reddish. It had been a more fiery hue when she was little. *Warrior red,* her father had said, tweaking a braid. She suspected that he'd been disappointed to see it darken over time.

She sat up—too swiftly. Her sight dimmed. She got light-headed.

"Ah," said a voice.

Her vision cleared. Sarsine stretched up from a chair (dove-gray wood, upholstery the color of matte pearl. This, too: familiar) and padded to a small table that held a covered tureen. Sarsine ladled steaming broth into a cup and brought it to her. "Hungry?"

Kestrel's stomach growled. "Yes," she said, marveling at such a simple thing as normal hunger. She drank, and felt immediately exhausted. The cup hung limp in her hands. "How long?" she managed to say.

"Since you've been here? Two days."

The windows were curtained and glowed with daylight.

"You've been fitful," Sarsine said, "and very ill. But I think"—the woman touched Kestrel's cheek—"that we've turned a corner."

This woman was good, Kestrel thought. All brisk confidence. Firm, matter-of-fact, with an undercurrent of care. A crease of worry about the eyes. Genuine, maybe.

"You need some solid sleep," Sarsine said. "Can you try?"

Kestrel liked this, too: how Sarsine knew that something that should be easy wasn't easy. It was true that wake and sleep in the past days (two, she reminded herself) had been broken and shuffled. She glanced up into Sarsine's eyes. Then stared. She saw clearly now what she hadn't noticed before. Her heart thumped.

They were the exact same color. Gray, like fine rain. Heavy black lashes. His eyes.

Her mouth, too. Not quite the same shape. But the cut of the lower lip, the corner lifted in the smallest of smiles . . .

"Well?" Sarsine said gently, taking the empty cup, which had become heavier than stone.

Kestrel reached for Sarsine's free hand and gripped it. She steadied under the unwavering gray gaze. *Not right,* part of her insisted. Not right to seek him in this woman's face. To seek him at all. But Kestrel did, she couldn't help doing it, and when sleep opened beneath her she wasn't afraid to fall into it.

It was night when she woke again. The lamp burned low. A large shadow lurked in the chair. Long, trousered legs stretched out, boots still tightly laced. His dark head crooked awkwardly against the carved trim of the chair's back.

Clean, asleep. Hard lines softer now. Face shaven. That scar.

He was *too* clean. Close enough that she could smell him. He smelled strange: vinegar and orange and . . . lye?

His eyes cracked open. Hazy for the length of one drawn breath. Then alert in the lamplight. He watched her watch him. He didn't move.

Her rabbit heart beat fast. She flickered between distrust and trust and an emotion less easy to name.

"Go back to sleep," he murmured.

She closed her eyes. Her rabbit heart slowed, curled up in its warren, and seemed to become fully itself: warm fur, soft belly. A thrum of breath in the dark.

When she woke again, the curtains were wide open. Midday. Yellow light. The pearl-colored chair was empty.

An unpleasant bolt shot through her. She didn't know what it meant, exactly, but it made her feel small.

She pushed herself up. A mirror stood on a nearby dressing table. Kestrel slipped from the bed: hollow, unsteady. The dressing table and its chair weren't so nearby after all. The distance between her and them yawned wide. When she reached the chair, she dropped down into it.

The girl in the reflection looked so shocked that Kestrel's first instinct was to touch her. To reassure. Fingertips met. The mirror was cool.

"Planning on breaking it?" said a voice.

Kestrel's hand fell, and her gaze jerked away to find Sarsine standing behind her in the open doorway. Kestrel hadn't been alone after all. The woman's expression had the thoughtful cast of someone who'd been watching for a while. She carried a bundle of fabric in her arms.

"That's not me," Kestrel said.

Sarsine draped the fabric (a dress) over the back of the pearl-gray chair. She came close and rested a hand on Kestrel's shoulder—warmly, yet at a careful distance from the raised marks she could probably see on Kestrel's back through her shift.

Kestrel glanced again at the too-thin girl with the sunken eyes. Cracked lips. The knobs of her clavicle.

"Here," Sarsine said, and gathered Kestrel's hair. She wove a quick, practical braid.

"He did that," Kestrel said suddenly. He had braided her hair, before. *That* (that?) was the unnamed, lost pleasure she had tried to remember. He had taken his time. A sensual slowness. The brush of his thumb against the nape of her neck. Mesmerizing. Then later, the next morning: all those little braids transformed into miserable knots.

"What?" Sarsine tied the braid with a ribbon.

"Nothing."

Sarsine met her eyes in the mirror, but said only, "Come, let's get you dressed."

"To do what?"

"To look more like yourself." Sarsine pulled her to her feet.

The dress was too loose. But it fit well in the shoulders and was the perfect length. The fabric. That pattern of sprigged flowers. "This is mine."

"Yes."

"But this isn't my home."

Sarsine's fingers paused in their buttoning. "No."

"Then what am I doing here? Where did you get this?"

Sarsine fastened the last button. "How much do you remember?"

"I don't know." She was frustrated. "How am I supposed to know *how much*? For that, I'd have to know what I've forgotten. You tell me."

"Better if you asked someone else."

Kestrel knew whom she meant. There it was again: his fingers sliding through her hair. It was true, what she'd suspected on the tundra was true. A lover? Maybe. Something tender, anyway. But tender like a bruise.

"No," Kestrel told Sarsine. "I trust *you*."

Sarsine knelt to put slippers on her feet. "Why?"

"You don't want anything from me."

"Who says I don't? A maid might seek any number of things from her mistress."

"You're not my maid."

Sarsine glanced up.

"Why are you doing this?" Kestrel asked. "Why are you kind to me?"

Sarsine dropped her hands to her skirted lap. She worried a thumb over the opposite palm. Then she got to her feet and helped Kestrel to a full-length floor mirror. Kestrel, fully tired now, and confused by a number of conflicting things, let herself be led.

"There," Sarsine said, once Kestrel stood before the reflection. "You look almost like a proper Valorian lady. That's what you are. When I first saw you, I hated you."

Kestrel stared at herself. She didn't see what was worth hating. She didn't see much of anything. Just a shadow of a girl in a nice dress. She whispered, "Am I despicable?"

Sarsine's smile was sad. "No."

There was a silence that Kestrel didn't want to break, because it seemed, for that moment, that there was a downy safety in not deserving hatred. Maybe she didn't need to be anything else. Maybe it was all a person needed to be.

Sarsine said, "Almost eleven years ago, your people conquered this country. They enslaved us. You were rich, Kestrel. You had everything you could want. You were happy."

Kestrel's brow furrowed. She recognized some of what Sarsine had said, saw it far off, hazy in the distance. But . . .

It was *want*, she realized. And *happy*.

"I don't know every detail," Sarsine said. "What I do know is that last summer, you bought Arin in the market."

"So it's true."

"You won him at an auction and brought him to your house. But the auctioneer, a man called Cheat—"

Kestrel felt an ugly pang.

"—*wanted* you to win. Arin did, too. Your father is the highest-ranking general in the Valorian army. Arin was a spy for the Herrani rebellion. He was crucial. Nothing could have been done without him. Or you. You gave him useful information, though you didn't mean to. You wouldn't have done it if you'd understood what Arin was after and what he'd do with what you told him. Valorians were attacked all over the city, taken by surprise, killed. Your friends, too."

Tears on dead skin. A girl in a green dress. Poisoned purple lips. Kestrel swallowed.

"After the rebellion," Sarsine said, "you were brought here."

Kestrel's voice came out strangled: "A prisoner."

Sarsine pursed her mouth, but didn't deny it. "You escaped. I'm not sure how. The next thing we knew, the Valorian army was here and we were under siege. But you came and presented Arin with a treaty."

Heavy paper beneath her thumb. Snow floating onto her cheeks. White paper, white snow, white heart.

"It offered us our independence as a self-governed territory under the emperor's rule. It seemed too good to be true. It was. Several months later, people in this city began to fall ill. I did, too. We were being slowly poisoned by tainted water from the aqueducts. The emperor wanted to kill us without risking any of his soldiers' lives. We know this— and stopped it—because of you. You were passing information to Tensen, Arin's spymaster in the capital. Arin didn't know who Tensen's source was. Tensen refused to name her, and instead called her by a code name: the Moth.

"You were caught. A Herrani groom in the mountains brought news that a woman in a prison wagon bound for the tundra had given him a moth and asked him to give it to Arin. Arin went for you. Here you are."

Kestrel's teeth were set, her shoulders stiff. She didn't remember most of what Sarsine had said, wasn't sure what to make of the few vague images that pulsed in her mind. She fought fatigue. "That's crazy."

"Implausible, I know."

"A story." Kestrel groped for the way to say it. "Like something out of books. Why would I do such things?"

It was you, she'd told him on the tundra. *You're the reason I was in that prison.*

Yes.

Flatly, Kestrel said, "I sound very stupid."

"You sound like the person who saved my life." Sarsine touched three fingers to the back of Kestrel's hand.

Kestrel remembered what that gesture meant. The knowledge opened inside her. The gesture was Herrani. It meant gratitude, or apology, or both.

She plucked at the loose dress. Her thoughts whirled. Her eyelids were heavy, lowering. She tried to imagine her former self. Enemy. Prisoner. Friend? Daughter. Spy. Prisoner again. "What am I now?"

Sarsine held both of Kestrel's hands. "Whatever you want to be."

What Kestrel wanted to be was asleep. She wavered to the nearest piece of furniture—a divan, but the blackness came too quickly for her to see it for what it was. It was just an object that wasn't the floor. She surrendered herself to it and sank swiftly into sleep. A cushion. A drawn coverlet. A dress that had been hers.

Someone had moved her back into her bed. Not Sarsine.

It was dark, but a low-lit lamp had been left. The chair was empty.

She lay curled on her side. Her back had healed into a dull ache. A few deep grooves stung. On the tundra, she hadn't noticed pain much while the drugs were still in her.

Then they weren't, and the sickness and craving had been worse than anything else.

The ache gnawed through her back, coming up through her heart. She eyed the empty chair.

It occurred to her that after the last time, when she'd woken in the night, he'd decided to keep a better distance.

It occurred to her that the cold, small thing she felt was abandonment.

Which should have made her queasy with anger at her own confusion. Who was she, that she would strike the person who had saved her, and then feel bereft at his absence?

She wasn't a person, really, but two. The Kestrel from before and the one now, each grating against the other like halves of a split bone.

She turned onto her other side, faced the wall, and reached to touch, for the first time, the ridges on her back. Wincing flesh. Long, clotted scales. Repulsed, she withdrew her hand and tucked it close to her breast.

Go back to sleep, she commanded herself.

She didn't need the nighttime drug anymore. Not exactly. Yet the thought of it made her throb with longing. If offered a cup, she'd gulp it down.

The following day (at least, Kestrel *thought* it was the following day. It seemed entirely possible that she might have slept straight through more than one night), Sarsine helped her walk to the breakfast room. The table bore ilea fruit, bread, tea, milk, a set of iron keys, and one other item, muslin-wrapped.

Large. A clunky-looking shape. Set right next to the keys at the head of a plate.

"For you," Sarsine said.

"Is it Ninarrith?" The word came to her, alien in her mouth. From the ancient Herrani tongue, she remembered, which was so old that it was its own language. No one spoke it, though a few words lingered. Before the war, Herrani used to give each other gifts on Ninarrith. A holiday.

"Not yet." Sarsine peered at her.

"What?"

"It's an odd thing for you to remember."

"I can remember some things."

"It's been eleven years since we've celebrated Ninarrith."

"What does the word mean?"

"It's two words, joined together. For 'hundred' and 'candles.' The holiday marks the last day the gods walked among us. We celebrate the hope of their return."

Kestrel pulled at the memory, drew it out, thick and slow. "My nurse. She was Herrani. I celebrated with her in secret." She wondered what would have happened if they'd been caught. Fear puddled in her heart. But there was no one to catch her now, no one here who'd punish her. "I loved her." Yet she couldn't remember the woman's name anymore. Kestrel's fear condensed into loss. She tried to smile, felt it waver.

"The tea will get cold." Sarsine bustled unnecessarily with the pot, and Kestrel was grateful to have a moment for her expression to be whatever it was without the burden of someone else's gaze.

She told Sarsine, "I'd like to celebrate Ninarrith with you."

"If we're here come then," the woman said darkly, but shook her head when Kestrel peered at her. "Go on. Take them."

The keys were heavy.

"They're for the house," Sarsine said. "A full set."

Their weight on her palm. Something she thought she should remember.

She set the keys aside. "And this?" She ran a finger down a crease in the muslin of the clunky, wrapped thing.

Sarsine lifted her brows—a little sardonically, Kestrel thought, although the edge of the woman's expression appeared less to do with Kestrel and more to do with a knowledge Sarsine had and Kestrel didn't. The black brows, their quality of curbed cynicism, dry amusement . . . again Kestrel recognized him in her. He'd looked at Kestrel like that, before. She wondered why she felt comfortable with Sarsine and not with him, and if that ease was despite the resemblance, or because of it.

"See for yourself," Sarsine said.

It was a dagger, bright beneath the opened muslin. Nestled in its scabbard, hooked to a slim belt. The leather of the belt was sturdy yet supple, not made with any particular elegance but with an eye for durability and comfort. There were few holes for the buckle's tongue: a sign that the maker was assured of the belt's fit. The scabbard, like the belt, was clean and strong in design, not given to the fanciful, though the ferrule was more severely pointed than Kestrel had seen before (yes, she realized. She knew daggers well). Not so sharp that it'd be likely to hurt the bearer, but pointed enough to do damage if the scabbard were gripped in the fist and driven into an opponent. And the scabbard wasn't entirely without decoration. Just below its throat was a symbol: two rings, one fitted inside the other, distinguishable only because the raised texture of each was different. The symbol was echoed on the dagger's hilt, in the round of the pommel, which was weighted enough to kill if brought down on certain parts of the skull. The hilt—Kestrel wrapped her fingers around it—was a perfect fit for her hand, cross guards hooked to protect the fingers.

She pulled the blade free. It was very Valorian. Save for the straightened point and that unknown symbol, its every element showed the Valorian style, from the hooked cross guard to the double edge to the blade's beveled shaft. The steel's faint blue hue showed its quality, but Kestrel would have known it anyway. The dagger felt light in her grip, agile. Beautifully forged. Balanced. Fine in its proportions. Made by a master.

Kestrel touched a thumb to its edge. Blood sprang to the skin. "Gods," Kestrel said, and sucked at the cut.

Sarsine laughed. "A convert now, are you?"

Kestrel was startled. She'd forgotten about Sarsine. She frowned, unsure why she'd said what she had. It had been the kick of instinct. Or maybe someone else's instinct, rooted inside her, inhabiting a hidden space that made it feel natural for her to invoke gods she didn't believe in. She pushed the blade back in, set the whole thing back on the table with a *thunk*.

"Why are you giving this to me?" The keys she understood. She was not meant to be a prisoner here, but a guest.

More than a guest, if she read the gift rightly. Guests don't have access to their host's every room.

But the dagger . . .

"I could kill you with this," she said. "Right now."

"Oh, I don't know." Sarsine still looked amused. "You're hardly in fighting form."

"That's not the point." It was starting to upset her a little, the keys and the dagger together. The way each gift, in its own way, showed a trust absolute.

"The thinking," Sarsine said carefully, "was that you shouldn't feel defenseless."

Kestrel opened her mouth, then shut it, not realizing until then that this *was* how she had felt, and that the first emotion that had claimed her after falling under the visual spell of the dagger was a sense of security.

Sarsine said, "We—"

Kestrel looked at her sharply.

"I'm not worried that you'll hurt someone else," Sarsine said. The phrasing of the words indicated exactly what the worry had been—or maybe still was.

"I see." Her mouth thinned. "I don't need a dagger for suicide. But I wouldn't do it. I'm no coward."

"No one," Sarsine said, "thinks that you are a coward."

Kestrel took the sheathed dagger onto her lap, gripped it with both hands. It felt irrevocably hers. It would pain her to give it back. She thought from the way Sarsine looked at her that the other woman understood this. Kestrel relaxed her hold. The dagger was hers, and it was all right. She was trusted with a weapon, and that was right, too.

Sarsine drank her milk.

Kestrel said, "Is this dagger like the dresses?"

"I'm not sure what you mean."

"It was made for me. Do you have other things of mine from before, like the dresses? Like this?"

Sarsine hesitated, as if she wanted to speak but the words lodged in her throat. Finally, she said, "Your piano."

The instrument rose before her eyes: black, massive, too large for her heart, which suddenly strained with desire. "Where?" she managed.

"Downstairs, in the salon."

The surge of remembered music. The arch of her fingers. Glittering notes.

"I want it," Kestrel said. "Now."

"Honestly, I'm not sure you'd make it down the stairs."

"But—"

"You could be carried, though not by me."

"Oh."

"You're not *that* light."

Kestrel was silent.

"Shall I arrange for it?"

She knew whom Sarsine would ask. "No."

"Then eat your breakfast."

She did, without another word.

Sometimes she'd step gingerly out onto her memory and it would creak and sway beneath her like a bridge that couldn't bear her weight. She'd retreat into what she knew best: the prison. There, she'd learned to love the earth beneath her cheek. Dry, cool. The sunless smell of it. The way it heralded sleep. She'd drink the nighttime drug. She'd swallow and swallow. Then she'd drift, and love the guard who led her, and love the moment right before sleep, because it was only a moment, and in one mere moment she wouldn't have to think about how she'd given in—and given up. She'd never had any other kind of life. This was all there was.

Sleep was there. It shoved her down. Pressed her lungs. The drug crept soft fingers across her mouth and shaped it into a loose smile.

No one stayed with her anymore at night. Not Sarsine. Not him. And she didn't need company, she was no child. She wasn't frightened by nightmares, or by the way she couldn't remember them after she woke, like now.

Her fingers trembled as they reached for the low-burning lamp on the bedside table. She took the lamp. The keys. She pulled on a robe and made her way through the suite, through the sunroom, and out onto the rooftop garden. Her feet were bare on the egg-shaped pebbles. The darkness was velvety, and warm enough that Kestrel knew that she shouldn't be cold.

She should know whether it was cold or warm.

She should know whether it was normal to be nervous. Would her pulse race like this if she were still the same person she used to be?

She tried the heavy keys on the ring until she found the one that fit into the door set into the opposite wall of the garden. Opened it. Saw another garden, just like hers. She tried to walk on the pebbles without making noise. Failed. It occurred to her that the pebbles were there for the very purpose of making noise. She thought about this, about why someone might want to hear another person coming, and this distracted her from the forgotten nightmare that seemed to have snapped her in two.

She felt like she was both her body and her shadow, like she was her own ghost.

She had done all this before. Had opened those doors, had crossed these twin gardens.

His sunroom was dark.

She opened its door anyway. Moved past the potted plants. Lamp lifted, she found the door to his suite. The hallway. Her footfalls were silent now, treading plush carpet. A set of silent rooms. The furnishings masculine in a way that didn't look like what he would have chosen, yet suited him. Or what she knew of him.

Which was little.

The lamp lowered. She wasn't sure what she was doing. Maybe she wanted to frighten him awake, to rip him out of sleep. Make him feel the way she'd felt when she'd woken minutes ago. She imagined screaming into his sleeping ear.

Or what if she woke him a different way? She seemed to see herself as if looking at a painting of a girl from a tale, kidnapped by a creature who showed his true form only at night. The girl held the lamp over the bed. Crept closer. A drop of hot oil fell to his bare shoulder. He woke.

Maybe Kestrel had come for answers. He had them . . . or pretended that he did.

Maybe this was a very bad idea.

She entered the room that she knew must be his bed-room.

It was empty. The bed was large and neatly made.

The windows, she realized now, were all shut. The air was stale. No one had been in this suite for days.

Her arm was tired. Her whole body was. She set down the lamp, the keys.

She touched the pillow. It was just a pillow. She touched the blanket. A blanket. The bed: a bed. Nothing more and nothing less than the thing she needed now. She sank into the bed. She told herself that she didn't care what it meant that she did this.

She lay on her stomach because she no longer slept on her back. She pressed her face into the pillow. His scent was there. She was stupid to have come, yet didn't have the strength to leave.

The ghost of him between the sheets. The shadow of her old self curled into the shadow of him.

Kestrel woke at dawn because she'd always woken at dawn in the prison. She saw where she was. She felt flat. The light was pink and pretty. Insulting.

It was habit, she told herself. That's why she'd come here last night. There'd been no mystery, no tangle of reasons to untangle. It was simple. She'd gotten used to sleeping next to him on the tundra. She had been cold and he had been warm. Habits die hard. That was all.

But she felt humiliated when she slipped from his bed. This time, she did remember what she had dreamed.

She straightened the sheets and made everything as it had been. She made sure there was no trace of her presence when she left.

"So you're his sister," Kestrel said, some days later.

Sarsine had coaxed her into her suite's sunroom. Kestrel's skin looked amber in the light. As the heat sank in, she realized that she wasn't sore anymore, except in the worst places. She wore the dagger. It rested against her thigh.

"No." Sarsine laughed. "Nor his lover."

Kestrel frowned, uneasy. She didn't understand the laugh or Sarsine's quick leap to something that hadn't even been suggested.

"It's what you asked when I first met you," Sarsine explained. She blew a cooling ripple into her tea. " 'Sister, or lover?' I'm his cousin."

"Where is he?"

Sarsine made no reply—not, Kestrel thought, because she had no intention of giving one, but because she was finding her words, and in that pause Kestrel remembered his empty suite and no longer wanted to know the answer to her question. She shoved a new one into its place. "Why *not* his lover?"

Sarsine choked on her tea.

"Cousins sometimes marry," Kestrel said.

"*Arin?* Gods, no." She was still coughing.

Kestrel didn't like her own impulse to keep opening and closing and opening again the subject of him.

"I love him," Sarsine said, "but not like that. I was an

orphan. My mother's brother took me into his home. Arin's parents were kind to me. His sister wasn't. And Arin . . ." She shook droplets of spilled tea from her fingers, then stopped, thinking. "As a child, he was a little world unto himself. A reader. A dreamer. Skinny thing. Whenever I managed to convince him to come out of doors, he'd squint like he'd never seen the sun. But he'd come out to please me.

"I was in the countryside with my nurse when the Valorians conquered this city. My parents had an estate south of here. It was thought that I'd want to choose some of my things to be brought here before the country house was closed. The Valorian general—your father—attacked the city first. The countryside after. My nurse and I had tried to close up my parents' house and hide inside. The shutters were ripped open.

"I don't know what became of my nurse. I never saw her again. I was forced to work on my family farm. There's work even a ten-year-old can do. Then I was sold to another country estate. It hurt to leave, though it had hurt to stay.

"I could make myself do what was wanted. Not everyone can. Arin couldn't. Never for very long. But I wasn't tied to a whipping post. I was good and sweet and I did things that maybe, in the end, were worse than punishment. One of my masters decided, eventually, to bring me to the city.

"Before the war, on my last day before I left this house to drive into the countryside with my nurse, Arin gave me a flower he'd pressed. It was pink, spread in a fan. I put it in a locket. I got into the carriage. Later, I lost the locket, lost the flower. But I remember it."

"Why are you telling me this?"

Sarsine looked at her in the too-strong light. "So that you will understand me." She added, "And him." She paused again. "You asked where he is."

"I don't care where he is."

"He's been away. He's just come back."

After these words, Sarsine abruptly took her leave.

The obviousness of Sarsine's hint to go see him so annoyed Kestrel that she nearly did nothing. The annoyance grew, became larger than life. If Sarsine had put that pressed flower in Kestrel's hand, she would have crushed it in her fist, would have been glad to see the arrowed pink flakes. She felt exactly the same as when she'd woken in his empty bed.

Ultimately, it was anger that got Kestrel to her feet and out the door.

As she strode down the hallway that led from his sunroom, and then into another chamber, she heard muffled thumps coming from the recesses of his suite. A short, metallic clatter. Quieter sounds.

Silence.

Then the quality of the silence seemed to shift. It changed the way a thought does: from soft idea to exploration to firm decision.

To footfalls, coming toward her.

Her pulse jumped. She had frozen in place. She held on to her anger . . . and somehow lost it when he appeared at the threshold of the room she had entered. He didn't look like she'd expected. Boots off, jacket half undone. Grimy. Unshaven, the scar a white line cutting into the black.

Startled, he stared. Then smiled a little. The smile was sweet. It was so different from what she felt that it surprised her how two people in the same room could feel such different things. As she thought about this difference, it became clear to her that she no longer knew what she felt.

She recognized the rusted smears on his skin. It was easier to focus on this. Simpler to decode. She remembered that earlier, metallic clatter. He had come from war.

"Did you win?" she asked.

He laughed. "No."

"Why is it funny that you lost?"

"It's not that. It's just . . . the question is very much like you."

She lifted her chin, felt her body go hard again. "I'm not her. Not anymore. I'm not the person that you—" She shut her mouth.

"That I love?" he said quietly.

She made no reply. He looked down, rubbed at his dirty hands.

"Excuse me," he said. He moved to leave the room, then hesitated, one finger on the curved wooden ripple of the doorjamb. "I'm coming back." A note in his voice made her realize that it had been obvious to him that he'd come back, and that it hadn't been to her, and that his pause had been from the understanding that what was obvious to him wasn't obvious to her. "One moment. Please don't go."

"All right," she said, surprising herself.

He left. Nervousness swarmed inside her.

She refused to be ruled by nervousness. That refusal held her there a little longer. Then: the realization that despite the way he'd looked, he'd had a kind of gentleness. It gentled her, and even if this was exactly what he had hoped, she found it hard to resent someone for being gentle.

She was still thinking about this when he returned. His jacket was changed for a fresh shirt. Soft shoes. Hands and face clean. A scrolled paper tucked under his arm. He unrolled it onto a small, octagonal table (delicate, with worked legs. For two. A breakfast table).

The paper was a map. "We lost Ithrya Island," he said, pointing south. "It's uninhabited, but . . ." He pressed a palm down on the buckling paper and looked up at her. "Do you want to know this?"

"Is there something wrong with me knowing?"

"No. But you might not like it. My people are at war with your people."

Her people were the ones who'd held her captive. They had hurt her. She crossed her arms over her chest. "So?"

"Your father—"

"Don't talk about my father."

Her pulse was high again, stammering in her ears. His dark brows had gone up—his hand, too. The palm had risen off the map, fingertips still pinned down. His skin was clean, but the fingernails were ringed with black. Odd. She concentrated on that. As she did, she evened out. It calmed her to concentrate, and to find his blackened nails familiar. At least she could *recognize* familiarity, even if she couldn't translate it. She said, "You didn't wash your hands very well."

He glanced down at his hand. It came entirely off the map. The paper curled up. "Oh." He swept a thumb once across his nails. "That. That doesn't come out for a long time."

His eyes went, strangely, to the dagger at her hip, then darted away, making her think that he was thinking of the battle he'd just been in.

She said, "Does losing this battle mean you'll lose your war?"

"Maybe."

"How many did you kill?"

He shrugged. He didn't know.

"Does it bother you?"

He met her eyes. Slowly, he shook his head.

"Why not? Do you like killing?"

"They want my country."

"So you do like it."

"Lately, sometimes."

"Why?"

"There are many reasons."

"That's no answer."

"But you are one of my reasons, Kestrel. You don't want to hear that. I think you might be pushing me to say something that will make you leave."

This gave her pause. She thought of how painstakingly she had neatened his bedsheets to erase her presence.

"I don't—" The words caught in her throat. She let herself sit at the table and studied a symbol carved onto its surface. The symbol of a god, probably. The Herrani had many. "I don't understand why I've forgotten so much."

"You were drugged." There was something unspoken in his voice.

"You think it's more than that."

He took the other chair, but sat at a distance, his body

turned from her, directed toward an eastern window, face in profile, scarred side hidden. As he spoke, it occurred to her that maybe he, too, felt like two people, that maybe everybody does, and that it's not a question of whether one's damaged, but of how easily or not that damage is seen.

She studied him. Captor, rescuer, culprit.

He kept talking. She began to listen. It was a terrible story, told softly, never stopping. He barely paused for breath. As he described the night of the Valorian invasion and himself as a child, she began to see how natural the reflex of self-blame was for him. Ingrained. Insidious.

You're the reason I was in that prison.

Yes.

It occurred to her that he might have taken blame he didn't deserve.

It occurred to her that she had already guessed this even before he'd begun telling his nakedly awful story.

And that maybe she had been cruel.

This thinking was not the same as trust. Still, she listened. After he finished, she listened to his silence.

He spoke again. "Maybe, for you, it's not just the drugs. Maybe . . . there are things that you can't bear to remember." He glanced into her eyes, then away, and she saw that it wasn't because he was afraid of letting her see how he could or could not bear his memories, but because he was afraid of what her own lost memories might be, and didn't want to show this fear, for fear of frightening her.

She said, "I didn't choose to forget."

The corner of his mouth lifted. It wasn't a false smile, but only as true as it could be. He spoke lightly, like some joke had been played upon them both. "I don't choose to remember." He shifted to face her fully. "May I ask you a question?"

She thought about it. She wasn't sure.

"I'm not asking for information," he hastened to say. "I don't want anything. Or, I suppose I do want something, but it's to *understand*. That's different, isn't it, from asking for a favor, or . . . an emotion?" He stopped, blocked by the difficulty of holding himself to honesty and finding the way language fails, sometimes, to get honesty right. "Maybe it's not different. You don't have to answer."

"Just say it."

"You've not wanted me to talk about what you can't remember. Not to ask. Not to tell. You're . . ." He didn't say the words. Kestrel thought them anyway. *Angry. Terrified.* "Is it because you really don't want to hear it, or . . . because you don't want it to be *me* who tells you?"

"I want to ask a question of my own first."

This took him aback. "Of course."

"On the tundra, you said that it was your fault that I was in prison."

"Yes."

"How?"

"How . . . ?"

"Did you tell someone I was spying for Herran?"

He recoiled. "No. I didn't know. I wouldn't do that."

"What exactly did you do?"

"I . . ."

"I have the right to know."

"You lied," he burst out. "You lied to me, and I believed

you. I didn't ask you to risk yourself. I never wanted you to do any of what you did. I never would have wanted *this*." His mouth was tight, eyes wide: flooded with something hot and rich and hurt. "I had so many chances to see what you were doing. And I didn't. I didn't stop you. I didn't help you. I despised you."

She said, "I lied."

"Yes."

"Tell me my lies."

"Gods." He raked a hand through his hair. "You lied about the treaty. You agreed to marry someone else so that I could have a *piece of paper*. You tried to help the eastern plainspeople, yet let me think that you were responsible for their deaths. The way you acted. Selfish. Horrible. You worked for my spymaster and you lied about that, too, and *he* lied to me, and it makes me hate him now. I hate myself for not seeing it. He knew. He let you. You committed treason, Kestrel. How could you do that? You should be *dead*." His voice lowered, dug in deep. "The worst—I don't know—the worst is that you lied about—" He stopped himself, drawing a ragged breath. "You lied for a very long time."

There was a silence. Slowly, Kestrel said, "I did all that for you."

He flushed. "Maybe you had other reasons."

"That's the one you care about."

"Yes."

She warred with what to say. It was strange to talk about reckless choices she didn't remember. It helped to see his anger, the way it blistered the surface of things. It was a relief not to be alone in her anger. It was folly, what her old self had done, but brave, too. She could see that. She could see how he saw it, and how it made things worse for him.

Easier, though, for her: to know she hadn't always been this husk of a vanished person. Then harder, to glimpse who she'd been. She saw the great difference between that person and the one sitting in a chair because she was too weak to stand. Emotions whirlpooled inside her. "Your question."

"Never mind."

"I'll tell you."

He shook his head. "Not necessary."

"It *is* you. It's true, I haven't wanted it to be you who tells me things I can't recall. Not you." She saw his flinch, and the effort to hide it. Tears sprang to her eyes. "Who are you, that you get to know so much about me that even I don't know? Why do *you* get to tell me who I am? How did you get so much power? I have none. It's not fair. You are unfair." Her voice broke. "*I* am unfair."

His expression changed. "Kestrel."

She held her breath until her lungs ached. She couldn't speak. Here was the truth, it peeled itself open: *she* was the reason she was in that prison. She had made some fatal, unknown mistake. Arin looked like a good culprit, but he wasn't the right one.

She was. It had been her fault, hers alone.

He reached across the table. His warm hand dwarfed hers. She saw it through her swimming vision. Those black-rimmed nails.

Blacksmith.

A sudden understanding held her still. She became aware of the weight of the dagger at her hip. Her sight cleared. She looked at Arin. He looked young. And too careful, and worried, and uncertain, and . . . something new was emerging, she saw it. It changed the quality of his expression the way light changes everything. A small sort of hope.

"Maybe," he said, "we could try being honest with each other."

She wondered what was in her expression that hope would grow in his. She wondered what he saw. "Arin," she said, "I like the dagger."

He smiled.

"THEY HAVE A FOOTHOLD IN THE SOUTH NOW," Roshar said.

"I know," said Arin.

"I doubt you know anything that doesn't have to do with that wraith of yours."

"Enough."

They had been talking like this for some time, Roshar gradually dropping his veneer of needling humor to vent real frustration, Arin growing quiet, entrenched. They were in an office adjacent to the library, the table between them blanketed with maps and papers. The room had been chosen for privacy. Probably no one could hear them beyond the locked door. Or if people did, down the first floor's north hallway, they heard not words but muffled tones. Despite the hot day, the diamond-paned windows remained shut because Roshar had complained of a chill. In truth, the prince hadn't wanted their conversation to carry into the garden. But this meeting, which was supposed to develop tactics to keep the Valorian general off the peninsula's shores, was deteriorating to the point that Arin wouldn't have been surprised if Roshar broke something, possibly one of the windows, if only because they'd make the loudest noise.

"We lost that island, and you . . . where *are* you?" Roshar's tight hands opened and spread wide. "Are you even here? No, you're not. You're upstairs, roaming her halls, roaming her head. Arin, this needs to end."

But Arin said nothing.

Roshar swore at him in Dacran, the curse so intricate and colorful that Arin didn't even try to make sense of the grammar.

In the silence that followed, Arin thought about how the god of death had deserted him. He had strained to hear his god. He'd also prayed to the god of war—confederate of death, drinker of blood—but the prayers had found no favor. Ithrya Island had been lost. It was now occupied as a Valorian base, south of Herran. It wouldn't be long before the general's army tried to land again on the peninsula—though *where* was uncertain.

Roshar said, "My sister is going to have some hard questions for you."

Arin couldn't avoid remembering the queen's kiss last spring. He'd pressed her against the shut door. She had wanted him. Kestrel had said that she didn't. He hadn't wanted Kestrel either, not then. Or so he'd thought. His gut twisted with shame.

"Arin, you will do me the courtesy of responding when I speak."

"Your sister is none of my concern."

The prince pressed palms to his face so that his hands

made a mask that showed only his disbelieving eyes. Then his fingertips crept up and rubbed against squeezed-shut eyelids.

But what could Arin say? He couldn't explain how it felt, mere days after Kestrel had come to his rooms and said that she liked the dagger, to hear the rich cascade of the piano played in a far-off room. To hold his breath as he heard the initial stammer of notes. Then: mistakes worked through. Rhythms made right. He'd felt this new thing, giddy and bright. It spun inside him, soft and warm and summery.

"We have used this city as a base." Roshar dropped his hands. He'd switched to Arin's language. He was speaking with the kind of bell-like tone one uses with children. "It's been a convenient point of return. We're here now because the bay provides a good base to attack or defend anywhere along the eastern coast between here and Ithrya. And the city, as the general's greatest prize, must be protected. But the general's not likely to bite at it, not yet. Not when we've avalanched again the mountain pass he used for the first invasion. Not when our fleet is in this bay. He can seize the easy fruits of your countryside and march north, inland to the city, where he'll breach the wall and take what he wants that way."

Arin didn't disagree.

"I'm heading south soon, little Herrani. I don't plan on returning to your lovely home with its new and fascinating guest. Will you see fit to join me in defending your very own country, or will you waste away here with your Valorian ghost until her people break down your doors and murder you both?"

"I'm coming with you," Arin said . . . but not immediately, and with the prick of offense that comes when an accusation hits home.

"*My prince.* 'I'm coming with you, *my prince.*'"

But Arin wouldn't say it, not even in the same mean mock-play of Roshar's tone. He swallowed, throat tight. His mouth had the same taste it had years ago when a Valorian had shoved a horse bit into it.

"I do hope," Roshar said, "that what you lack in grace and self-preservation will be recompensed by a return to your usual brutal and uncanny gift for battle. I want you to kill them all. Can you do that for me?"

"Yes."

"What about your gun?"

Roshar's word for Arin's invention was accurate in the vaguest sense, since the term had long been used to refer to any shape and style of cannon.

"Our supply has increased," Arin said, "but I'm worried about the device's accuracy." He shuffled through the papers on the table until he found the sketches for the weapon. He selected a particular page and traced the sketch of a barrel and matchlock. "If we use what we have now, we'll risk hitting our soldiers when we fire. We can surprise the Valorians with this weapon only once, and—"

A slender hand reached between them to take the sketch.

Roshar spun around. Arin didn't move.

Kestrel stood there, ignoring the prince, who had sucked in his breath and hardened his expression into a death's-head mask. She glanced up at Roshar once, coolly, then continued to study the design. She hadn't looked at Arin at all. Her slippered feet sank into the plush, vividly patterned carpet as she stepped quietly away from them and closer to a window. A shaft of light hit her cheekbone, made the paper glow. It set her hair on fire. Arin's stomach twinged. His throat tightened. Her eyes were still too shadowed. But she'd gained weight and looked less frail. Once again, Arin dared to hope.

He had forgotten what she was looking at until she spoke. "The ordnance is wrong."

"What?" Roshar was just barely keeping his composure.

"It's round. You're planning on shooting a ball like a cannon does. But this is not a cannon. Cannons aren't intended to be especially accurate. They're designed to do the most amount of destruction in a generalized space. This thing—a gun, you said?"

Only now did Arin wonder when she'd entered the room, and how much she'd heard. He didn't think she understood the eastern language, but he and Roshar had been speaking in Herrani for some time now.

"This seems designed for specific harm to a person or that person's parts," Kestrel said. "In that sense, it's like a bow and arrow. An arrowhead is not round. It's tipped. That makes the arrow fly true. It drives into the flesh. If you want greater accuracy, that little cannonball should not be a ball. It should be conical, perhaps. Tipped."

She returned the sketch to Arin. Then she left as silently as she had come, closing the door behind her.

"Arin." Roshar's voice was menacing. "That door was locked."

"I gave her the keys."

Roshar exploded.

Kestrel was on the grounds at the edge of the orchard when he found her. The eastern prince kept his distance, but he was unmistakably there to speak with her. Ripe ilea hung heavily from the trees. Some of the purple fruit had fallen to the grass. Wasps climbed over it. They didn't bother her, but the sun made her tired.

"What do you want?" she said when he approached.

"I'd like to know how much you know." Roshar saw her expression. What he saw changed his. A little more gently, he said, "It's a matter of safety."

"Mine, or yours?"

"I care about as much for my safety as I think you do for yours."

"His, then."

"This is war. The safety of many people is at stake."

"If you play war safely, you'll lose," she said, then was uneasy. Those words hadn't felt like hers. They belonged to someone else, a person who knew war well and enjoyed discussing it with her.

She shook her head. She didn't want to think about that. It made her dizzy, pricked by invisible pins. She focused on the prince: his mutilations, his finely drawn black eyes. "How do you speak my language so well?"

Roshar raised his brows.

"I mean, his." She knew that Herrani wasn't her first language. Still, it often felt that way.

"I was enslaved by your people. Then I was sold into this country."

She looked again at the missing nose. The slitted, reptilian nostrils. "Did they do that to you?"

He smiled with his teeth.

Testing the truth of it as she spoke, Kestrel said, "I knew that they did that to runaways. I don't remember seeing it happen."

"You might not have. You were a lady. Part of privilege is not having to look at ugly things."

"You're not ugly."

"What a sweet little liar you are."

"Except when you smile. You make yourself look like a grinning skull. You do it on purpose."

"Not so sweet, then."

"Not a liar."

"But you *were* a liar. A very good one, if what I hear is true. Who's to say you're not lying about your lost memory?"

She gave him a look of such plain hatred that he drew back. The wasps buzzed.

"I have a confession," he said. "Sometimes I offend on purpose. It's like my smile."

"That's not an apology."

"Princes don't apologize."

In a swift move, she had her dagger in her hand at his throat. He jerked his head back with a hiss.

"Apologize," she said.

"I'm not sure giving you that dagger was wise. You're not exactly stable."

She pressed the dagger. He stepped back. She stepped forward. "Everyone says I've done these marvelous things. Traitor to my country for the greater good. I was so *noble*." Her mouth became a sneer. "Poor girl. Poor Kestrel with her worthless weak body, her empty mind. Why would I lie now?"

"To torment him."

Startled, she lowered the blade.

Roshar said, "You torment him."

"Is that why you're here? To protect your friend from me?"

This time, Roshar's smile was a mere twist of the mouth.

"I don't want anything from him," she said.

"That might be part of the problem."

She spoke as if she hadn't heard. "I don't care about your war."

"Did you, or did you not, just advise us on how to improve a weapon designed to riddle your people with holes? A weapon that if we are very lucky will kill your father."

"My father." The blue sky went black. Wasps buzzed inside her head. She opened her mouth to speak. Nothing came out.

"Yes," Roshar said. "He's leading the Valorian army. Didn't anyone tell you?"

The hand that held the dagger sagged. She thought about her conversation with Arin in his rooms. He had tried to tell her.

Roshar touched her shoulder. Her vision cleared, but her heart was racing. He said, "I apologize. I'm sorry for what I said earlier."

She felt far away and horribly grounded at the same time, like her heart had been torn from her body and lost, and she didn't know whether she was her heart or her body.

"Kestrel?"

It was one thing to perfect a weapon that would kill her people. It was another to discover that she hadn't considered her father, had never even thought about his role in this war, though she'd had enough information to guess it without being told.

She realized she didn't regret perfecting the weapon. Part of her *wanted* her father to be a target. Her own father. What kind of person was she?

Abruptly, Roshar said, "I don't remember how I used to look."

It took her a moment to absorb what he had said.

"When I look in a mirror, this is all I see," he told her. "There's no memory of what I was before."

The scent of ilea fruit was heady. She forgot her father. She did not want to remember him. Bringing her gaze up again to Roshar's face, she met his lovely, untouched eyes. And saw the satiny brown skin of his cheek. She asked, "Do you miss who you were?"

At first, she thought his reply would be mocking. Yet he simply shrugged and spoke in a voice that was light yet thin. "Oh, what's the use of missing?" He squinted one eye and, apparently aware of how the mood had changed between them, he said, "You're good with a blade."

"No."

"Yes."

She shook her head. "I never was."

"I said *good*, not divinely talented. You've got an ease that comes from training for a long time."

"Is that what you see, or what you know about me from before?"

"What I see. I didn't know you before."

Kestrel watched him smile yet again, softly this time. She waded into the sheer relief of being with someone who knew her only as she was now.

The piano and the horse were hers in an uncomplicated way.

They didn't talk, which helped. It wasn't that they expected nothing from her. Even the piano seemed expectant, each key ready for the strike. Javelin chewed her loose sleeve and slobbered and shamelessly leaned in for her caress. Yet both the horse and the piano knew her and didn't care how she compared with her former self. They were hers. She was theirs. There were no questions.

She saddled Javelin. It wasn't easy. But if she lifted the saddle to his back every day then a day would come when her weak arms were strong. She tightened the girth. An irrielle bird hopped in through the open stable doors, pecking at the dirt. It cocked its head, watched Kestrel with tiny green eyes. Tipped its long, narrow tail. She got a mounting block, which she thought she probably hadn't used since she was a child, and set her foot in the horse's stirrup. The stallion was enormously tall. Mountainous, really. A warhorse. He shouldn't suit her, but he did.

She pulled herself up clumsily, but the horse didn't seem to mind. The bird launched itself back out into the unclouded sky, dipping and weaving. Irrielles don't fly straight.

Kestrel took the reins and spurred the horse to follow the bird.

She rode away from the house, taking a path that led to another path. She didn't recognize it. It wasn't long until she was surrounded by trees in full leaf. The path stretched out into a green tunnel. She rode for some time. She saw a day owl with her owlets. There was little wind. It wasn't too hot. Good weather for war.

She'd heard enough of the conversation between Arin and Roshar a few days earlier. They were biding their time here. If she were them, she wouldn't stay long.

Her stomach swayed. It matched the horse's movement. She loosened the reins, letting Javelin go as he pleased.

But she found that he was surging forward, hooves clopping. Arin's house lay far behind. The path forked. The horse went left. He was stepping surely. He was, she realized, going somewhere he recognized and she didn't.

She jerked his head around and ground him to a halt. He snorted, hooves shifting.

Kestrel was sweating. Her dress stuck to her skin. She made Javelin go back the way they'd come—fast, then faster, his hooves beating the rhythm of her terrified heart.

She somehow wasn't surprised to find Arin waiting alongside a stream close to his house, but she was surprised that she was grateful. Her heart still stammered inside her chest.

Arin had no horse, though a bit of stable straw stuck to the sole of a boot. He was crouched by the water, fingertips sunk only past the first knuckles. Barely in the water at all. Just feeling the slight current, she thought. He hadn't glanced over his shoulder. Still, he was aware that she was there. He listened to the slowing thump of Javelin's hooves. Arin's hair hung in his eyes.

She had wanted to sweep it aside. She remembered this. It had been on the first day. When she had bought him. She had wanted to see him clearly.

She stopped her horse.

Arin straightened, water dripping from his hand. He came close, put his fingers into Javelin's mane, and met her eyes. She was held in the palm of that memory: curiosity, hesitation, a sense of wrong, a violation. Yet still the compulsion to *see*. This person. She remembered his rigid shoulders, hard mouth. He had avoided her gaze. His whole body: a silent snarl.

He wasn't like that now. He looked up at her, his expression was unguarded, growing worried. "What's wrong?"

"Nothing." Javelin shifted beneath her.

Arin frowned. "Do I frighten you?"

"No."

"Your face is bloodless." He touched her hand. She saw that she was clenching the reins and let them slacken.

"It's not because of you," she said. Then, because she had decided to be honest, she said, "Yes, you, a little." She stopped, confused, unable to explain to him or herself the difference between the fear that had sent her tearing back down the horse path and the bright stitch of nervousness that traveled up her skin now as she looked down at him. "In the woods, Javelin wanted to take a path. I didn't. It upset me."

His eyes went crystalline. "Where was this?"

"Is there something dangerous in the woods?"

He grabbed the pommel and mounted the horse behind her. "Show me."

She kept the reins. He drew his sword. It was a different sword than the one he'd had on the tundra. She thought about that, which kept her from thinking about how dread mounted in her throat as they rode, how her breath was again too fast. The damp dress still clung to her, and as she strained to be alert to everything around them, each little life that moved in the woods, it was hard not to be aware of him, too.

But there was no telltale snap of a twig. No enemy shadow in the trees. Kestrel almost wished there were. It would explain the terror that had seized her . . . and seized her again as they stopped at the fork in the path. The stallion stamped.

Arin sheathed his blade.

"What is it?" she asked.

"It's the way to your house." She felt his voice travel up her back. There was a long pause. "We could go."

"No."

"Nothing's there. It's empty. I'd be with you."

"I don't want to."

He took the reins from her frozen hands. He turned back Javelin, who showed more reluctance this time. Arin kept the pace slow, at a walk.

They were silent as they rode. Then Kestrel heard herself say, voice low, "I feel foolish."

"No, Kestrel, you're not."

"There was no reason to be afraid."

"Maybe we just don't know what your reason is."

Javelin, whose ears flicked crankily to have been thwarted twice in his plans to take the fork in the road, whuffed and shook his head. "Shh," Arin told the horse, and hummed a few low notes. Then he stopped and was quiet before saying, "Even if you had no reason at all, fear isn't foolish. I get frightened, too."

She remembered how he'd held his sword earlier. "You thought there were Valorians in the woods. You weren't frightened then."

"Not exactly."

"Then what are you afraid of?"

"Spiders," he said gravely.

She elbowed him.

"Ow."

She snorted. "Spiders."

"Or those things with a thousand legs." He shuddered. "Gods."

She laughed.

Quietly, he said, "I was afraid when I came to the stable and saw that Javelin wasn't in his stall."

Startled, she turned her head, catching a glimpse of the line of his jaw and the shadows of his throat. She returned her gaze to the road. Lightly, she said, "Worse than spiders?"

"Ah, much worse."

"If I ran away, I wouldn't get very far."

"In my experience, it's a very bad idea to underestimate you."

"But you didn't try to ride me down."

"No."

"You wanted to."

"Yes."

"What stopped you?"

"Fear," he said, "of what it would mean for me not to trust you. I saddled a horse. I was ready to ride . . . but I thought that if I did, I'd be nothing more than a different kind of prison to you."

His words made her feel strange.

He changed his tone. There was mischief in it now. "Also, you're a little intimidating."

"I am not."

"Oh, yes. I didn't think you'd appreciate being followed. I've seen what happens to people who get on your bad side. And now you know my weakness, and will drop spiders down the back of my shirt if I cross you, and I'll have a hard life indeed."

"Hmph," she said, but she had calmed. Her bones didn't feel so jammed up against each other in tensed certainty of a blow about to fall. There was the day. It was green and blue and gold. There was the powerful slow horse. His steady step. A murmur in the trees. Branch and twig. Arms on either side of her. Roots buckling up and disappearing back into the ground.

Words clogged in her throat. But there was a soft feeling in her chest, a warmth that gave her courage to speak.

"You said that we don't know the reason I stopped Javelin from taking the path to my house. What do you *think* is the reason?"

He hesitated. Finally, he said, "I have no thoughts."

"You *always* have thoughts."

She felt some quality of surprise in him. He'd been surprised by the familiarity of her tone.

"Tell me," she said.

"I'm thinking that I don't want to assume anything. It's—" He broke off. "Dangerous for me. Where you're concerned."

As they neared his home, they had an easy rhythm in the saddle. He rode one-handed now. She was a bit sorry for Javelin, who had to bear both their weights. She'd make it up to him. She knew where the carrots were kept.

But eventually her mental list of which treat to offer and which curry brush to use came to an end. She was left with images that wouldn't go away.

The fork in the path. Arin by the creek. That brief memory of the first time she'd ever seen him. His refusal to look up. His face bruised, armored by hatred.

She said, "Was I horrible to you when you worked for me?"

"No."

"Did I hit you?"

"Kestrel, no. Why would you ask that?"

"I remember you bruised."

"You didn't do that. You wouldn't."

"Well," she pointed out, "I *have* hit you in recent memory."

"That was different."

She remembered how powerless she'd felt when she'd struck him. She thought she understood what he meant. "How was I, then, when I owned you?"

There was no sound but the leaves and Javelin's hooves on the dirt. The trees thinned. Arin's house rose into view.

Kestrel said, "You hated me."

He stopped the horse. "Please look at me."

She turned in the saddle and did, meeting his gaze.

"At first I hated you," he said. "It was for what you were, not who you were. I didn't know who you were. And then I did, a little. You seemed kind. Kindness isn't good in a master. Not to me. It's another way of making you beg. You become grateful for things you shouldn't be grateful for. When I was a child I was so grateful for it. Then I grew, and I almost preferred cruelty because it was closer to the truth, and no one hid behind the lie of being *nice*. I broke rules. Especially with you. I kept pushing for you to punish me. I tried to force your hand. I wanted you to show your true self."

His expression was difficult to read. The crook in her neck was painful. She dropped her gaze to Javelin's mane.

"But this *was* your true self," he said. "Intelligent, brave, manipulative. Kind. You made no effort to hide who you were. Then I found that I *wanted* you to hide it. This was the luxury of your position, wasn't it, that you didn't have to hide? It was the doomed nature of mine, that I did. And that's true. Sometimes a truth squeezes you so tightly you can't breathe. It was like that. But it also wasn't, because there was another reason it hurt to look at you. You were too likable. To me."

She wasn't sure what to say.

"I'm trying to be honest," he told her.

"I believe you. But it's hard to believe you could have really known me. Some of what you say doesn't make sense."

"Which part?"

"My character seems contradictory."

"Why?"

"I don't think you can be manipulative and kind at the same time."

He laughed. "*You* can."

There was a silence. Javelin shifted beneath them.

Arin touched a fingertip to the nape of her neck. He found, beneath the edge of her dress at her shoulder, a healed scar, thin and long. The skin where the whip had fallen was deadened, but the skin that bordered it was alive, and shivered. She was glad that she no longer faced him.

"You are changed," he murmured, "and you are the same. Honorable. I honor you."

That shiver dissolved into fear. Fear, for the fork in the path that loomed in the forest behind them. For what it meant that Arin knew her before and knew her now and honored her.

She did not ask him to honor her. She was suspicious of honor.

She nudged her knees into Javelin's sides. Arin's fingertips fell away. The horse headed for the stables.

Arin said nothing more to her that day, beyond an offer to curry Javelin. She accepted. She wanted to be alone. Even when she retreated into the house, her skin felt vibrant. Wakeful, unruly. Like it would give her no quarter. It would insist and insist, all because of a touch that had seemed intended to soothe.

But it was not soothing.

Although the day had not been without comfort, Kestrel kept the last potent moment of it in mind. She decided that Arin was the opposite of relief.

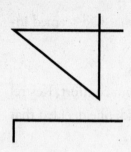

ARIN WAS GONE AGAIN. HE LEFT KESTREL A
note that announced his departure but gave no reason for it
nor an indication of how long he'd be away. She assumed it
had something to do with the war, and that he hesitated to
explain anything in writing, which begged the question of
why he hadn't spoken with her, which in turn reminded her
of how she'd flinched from his touch.

She understood the note. But she didn't like it.

She asked Roshar where Arin was and why.

"Nosy, nosy," said the prince. His tone was arch. Friendly
enough. Still, it drew a clear hard line that warned she'd
waste her time pressing for more information.

They were playing Borderlands in the parlor. The windows were open and a storm was brewing, but the rain hadn't
come yet. Dark clouds knotted on the horizon. The wind
that stirred the curtains smelled raw. Roshar shifted, and
shifted again, eyeing the game pieces.

Arin hadn't taken Javelin. No horses were missing from
the stables. She'd counted them.

Roshar glanced at the darkening sky.

"Is he at sea?" Kestrel asked.

"Dear one, what do you care?"

"You're nervous."

"I'm nervous about *you*. You're going to beat me."

"I thought you were at war. You should have better things to do than stay here and play Borderlands with me."

He lifted one brow, but merely said, "Your move."

She made it. It had been a pleasure to discover that she remembered how to play. *How* was not a problem for her. She knew how to do things. Play a game, play the piano, ride a horse, speak a language. If there was anything she no longer knew *how* to do, she wasn't conscious of it.

The issue was *what*. Her memory was a gaming set where she could see the board and knew the rules of the game yet didn't recognize all the pieces.

She said, "Who commands the Dacran-Herrani alliance?"

"Need you even ask? Do I not exude an air of irrefutable authority?"

"What's Arin's role?"

"That," he told her, "is a good question."

The wind billowed a curtain. She moved her engineer, keeping her eyes on the board. "I'm surprised your people support the alliance."

He shrugged, muttering something short and irritable in his language.

"Dying for someone else's people is not usually how war works," Kestrel said. "What exactly does your queen want from Herran?"

"That deadly little invention of Arin's, for one."

"You have that already. He's given you the plans."

"The empire must be kept at bay. If they take this peninsula, it's only a matter of time before they take the east."

"Is your sister intelligent?"

He gave her an impatient look. She saw his answer. "Then she must want something more," Kestrel said. "Does Arin know what she wants?"

Roshar's green-rimmed eyes narrowed. "Arin knows a good deal when he sees one. We're the best thing that could have happened to him."

"Yes, clearly. You are great benefactors. If you care so much for his well-being, why have you sent him to sea in the middle of a storm?"

"Arin sent himself."

She fell silent. Roshar made his move. "Tell me, little ghost: do you enjoy my company?"

She was surprised. "Yes."

"I enjoy yours, too. I can see why you like me. I'm intelligent, charming—not to mention handsome."

"And skilled at preening. Let's not forget that."

"Lies, all lies." He met her eyes across the gaming board. "The reason you enjoy my company is because I look like how you feel."

"That's not it," she said, though when she looked again at his damaged face she realized that what he'd said was true. Yet it was only partly true, and she didn't know how to put the other parts into words.

"Arin is my friend," Roshar told her. "I trust him with my life, and he trusts me with his. That's rare. I won't have it questioned by someone who, for all I can tell, has no love for him." He knocked over his general: the gesture of surrender. The marble game piece rolled. "Go away, little ghost. Go haunt someone else." But he was the one who left.

Rain tapped the panes. She went to draw the windows shut, then paused, seeing how the trees bent, lashed by wind blowing in from the sea. It smelled like a cut-open oyster.

Dear one, what do you care?

A small serpent of worry lifted its hooded head inside her.

Rain drove into Arin's eyes. The deck heaved. It wasn't a green storm, but just as bad. They'd seen the signs. They'd been warned against sailing by the Herrani captain who'd taken Arin east last winter.

"We must," Arin had told Roshar. "The general holds Ithrya. He'll use it to supply a strike at the mainland and can sustain that attack only if he's able to supply his forces. He's stockpiling Ithrya. We must break his supply lines with the Valorian capital. I'll sail to the Empty Islands between our western shores and Valoria."

"You're no sailor."

Arin spoke as if he hadn't heard. "A Herrani ship, with Herrani crew."

"I'll send Xash."

Arin shook his head. "My people have recovered. They want to fight. As it is, your soldiers wonder when we're going to pull our own weight."

So Arin's ship had set sail.

Now it quaked under each hit from a monstrous wave.

The sea swelled into purple hills and valleys. The sails had been stowed lest they be shredded by the wind. The captain had set a drogue in the water to slow the ship and stabilize it, but its prow punctured wave after wave. The deck was slick. Arin struggled to keep his footing. He slid, hit the railing, and gripped it. Vomited.

"God of madness." The captain seized Arin's upper arm and hauled him upright. The captain was three times Arin's age and growled with that lilt that Herrani sailors had had before the war. "Get below, boy. What good're you on deck? You know nothing of the sea." Then the captain's attention darted away, and he was gone.

The captain was right. Arin was headed toward the bolt-hole, his face stinging with salt and rain, eyes burning, when it struck him that he was too seasick to be afraid. This made him remember his conversation with Kestrel as they'd ridden her horse, and how, if he'd had to touch her, he should have known better than to touch her where they had hurt her, even if he had wanted to say, without words, that he understood how they had hurt her.

His boots skidded. The world was a dizzy, wet blur. The ship shuddered and leaned on its side. Again, Arin tumbled against the railing. This time, he went over. He plunged into the seething water below.

HE PUNCHED TO THE SURFACE. BROKE IT.
Gasped. Was shoved under again by a swell of water. His
lungs blazed.

This time, when he came up from the silence into the
roaring air, he was smarter. He broke the laces of his boots
with a savage yank, kicked the heavy things from his feet.
He sucked in his breath, swam straight through the next
wave, and struck out for the tempest-tossed ship, which wasn't
far. The water was blood-warm. It tugged at him. Dragged
and pushed. His shoulders ached. He swam through another
wave. He prayed. He was closer.

A rope? Could someone lower a rope from the deck?

Maybe . . . if anyone had even seen him go over.

He kicked harder. *Don't leave me,* he prayed again to his
god. *Not like this.*

There was no sound but the sea.

I'll serve you, Arin promised.

His god didn't answer. Arin was close enough to see the

barnacles on the ship's hull. He looked up. No one looked down. He pushed forward.

How can I serve you, if I drown?

And now the fear. Weariness. His limbs felt as if they were plowing through mud. Salt in his throat. His lungs. His death wasn't supposed to happen this way.

By the sword. Please.

Not like this.

Not alone.

Not yet.

A current sucked him away from the ship.

Arin almost surrendered himself to it. You can't fight the will of the gods, and never this god.

A tattered desolation fluttered through him. Again: *Not alone, not yet.* But he *was* alone. He had been alone for a long time.

I wish, he thought, *that I could hear your voice again.* He wondered if he would, in the end.

The current still gripped him. But it turned on itself. It flung Arin forward, muscling him swiftly through the water until he slammed against the hull's side.

He almost blacked out. Head ringing, vision weird, Arin went up and down. He swallowed water. Scrambled against the hull. His hands sought something, anything.

And hooked hard. Squeezed.

The hull ladder.

Arin looked up and saw the line of rusted rungs leading up the hull. For a moment, he couldn't move. He was rapt with wonder.

In your name, Arin swore. *I'll bring glory to you.*

Shaking, grateful, he climbed.

The next day broke clean, like it had been spat on and polished to a shine.

The black powder stored in the magazine deep in the ship's hold had stayed dry. Some sacks, though, had been kept at the ready on the gundecks. They were soaked. The sea had swamped the gunports before the sailors had hauled back the cannons and bolted the ports.

Arin and some of the sailors opened the sacks and spread powder out in shallow pans laid out on the quarterdeck. The sun was hot on his bare shoulders. He bowed with the weight of a full sack. The powder was damp and cakey as he jostled it out of the bag and sifted the grit with his hands, spreading it into a fine layer. His palms became black. They looked familiar. Not so different from how they'd used to look after a day in the forge. A normal day.

But today was not normal. He kept his eyes on his task. The black powder, made from sulfur extracted from Dacra's northern plateau, was precious. The eastern supply was limited, so it was important that the powder, useless when wet, dry well. It was important that Arin take care. And it was very important that he keep his gaze averted from the other sailors, who kept sneaking glances at him.

Because Arin was not normal. No one fell into the sea like that and lived.

He felt the stare from the girl scraping scales from a

freshly caught fish half her size. Other sailors stared, too. The ones mending a sail and tarring the rigging. Those nearest to him, emptying their sacks.

Sweat dripped from his brow and vanished into the powder in its pan near his bare feet. Arin wondered when that powder would be used. He wondered what damage it would do, and if, when the powder exploded, some essence of himself would burn with it.

He wondered if this was a normal thought.

The sacks were now empty. He brushed his black palms. He needed to rinse. He was a walking fire hazard. A bucket of seawater was kept near the mainmast. He went to it, dunked his arms in up to his elbows, and splashed a little over his shoulders, feeling the water go down the runnel of his spine. He'd itch once the water dried to salt.

"You look none the worse for drowning."

Arin straightened to see the captain leaning near the shrouds, watching him. Arin remembered the man's expression during the storm, when Arin had hauled himself over the railing, slopped down onto the deck, and retched a bellyful of seawater.

Arin asked, "How long until the Empty Islands?"

"Ithrya's near, but we must give her a wide berth. Two, three days, then, to sail south around Ithrya and up to the islands. Should the winds stay fair."

"Do you think they will?"

"Ask them, why don't you, and see if they will for *you*."

The sun was in the captain's face. Arin couldn't read his expression. The man's voice could have either been mock serious, or dead serious. Arin cleared his throat. "The gunpowder should be dry by day's end. No one's to smoke. Even one stray spark—"

"We're not daft, boy."

Arin rubbed the nape of his neck, nodded, and thought the conversation was over. He looked out at the sea. Green and dazzling, like his mother's emerald. He remembered the day he'd traded it away, and wished he'd kept it. He thought that everyone should have one precious thing to hold with his whole heart, to know to be incontrovertibly his own. He held the emerald in his mind, felt its cool facets. He imagined placing it in the palm of a hand he knew well, and wondered if it would be accepted, and how it would feel to have someone else hold what he held with his whole heart.

He blinked, looked away from the horizon. He was sea-dreaming. Imagining things that would hurt him later.

Now, even.

"There've been stories about you." The captain was squinting at him. "Well before the storm."

It disconcerted Arin, the way people had begun to look at him. There was this shining expectation. He wasn't sure how much of it really had to do with him. Maybe when people have nothing precious, an idea takes its place. Arin wasn't ready to be an idea. *They're just stories,* Arin wanted to say, but the words died on his lips. He knew better than to deny his god.

It was as if the captain had heard Arin's thoughts. "God-touched, you are."

Arin said nothing, yet beneath the shyness lay an undeniable pleasure.

The ship slipped between the Empty Islands and dropped anchor to the east of one island large enough to hide the ship from view of any vessel that might come from the Valorian capital. The crew waited.

Arin still had no shoes. His feet were too large for the few spare boots on board. He ripped rags, tied them around his feet, and walked carefully.

He tried to go over the plan with the captain, who interrupted him with a dismissive flick of the hand. "That's not a plan. That's simple piracy. You needn't teach me that."

Arin was taken aback. "Before the war, the Herrani were the best at sea. We gained wealth through sea trade. We weren't pirates."

The captain laughed and laughed.

The ship came. It sailed from the west. A large vessel, weighty with double gundecks.

The cry came down from the crow's nest aboard Arin's ship. The crew heaved at the capstan, weighed anchor, luffed the sails, and drove toward the Valorian vessel.

Arin's ship was lighter, which made it faster. But it was lighter because of its single gundeck. Catching up to the Valorian vessel wasn't the hard part. Boarding her without being blown out of the water would be. If the Valorians were surprised to see the Herrani ship move out from behind the island and ride in their wake, their surprise wouldn't last long. They'd be ready for an attack.

Arin went below to the gundeck. The gunports were open now, the mouths of a row of cannons yawning wide. Arin and the crew prepared them. Black powder down a cannon's belly, a wad of cloth jammed in tight and shoved home with a rammer. The cannonball. Arin cradled it between his palms, smooth and heavy, then pushed it in. All rammed down. He primed the cannon. Hauled on the gun tackles. The sailors dragged each cannon forward until its barrel slid into the gunport and its carriage met the bulwark.

Arin snuck a look out the port. He didn't see the ship yet. But he probably wouldn't see it until his captain brought his ship broadside to broadside, the gunports of one ship mirroring the other.

He looked away and caught sight of the gray face of the sailor nearest him. Sweat trembled on the man's brow. He looked ill. He didn't look how Arin felt. Arin wished he could share what he felt: a dark greed.

The ship slowed. They must be drawing abreast of the Valorians.

His lungs were taut, eager. The world was made simple. Arin, who with other things had gone so badly wrong before, who had judged and misjudged and misunderstood, wouldn't fail at *this*. Maybe it was his god, or maybe it was only ordinary human determination, but his need to fight felt ready and strong, like sprung steel that wanted to cut its way out of him.

He smiled encouragingly at the sailor.

A blast burst through the bulwark. The sailor exploded into bloody chunks. Shards of wood whizzed through the air, driving into Arin's flung-up arm.

"Fire," Arin shouted. He lit his cannon, got out of the path of its recoil. It shuddered and boomed. The sailors were doing the same, and then doing as Arin did: dragging the shot cannon back, swabbing it out, stuffing it again, dragging it up against the bulwark. It went on like that for some time. It was impossible to see what damage the Herrani inflicted. Another blast ruptured a hole in the bulwark. They were high enough above the waterline not to take on the sea, and the Valorians would want to seize his ship as much as he wanted theirs, but they'd sink it if it came to that. Arin reloaded. Fired.

Then he stepped wrong. A sharp object pierced his rag-covered foot. He glanced down at his right foot. The rags were staining red. He paused, slow now for some reason he couldn't quite comprehend, but Arin had come to trust these moments when part of him understood something before his mind did. He reached down, dragged out a bloody bit of metal (a bent nail?), and gave it a good brief stare. An idea spread within him, curved. A malevolent sort of smile.

He grabbed the nearest sailor. "You. Get below, find rags. Make small bags of them. Stuff them with gunpowder and anything little and sharp. Nails. Tie it all up, set a joss stick down the neck of each bag, and bring them all back here, ten at a time. Light them, throw them out the gunports. Try to get them into *their* gunports, when they pull their cannons back to load them. Understand? *Go.*"

Then Arin looked for the sailor whose expression looked most like his own must, and told him to take charge. Arin was going to board that Valorian ship.

Up onto the deck, into the blue and smoky black. Sword

in the right hand, dagger in the left. Valorians on his ship already. Their vessel was close enough to board. Arin ducked. Sliced. His sword beat back a thrust and he drove in with his dagger, found a soft belly. Steaming liquid up to the wrist, running to the elbow.

Arin worked his way to the railing. He heard crossbow quarrels. They didn't touch him. His god rose within him: silent, approving. Arin leaped onto the Valorian ship. A blade came at him. He caught it with his own, parried, snaked his sword up for a thrust into the man's arm where the leather armor joined. Dagger to the neck. Both weapons snatched back out of the flesh, the metal oily red. Body at his feet.

He saw a package launch out of the Herrani ship's gun hole. Then another. An explosion belowdeck trembled the boards. Another.

Then, incredibly, over the din of cannons and screams, he heard a slight sound. He spun, and came face-to-face with a Valorian. A woman. Fair hair, dark eyes.

He dropped his guard.

She went for his neck. He jerked away at the last moment, caught the sword in his left shoulder. A surge of wet, running pain.

"No," he said in her language. "Wait."

She thrust again.

He parried her this time, his sword coming instinctively up, his good arm bending her blade back, not even pushing hard. A part of him watched this in horror, saw how easily the woman's arm bent. She was his age. Her face was not like Kestrel's but not very different either. As if she were Kestrel's sister.

It wasn't that he'd never seen a woman in battle. He'd just never killed one.

He knocked the sword from her hand.

He saw his sister's corpse in the street. His mother's jetting blood. His arm moved. He screamed at it to stop. Then he didn't see anything until he saw that he'd dropped his sword. His dagger? Gone, too.

The Valorian had her dagger in her hand. There was the flash of an incredulous, vicious grin. Then she drove the heel of her boot down onto his rag-covered foot and stabbed toward his heart.

His foot seemed to explode. He reeled, then somehow managed to turn the movement into a sidestep away from the dagger's thrust. He snatched her wrist. Forced her hand to open.

With her free hand, she punched his throat.

Arin.

Dimly, gasping, he became aware of the bright arc of her dagger coming toward him.

You're going to get yourself killed.

He swerved away. The weapon came again, cut him. He couldn't tell where.

In my name, you said.

You swore to serve.

Arin went low.

Are you not mine? Am I not yours?

His hand fumbled and grabbed.

To whom else would you ever belong?

Listen, my child.

My love.

Listen.

His ears were loud with silence. He saw.

Wide brown eyes. A slender body folded over his sword.

Which was in his hand.

The bloody dagger fell from hers.

Afterward, the captain directed the plunder of the ship. It was well stocked with food—and, more important, black powder.

The captain was pleased. He called Arin's little explosive bags a gods-given stroke of brilliance. They'd surprised the Valorian gunners, who took nails in the flesh and couldn't see through the smoke. "Very nasty, very nice."

Arin said nothing.

The captain studied him, lingering over the bloodier parts. "You'll heal fine." He squinted down at Arin's feet. "You need boots."

Arin shrugged. He realized that he didn't dare speak. He felt hollow, horrified at what he'd done even though he would have been killed if he hadn't, and it shouldn't have made a difference whether a Valorian he fought was a man or a woman. If he'd been asked before this whether both men and women had the right to war, he would have said yes. If asked whether men and women were equal, he would've said yes. Should they be treated the same? Yes. By that logic, no mercy to men meant no mercy to women. But Arin didn't feel logical. He disgusted himself.

She'd been fierce, determined. Kestrel would have been like that.

Fear opened wide inside him, funnel-shaped, draining away everything else.

Her father had wanted the life of a soldier for her. She'd nearly agreed. He imagined her at war. His throat tightened.

"Here." The captain had come back. Arin hadn't noticed him leave. The man held out a pair of boots. "Try these."

No need to ask where they'd come from. Bodies were all over both ships. The captain surveyed the scene. "This is good work. If we keep at it, their general won't have an easy time attacking the mainland. Soldiers can't fight if they can't eat."

What would happen if Valorians landed on the peninsula? If they pushed, unchecked, to the city? His cousin. His friends.

And what of Kestrel? Escaped prisoner. Traitor to her people. Would her father spare her? Arin couldn't even ask himself the question. That question would lead to other questions, and a worming sort of knowledge reminded Arin that the general hadn't acted to save his daughter from prison, which meant that either he didn't know she was there, or he knew and didn't care, or . . .

No. Arin had sworn to himself not to try to guess what Kestrel couldn't recall.

But he was sick, he was sore.

He was certain that the general would have no mercy.

So there was no room for Arin's mercy.

Arin put on the boots.

They'd seized another ship and anchored it off the eastern shore of an island, as they had with the first, when Xash arrived. He sailed up alongside Arin's ship and boarded. "I'm taking over," he told Arin. "Return to the city."

This was unexpected. Possibilities teemed in Arin's mind, and he didn't like any of them.

"My queen has arrived in your city," Xash told him. "She wants you."

IT WAS NOW CLEAR WHY ROSHAR HAD STAYED in the city. He'd been waiting for his sister.

The queen wasn't what Kestrel had expected. She'd imagined someone older, but this woman looked no older than Roshar.

Kestrel had gone down to the harbor with the rest of the household, as surprised and curious as the others. The crowd had eyed her from the moment she slipped in among them. She didn't know what stories had been told about her, but whatever they were, they made the Herrani and Dacran strangers look at her with fascination, but leave her alone.

Roshar's gaze had cut her way when he'd ridden past her into the city. Kestrel didn't recognize what his expression meant. She saw a flash of discomfort, then his face had shuttered and he'd ridden on.

He was all ease now, on the pier at his sister's side. Kestrel watched him offer pleasantries she couldn't hear and wouldn't understand if she did. She'd never learned the eastern language.

Her father had wanted her to learn. She remembered this. She didn't like the queasy feeling remembering gave her.

He had pressured her. She had refused.

It's dangerous not to know the language of your enemy, he'd said. *When you go to war—*

I won't go to war.

The words throbbed in her brain.

Kestrel felt Arin's absence. She wondered what he would make of this woman on the pier. But then Kestrel reminded herself that Arin knew the queen already, must know her well, quite well, if he'd been able to persuade her to take his side in war.

The queen (her name was Inishanaway, Kestrel heard someone in the crowd murmur) listened as her brother spoke. Her face was so still that it was easy to see its magnetic quality. A deep sort of mouth, ears so small that they looked like ornamentation, the nose softly shaped. Yes, beautiful, Kestrel decided, yet she didn't understand why that thought dug hard into some vulnerable place.

Kestrel wanted her horse. She wished she hadn't tethered Javelin in the marketplace and continued to the harbor on foot. She wanted to ride away. Now.

Foolish. If she felt dingy and small, it was her own fault for comparing herself where no comparisons could be made. She'd seen a mirror.

As she tried to understand it—this compulsion to compare—she began to realize slowly that the queen's features were familiar. It wasn't because they resembled Roshar's, though they did.

A little sister. Kestrel had known her at court. Risha, the

eastern princess, the youngest child of the three, beloved of the Valorian crown prince . . . who had been engaged to Kestrel.

Kestrel felt dizzy under the lemon-yellow sun. A sour taste in her mouth. Her father had been pleased, she remembered. He had hoped for Kestrel to marry Prince Verex, had hoped for it even when they were babies. His daughter: an empress.

She told herself that now she understood her fascination with the queen. It had been the familiarity, which Kestrel had needed to place. Or maybe it had been discomfort, to be powerless and behold someone with great power.

Maybe. But she still couldn't explain the rotten ooze in her heart.

Kestrel saw Roshar's gaze touch upon her, and dwell. He said something only the queen could hear. The woman's eyes went to Kestrel.

Roshar murmured in his sister's ear, his smile as light as a little knife.

There was an obvious reason for the way the queen looked at her: Kestrel was Valorian. She was to be questioned, doubted. Picked apart. Kestrel felt the dissecting gaze. She had a sudden image of herself as her namesake: a small hunting hawk, feathers plucked, wings lifted, spread back, pinioned.

Kestrel crossed her arms over her chest. The sun was hot. She was thirsty, throat dry. She stared right back at the woman and understood that the way the queen looked at her wasn't because Kestrel was Valorian, or her father's daughter. It was because of a secret Kestrel didn't know, and wasn't sure she wanted to know.

"Ah, Kestrel. I hoped to find you here."

She looked up from currying her horse and glanced over Roshar's shoulder, but no one lingered behind him. They were alone in the stables. She blew a wisp of hair out of her eyes and kept at her task.

"I have a favor to beg," he said.

"No need to speak so prettily, princeling."

"My sister . . ."

Kestrel felt it again: a sore wariness. Something was coming. Something sure to hurt.

". . . I had thought she'd reside in the palace of the former governor. However, it seems to not quite meet her standards."

"It's grander than anything else in the city."

"She likes *this* home."

Kestrel stopped brushing Javelin's coat. "What does that have to do with me?"

Roshar coughed, clearly uncomfortable. "Your suite."

"Oh."

"It's the only set of rooms suitable."

"I see."

"Would you mind?"

With a flash of feeling, she said, "This is Arin's home."

Roshar muttered in his language.

"What did you say?"

He met her eyes. "I said, 'Yes, precisely.'"

Javelin knocked his nose against her shoulder. Her fingers tightened around the curry brush. There was no *precisely*. There were only undercurrents of meaning to this situation that pushed Kestrel into a place she couldn't name. She forced herself to shrug. "I'll move my things." The thought of that day on the horse path rose unbidden in her mind: the fork in the road. The general's villa. She almost saw the house in her mind. *Her* house. Then came the fountaining fear, and Kestrel knew she couldn't go there, she never would, not even if there was no place for her here. "I'll speak with Sarsine."

"Yes." Roshar was relieved. "Thank you." He moved to leave.

"Did Arin tell you to ask me this?"

Roshar turned, surprised. "Of course not."

Questions rose within her. She was too proud to ask them.

"Arin," Roshar added, "is likely to kill me when he returns. But I never have any peace when my sister doesn't get her way. Death might be preferable. Be a good friend and make my next few days pleasant ones, for they'll be my last."

"Then he'll be here soon."

"My sister has summoned him."

Kestrel stared at Javelin's brown coat. She rubbed a dark dapple on his shoulder.

"Arin turned pirate for a while, but all for the best of causes," Roshar said. "Now that the queen has assumed command of the city, I won't linger. Neither will he. We'll both head south. After his royal audience, of course."

Her eyes pricked. She brushed a thumb against her fingers and looked at the dust from the ride through the city, then glanced up and found Roshar studying her, his expression sympathetic but also searching, and when she understood what it was he sought she became determined that he not find it. Her eyes cleared. She took the house keys from the pocket of her riding trousers and unhooked the key to the suite in the east wing. She offered it to Roshar. As she dropped it in his palm she knew perfectly well what had hurt her at the sight of the queen.

She did not give him the key to the rooftop garden.

"You'll share my rooms," Sarsine decided.

"All right."

"We can't offend her."

"I know."

Sarsine looked at her closely. "Arin would offend her. He wouldn't agree to this if he were here."

Kestrel wasn't so sure. She thought that Roshar knew a secret about the queen and Arin that Sarsine didn't. She said, "It doesn't matter to me."

But it did.

Four days later, Kestrel was in the kitchen gardens on the grounds. She weeded. She liked it. She enjoyed knowing what belonged and what didn't. There'd been a few mistakes at first, particularly with cooking herbs, but she knew what she was doing now. There was a pleasure in snapping pea pods from their stems and dropping them into her basket. She liked the bitter, ashy scent of the stunted plants that bore striped erasti, a fruit that grew only on this peninsula and only in this month. It was used in savory dishes. Kestrel picked them carefully. The cook, who'd been amusedly gentle with Kestrel's gardening and her mistakes, had sucked in his breath when she'd first brought in a basket of erasti. They'd been unripe. "You must wait." His tone was as close to chastisement as it ever got. "Leave them on the vine until they look like they'll explode if you touch them."

Her skin had burned on the first day of gardening, then peeled. She tanned. At first, she'd used a little knife to scrape out the dirt beneath her nails. Now she didn't bother.

Today the wind was high. The earth was soft. She didn't hear Arin approach.

"I've been looking everywhere for you."

Kestrel glanced up at him. The wind swirled her hair into her face. She couldn't see his expression and wanted to hide her own. She didn't like what she felt. Relief, that he was safe. And a very different emotion: simmering, awful.

He said, "I need to speak with you."

She knew from his tone what this was about. Knew that she had been right. She turned back to the plants. "I'm busy," she told him. Green juice trickled down her wrist. The fruit went into the basket.

He crouched next to her between the plants. Gently, he pushed the stray, windborn strands of hair from her face. His thumb touched her cheek. She looked at him then. He was unwashed, hair knotted, clothes rimed white with salt, his jaw green and yellow from an old bruise. His boots were Valorian, high and hooked.

She didn't want to see how the sun jeweled his eyes, or for her skin to feel suddenly alive simply because he had touched her. She didn't want him to look at her as if there were a door inside her he wanted to open and enter.

She said, "You should marry the queen."

He dropped his hand. "No."

"Then you're a fool."

"I've asked Inisha to move into the governor's palace."

"Twice a fool. Beg her back."

"Listen, please. When I was in the east, I thought all the wrong things of you. And you were engaged. You wouldn't change your mind. I asked you . . ." Arin stopped.

She heard the memory of his voice: *Marry him. But be mine in secret.*

She ached at the memory of it, saw her hurt mirrored in his eyes as he remembered it, too, saw the echo of his expression last winter, in a tavern. He had begged for scraps. Hated himself for it. Asked anyway.

"It was a kiss," Arin said. "Nothing more. There are no promises between me and the queen."

"You have no sense of self-preservation." Her heart was pounding hard. "If you've made no promises, you had better make them now. Why do you think she has allied with you?"

"Why doesn't matter."

"Of course it does." She leaped to her feet. He followed her, caught the hand that held the basket. "Was it a ploy?"

she demanded. Her heart was beating in a double rhythm now. Fear and anger, fear and anger. "Did you kiss her so that she'd believe your alliance would be permanent?"

"No."

"Then why?"

"Because I wanted to!" The words burst from him. "Because she wanted me, and it felt too good to be wanted."

Kestrel took a shuddering breath. How was it possible to be wounded by someone she didn't even love? The wind rode high. It whipped hair across her mouth. She waited until she could speak evenly. "I think that you don't understand the politics of this situation. Did you expect the queen to come to Herran?"

"No."

"Did Roshar?" But she knew the answer.

"Yes."

"Yet your friend didn't tell you."

Arin paused. "No."

"Why is she here?"

"To take command of the city."

"Arin. *Why is she here?*"

He was silent, and she saw from his expression that he guessed what she was going to say.

"She's here," Kestrel told him, "to show her soldiers that this land is as good as hers. The Dacrans don't like the alliance. They don't see what they get out of it. But they will begin to see, once she establishes herself in this city. It's not just for your new weapon, or for the sake of keeping the empire at bay that she agreed to help a small country with a weakened population. It's because if you win this war, she can annex Herran and make it part of the east."

He didn't deny it. "She doesn't need *me* to do that," he said finally. "She could take it by force. Using me wouldn't help much."

She saw what he meant. It was true: Arin's people loved him—she'd seen it, it was plain and powerful, the love flared up every time he smiled at someone, said a brief word—but he was no governor. No resurrected member of the massacred royal family. His political power was uncertain. Kestrel didn't think she was wrong about the queen's designs on this country, but her stomach clenched as she recognized how unavoidably, obviously true it was that the queen had wanted Arin for himself alone. "She must enjoy you, then. Maybe marriage isn't exactly what she wants from you. Still, you should give her what she wants. You might get a nice future out of it. At the very least, you should ask."

His expression seemed to shrink and tighten. "I won't."

She hitched the basket into the crook of her arm. "I must go. The cook needs these supplies." She was mortified to hear her voice break.

Arin's face changed. "Kestrel, forgive me."

"There's nothing to forgive."

"I'm so sorry."

"I don't care."

He shook his head, eyes not leaving hers. He was wholly altered now, quiet with surprise, alive with some new idea. He touched fingertips to her cheek, traced the path of a tear. "But you do," he said wonderingly.

She broke away.

"Wait."

She kept her back to him as she hurried, basket banging against her hip. "Don't follow me." She wiped her dirty wrist across her face, heard her breath escape in an ugly sound. "I will never speak with you again if you follow me."

He didn't.

Kestrel turned down the lamp and climbed into the high bed next to Sarsine. She could have slept on a divan in another room in the suite, but Sarsine wouldn't hear of it, and Kestrel, though shy, had been touched.

Sarsine turned beneath the light blanket and studied Kestrel, her loose hair and lashes and brows very black against the white pillow. She was looking at her in a way difficult for Kestrel to name, though maybe only because her own emotions were such a mess. Sarsine looked too much like Arin.

Abruptly, as if changing a conversation, Kestrel said, "I used to share a bed with my friend Jess."

"I remember her. You saved her life."

"No, I didn't."

"I was there. She'd been poisoned. She would have died if not for you."

But all Kestrel could recall was Jess's accusation of betrayal. She tried to explain to Sarsine, but didn't have enough pieces of the story for it to make sense. Sarsine listened, then said, "Maybe you both changed too much. Or you'll see her again one day, and things will be clearer between you. But

I saw what you did for her. How you loved her." Sarsine pulled the blanket up over Kestrel's shoulder.

Protective. That was the word for Sarsine's furrowed brow, her gentle mouth.

"Does something else trouble you?" she asked. "You can talk to me. I can keep a secret."

Kestrel felt her eyes glitter. She started and stopped and finally said, "I don't know how to say what's wrong. I don't know anything."

"I'm your friend. That much, you can know for certain." Sarsine touched Kestrel's cheek, letting silence be a comfort. Then she blew out the light.

But Kestrel couldn't sleep. Sarsine was an eerily quiet sleeper. Kestrel was used to Jess, and remembered how her friend would kick. Jess muttered as she dreamed. Kestrel missed her, remembered and missed her at the same time, which made her wonder if memory is always a kind of missing. The pillow was hot and damp beneath her cheek.

Kestrel imagined a melody. A tight rhythm, each note crisp and clean. She imagined how she'd play it. The control. Little bright pops of sound. She focused on that, because if she didn't, she knew where her thoughts would go next . . . though as soon as she glimpsed what she'd have to avoid, it rose up within her in full being.

Jess's rejection. It had been in Jess's townhome in the Valorian capital. Fawn-colored curtains. Kestrel couldn't remember all the exact words, but she knew now why the friendship had broken. She heard herself quietly saying the very things that Jess would never forgive, saw her former self choosing against her own people, her friends, her father.

He has done this to you, Jess had accused.

No one has made me change.

But you have.

Kestrel turned onto her other side. Arin had been in the queen's city then. She knew that now.

She sat up, flung the sheet aside.

It was not natural. It wasn't possible that she'd given up so much. And for what?

She was ready to believe in enchantments. How else could it be that her body still felt the pull of Arin, seemed to remember him all too clearly when her mind didn't, and sent her to his empty bed, sealed her between his sheets, made her care where he went and what he risked and what he did and with whom?

She reached for her set of keys.

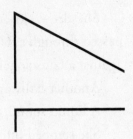

SHE WENT SWIFTLY THROUGH THE DARK HOUSE, her feet bare and noiseless on the tiles, the carpet, the steps. Up one flight, hand skimming the balustrade. At the landing, her palm spun around the newel. She went left. She knew Arin's home well.

Knew it now, knew it then. She felt time layer. The present slipped over the past.

She'd never taken this path before. But she'd thought about it.

She flipped through the keys, found the right one, set it into the outermost door of Arin's suite, and opened it.

She stepped into white light. It startled her, seemed hallucinatory, impossible, as if she'd dropped into a silver pond. But then she glanced up and saw a skylight above the entryway. The moon hung low and large. Though the oil lamp sconces were unlit, the hallway was almost as bright as day. At the other end of it: darkness.

A brief clinking sound came from the recesses of the suite.

She drew closer to the shadowed end of the hallway, passed through a dark receiving room. She barked her thigh against a console table and swore under her breath.

Another hallway, a turn. Then . . . a soft glow. A lamp. A liquid sound. A muffled thump. Glass on wood?

She stepped into the lamplit room.

Arin looked up from where he sat. His fingers tightened around the glass in his hand. He stared.

She flushed, realizing that she'd forgotten to throw a robe over her thin nightdress.

Or *had* she forgotten? Had she not decided in some way too quick for thought that this was exactly what she'd wanted? She glanced down at the shift's hem, which hit just below the knees. The cloth was as sheer as melted butter. Her flush deepened. She saw the expression on Arin's face.

He glanced away. "Gods," he said, and drank.

"Exactly."

That brought his gaze back. He swallowed, winced, and said, "It's possible that I've lost any claim to coherent thought, but I've no idea what you mean."

"Those gods of yours."

His dark brows were lifted. His eyes had grown round. The glass in his hand was a tumbler, the liquid a thumb's width high and deep green. It looked like the blood of leaves. He cleared his throat. Hoarsely, he said, "Yes?"

"Did you pray to them?"

"Kestrel, I am praying to them right now. Very hard, in fact."

She shook her head. "Did you pray to your"—she rummaged through her memory—"god of souls?" She was ready to believe in a supernatural reason. It would explain his power over her.

He coughed, then gave a short, rasping laugh. "That god doesn't listen to me." He set the tumbler next to the carafe on the table. He paused, thinking. In a new, slow tone, he said, "Except perhaps now." He dropped his cheek into an open palm and rubbed fingers into one closed eye. He nodded at the chair across the table from him. "Would you like to sit?"

Now that she was here, she wasn't sure she actually wanted to get closer to him. Her pulse had gone erratic. "I'm fine here."

"I'd really rather."

"If I make you uncomfortable, why don't you leave?"

He laughed again. "Ah, no. No, thank you. Here." He slid the glass across the table. The remaining liquid sloshed but didn't spill. When she sat, curious (what would the blood of leaves taste like?), he said, "You might want to try only a bit first."

"That's not wine."

"It decidedly is not."

"What is it?"

"An eastern liquor. Roshar gave it to me. He said that if you drink enough of it, the dregs start to taste like sugar. I suspect a prank."

"But you've no head for drink."

He looked as startled as she felt. "Of all the things, you remember *that*."

She had remembered something else, too, as she'd tried

to sleep. She'd come to ask him about it, but the words stuck in her throat. Instead, she appraised him. "You seem clear-minded enough."

"It's early. Still, I don't know. This conversation feels just shy of a delusion."

She fiddled with the glass. "I want to understand a few things."

"Ask me."

She wasn't yet ready to share what she remembered. She set the glass down. "What did you tell the queen?"

"I told Inisha about you."

"What, exactly?"

He hesitated. "I'm afraid to say."

"I want you to."

"You might leave."

"I won't."

He stayed silent.

She said, "I give you my word."

"I told her that I belong to you, and no other. I said that I was sorry."

She couldn't help the rush of pleasure . . . and jealousy. His words *did* make her want to leave. She felt so unalterably his. It was bewildering, because she didn't know him, not really, and he knew two halves of her that she couldn't fit together.

He was waiting for her to speak. He was so still. She realized he was holding his breath.

She said, "That's political suicide."

He smiled a little.

"How did she respond?"

"She said, 'You overestimate your importance.'"

"Is that why you're drinking?"

"Kestrel, you know why I am drinking."

She looked into the shadowed corners of the room. Talking with him was like having a flower unfold inside her chest, then close up tight. Creep open. Collapse in on itself. Voice low, she said, "Why do you call her Inisha? That's not her name."

"It's . . . her little name." The pause made Kestrel think that he'd been translating a Dacran term in his mind before speaking it, but also that he'd been translating her question, and recognizing the implied intimacy it exposed between him and the queen. He held Kestrel's eyes. "There never would have been anything between her and me if I'd known the truth about you. I should have known it. I can't forgive myself for not knowing it. As it was . . . yesterday, in the garden, you asked if I used her for political gain. I didn't. I used her to forget about you. You probably don't want to know that. It's ugly. But I must tell you, because there's been too much hiding. More would break me."

She looked at the green liquor left in the glass. It was green. It was liquid. This was a glass. To hide from her would break him. Simple things, so apparent, so not anything other than what they showed themselves to be. She dipped a finger into the liquor's dregs and touched it to her tongue. It burned.

Arin made a sound.

She glanced up. She didn't know where her voice had gone. She was nervous. Her flesh was resonant with the knowledge of what she wanted to understand and what she'd come here to find out. It was much riskier than what she'd already asked. She stood.

He watched her pace toward him.

She stopped just short of his chair and looked down at him. Her loose hair slipped over her shoulder. "I remember something. I'm not sure if it happened or not. Will you tell me?"

"Yes," he whispered.

"I remember lying with you on the lawn of the imperial palace's spring garden."

He shifted. Lamplight pulsed over his face. He shook his head.

"I remember finding you in your suite." This memory was coming to her now. It had a similar flavor as the last one. "I promised to tell you my secrets. You held a book. Or kindling? You were making a fire."

"That didn't happen."

"I kissed you." She touched the hollow at the base of his neck. His pulse was wild.

"Not then," he said finally.

"But I have before." There was a rush of images. It was as if the melody she'd imagined while lying in the dark had been dunked in the green liquor. All the cold stops gained heat and ran together. It was easy to remember Arin, especially now. Her hand slid to his chest. The cotton of his shirt was hot. "Your kitchens. A table. Honey and flour."

His heart slammed against her palm. "Yes."

"A carriage."

"Yes."

"A balcony."

Breath escaped him like a laugh. "Almost."

"I remember falling asleep in your bed when you weren't here."

He pulled back slightly, searched her face. "That didn't happen."

"Yes it did."

His mouth parted, but he didn't speak. The blacks of his eyes were bright. She wondered what it would be like to give her body what it wanted. It knew something she didn't. Her heart sped, her blood was lush in her veins.

"The first day," she said. "Last summer. Your hair was a mess. I wanted to sweep it back and make you meet my eyes. I wanted to see you."

His chest rose and fell beneath her hand. "I don't know. I can't—I don't know what you wanted."

"I never said?"

"No."

She lowered her mouth to his. She tasted him: the raw burn of liquor on his tongue. She felt him swallow, heard the low, dry sound of it.

He pulled her down to him, tangled his hands in her hair, sucked the breath from her lips. She became uncertain whose breath was whose. He kissed her back, fingertips fanning across her face, then gone, nowhere. Then: a light touch along the curve of her hip, just barely. A stone skipping the surface of the water. "Strange," he murmured into her mouth.

She wasn't listening. She was rippling, the sensation spreading wide. Stone on water, dimpled pockets of pressure. The wait for the stone to finally drop down.

Suddenly she knew—or thought she knew—what he found strange as he traced where a dagger should have been. To see a part of her missing. She felt her missing pieces, the stark gaps. She was arrested by the thought (it pierced her, sharp and surreal) that she had become transparent, that if he touched her again his hand would go right through her, into air, into the empty spaces of who she was now.

She didn't want to be empty, didn't want to vanish. She wanted to be whole.

She said, "I want to remember you."

An emotion flared in his face. He braced her hips, tugged her closer. His lids were heavy, eyes dark. His mouth was a wet gleam. She didn't recognize his expression. It was new. She leaned in and drank the newness of him.

Their kiss turned savage. She made it so. She felt his teeth, reveled in the sure knowledge that it had never been like this between them. Yet at the same time, she felt each kiss they'd shared before, felt them live inside this one. His mouth left hers, rasping down her neck. He buried his face in her skin.

She sought his mouth and found that he tasted different now. She was tasting the taste of her skin on his mouth. Coppery. She dipped her tongue into it again.

"Kestrel."

She didn't answer him.

"This is a bad idea."

"No," she said. "It isn't."

He pulled away, closed his eyes, and dropped his head to press his brow against her belly. She felt rich with the words he muttered against her nightdress. His mouth burned through the cloth.

His chair scraped back. He no longer touched her. "Not like this."

"Yes. Exactly like this." She tried to find the words to express how this helped, how he somehow mapped the country of herself, showed the ridges, the rise and valley of her very being.

"Kestrel, I think that you're . . . using me a little."

She stopped, unpleasantly startled. It occurred to her that what he'd said was another version of what she'd been struggling to say.

"It's not, ah, a hardship." He gave a rueful smile. "It's not that I don't want—" She'd never heard him stammer. Even with her untrustworthy memory, she knew this. You're easy to know, she wanted to say. Memories of him came quickly. It didn't hurt, not as much as she'd feared before, on the tundra, or in his empty bed. At least, it didn't hurt anymore. It was better. Better than . . . other things.

A faceless horror. A monster. Inside her. It thickened, grew into a featureless, blunt shape. She wouldn't touch it. She'd go nowhere near it.

Arin had been right, that day when he'd suggested that there was something too horrible for her to remember.

"It's not enough," he said. It took her a moment to realize he was continuing his refusal and not responding to her thoughts, which were so loud in her head that she felt as if she'd shouted them.

She said, "What would be enough?"

Color mounted in his face.

"You can tell me," she said.

"Ah," he said. "Well. Me."

"I don't understand."

"I want . . . you to want me."

"I do."

He pushed a hand through his rough hair. "I don't mean *this*." He gestured between them, his hand flipping from her to him. "I . . ." He struggled, knuckled his eyes, and let the words come. "I want you to be mine, wholly mine, your heart, too. I want you to feel the same way."

Her stomach sank. She'd sworn to herself not to lie to him.

He read her answer in her eyes. He dimmed, and said nothing either. But he brushed hair from her face, lifting away strands that had caught in her eyelashes and between her lips. His fingertip painted a slow line over her lower lip. She felt it down her spine, in her belly. Then his hand fell away, and she felt alone.

"I leave tomorrow morning with Roshar," he said. "It'll be some time before I return."

An ember of hurt. An old feeling, as old as her whole life. She was always being left. War always won. She saw herself: a little girl, holding up a level, sheathed sword nearly as long as she was tall. Her arms ached. She must not drop it. The man on the horse would take it soon. He glanced down, and she wondered if he was waiting to see how long she could hold the blade steady. He smiled, and her twinned heart— the girl, the woman, her past, her present—burst with pride and sorrow and rage.

"Take me with you," she told Arin.

A shadow crossed his face. "No. Absolutely not."

"I can help. I know my father's system of running scouts, his tactics, codes, formations—"

"No."

"You don't have the right to choose for me."

"It won't happen." He caught his anger, became aware of it as well as hers, and said more gently, "It's too dangerous."

"I can take care of myself."

"I can't lose you." Grief slashed through his voice. "Not you, too."

The story he had told her about the night of the invasion flickered in his eyes, darkening them.

Her father had done this to him. She remembered her father, felt the memory squeeze her—a crunch, a creak of bone—and then seemed to feel how Arin guessed where her mind had gone. She felt what the direction of her thoughts did to him.

She had begged her father to let her go to war with him. He'd promised that one day she would, but then she had grown and no longer wanted what he wanted, and wanted him to stay instead, and he wouldn't.

Arin's story and hers twisted together into patterns she couldn't follow. Their silence grew.

Quietly, Arin said, "I'll stay."

Her eyes flew to him. It was so unexpected that she was shaken out of her thoughts.

"If you want," he said. "I could stay. We'd be together."

"If you stay here while the Dacrans march south to fight your war, the alliance will crumble."

He studied his hands.

"Unless you do it for the queen."

He gave Kestrel a reproachful look.

"Then you can't," she said.

"Do you want me to stay?"

Kestrel wondered if every question is a way of putting yourself at the mercy of someone else. "It would cost you too much."

"Think about it. Will you think about it? We're to leave at dawn. Meet me then at the brook, the one near the horse paths, to tell me what you've decided."

Her answer should be no, yet she couldn't make herself say it.

"Meet me anyway," he said, "even if it's to say goodbye. Will you wish me well?"

Kestrel saw the ripped grass of the battlefield, stained with gore. Him: broken, bloody. Skin ashen. His blank gaze fixed on something she couldn't see. His light gone.

Stay, she almost said. Then an invisible hand clamped down over her mouth and warned again about the political consequences. Either way, Kestrel read his doom. Death in battle, or the slower death of the alliance collapsing and the empire's victory.

Tears welled in her eyes. She turned so that he wouldn't see them.

"Won't you wish me well?" Arin asked.

"I will. I do."

He seemed uncertain. "If I don't see you at dawn, I'll take it to mean that you want me to go."

"I'll be there," she told him. "I promise."

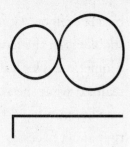

SHE COULDN'T SLEEP. SHE ROAMED THE DREAM-
ing house, saw copper pots gleaming in the dark kitchen
like a row of hung moons. Her feet made mouse sounds
on the staircases. She found the library, remembered touching the spines of the books when she'd lived here before. She
touched them again. She remembered and touched them,
touched and remembered. Her piano was a large shadow
in the parlor. Arin had brought it from her home. This was
before the prison, before the imperial palace. He'd asked her
to stay and share his life. She'd left him, had gone down to
the harbor and stolen a fishing boat. The stormy sea. The
emperor. A choice.

The capital: stiff lace, sugar, snow. Thick blood, skinned
fingers. A white knuckle joint.

Choose, the emperor had said when she'd stood before
him for the first time and saw his cold cunning. She'd chosen to marry his son. Her father had been proud.

Memory crept over her skin in a prickling rash. Through
a silvered window, Kestrel saw the harbor. The bay was a

bucket of light. Although she wasn't cold, she chafed her bare shoulders in the habit of someone who'd once been cold for a long time. Her hands paused in their movements when she realized what she was doing. Again she wondered at it: the way the mind and the body have different sets of memories that aren't necessarily always aware of each other.

She was not cold, yet she *felt* cold. There was a lump of ice in her heart.

She didn't know what she would say to Arin when dawn came. The choice he'd offered became so large that she couldn't clearly see either *stay* or *go*, only *choice*.

She was afraid of choices. She had paid dearly for them.

She looked at the harbor and remembered standing there last winter, her breath a fog—Arin's, too. Her hand on a jagged shard of pottery, sharp as a knife. The fishing boat rocking at its dock. He'd let her escape, had chosen her freedom and his probable ruin simply because he couldn't bear the thought of forcing her to stay.

Arin wasn't the ice in her heart. He didn't cause the fear that kept her from knowing who she was and what she'd done and what had been done to her.

Who *was* Kestrel? She turned over what she knew, studied the pieces of her old self. *Honorable*, Arin had said. *Brave*, she'd thought before. She imagined this Kestrel, a creature straight out of stories, and wished that she could be like her.

Her feet were moving. They were heading to Sarsine's rooms. They stole over the floorboards as she opened doors, opened a wardrobe, fastened clothes. She pulled on boots.

The soldiers would ride south at dawn. She had several hours. The moonlight was strong. Bright enough.

She left the house by a back door for servants. She quickened her pace over flagstones, through the garden, and across the grounds to the stables.

The high dark grass rippled around the villa in the warm wind. She let Javelin walk toward the house. Somewhere on the grounds must be a pond or creek she couldn't see. Frogs sang. The full moon shone overhead, its light diminishing the stars.

The house was grand in its silence, its windows shut tight. A shudder shook her, and she understood the nature of her fear a little better than she had before. It wasn't formless. It was sharply specific. It was the fear of pain.

She swung a leg off Javelin and dropped down into the grass. It itched. She pushed through it, let it tickle, annoy. *Look at the grass,* she thought. *It is grass. The house is a house. The moon, a moon. They are themselves and nothing else.*

Her feet found a flagstone path hidden beneath the grass. She pushed forward, holding a dead lantern she'd taken from the saddlebag. She longed to light it yet dreaded what it might show. The house—the *house*, the second-floor windows, those eaves, that portico, all so clearly and sickeningly *hers*—held a secret she must understand.

She felt naked when she came out of the grass. She looked back over her shoulder, saw the dark arch of Javelin's neck. Then she met the blank black eyes of the villa's windows.

Nothing's there, Arin had said. *It's empty.*

No, it wasn't.

Something was in there. She felt it swell against the walls.

I'd be with you, Arin had said that day on the horse paths. She knew that she could turn around this very moment, return, wake him. He wouldn't question her. He wouldn't say *wait.*

Some horror, she'd tell him and then stop, unable to say more.

I'll come with you, he'd answer. *You won't be alone.*

A door whined open at her unsteady touch.

The smell was an assault. She gagged on the familiarity of it. Redolent. Orange-scented wood oil. Windows washed with vinegar. A clean house, *her* clean house, the cleanliness of every day of almost all her life. The childhood smell she didn't realize was from her childhood until she had forgotten it and encountered it again.

It stripped away whatever strength she'd had. She almost stumbled from the entryway and back out into the night.

Then a thought brushed her panicked consciousness. It was gentle, and gave her pause. It said that the smell's familiarity wasn't just the fermented memory of many years. She'd also encountered this smell (orange, vinegar, lye) recently. In some small way, one difficult to determine.

She lit the lamp. The house burst into being.

It was empty. Jagged shadows. Glittering tiles.

She passed into a parlor, feeling pushed. The echoes she made here were quieter. This room had a wooden floor, paler in places where furniture had been. Its varnish gleamed.

The house, though abandoned for months (grounds unkept, grass hip-high), was clean. No dust. She went from room to room.

She stopped in one that had windowed double doors facing the garden. Sheet music lined inset shelves built specially with narrow dividers to hold the thin booklets, which were neatly organized. Though not—she realized as she went through them, the music echoing inside her as she traced a marked passage—not *exactly* as she had organized them.

The Herrani music was arranged by composer (she saw her old self, that elegant ghost, slipping the music into its slots). The Valorian music—little though there was of it—was organized in the same way. But that wasn't right. She wouldn't have classed the Valorian music like that. Valorians ordered books by the binding's color, which was coded by subject. They organized music by kind.

Kestrel went through the music again, recalling how she'd missed these pieces when she was in the capital, but didn't ask for them, because to ask was to admit that she missed something from her home, and it was too hard to think about what she missed, and too dangerous to reveal that she missed anything at all.

Another person had painstakingly organized these booklets. Not her. Not a Valorian.

She heard the memory of Arin's voice. *I have no interest in the music room.*

It hadn't been true then. It wasn't true now.

She understood now what had stopped her from leaving the villa. It had been a feathery sort of almost-idea, its fronds still floating in her mind. *You know where you've smelled that too-clean smell before. Orange, vinegar, lye.*

Arin. It had been when she was sore and broken and in between dreams, and he slept in a chair beside her bed in the suite that had belonged to his mother. He had woken. *Go back to sleep,* he'd murmured. He'd had a strange scent. An alkaline tang. Clean, she'd thought then. Too clean.

Soft gold lamplight. His voice, its low timbre. The gleam of eyes. Slow silence. Then sleep.

Kestrel lifted the lamp higher, though she didn't need its light like she had when she'd first entered the house. It was easier to see now. This room was just an empty space where things had once been, and the dread of those things no longer overwhelmed her, because she no longer felt alone.

She explored the house.

Night lifted. Shadows dwindled into their corners. Kestrel didn't notice this—or, if she did, she thought it was because her mind saw better, not her eyes.

She waded through her memory. Her mother. Her nurse, Enai. A love so full that it welled up beneath her breastbone.

Her suite. Painted walls. In the bedchamber, where a curtain had hung: the scratched lines of a name. *Jess.* They'd done it with a pin when they were little. There was no curve to the scratched letters. Each *s* was all angles. Kestrel touched the name, and knew she'd find her own on the wall of Jess's suite. She recalled the pin digging into paint. Her eyes stung.

The lamp burned low. It gave off a hot ceramic odor. She knew, vaguely, that time was running out, but she was so lost in time that she knew it was running out without really knowing what this meant.

She walked quickly now. There was a tug on her heart, like it had been tied with twine and someone had jerked a loose end. Again: the fear of pain. The surety that it would come. A drag forward. She dug in her heels and stopped.

Gray light glowed in the windows.

She remembered her promise to Arin. The worry in his voice: *Won't you wish me well?* She thought of the person who had cleaned her home for no other reason, as far as she could tell, than that this home was hers and he didn't want it to be dirty. She thought of how he'd feel to leave the city with his question unanswered, his offer disregarded, with not even a wish for his safe return.

The awfulness of it hit her with a cold, fresh slap.

She could make it to him by dawn if she left now.

She strode down a hallway, fast footsteps ringing loud. She reached a landing, ready to race down the stairs and back out into the grass.

But the twine tied inside her cut harder, pulling tight. Before she knew it, she'd crossed the landing and entered a narrow, mirrored gallery, her shadow flitting alongside her. At the end of the gallery was a door. Behind the door was a suite. Dark wainscoting lined the walls, and she remembered silk curtains on the now bare rods. *Your mother chose the color,* her father had said, looking at the curtains as though he couldn't say what their color was.

Kestrel was in her father's rooms.

She groped her way back to the stairs, retreating. She'd lost her lamp. She stumbled past a small ballroom. A dining hall. The parlor. She gripped the knob of a door: the library.

She remembered him better in the library than in his suite, to which she'd rarely been invited. He didn't brook intrusion. The library was achingly familiar, even with the books missing. There was no sign of violence here. Still, it felt as if violence had been done, as if the books had been gouged out of their inset shelves. There used to be a translucent red paperweight that had sat on a squat marble-topped table. The paperweight had been made from blown glass. She recalled the whorls beneath her fingertips. He'd used it to hold down maps. She didn't know where it was now.

She sat on the floor where a chair had been. As the pearled dawn touched her wet eyes, searing the room orange and pink and yellow, Kestrel knew that she'd come to this house for only one true reason: to find her father.

Her memory limped up to her. It crawled into her lap. Kestrel didn't remember everything, but she remembered enough.

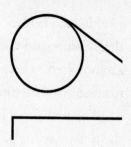

ARIN ARRIVED EARLY AT THE BROOK IN THE gray hour before dawn. Sat on the grass. Had thoughts that kept forcing each other from his head.

Nervous. He pressed his palms hard against the earth. He was too nervous.

She didn't come.

He watched the water glint with the rising sun. The brook gently coursed along its path. Birds sang out. An irrielle called, notes flat and sweet. It repeated itself. There was no answer. It continued, the sound casting a spell. The bird sounded caught in its own enchantment.

He waited as long as he could. Eventually, a quiet part of him admitted that he had doubted all along. He'd never really expected she would come. It had been doubt, hadn't it, that had kept him from sleeping after she'd left his rooms? Not the difficult pleasure of her presence there, or how her absence felt. Not the anticipation of war, nor the possibility that she might lay claim to him.

Be honest, now.

He held himself to honesty. Held hard. Conceded. Yes, the pleasure and difficulty and absence and anticipation had all conspired to keep him from sleep last night. Still, doubt— fizzy, sour—had also been part of it.

And now some heavy emotion. Round. About the size of the hollow of his palm. An emotion he seemed to have kept in an invisible pocket, and now took out to see fully.

Just a small sorrow, he told himself. Small, because expected. What else could he have expected?

He plucked a few blades of grass, rubbed them between fingers and thumb, and inhaled the young scent. Then— he knew it was odd, he wanted the oddity of it to distract him, or to give him one last thing to do before he left, because maybe she would arrive in that final moment, if he waited but one more moment—he put a blade of grass in his mouth and chewed. It tasted soapy. Clean.

She wasn't coming. She probably had never had any intention of coming.

He went to ready his horse.

Arin drew up short several paces from the stables. Soldiers— perhaps a hundred strong, on horse and on foot—gathered on the hill. The morning was loud with the huff and stamp of horses, the rough irritation of people who got in each other's way, the click and tap of metal and leather, the slap of a saddle dropped on a horse's back. None of this surprised Arin. What surprised him was the sight of Roshar, standing with two saddled horses, smiling at him.

Roshar approached, the horses walking behind. "You're late. Sleep in, did you?"

Arin said nothing.

"Here you are." Roshar passed the reins. "You ride this one sometimes, I've noticed. He's good. Not as good as mine, but he'll do. I thought you'd want to leave that big warhorse behind. Hers, isn't it?"

"Javelin stays."

"Of course," Roshar said easily. "Well. Wasn't this thoughtful?" He swept his hand at Arin's saddled horse.

"Yes . . . though a little unlike you."

"Never say so. I am the soul of thoughtfulness."

Arin found himself smiling faintly back. He mounted the horse.

Everyone ordered themselves behind him and the prince. They would make their way down to the city, gathering soldiers as they went. Eventually they'd reach the harbor, where eastern soldiers who'd come on ships waited for them. Then the march south.

But first they passed along the path to the house. A few people lined the path, having learned or guessed of the soldiers' leaving.

Kestrel wasn't there. Sarsine was, and the queen. Inisha lifted one sardonic brow at him, and said, "Careful."

But Sarsine. She looked different than he'd ever seen, like she knew he wasn't sure he'd come back this time. He thought that his promise to his god might be absolute. She was weeping. She held out flowers, tiny ones that grew at the base of trees, in their shadows. The kind you had to get on your hands and knees to see properly. They had been his favorites, long ago.

He took them. From his height on the horse, he leaned to brush away her tears. "Don't," he said, which only made her eyes swim again.

"I love you," she said. He said that he loved her, too.

The horse moved forward. His hand fell away. The distance grew between them.

Don't you worry, murmured a voice within him. *I take care of my own.* Yet the god of death sounded ominous.

I heard you, the god added. *Last night. A promise to stay? To miss it all? Arin, you made* me *a promise. Glory. In my name. Or do I misremember?*

Arin said nothing.

Ah, Arin. You're lucky that I like you.

Why do you? Arin asked, but the god just smirked silently inside him.

The ships stayed in the bay. The queen would defend the city. Arin tried to dismiss the thought that she could easily claim it for her own. He had no choice but to trust her.

A few thousand marched south. They could only travel as fast as foot soldiers walked and supply wagons trundled. The roads were good. They were Valorian, made after the invasion by slave labor. They were paved for war.

"You haven't asked me about Arin," Roshar said as he rode alongside him.

"What?"

"The tiger. Not the surly human. I thought it was best

to leave him behind to keep my sister company. Since you won't."

Arin shot him a look.

"Did I *say* I wanted you to be my sister's pet? Did I not merely imply it in order to get under that ridiculously thin skin of yours? I prefer to have you here."

"Why?"

"It would have been a mistake to stay. Don't tell me you didn't consider it. She—"

"You mean Kestrel."

"I mean *both* of them. I'll say nothing of your little ghost. You'd chuck me off my horse and then I'd have to kill you for insubordination, which would set the tone nicely for the army's underlings but would be messy and inconvenient."

"Make your point."

Roshar turned serious. "Watch your back, especially around my sister."

Arin's gaze flicked over him. He didn't think Inisha would appreciate that warning. "Are you disloyal to her?"

Roshar's smile said that he found it charming that Arin would ask such a direct question and expect a direct answer. "Never."

The sound of the army—the creak of wagons, the hooves, boots, bits of conversation in two different languages—hammered the thoughts from Arin's head. But he still carried that emotion with him, the one he'd found by the brook. It knocked against his breastbone: a small, heavy stone.

Yellow thorn bushes bloomed by the side of the road.

Once, he saw a fox and her kits tumble out of a bush and scramble across the road in front of him. He'd stayed his horse, feeling foolish—then relieved to see them dodge several sets of hooves and make it safely to the other side.

"The Valorian general might try again to land at Lerralen's beach," Roshar said.

"It'd be costly."

"True, but it's still the best location for a large invasion. He's got the numbers to do it. If reports are right, our force is the smaller one. Still, we *are* better looking, which is a significant advantage."

"I think that it's not just about winning for him." Arin remembered Kestrel at the gaming table. "He likes to win with style. Make you feel the fool for ever thinking you could compete. He could push all his troops up onto that beach and bleed them out, and still win, and come up north to take the city. Brute force victory. A nasty one, though, with heavy losses. And a little too straightforward. He prefers a trick. He already played one with the cliffs. Unless he's got another trick up his sleeve for the beach, I wouldn't focus our forces there."

"If we have none in position at Lerralen, he'll walk right onto the peninsula with no resistance."

"Send a division."

"Two-thirds?"

"Plus most of the supplies, and infantry. Stationed there. The rest of the army keeps moving south—light, fast, mainly cavalry. Small cannon. And guns."

"Where would you put your people?"

"Where you want them."

Roshar's eyes went exaggeratedly round. "How very accommodating of you."

"So long as they're under my command."

"Why not," Roshar said graciously, "so long as you are under mine?"

Night. Without commenting on it, Arin and Roshar had pitched their tents near each other. A small fire crackled. A chill had crept into the air; the weather was changing.

Roshar lay on his back, the dip of his neck bolstered by a tied bedroll. He smoked. "I've been thinking."

"Dear gods."

"It occurs to me that you have no official rank, and that I, as your prince, might give you one." He said an eastern word Arin didn't know. "Well? Will it suit?"

"Depends."

"On?"

"Whether that word was some horrific insult you're pretending is an actual military rank."

"How mistrustful! Arin, I have taught you every foul curse I know."

"I'm sure you've saved a few, for just such a time."

Roshar said something about pigs and Arin's fondness for certain questionable practices.

Arin laughed.

"I wasn't joking earlier," Roshar said. "I don't know how to translate that word. For your rank. It puts you third. After

Xash." The sea captain had requested the queen's permission to leave his ships under her orders, and that of his second-in-command. He wanted to be part of the land operation. "He has the experience. He fought the general in the mountains four years back. He's good. Also, he'd kill me if I ranked you above him."

Arin shifted a log and watched the darting sparks. "Thank you."

Roshar squinted up at him, dragging on his pipe. Its bowl blistered red. "You don't seem wholly pleased." Smoke curled around his face. "What is it? What makes you not glad for third? You don't like Xash? Neither do I. So what? You can't have second, and you damned well won't get first." He studied Arin more carefully. "No, it's not thwarted ambition that's bothering you. Not even wounded pride, which is usually the obvious interpretation where you're concerned. Not this time, somehow. Arin, you're not *nervous*, are you? You're perfect for this. You want it. Just earlier today you claimed command of the Herrani."

"I must. I'm responsible for them."

"And they love you. They think you're some holy gift from your gods. Very nice work, I must say."

"I didn't mean for that to happen."

"Even better. Makes it seem more authentic. Convenient, you understand, when sending people to their deaths."

Arin looked at his stolen Valorian boots and felt the fire's heat in his cheeks.

"Too late to have qualms about death and dying and killing," Roshar said. "You're in it. Some people were born to be in it."

Arin wondered if that's why Kestrel hadn't come: because she could smell death on him.

Roshar said, "You'll do well."

"I know."

Roshar crossed a leg over one bent knee, sat up slightly to knock spent ash out of his pipe by rapping it against a boot, then eased back against his bedroll. "I smell rain."

"Hmm."

"The leaves of the trees are cupped for it."

"You can't see that in this dark."

"I see it in my mind." The smoke from his pipe lingered. He folded his arms across his chest. His body looked close to sleep. "Arin."

Arin, who was sitting with his forearms propped on bent knees, fingers loose, felt nowhere near sleep. "Yes?"

"How do I look in the dark?"

Startled, Arin glanced at him. The question had had no edges. It wasn't sleek, either. Its soft, uncertain shape suggested that Roshar truly wanted to know. In the fired red shadows, his limbs looked lax and his mutilated face met Arin's squarely. The heavy feeling that Arin carried—that specific sadness, nestled just below his collarbone, like a pendant— lessened. He said, "Like my friend."

Roshar didn't smile. When he spoke, his voice matched his expression, which was rare for him. Rarer still: his tone. Quiet and true. "You do, too."

Alone in his tent, Arin must have fallen asleep at some point. He woke expecting Kestrel to be beside him. Her presence seemed clear and real, as real as when she'd stood before him in his rooms. That thin shift. The sear of her hot skin. *I want to remember you.*

Go back to sleep, he told himself. You can't hold her to any promise.

He curled onto his side. There was a clap of thunder. The sky opened. Rain pattered the canvas, and grew loud.

It didn't let up. Water streamed down the horses as they walked. Afternoon looked no different from morning, which hadn't looked a lot different from night. Everything was a muddled gray. Arin was soaked to the skin. Rain ran off his nose.

Progress was slow. Arin fell back to the middle lines and stopped to help shoulder a wagon wheel out of a slick rut between split paving stones. He'd just mounted his horse again when he realized that a halt must have been called. Everyone stayed where they were.

He rode up through the ranks to Roshar. "What is it?" he asked the prince.

"A parting of ways." Roshar nodded at the road ahead, and he pulled a waxed map from a tube in his saddlebags. Arin took a roughly woven blanket from his and sidled his horse along Roshar's, reaching the blanket over him and the prince as a shield to keep the worst of the rain off the map.

The road would soon fork. West lay Lerralen.

"I'm going to listen to your advice," Roshar said. "We split. Most to the west. Some south. Lay your bet, Arin. It's your country. Where will the action be?"

Arin studied the map, worrying his lower lip between his teeth.

Mmm, said death. *Those estates look nice.*

A few unwalled villages stood near them. The estates were far enough south that it'd be easy for the general to run his supplies from Ithrya onto the mainland.

"One of these," Arin said, rain dripping from his mouth. It felt like he was spitting. "If the general gains a foothold there he can strengthen his position, take almost everything he needs from the estates, except black powder. He could creep up, spread out, form flanks to the east and west. Scoop us up. Push to the city."

Roshar rolled and stowed the map. Arin lowered the blanket, which was soaked. He'd have a wet night.

Roshar looked up into the rain, blinking. "Almost feels like home." He squinted at Arin. "Do you want to go with Xash to Lerralen?"

Arin shook his head.

"That's what I thought."

The army divided. Arin rode south with Roshar.

Near dusk the rain stopped, but it had been falling so long that Arin seemed to still see it dribbling across his vision.

The diminished army set up camp for the night, swearing at the mud, the mood miserable. Arin's tent had stayed mostly dry in its tarp. A change of clothes, too, buried at the bottom of a saddlebag. Everything else was damp. He unbuckled his leather armor, which shed water and smelled like a soggy cow. Shrugged off his tunic. Had nothing to hang it with. He draped it to dry on a low-hanging branch of a nearby tree, then sighed when a breeze showered droplets down from high leaves.

Everyone wanted a fire, but the wood in the forest along the road was wet. Nothing would burn. Arin resigned himself to the damp. He pitched his tent, peeled a broad strip of thick bark off a tree (the unexposed side was dry), and sat on it rather than the mud outside his tent while he used his one dry shirt to wipe rain off anything metal so that it wouldn't rust: his sword, dagger, shield, armor buckles, the horse tack.

It felt nothing like summer. Arin was chilled, the skin along his back unpleasantly tight. A lock of wet hair flopped down along his cheek. He shuddered, brushed it away, and kept polishing with the shirt, rubbing at the bit and buckles on the bridle and girth. He warmed a little from the activity.

"Well, well, look at you." Roshar stood in front of him, hands on his hips, armor unbuckled but still on. "So industrious. Cold, too, I bet."

Arin ignored him.

"While you're at it," Roshar said, "want to dry my things, too?"

Arin paused, looked up, and made a gesture he'd learned in the east.

Roshar laughed. He squished his way toward his tent. Arin heard him call for one of his underlings. Then Arin stopped paying attention.

After a while, though, a prickle crept up his neck. At first Arin thought it was the cold. But he wasn't finished with his task, and so didn't pull the mostly dry shirt over his head, which was what he longed to do. He kept at what he was doing.

Slowly, he became aware of a surprised quiet stealing over the camp. The sodden thuds of a lone horse's hooves, approaching. Then someone—a Dacran—said, "Stay where you are!" Arin heard the crank of a crossbow.

He looked up just as the rider stopped.

There—high up on her stallion, hair plastered to her head, expression bleak—was Kestrel.

HE WENT TO HER, YANKING HIS CLAMMY TUNIC off the tree as he passed, shrugging into it.

Her hands clenched the reins, body stiff. She'd been riding for a long time. She had a stunned look that reminded him badly of the tundra. Everything about her was rigid and wrong.

He took her by the waist and lifted her down. Vivid with confusion and worry, he said, "What are you doing here?"

"I'm sorry. I didn't keep my promise to you."

"That doesn't matter."

"I gave you my word. A Valorian honors her word." She swayed slightly.

He flipped open Javelin's saddlebag. No food. No clothes. Not a match, not a bit of tinder. Not even a canteen. Just a burned-out lamp. "Kestrel, you're scaring me."

"I'm sorry."

He got her to his tent, ignoring the curious stares, and was grateful—without quite knowing why—that Roshar was nowhere to be seen. Arin grabbed his dry shirt from where he'd let it fall to the ground and dug his clean trousers out of a saddlebag. His canteen. Some hardtack, gone sticky with the damp. "Here." He pressed it all into her hands. "Change. Eat. I'll be outside."

She nodded. He was shakily relieved to get a response that seemed, small as it was, normal. Then she disappeared into his tent and he became anxious again.

Moments passed. There was a rustle from inside the tent. It subsided. He asked if she was all right. No answer. Finally, he was too concerned not to come inside.

She was sitting, staring into her lap, holding the unopened canteen. She'd changed into his shirt, then appeared to have reached the limit of what she could do. She still wore her wet trousers, the riding boots, her dagger. The hardtack lay to the side, untouched.

He knelt and took her freezing hands. "Please tell me what's wrong."

She opened her mouth but choked on the words. She looked brittle. He began to feel the way she looked. He tried a different question. "How did you know where we'd be?"

"I guessed."

Arin stared.

"I thought—maybe Lerralen—but my father, he . . . I know what he's like. So I thought—" She halted. He didn't like the way her voice collapsed when she mentioned the general. "The Errilith estate. Livestock, meadows, trees. Water. It'd make sense. To him. I worried. Maybe you wouldn't think of Errilith. Or you would and ignore it. But I hoped."

He felt a flash of wild fear. To wander vaguely south . . . unsupplied, alone, practically unarmed . . . on a gamble. A *guess.* It shook him. "You don't even have a map." He tried to say nothing else. He worried that she'd see the extremity of what he felt and recoil from it.

"I've seen the right maps, before. I remembered. I—" Her face contorted.

"You don't have to say."

"Let me. I want to. I went to the villa. My house. After I left your suite. I didn't mean to stay there so long. I'm sorry."

"You've nothing to apologize for."

"Yes. I was so *sure.* On the tundra, I blamed you. The blame: rotten inside me. But when I went home, I remembered. The prison wasn't your fault. It was mine. It was his."

Arin went cold. His suspicion took its final shape. "Your father."

"Yes."

"Your father betrayed you."

"I wrote a letter to you when I was in the capital. So *stupid,* to put it all in writing. Everything I'd done. The information I passed to Tensen. The way I worked against the empire. What I felt. My father read it. He gave it to the emperor." She was weeping. "And I know, I *know* that it hurt him, that I broke something, that he felt it break. Maybe I wasn't *me* anymore, to him. Do you understand? Not his daughter. Not anyone he knew. Just a lying stranger. But how could he? Why couldn't he love me most? Or enough. Why couldn't he love me enough to choose me over his rules?"

Arin pulled her onto his lap. He held her shaking form, tucked his face into the crook of her cold neck as she sobbed against him. He murmured that he loved her more than he could say. He promised that he would always choose her first.

She was exhausted, and she fell asleep quickly. Arin sat beside her for a few long moments after. Murder rose in his heart.

The general was out of reach, for now. But someone closer by would do.

He left the tent and didn't have to go far. Roshar was waiting for him. "I hear we have an unexpected guest," said the prince.

Arin clamped a hand down on his shoulder and drove him into the trees.

Roshar—oddly enough—made no sound until enough distance had been put between them and the army. When they wouldn't be overheard, he said cautiously, "Arin, why are you . . . manhandling me?"

"You knew."

"Specificity, please."

"On the morning we left, you knew that her horse wasn't in the stables. That's why you saddled a horse and brought it to me: so that I wouldn't notice that she was gone. You are a liar."

"That's not a lie."

Silence.

"Arin, you are *crushing* me. Fine, yes, all right. I might have *gently deceived* you, in the name of your greater happiness. Is that really a lie? Or if it is, isn't it a very, very small one?" He showed with his fingertip and thumb just how small.

"You don't know what makes me happy."

"I know that you're not. I know that you've no sense of reason where she's concerned. Maybe I *did* observe that Javelin wasn't in his stall that morning. Maybe I knew how things would unfold: how you'd notice, and go tearing off after her, wherever she was, and my sister would learn of it. What would my soldiers think if I waited for you? Or if we marched south without you? It'd all fall apart. So yes, I lied. I'd do it again. My only other option was to watch you throw everything away for the sake of someone who doesn't even love you."

Arin released him. He felt brutally gutted.

"You wanted the truth," said the prince.

Arin thought of Cheat, Tensen, Kestrel. He wondered if some part of him was drawn to lies. What was it that made him so easy to deceive?

"Oh, Arin. Don't look like that. I apologize."

He stared at his friend, who was still his friend. It struck him that Roshar had gone quietly into the trees because if he had protested, his army would have cut Arin down.

Arin apologized as well, then said, "It's not you who angers me."

"Oh no?"

"You're just a close target."

"How flattering."

"Kestrel was caught by her father. He had proof that she was spying for Herran and exposed her to the emperor."

Roshar considered this, his expression guarded. "A new memory?"

"Yes."

"What else does she remember about the general?"

"I'm not sure."

"You should ask."

"No."

"This isn't prying, Arin. This is gathering information potentially relevant to our current operation. I'm happy to talk with her if you won't."

"Leave her alone."

"You underestimate my charm. Granted, she once pulled that dagger on me, but we've put that behind us. She likes me. I am very likable."

Arin didn't want to tell him about her raw eyes, or the stripped, thin quality of her voice. The way she'd wept, the utter abandonment. Her face: so alone, no matter what he said to her.

"She's in no shape to talk to you," he said flatly. "She rode for two days and a night with no food or water except maybe what she gathered along the road—*if* she bothered to do that. She didn't even know for sure that she'd find us. She guessed where we'd go and pushed herself to catch up."

The prince lifted his brows. "Impressive."

His tone made Arin wary. "What do you mean by that?"

"She's got a knack for survival."

It struck Arin that Roshar could have pressed Kestrel for information before, back in the city, and if he hadn't, it wasn't likely out of deference to her ill health and recovery, or because he'd assumed there was nothing to be gained from digging around in Kestrel's uncertain memory. It was because Roshar wouldn't have trusted what she had to say . . . then. If he trusted her word now it was only because she'd been damaged by their enemy. Which made her—Arin saw the idea take shape in Roshar's eyes—a motivated asset to their cause.

"I don't like what you're thinking," Arin said.

"She could be useful."

"You will not *use her*."

"The general's daughter? We'd be fools not to. You talk about her as if she's made of spun glass. Know what I see? Steel."

"You won't make her part of this war. I'm taking her back to the city."

"No," Kestrel said from behind them. "You're not."

Arin turned.

The sight of her. It wasn't just that she looked lost in his too-large shirt, or how her eyes were tired holes. It was the set of her jaw. The way she lifted her chin. He'd seen this before. All the ships that shattered against the rock of her determination. How she'd break herself, too, if she must, to get what she wanted.

Lock this slave up. Her words, uttered the day she'd fought a duel for his sake, still hurt. What had followed: the clench of helplessness. Being outnumbered by her father's private guard. The first blow. The way she hadn't looked back as she'd let the door shut behind her. Humiliation. A sort of appalled admiration. Indebtedness. Later: her, injured and limping across the villa's lawn.

It had changed him. Exposed something running inside him like a vein of soft gold. A slow attraction. Growing, despite himself, into care . . . and more.

That incident last autumn when she'd tricked him, had

him locked in a cell while she rode to the duel, loomed in his mind as a little story that told the larger one of how she'd been broken, and he'd been kept safe, and how his safety and her brokenness had broken him.

Now she stared him down. His gaze traced the fall of a single, newly plaited braid over her shoulder, its color obscure in the twilight. He recalled the fold of the dead Valorian girl's body over his blade. His sister being dragged to the cloakroom.

"You can't stay," he told her.

"It's not your choice."

"It's not safe."

"That doesn't matter."

"I won't allow it."

"You don't command this army."

Roshar smiled.

"No," said Arin. "Don't."

"What do you propose, my lady?"

"My prince, I wish to enlist. I swear to serve, and rout your enemy, and wash my blade with his blood."

"How savagely Valorian of you. Is this the traditional military oath? I like it. I accept."

She nodded slightly and cast Arin an unreadable look—tinged, perhaps, with something like regret, though it was hard to know exactly what had affected her. Maybe it was his expression, or maybe a memory floating invisibly in the darkening summer air, seen only by her.

She left them.

"If you send her into battle," Arin told Roshar, "she'll fall in the first wave."

"Why, because she's half your size? I'll wager she's had more training than the average foot soldier."

"She has no talent for it and little experience."

"She wants this, Arin. I don't blame her for wanting it, and quite frankly I think her help could be crucial."

"Her *advice*. Let her advise, then. Enlist her, rank her, if you must. But keep her out of combat."

"All right," Roshar said. "For you."

Arin turned to leave. His head was brimming, his heart sore.

Roshar touched his shoulder, surprisingly gentle. "I know you want her to be safe forever, but it's just not that kind of world."

Arin begged a pair of Herrani officers to share a tent. He shouldered the spare one, loosely bundled. He found a woman about Kestrel's height and bartered a little boot knife for a set of decent clothes. He rummaged through supply wagons and stared dully at the extra suits of armor: all far too large. Swords: too heavy. He considered a gun among the many rows of them, hidden in a false bottom below bales of horse feed. Unsure, he left the guns where they lay. Finally, he snagged an eastern crossbow. Even if Roshar kept his word and tried to keep Kestrel from any real military action, there was always the possibility of a surprise attack.

He brought everything to Kestrel. It was full night. Light from a nearby fire flickered in her face. He tried not to look at her. He crouched and began to set the tent's frame. He drove a stake into the earth. Drier now.

There was a pause after he hammered the first stake in. He straightened.

"I thought . . ." Kestrel's voice trailed into the dark. She didn't say what she thought. She touched his wrist, light as a moth.

Arin flinched. He didn't mean to. He wanted to undo it, yet flitting through his mind was a nightmarish sequence of images: a masker moth, the signed treaty in Kestrel's wintry hand, the Valorian girl he had killed at sea. His mother's bloody black hair.

Kestrel drew back. He seemed to feel her echo his hurt. "I can do that." She took the stone from his hand. "My father taught me how to pitch a tent. I remember."

What else do you remember? Arin wanted to ask, and was repulsed by himself. He knew how much what she *did* remember wounded her. He hadn't thought it'd be possible to hate the general more, yet there it was: a hot jet of hatred. He said, "I won't spare your father."

The shadows were too deep between them. He couldn't read her face. She said, "I don't want you to."

THEY CONTINUED SOUTH. ARIN KEPT HIS DIS-
tance from her. Once or twice, she rode Javelin alongside
his horse. It went badly. He didn't know how to fix himself.
He couldn't accept this.

The first time she drew her horse up to him, he burst
out, "For gods' sake, you don't even have armor."

"I know you're worried," she said quietly.

"Your father wanted you to enlist. You fought him. Your
music. You loved it more. You told me once that you didn't
want to go to war because you didn't want to kill."

"This is important to me."

"You wouldn't have done this before."

"I know. I've changed."

He heard the truth of this in a way he never had. She'd
said this many times, even insisted on it: the woman he'd
known was gone. He heard again his promise to her in his
tent. He felt the absence of hers.

Yet it was wrong to feel hurt in the face of her larger grief,
and the wrongness of it made him feel small. He looked at

the sun in her hair, the ease of her seat in the saddle. Beyond her: a file of cavalry, an eastern pennant snapping blue and green. Fear choked him. It was hard to hear what she said next. A promise to be careful, to take no risks. It was so impossible and absurd to make any promise like that in war that he couldn't even reply.

Eventually, she fell silent.

The next time, also on the road, he noticed her weaving Javelin through the ranks to approach him. He twitched his horse left and found a reason to be somewhere else. At night, he waited until she had pitched her tent. He made sure not to set his nearby.

She continued to glow at the edge of his vision. When camp broke at dawn, he'd catch sight of her bright hair, notice her talking effortlessly with the Herrani, or trying to learn Dacran from the easterners. He watched the soldiers' wariness dissolve. They began to smile at her arrival, to like her despite themselves and her appearance: the very image of a Valorian warrior girl.

She kept close company with Roshar. Arin saw from afar the way the prince teased her. Heard her laugh. It squeezed a fist inside him. At dusk, the pair of them played cards. Roshar bled the air with a string of eastern curses when he lost.

On an evening when they were about ten leagues from Errilith, Arin came to Roshar's tent, which was large enough to accommodate a small table, a set of canvas-backed chairs, and a collapsible bed woven in the style and colors of the nomadic plainspeople. The ticking had feathers, not straw, and the table offered roasted fowl, hulled red berries, and a bowl of eastern rice rendered a shocking orange by a spice Arin had tasted before, and found tangy, sweet, and a little bitter. There was a gourd of wine and two pewter cups. Two plates.

"And lo," Roshar said from where he lounged in his teak chair with its swoop of green cloth. "The rains opened, and the stranger was a stranger no more."

Arin looked at him.

"Poetry," Roshar explained, "though it doesn't scan so well in your tongue."

"You're expecting someone."

"Maybe. You'll do for now. Sit with me."

"Kestrel?"

"Pardon me?"

"Are you expecting Kestrel." The question came out flat.

Roshar coughed. "Nooo," he drawled, but Arin didn't like the humor in his voice. He sat anyway and watched Roshar prepare a plate for him, which wasn't at all expected of an eastern prince and his guest, but Roshar sometimes liked to play the prince and sometimes didn't. "Kestrel has raised the issue of Valorian scouts. We can't expect to be wholly unnoticed, tramping along the main southern road."

"There's been no attack." Which was what Arin thought would ensue if the Valorians became aware of their movements.

"She wagers that the general has noticed the concentration of our forces at Lerralen. Whether he knows of this contingent is unclear, but he might be refraining from attacking us because he doesn't want to position forces north of Errilith when his supply lines run south of it. Or maybe he thinks we'll choose to defend the wrong estate and he can seize his prize unchallenged. Why confront us now and pay the price in blood if we'll waste our energies elsewhere while he takes what he wants? Of course, Errilith could be the wrong estate."

"If Kestrel says that's the one, she's right."

"I agree." Roshar drank his wine.

Arin tried to eat.

"Have you ever bested her at cards? Borderlands? Anything? She *murders* me," Roshar complained.

"You spend a good deal of time with her."

Roshar's cup paused in midair. "Arin."

Swift jealousy. A caged resentment.

"I'm not—shall we say—*interested* in Kestrel." The prince's expression changed slightly, and in the pause that followed, a slow thought occurred to Arin, one that offered an entirely new explanation for why Roshar's soldiers had done nothing when Arin had pushed him into the shadowed trees. "Women don't interest me that way," Roshar said.

It seemed to Arin that he had understood this for a long time without actually realizing that he did. He caught Roshar's expression, which on another man Arin might have called tentative, but on the prince looked closer to soft curiosity. His black eyes were quiet. Arin felt things shift between them into more intricate patterns than before. "I know," Arin told him.

"Oh *do* you?" A wicked grin. "Would you like to know for sure?"

Arin flushed. "Roshar . . ." He floundered for what to say.

The prince laughed at him. He filled Arin's cup. "Drink fast, little Herrani. As you astutely observed, I have someone else coming tonight, and while your company is almost always welcome, his is company I will best enjoy alone."

Kestrel waited outside Arin's tent. It was a muzzy sort of night, too warm for a fire. The camp was a dark terrain. He didn't see her clearly, just the shape of her.

"I brought you something." She held out her hand and dropped a round object into his.

He knew it instantly. He ran fingers over its firm, lightly pebbled surface. "An orange."

"I found a tree not far from camp and took as many as I could carry. Most I gave away. This one, I thought we could share."

He jumped the orange from one hand to the other, marveling at it.

She said, "I didn't know whether you like them."

"I do."

"Did you tell this to me once? Did I forget?"

"I never told you. Actually . . ." He rolled it in the well of one palm. "I love them."

He could have sworn that she smiled in the dark. "Then what are you waiting for?"

He dug his thumb in and peeled it open. Its perfume sprayed the air. He halved it and gave Kestrel her share.

They sat on the grass outside his tent. They'd camped in a meadow not far from the road. He touched the grass, sleek beneath his fingers. He ate. The fruit was vibrant on his tongue. It had been years. "Thank you."

He thought he saw her mouth curve, and he was washed by a breathless nervousness. He spat a seed into his palm and wondered what little kernel lay in the folds of this moment. Then he told himself to stop thinking. An orange. A rare enough pleasure. Just eat.

After a moment, he asked, "How are you?"

"Better. Before . . . it was like I was trying to navigate a new country where there was no such thing as the ground. At least now I know where I stand." He heard the sound of her brushing her hands clean, and then the sound of things unsaid, of words weighed and found wanting. Sorrow, radiating from her. The low throb of it.

Gently, he asked, "Are you truly better?"

He heard her breath catch.

"You don't have to be better."

The silence expanded.

He said, "I wouldn't be."

Her voice was a mere thread. "How would you be?"

He thought of the wrongness of loss, how as a child he'd step right into it, and fall, and then would blame himself not only for everything he hadn't done when the soldiers had invaded his home, but also for his fathomless grief. He should see the gaping holes in his life. Avoid them. Step carefully,

Arin, why can't you step carefully? Mother, father, sister. What could you say about someone who walked daily into his grief and lived at the bottom of its hole and didn't even want to come out?

He remembered how he'd begun to hate himself. The sculpting of his anger. He thought about how certain words mean themselves and also their opposites, like *cleave*. Come together, split apart. He thought about how sorrow limns the places where parts of you join. Your past and present. Loves and hates. It sets a chisel into the cracks and pries. He wanted to say this, yet worried. He feared saying the wrong thing. He feared that his anger for her father might twist what he wanted to say. And he wasn't sure, suddenly, if he should answer her question . . . if by answering it he might, without meaning to, push his own loss into the place of hers, or make hers look like his.

He stared at the dark outline of her face. Her question overwhelmed him.

Until it didn't. Until he seemed to be able to see in the dark. He knew how she must be tightening her jaw, how she was curling her nails into her palms. He knew her. "I think that you try hard to be strong. You don't have to be."

"He would want me to be strong."

This made Arin too angry to trust himself to speak.

She said, "I've been trying to tell you something since I've come here."

And he had avoided her, letting her know in more ways than one that she needed to leave. He felt ashamed. His hands were empty; the orange rinds had fallen to the dirt. "I'm sorry. I've been unbearable."

"Just scared. And there weren't even spiders involved."

This was like her: the way her voice became light when something was hard.

"Please," he said, "tell me."

"I remembered more about my last day in the imperial palace than I said when I first joined your army. I thought that maybe it would hurt you, if I said."

"Tell me anyway."

"You came to me in the palace music room."

"Yes." He remembered: his palm flat against the music room door. Opening it, seeing her face go white.

"My father heard our conversation. He was listening in a secret room, one built for spying, hidden behind a screen in the shelves."

Understanding gripped him. It all rushed sickeningly through his brain. The gesture of her slim hand lifted, trembling, to ward him away as he stood on the threshold of the music room. He'd barreled ahead. She had told him to leave. He had come closer.

"I tried to warn you that he was there," Kestrel said. "Nothing worked."

She had reached for a pen and paper. A note—he realized now. She'd meant to write what she couldn't say out loud. He'd wrenched the pen from her hand and dashed it to the floor.

This was how it must feel, he thought, to take a knife to the gut.

Kestrel was talking rapidly now, voice unsteady. "He hadn't come to spy on me, only to listen to me play. It was hard for us to talk with each other. Easier to have an open secret between us. He would come and listen, and he could pretend that he wasn't really there. But I was happy to have him hear me. Then you opened the music room door. I felt . . . I remember how I felt. I didn't mean what I said. I was insulting. I'm sorry."

"Don't say that. Not to me. I failed you."

"I never trusted you enough to give you the chance to fail me, or not fail me. I *am* sorry. I was cruel. Not only to protect you from my father. I wanted to protect myself, too. I couldn't bear for him to know. But what if I'd given up on all those secret ways to try to tell you he was hiding behind the screen? I could have just *told you*. I could have admitted to what I'd done and let him hear it. Yes, I agreed to marry the prince so that you could have your independence. Yes, I was Tensen's spy. Yes, I loved you." There was a silence. Fireflies lit the distance. "Why didn't I say that then? I wonder what would have happened if I had."

And now? he wanted to ask. *Do you love me now?* He felt her uncertainty. He felt—as if it had already happened, and he'd already asked—the damage of forcing the question.

She spoke as if she'd heard it anyway. "You are important to me," she said, and touched his face.

Important. The word swelled and deflated. More than he'd thought. Less than he wanted.

But this: her touching him. How his blood jumped. He stayed very still.

No more mistakes. He couldn't afford any. He would do nothing.

Something.

No.

She found the curves of his closed eyelids, the shape of his nose, the divot above his mouth, the rasp along his jaw where he hadn't shaved. His skin began to dream. Then his pulse. His flesh. Right down to the bones.

She shifted on the grass. Green and orange perfumed the air. It was on her skin. She tasted like it, too, when her mouth brushed his, and their noses bumped awkwardly, and he wished he could see her as she breathed a laugh and his hands went into her hair despite himself, despite what he'd told her the night before he'd left his home about what was enough and what wasn't. The tang of citrus on her tongue. He forgot himself. He moved her beneath him and felt their bodies mark the grass.

A fluffy breeze stirred the heavy air, floating over the arch of his back. She tugged up his shirt and he went down onto his elbows. The hilt of her dagger dug into his belly. He stayed where he was, her palms warm water flowing over his skin. He didn't want to make a sound. Even his blood seemed loud as he kissed her.

Then a campfire lit the near dark. Startled, he pulled away.

He could see her face better now. Slow eyes, a blurry mouth, and a question stealing across her expression. He'd imagined this before, or something close to it.

Close enough, he decided, but then had the sudden worry that if before she had come to him in his suite because she had wanted to remember, maybe this time, knowing what she knew now, he was just a way for her to forget.

He pushed himself up.

He heard a rustle as she sat up, too, and wrapped her arms around her trousered knees. He kept his eyes off her.

He straightened his shirt, but it felt odd, like it didn't fit him anymore. The sticky air cooled between them. He pushed damp hair off his brow. His limbs—so certain of themselves only moments ago—became an awkward jumble.

Kestrel said, "Will you tell me about the day we met?"

This was unexpected. "It wasn't a nice day."

"I want to know everything from then until now."

Still unsure, Arin said, "But you haven't before."

"I trust you. You won't lie to me."

So he began to tell her, with a hesitancy that eventually steadied as the nearby campfire died down and the night surrendered fully to its creatures: the singing insects, the almost soundless flap of bat wings, a breeze that flowed with the mellow scent of cooling earth. As he spoke, it seemed to him that this was really the only story he wanted to tell.

He kept nothing from her.

Somehow they ended up lying down again, side by side, the grass dense beneath them as they talked. The moon above was large yet intimate. Questions and answers were lifted out into the dark. Sometimes Kestrel recalled a moment Arin described, and then it felt to Arin as if he'd looked into a mirror and saw her instead of his own reflection.

They talked long and late.

AS THEY NEARED THE FIRST VILLAGE ON THE
outskirts of Errilith, Kestrel considered it: why didn't she
know what she felt for him?

It shouldn't be hard to figure out. She knew enough—
remembered enough—of her past to guess the strength of
the emotions she had hidden. Yet the tether between her
and the past felt like it could snap with a mere twist.

One memory ruled her mind: how her father had pushed
her away from him as her heels skidded the floor and she
begged.

Arin's horse, galled by something unseen, tossed its head.
He muttered at the creature—crooned, practically; even at
its roughest, there always was a musical quality to his voice—
then glanced slantways through the sun at Kestrel. His
brown hair fell over his scarred brow.

They'd slept little the night before. But she didn't feel
sleepy, not now, as he regarded her.

A thought etched itself in unreadable patterns across
his face. There was a delay, and she grew nervous as she

wondered whether what changed his expression was regret, and if it was regret, what did he regret? What they hadn't done last night, or the secrets they had shared?

Some of what he'd said still made her hesitate, like his role in the eastern fire that killed her friend Ronan. Even if Arin hadn't intended her friend's death, even if when he had learned of it, she had felt Arin's regret, she knew that the regret was for her sake, not for Ronan.

It was disorienting to be reminded of things she hadn't known she'd forgotten. To have a friend, a whole person, Ronan, rise up inside her only to vanish. She remembered how she'd mourned him. She mourned him again.

Kestrel held Arin's gaze. She didn't break it as he held himself loose in his saddle. His body rocked slightly in rhythm with the stride of his horse. She wasn't sure she wanted him to speak now. His voice had the power to call whole memories into being. Even when he was silent, she was awake to the supple quality of his voice: grave, slow, graveled, graceful. Clear, sometimes so transparent with feeling that she wondered how he had ever deceived her in those first months in her household. With a voice like that. It shouldn't have been possible.

He studied her. This, too, should be impossible: the way a kind of wonder tinged his expression. Surprised. A little amused.

Arin reached across the narrow space between them. With a dusty finger, he briefly touched her nose. "You freckle in the sun," he said, and smiled.

She felt suddenly light and sheer, as if this moment were encased in golden glass.

Maybe love was easy, she thought.

Maybe her past wasn't as vital as her present, she thought.

But then she heard her father say that she'd broken his heart, and she could no longer believe that either thought was true.

Arin was against riding through the village. Kestrel heard him argue with the prince. Scouts had run ahead and learned that the general's army had seized, uncontested, an estate just south of Errilith. The Valorians would move north soon, and fall on Errilith's farmlands. They'd butcher the sheep. Seize grain. Add another link in the supply chain running from Ithrya Island. Fortify themselves for a farther push north toward the city.

"We need to position ourselves in the hills outside the estate," Arin said. "Now."

"What," Roshar said, "would you leave the village undefended?"

"Of course not. Garrison a contingent. You don't need to parade the whole army down its streets."

"The whole army? Not so. You forget: three-quarters of our forces lie at Lerralen. We brave few are all that stand between these villagers and bloody dominion." Roshar sounded merry.

"This is not a play," Arin said through his teeth.

Kestrel didn't understand Arin's discomfort until the prince said, "Let them get a look at you."

Even then, Kestrel didn't fully understand until she saw it happen.

Although the Herrani and easterners usually marched in discrete brigades, Roshar gave orders for them to mingle. On the road outside the village, he took a personal artistic interest in arranging the visual appearance of, as he put it, "friendship in the face of adversity"—a phrase that made Arin cringe.

Roshar bullied Arin into the front of the ranks alongside him. The prince caught Kestrel's eyes. She saw the gleam of strategy in his and responded to it. She held Javelin slightly back. They entered the village, Roshar and Arin riding abreast.

Villagers lined the main road, packed thickly, small children lifted onto grown shoulders. When the villagers saw Arin, their eyes widened with excitement. There was a murmur. People surged forward. They tried to touch him.

Arin's horse didn't like it, and it huffed and stamped. Arin hissed fiercely at Roshar in the eastern tongue; it sounded like a curse.

"If you're so worried they'll be trampled," Roshar drawled loudly in Herrani, "get down off your horse and greet your people."

Arin glanced over his shoulder at Kestrel: a wordless plea. Then he dismounted and she lost sight of him in the sea of people.

She drew Javelin up alongside Roshar. "What are you doing?"

"Don't you think our boy deserves some love?"

"I think you're using him to make yourself and your people look good by association."

The prince smiled, spreading his hands helplessly.

Kestrel dismounted and made her way through the villagers. She used her elbows. A few sharp words, too, which drew surprised looks that quickly hardened into shock. She saw them see her Valorian features.

Suspicion and hatred unfolded on their faces. They hadn't noticed her when she'd ridden with the army. Their eyes had been on Arin. But they noticed her now.

"Please let me through," she said.

The press of bodies grew more solid. This wasn't the city, where everyone knew about her. All the villagers knew was their own past engraved in her eyes, her hair, the shape of her face. Murder and oppression, mixed right into the color of her skin.

"You," someone said, hard and flat.

Wary, she backed away. People surrounded her.

Someone from behind seized her hand. She yanked it free, pulse high and stuttering. She tried to turn, then heard, "Kestrel."

Arin shouldered someone aside and reached for her hand again, gripping it firmly this time. She felt a rush of relief—and foolishness, for thinking to help Arin and becoming the person who needed help. But the crowd's anger wasn't going away. If anything, it intensified.

"What is she doing here?" Kestrel couldn't tell who'd said it.

"She's my friend," Arin answered. "Give her room."

They did.

It was strange to look at Arin through her own eyes and also through theirs, to see the real and imagined person, and to know that what they imagined him to be *was* true, even if it wasn't the whole truth. There was a solid command in his voice, his frame. There was the aura of Arin's singularity, the way he seemed like no one else, like he was a little more than human. But there was also his anxiety, traveling through their interlaced fingers, and the hunted quality to his expression. His mouth wasn't right. She didn't think they saw that.

"Stay with me?" he murmured in her ear.

"Yes."

With her beside him, he walked among the villagers. They kept touching him. Each time, she felt the slight tremor of his reaction, quickly stilled. He tried to be at ease, yet mostly failed. She wasn't sure if the villagers noticed. They smiled, asked questions, voices riding high. Arin didn't let go of her hand.

At least, he didn't let go until a woman pressed her swaddled infant against his chest. Awkward, quick, Arin brought both arms up to hold the baby against his leather armor. He stared at the mother as if questioning her sanity.

"Bless him," the woman said.

"What?"

"Bless him by your god."

Arin looked down at the cradled boy, who slept, eyelids delicate, his cheeks round with health. A tiny flower of a hand peeked out of the swaddling. It flexed and curled against the cloth. Hoarsely, Arin said, "My god?"

"Please."

"But you don't know. Who, I mean. My god—"

"It doesn't matter. If your god cares for my son the way he cares for you, that's all I want."

Arin's eyes flew to Kestrel's.

"Is there any harm?" Kestrel asked, but still he wouldn't do it.

Sternly, the mother told him, "You'll offend your god if you don't share his blessing."

Arin shifted the baby more securely against him. Fingers tentative, he touched the baby's brow. The child sighed. Arin's face changed. He softened, grew luminous, the way certain early hours of certain days are pearled, quiet, and rare. Kestrel seemed to feel with her own fingertips the baby's fresh skin beneath Arin's touch.

The baby opened his eyes. They were Herrani gray.

Arin murmured words too low for Kestrel to hear. Then he settled the baby into the waiting arms of the mother, who appeared satisfied. She made the Herrani gesture of thanks, which Arin returned. There was something about the way he did it that reminded Kestrel that the gesture could mean an apology as well.

Arin's hand found hers again. He felt slightly unfamiliar. Something had changed between them.

She knew why it changed her to see Arin hold this child. She understood the question that had opened inside her, but she was unprepared. She hadn't thought of this. Her heart raced with an emotion too complicated for either fear or happiness.

She released Arin's hand. "Ready to go back?" Her voice didn't match how she felt. It was cool, even careless. She realized that this particular voice was perhaps her most treasured armor.

Arin's expression closed. "Yes."

The crowd cleared a path for them. They returned to their horses and mounted.

"See?" Roshar said, "wasn't that fun?"

Arin looked ready to shove the prince off his horse.

The army moved from the road into a meadow that swelled into hills. It was near misery for the horses that dragged the light cannon and supply wagons, but Roshar wanted the high ground. Kestrel wanted the cover of the forest edging the higher hills, as well as the proximity to Errilith's manor with its fortified walls—visible, but a day's ride away. Arin didn't say what he wanted. He said little of anything.

A stream swiveled down through the meadow: a clear rill bordered by tufted grass. The air pulsed with the sound of cicadas. Roshar called a halt.

Kestrel let Javelin drink and dropped to her knees beside him, cupping water to her mouth, down her sweaty neck. Delicious, chill. "The water," she said to no one in particular. Her father would want this estate for its abundant fresh water even more than for the stores behind the manor walls, or for the sheep ranging the hilltops. This much water this far south was a prize.

Arin's horse nosed past her to reach the stream. She looked up, expecting to see its rider, but Arin wasn't there.

She found him sitting far off on a knoll overlooking the slopes that curved and gentled down. The village sat in the distance like a gray pebble.

Arin glanced up as she approached. One tree shadowed

the knoll, a laran tree, leaves broad and glossy. Their shadows dappled Arin's face, made it a patchwork of sun and dark. It was hard to read his expression. She noticed for the first time the way he kept the scarred side of his face out of her line of sight. Or rather, what she noticed for the first time was how common this habit was for him in her presence—and what that meant.

She stepped deliberately around him and sat so that he had to face her fully or shift into an awkward, neck-craned position.

He faced her. His brow lifted, not so much in amusement as in his awareness of being studied and translated.

"Just a habit," he said, knowing what she'd seen.

"You have that habit only with me."

He didn't deny it.

"Your scar doesn't matter to me, Arin."

His expression turned sardonic and interior, as if he were listening to an unheard voice.

She groped for the right words, worried that she'd get this wrong. She remembered mocking him in the music room of the imperial palace (*I wonder what you believe could compel me to go to such epic lengths for your sake. Is it your charm? Your breeding? Not your looks, surely*).

"It matters because it hurts you," she said. "It doesn't change how I see you. You're beautiful. You always have been to me." Even when she hadn't realized it, even in the market nearly a year ago. Then later, when she understood his beauty. Again, when she saw his face torn, stitched, fevered. On the tundra, when his beauty terrified her. Now. Now, too. Her throat closed.

The line of his jaw hardened. He didn't believe her.

"Arin—"

"I'm sorry for what happened in the village."

She dropped her hand to her lap. She hadn't been conscious of lifting it.

"That shouldn't have happened," Arin said.

The crowd's anger toward her had been unsettling, but not surprising. It wasn't only that that troubled him. "What exactly *did* happen? With the mother and her baby."

He tunneled fingers through his hair and rubbed the heel of his hand against his brow. "A misapprehension."

"That you're god-touched?" Kestrel had heard the rumors.

"No, that's true. I am."

She stared.

"But I don't think the mother would be happy if she knew which god." He glanced at her, catching her surprise. "My twentieth nameday was on the winter solstice." The start of a new Herrani year. "But I'm older than that by the way Valorians reckon time. I was born nearly two full seasons before. My mother waited to name me. It was her right, the priests didn't disagree. The nameday is meant to celebrate not only the baby, but also the mother's recovery. Women recover differently, so the mother decides when. But in the year I was born, each new mother found a reason to wait until the year turned. You know, don't you, the way we mark time? Each year belongs to one god in the pantheon of the hundred, each hundred years measures an era. The sign of each god rules once every hundred years. My year—my birth year—belonged to the god of death."

"Arin," she said slowly, seeing his anxiety, "do you think you're cursed?"

He shook his head.

"Your mother named you in the following year. That's *your* year, then, isn't it? Herrani celebrate the nameday, not the birthday. It shouldn't matter when you were born."

"It matters."

"Why?"

"My whole family. I survived. There's a reason."

"Arin—"

"I didn't know then that I was marked."

"Arin, the only reason for what you suffered is that my father is a monster and he wanted your country."

"It's not so simple. I hear the god of death in my head. He advises me, comforts me."

Kestrel wasn't sure what to believe.

"I don't know what his blessing means," Arin said. "Do you see? When I look at what happened to me. What I've done. What I do. His favor is hard."

"Maybe the voice you hear is your own," she said gently, "and you just don't recognize it."

He made no reply.

She didn't like his belief that death had marked him. His fear—and pleasure—troubled her. A deep, alien satisfaction lurked in his eyes. "Isn't it possible that you've made this up without meaning to?"

"I'm his. I know it."

"And the baby in the village?"

Arin winced. "It would have been a sin to deny the mother. I couldn't. You understand, don't you? I should have told her, but if I had and she withdrew her request, that might catch the god's attention, and what might he do then? If she'd known it was the god of death, she never would have asked."

Kestrel tried to set aside his intricate understanding of cause and effect. It felt beyond her, and dangerous, operating on the whims of an unpredictable deity. "The mother knew whose blessing she sought," she said. "It can't be that hard to guess your age, give or take a year. Which god ruled your nameyear?"

"Sewing."

She squinted, then laughed.

He smiled a little, yet said, "You shouldn't laugh."

She laughed harder.

"Actually, I sew quite well."

"Perhaps. But you don't exactly seem like the god of sewing's chosen one. The baby's mother knew what she asked for."

The wind stirred the tree. Shadows moved in patterns around them.

Kestrel's heart was in her throat even before she knew what she'd say. "Would you do what your mother did? Would you delay the naming of your child for the favor of one god or another?"

There was a startled silence. "My child." Arin tried the words, exploring them. She heard in his voice what she'd seen on his face in the village as he'd held the baby.

She looked at the tree. It was a tree. A leaf, a leaf. Some things just are. They don't signal other meanings. They aren't like a god, casting its meaning over an entire year, or like a conversation, which is itself and also all the things that aren't said.

Her swift heart scurried along.

"It wouldn't be up to me," he said finally. "It would be my wife's choice."

She met his eyes. He touched her hot cheek.

A tree was not a tree. A leaf, not a leaf. She understood what he didn't say.

She stood. "Come, the stream is amazing. Aren't you thirsty? Your horse has better sense than you." A smile. Teasing . . . a little shy, too, yet discovering a newfound safety in showing shyness. She held out her hand.

He took it.

The army camped in the forest on the height of the hills outside Errilith's manor. Another stream coursed through the trees, wide and rough. It fed over rocks and went down deep. Kestrel went with the women soldiers to bathe. She thought about Sarsine, wishing she had the woman's steady, clear way of seeing things. With a twinge of guilt, Kestrel realized that Sarsine had no way of knowing how or why Kestrel had disappeared from Arin's house. Kestrel had been incapable of leaving any word behind and now it was too late. A message, no matter how obliquely worded, could be intercepted and understood. She imagined her father discovering exactly where she was. Her stomach shrank.

So instead she thought about what she'd say to Sarsine when she returned to the city. *I missed you,* she'd say. *I never thanked you for what you did for me.*

She shucked her clothes onto the grass. She needed to feel the water on her skin.

It was freezing. She ducked under, opened her eyes, and looked up through the wavering water at the blue and yellow sky. The cold made her remember that her father must have held her once the way Arin had held the baby. She held her breath and treaded hard to keep her weight below the surface.

It was cold, but the light was beautiful: broken and blurred by the water's rippled silk, as if the sky wasn't simply the sky but a whole other world. Magic, possible. Just within reach.

She washed her clothes and didn't wait for them to dry fully before putting them back on. She wrung out her hair and braided it.

Wending between the trees, she stepped noiselessly, finding moss or dirt or stone for her feet, never leaves or twigs.

You walk well, her father had said once.

Being quiet is hardly a requisite skill for battle, Father.

You could be a Ranger, he'd insisted, but this was after a spectacularly bad training session he'd watched. Her with a sword. The captain of her father's personal guard screaming at her. She knew her father didn't believe his own hope.

His voice echoed in her head, and her heart cramped. It felt as if she were underwater again, with someone holding her below the surface.

She shoved the memory away. There was only so much she could bear to remember.

A game. Make a game of it. How silently can you walk? Let's see.

Toe, not heel. Tree root. This patch of earth, darker and therefore soft. Spears of sun pierced through the trees. Her damp braid bounced between her shoulder blades.

But there was no one to witness her silence. No one to say *You walk well.* Although Kestrel understood the pleasure of doing something for herself alone, had played the piano for hours for her own ears and to feel the stretch and jump of her fingers, the reach of her long arms, she also knew what it was like to play for someone. It makes a difference. It's hard not to want to be heard, seen. To share.

A twig lay in her path. She paused, then deliberately stomped it. *Crack.*

"Pity." The voice echoed in the quiet clearing. "You were doing so nicely."

Roshar. Her eyes found him several paces away, leaning against a tree, watching her. She approached. There was blood on him.

"Sometimes, little ghost, you remind me of my sister," he said.

Her brows shot up.

He laughed. "Not that one."

Kestrel wasn't sure what connection he saw between her and Risha. Because his younger sister was a hostage in the imperial court? Maybe.

"Whose blood?" She tipped her chin in the direction of his spattered forearms.

"A Valorian scout. About your size. I came looking for you, thought you might like to try her armor. Stylish. Light.

Very Valorian. Good condition. Nary a scratch in the leather."

"What about the scout?"

"Hard to catch. Harder to subdue."

She gave him a level look.

Roshar tugged a cropped ear. "She's alive."

"When that scout doesn't report back, the general will know we're here."

"All the more reason to find out what she knows."

"Don't . . . press her."

"Kestrel," he said quietly, "the blood is from the fight when we captured her. Not torture."

"So you won't?"

"Now, it would be nice if information fell out of the sky. Given that it doesn't, it is still nevertheless comforting that certain people do horrible things so that other people don't have to. We should be grateful to such people. Or we should at least not ask questions when we don't want answers."

"She can't help us. Valorian scouts operate in relays. She doesn't report directly to the general's camp, but to a station between there and here. An officer remains at the station and sends hawks with coded messages back to the main camp, which keeps the scout from knowing too much: she won't know how the general's army might have shifted in formation, or what the conditions there are. She won't know the codes."

Roshar tilted his head, regarding her. "Do *you* know the codes?"

Kestrel nudged her memory. It pushed back. "I might have," she said slowly, "once."

"I'm sure the scout knows *something* useful."

"There's no point torturing her for information she doesn't have. Let her be."

His expression was difficult to read. "I'll do as you wish," he said finally. "For now."

"Thank you."

He slouched against a tree. "Do you forgive me for earlier?"

"That piece of pageantry in the village? I'm not the one you should be asking."

"It's good for Arin."

"Good for you, too."

His black eyes met hers. "You want to win?"

"Yes."

"If Arin is admired and my people are trusted, does that help or hurt?"

"Help," she acknowledged.

"Come try your armor. I think it'll fit."

Arin came into Roshar's tent just as the prince tightened the last buckle on Kestrel's armor. Arin was shaven, his hair wet. Whatever he was going to say died on his lips.

"Aren't you pleased?" Roshar said.

Arin immediately left, dropping the flap of the tent's opening behind him.

Kestrel found him by his fire at the edge of the camp. It had grown late. He'd pitched his tent on the outskirts. She realized that, at each day's end, he'd been setting his tent farther from everyone else.

He fed the fire. She crouched beside him, the leather armor creaking. He flinched at the sound. "I'm sorry," he said finally. "It's hard to look at you like that."

"I'm still me," she said, and was surprised at herself for trying to convince him that no matter how she seemed to change, she remained the same person. This wasn't her usual line of argument. As she thought about how she looked in Valorian armor, and whether she looked like herself or not, a germ of an idea began to grow.

"Promise me you'll stay out of harm's way," he said. "I don't want you on the battlefield."

"It's not fair of you to ask that when you'd never do the same."

"The risk is different for you and me."

She became angry. "Why, because you're god-touched? Because you're good with a sword and I'm not?"

"That's part of it."

"That matters less than you think. People who are good at fighting die in war all the time, and people who aren't can find ways to win." Her idea—the armor, the Valorian scout, a plan—took shape. Kestrel's anger carved its details and made it perfect.

"Yes," Arin said, "but even so, the risk for you is still different—"

"Stop saying that."

"It *is*." His face was unhappy. "There *is* a difference between you and me. If I die, you'll survive. If you die, it will destroy me."

Her shoulders sagged. She couldn't bear his hollow expression. The anger drained from her.

"Please," he said. "Promise me. You'll still play a role. Tell Roshar and me what to do, and we'll listen. But not the battlefield. You're to stay safe."

Slowly, she nodded.

"Swear."

"I won't be part of the battle. I give you my word."

She moved to leave. She'd not gone two paces before he stood directly in her path. His eyes were narrow. "A trick."

She spread her open hands. "You asked. I swore. We're done."

"You swore *very specifically*. I need for you to promise. You'll stay off the battlefield *and* be safe. Say it. I beg you."

"I'll make no promises to you that you won't make to me."

She pushed past him.

SHE ENTERED ROSHAR'S TENT. "I NEED YOUR help."

Blinking, he propped himself up on his bed. He said groggily, "And I need a real door. With a lock."

"I have an idea."

"I don't know you all that well, and *still* hearing you say that makes me very, very worried."

"Listen to me."

"If I do, can I go back to sleep? Being a fearless leader is exhausting."

"It's about the Valorian scout."

"You said she was useless."

"In terms of what she can *tell* us. But if we play things right, her capture will be to our advantage."

Roshar was fully awake now. "Go on."

"The general is in his position with his troops at the estate they captured. A scout station is set between his position and a target. An officer remains at that station with message hawks. Meanwhile, scouts run from the station to evaluate the enemy, then report back to the station. The officer sends a coded message by hawk to the general, so if a scout's captured, she can't share much with the enemy, and since scouts get close to the target, *they* can't launch a hawk. Too visible to us. We might shoot it down, then track and capture the scout. That Valorian you caught spying on us can't tell us any codes, and won't be able to say much about the general's forces. But she *will* know the location of the relay station and to whom she reports."

"You want us to hunt down and extract information from the officer?"

She shook her head. "Something better."

"Pray tell, little ghost."

"Send me in her place."

He stared.

Kestrel said, "I'll pretend to be her."

"Please understand. When I look at you as if you're crazy, it's not that I judge you for your insanity."

"I fit in her armor. I'm her size. I'm Valorian."

"You don't look like her. Just because you're Valorian doesn't mean the officer at the relay station won't notice that you're a *completely different person*."

"It's night. I can report to the officer while keeping my distance."

"I'm going back to sleep. Wake me when you're sane."

Impatiently, Kestrel said, "What color is her hair?"

"Different."

"How different?"

"Brownish. All right, maybe not *that* different from yours in the dark, but—"

"I'll braid my hair like hers, wear everything she wore. Did you search her pockets? She'll have had a token. Sometimes the general sends an officer to relieve the one at the station. Then the new officer and a scout—and there are many of these scouts, not just this one reporting to a station—present a token to confirm their identity. We might get lucky. There might be a new officer at the station, one who's never seen the scout but knows her only by name. Roshar, no one would expect someone in your army to impersonate a Valorian scout. Normally, it wouldn't be possible. Not for an easterner. Not for a Herrani."

"What if the Valorians know you're with us? That stationed officer might be aware of it."

"If my father knows, he'll do his best to keep it hidden from as many people as possible."

"Why?"

There was a lump in her throat. "He's ashamed of me. It would shame him, for others to know."

Roshar settled back into the bed, arms folded. "What would we gain if you pretended to be the Valorian scout?"

"Misinformation. Let's assume the general knows of our presence here. If he doesn't, he will soon enough. The issue isn't whether he'll attack. It's *how*. I can influence that. I'll say you have a light force, which other Valorian scouts—if they're eyeing us—will confirm. But I'll also say that I overheard plans that you'll entrench yourselves in Errilith's manor."

Roshar was already off the bed, leafing through the maps spread out on the table in the tent's center.

"He'd take the main road then," Kestrel said. "He

wouldn't expect resistance along the way—or at most he'd expect stealth attacks by small bands of soldiers. There to strike and run, to whittle away at him, like by burning the supply wagons. Nothing serious. Nothing he couldn't handle. Nothing that would stop him from taking the easiest—and most obvious way—to Errilith."

"There are hills along the main road outside the estate. I can set our forces on either side."

"Use the guns. They have a longer range than crossbows. If you position the gunners far enough away, they can shoot without ever being touched by Valorian fire."

"I'm sorry I said you were crazy, little ghost."

Kestrel remembered how it felt to lose to her father at Bite and Sting, at Borderlands, at anything he chose to play. The dig at her pride. A hurt certainty that she'd never be able to prove herself to him. Embarrassment for *wanting* to prove herself.

She remembered her hands clinging to his jacket, her whole self reduced to two claws as she pleaded with him.

War wasn't a game, but she wanted badly to make her father know how it felt to lose.

Roshar said, "Tell me what you need."

"A horse. Javelin might be recognized. Probably not—I don't intend for the horse to be seen—but better not risk it, and I want to get there while it's still dark. Scouts run on foot, so I'll have to tether the horse at a distance from the station. As for the station . . ."

"You need the location."

"And the scout's gear."

Roshar clicked his teeth; a chastising sort of sound. "The

gear is easy. If you want the location of the scout's camp, we need to revisit our conversation this afternoon about not-so-nice means of extracting valuable information."

"Don't."

"I don't enjoy it. But she's not likely to tell us just because we ask nicely."

"You can't."

He drew an impatient breath, and she knew what he'd say, knew the arguments, the costs and benefits. She knew that Roshar, with his mutilated face, understood what it was like to be subjected to pain. She wanted to say all this before he did, and to find a convincing reason that he was wrong. There was no reason she thought he'd accept. She couldn't think of another way.

Then she did. "Don't do it. Trick her instead."

Roshar squinted. "Explain."

"When Valorians enlist, they do so partly because of friendships. There are lovers in a camp. Even without that, there's a sense of belonging. People you'd die for, and do anything to protect. She'll have someone she cares about among the scouts. Take her token. Cast it with a mold. A bit of soap, maybe, or wax. Melt down metal to match the token and make a new one. Return hers, show her the other one. Say you found its mate on another scout who claims to be her friend. Promise to torture her fellow scout if she doesn't give up the location of the officer."

"She might care more about the officer than this other scout."

"Try."

He shrugged, then nodded. "I hope that in your bag of delightful schemes, you have one for how to deal with Arin."

"No."

"Dear ghost, he will tie you and me up and dump us both into a very deep hole before he allows you to do what you plan to do."

"No more *allowing*," Kestrel said, "and no more lies."

ARIN WOKE TO THE SOUND OF SCREAMS.

He shoved out of his tent and into the night. But the camp was calm, undisturbed—though soldiers near their fires seemed to have stopped in midconversation to eye the tent from which the screams came and then choked off into a sob.

Arin asked the whereabouts of the prince and was directed to a nearby tree, where Roshar leaned over the bound Valorian scout, hissing a threat too low for Arin to understand. The Valorian girl—just a girl, Arin saw, younger than Kestrel—had her eyes squeezed shut. She strained back against the tree, bare heels digging into the dirt and moss. She wore an eastern tunic and trousers. A bandage on her arm was rusted with blood. She opened her eyes: glazed with fear, darting all over, skittering across Arin's face as he froze. How wide they were, how dark, how like the eyes of the woman he'd killed on the ship.

Another scream broke the night. It came again from the tent.

Arin strode to the prince. "Roshar. A word?"

"I was wondering when you'd join the fun," the prince answered in Valorian. He grinned at the girl. "I'll be back."

When they were out of earshot of the scout, Roshar dropped his smile. "To be clear, this was Kestrel's idea."

"What the hell are you doing?"

"Faking a torture."

Arin thought he understood, and calmed down a little. "Is it working?"

"It might, if you don't interrupt again."

"Let me know if you learn something."

"Of course."

"Where's Kestrel?"

"She wants to be alone right now," Roshar said after a slight pause. "Better let her be."

But Roshar's tone made Arin remember how the prince had smiled at him, the reins of two horses in his hands on the grounds of Arin's home. This made him think of Kestrel's refusal earlier, before nightfall, to make him any promises. Ever since the sun had gone down, Arin's nerves had tightened with anxiety even as he'd warned himself not to push things, to be different from how he usually was, to not overreact or feel too much or say too much. *Let her be,* he'd told himself, exactly as Roshar was telling him now. But another scream rose in the distance, and even though Arin knew that this was a trick, it was *Kestrel's* trick. Her tricks tended to be shaped like a nest, each twig and straw in place, hiding a dangerous creature Arin never saw until it was too late.

Arin said, "Where is she?"

Reluctantly, the prince said, "She hasn't left yet."

"Left? What? *Where?*"

"Ask her. She'll tell you—against my better judgment, I might add." Roshar nodded in the direction of his tent.

Arin took one rapid stride toward it. The prince's hand came down hard on his shoulder. "Arin, her plan is a good plan."

Arin shrugged off his grip and walked away.

He found her sitting on Roshar's cot, lacing up high Valorian boots. She wore trousers—the scout's trousers. Kestrel had bound her breasts with tight cloth. Her midriff was bare, her shoulders and arms, too: skin a dark gold fired by the lamplight.

She'd heard him enter, yet kept her head down, ignoring him, her braid hanging heavily over one shoulder. It swayed slightly as she jerked laces over the boots' hooks and cinched them. When she reached for the Valorian tunic and jacket on the cot beside her, he caught the trace of a mottled line on her shoulder, saw the lash that curled up over her neck. She paused—had she heard the sore thump of his heart? Or the way he'd swallowed, caught in the nightmare of those scars, in the memory of seeing them for the first time, in his awful imagining of how they'd been made?

She stood and turned her back to him. Just before she drew the tunic over her head, he saw almost the full maze of marks, white and raised. She put on the earth-colored jacket. All the scout's clothing, dyed to match the woods.

"Kestrel." His voice was rough.

She faced him and told him her plan. When he started to

argue (he couldn't even hear what he said; his pulse was shuddering, the blood draining from him), she said, "Trust me."

He did, he wanted to say so, then realized that he didn't, that he could not and would not, if trusting her meant *this.* "No."

She was angry now, too. "You can't keep me in a cage."

"I'm not—" Yet that *was* what he meant to do, in a way. Even as he saw the wrongness of that, he couldn't imagine letting her go. "It's too dangerous."

She shrugged.

"Why do you insist on risking yourself? You were caught once. You're not infallible. Are you trying to prove that you are?"

"No."

"Are you trying to punish me?"

"No."

"I deserve it, I know, but—"

"This isn't about you."

"You are going to get caught!"

"I don't think so."

"You'll be killed. Worse. I can't—"

"Yes, you can. You had better."

"Why?"

"Because this is *me*." Her eyes were wet. "This is the sort of person I've always been."

He wanted to tell her that wasn't true. *You remember wrong,* he could say, and this time he'd be the one who was a good liar.

Kestrel said, "I want to be like her."

No, you don't, he'd persuade, even though he'd never

been able to bear the way she thought of herself as two people. *Not like her at all.* His stomach curled.

"Am I the only one who's supposed to worry?" she asked. "As I did when you went to sea. As I will tomorrow. Every day after that. You can worry for me like I worry for you."

He looked at his hands. They trembled.

"Trust me," she repeated.

He felt the misery of his fear, the desperate certainty that he would lose her again. He trusted that certainty. He trusted his fear. It ruled him like a god.

"Arin."

He met her eyes. They were strange and familiar—rich, in his mind, with everything he knew about her, and with the mystery of her thoughts, which he'd never know for sure. He saw—the knowledge cracked open his shell of fear—that death wasn't the only way to lose her. He would lose her if he couldn't do this. He didn't trust her. He did not. Yet he understood that there are some things you feel and others that you choose to feel, and that the choice doesn't make the feeling less valid.

"Do you?" she asked.

He made his choice. "Yes."

She stepped into his arms. He held the rope of her braid gently. He was drowning. He was far below the surface. He'd forgotten how to breathe.

Then his lungs opened and his mind grew quiet and clear. "Come back to me," he murmured.

"I will."

SHE RODE HARD. CROUCHING LOW OVER THE
saddle, Kestrel pressed the horse to a gallop, drove it straight
down the main road from Errilith to the south. The map
was in her mind. She saw again the shaky mark made on
a forest two leagues from the general's camp. Roshar had
brought the map to her with the scout's token.

And now: the clatter of hooves. A cream of sweat on the
horse's neck. Wan moonlight. Hard to see pits and cracks
in the road. If the horse stumbled at this pace, it'd shatter a
bone. Toss its rider. Kestrel would break her neck on the paving stones.

She dug her heels in. She had mere hours before the sky
blued and lightened. There'd be no chance then to pretend
to be the scout.

Black trees jolted and wavered on either side of the road.
Her throat was dry. Sweat salted her lips.

She remembered Arin's hand slipping down the length
of her braid, letting go. The way he'd looked at her.

The trees gave way abruptly to grass and seemed to

topple back, crash noiselessly behind her as she sped forward. The horse's stride lengthened along the meadow. It felt like she rode over a black sea.

A smudge of trees in the distance. West.

Off the road now. Slower. Cantering over the meadow toward the western forest. She let the horse walk, felt its sides bellow and heave against her legs.

Low branches to duck under. Watch the knees. The trees grew close together; no path here. Straining to see through different shades of shadow, Kestrel picked a way through the woods until it didn't make sense anymore to ride.

It was when she tethered the horse (there was no sound of fresh water, and that was cruel, she hated to leave the horse like that, neck drooping, coat furred with sweat) that Kestrel first felt it. A slow fear, heavy, like sadness . . . which made her realize that her fear *was* a kind of sadness, because she couldn't be better than her fear. She had believed that she could be better when she'd stood before Arin and demanded that he trust her. When she felt, finally, the truth of his trust, warm and solid in his long limbs.

But this was how it ended: her, alone, stepping through the woods, afraid.

She paused, tipped her head back, and glanced up at the sharp stars.

See how brave they are, whispered the memory of her father's voice. She'd been very young when he'd said this. *Bright and still. Those stars are the kind of soldiers who stand and fight.*

A rush of anger.

Even the stars.

Don't just stand there, she told herself. Run.

She jogged through the trees. Her breath rasped. She abandoned what she'd been feeling and thought only of the mark on the map and reaching it while it was still dark.

It was the owl's hour. One last loop of the night, a final hunt before dawn crept in.

Kestrel slowed. Her legs were jelly. She drank from the canteen strapped over one shoulder and across her chest. Swished and spat. Her bad knee throbbed a little, but she realized—distantly, curiously—that her body had grown strong. The days of riding had hardened her legs. It felt good to run.

But her strength also reminded her of her weakness, of how easily her body had given out on the tundra. The unlocking of the prison gate. Relief, joy. Then the chase. Legs collapsing, mud, rope. The dress ripped open along her spine.

Kestrel capped the canteen, screwed it.

She ran again.

The sky was dark blue when she saw a flicker of orange in the trees. An oil lamp.

Her heart hit her ribs. She slowed her run, moving toward the clearing. The lamplight swung. She'd been heard.

"Hail," she tried to call as she threaded through the last copse of trees, her sides heaving. She had no breath. She coughed and tried again. "Hail Emperor Lycian, General of

Wolves, father of a hundred thousand children." It was his military title as well as his political one. Though the emperor hadn't fought in a war since the conquest of Herran, he retained his rank as first general, the only person to whom her father must answer.

"Alis?" called the voice behind the uplifted lamp.

"Stay back. Sir."

"You sound strange."

Kestrel dug out the token. "Catch." She flipped it into the air and heard the man snag it—or heard, rather, the nothingness of the coin not hitting earth.

The lamp moved closer. Kestrel couldn't see the features of the man who held it, only his tall broad form as he approached.

Kestrel coughed. "No, please stay where you are, sir. I'm sick."

"Come to my tent, then, and report there. Rest."

"It's a disease, something eastern. The barbarians brought it. I might infect you."

The officer's boots came to a gritty halt. "What kind of disease?"

"It starts with a cough." Kestrel hoped it'd explain any difference in voice. "Then pustules. The sores weep. I hadn't realized that one of the wagons held bodies. I'd crept close to their camp and looked inside the supplies to see how well fortified they were." It felt strange to speak in Valorian again. "The rebels mean to withstand a siege. They have plague bodies to launch over the walls of Errilith manor. They'll infect us when we attack. They seem to be immune."

"You need a physician." He sounded genuinely concerned. "We can quarantine you."

"Please, let me continue to do what I can for our victory." Kestrel conjured the ghost of her very young self as she spoke. She remembered that little girl, so eager to be her father's warrior. She spoke with that girl's voice. "As long as I can stay on my feet, I can still scout. I want to. Let me bring glory to the empire."

He hesitated, then said, "The glory is yours," which were the traditional words offered when a soldier accepted a mission almost certain to end in death.

The Valorian officer shifted in the shadows and was quiet. The sky appeared to grow a little lighter, but Kestrel told herself that it was her imagination, that the sky couldn't possibly do that in the span of two heartbeats. She was letting anxiety rule her.

"Your report, then," the officer said. "Tell me their numbers."

"One thousand soldiers. Maybe fifteen hundred." Roshar's force near Errilith numbered nearly twice that amount.

"Components?"

"Little cavalry, mostly infantry." True. "From the looks of it, young." True. "Inexperienced." Not true. "Light cannon, and not many of them." True, unfortunately. "Some tension between the Dacran and Herrani factions." Less than she'd expect. "Tension over who should command." Not true. Not exactly. Sometimes, though, she caught the way the prince eyed Arin with pensive hesitancy, as if he secretly believed Arin to be a wholly other creature than human, that a day would come when Arin's skin would split and whatever was lurking inside him would climb out.

In fact, most people looked at him that way.

"Position?" the officer asked.

"By now they'll have reached the manor."

"Tell me about the formation of their units, their positions within the army."

Kestrel answered, relieved. He seemed to believe her. This was easier than she'd thought. She mixed her lies and truths, setting them down like planks of joined wood, sturdy enough to bear the weight of this man's trust.

But when she stopped speaking, the silence lasted longer than it should have.

"Alis," said the officer, "where are you from?"

She pretended to misunderstand the question. "Sir, I came from the rebels' camp."

"That's not what I mean. Where are you *from*?"

Her confidence vanished. He suspected her. She didn't know anything of the scout's history. Kestrel had taken the token and the map and had left as quickly as she could.

Carefully, Kestrel told the officer, "I thought you already knew."

"Remind me."

The lamplight was strong enough that he'd see if she began to inch a hand toward her dagger. She stayed still. Gambling, she told him, "I'm a colonial girl." The odds were with her; almost all of Valoria was a colony.

"But from where, exactly?"

She coughed again, making the sound murky and wet,

and tried to think. "From here." Scouts deployed in Herran would have to know the language. Ideally the terrain, too. The scout—Alis—had been young, Roshar had said. Green, to be so easily caught. If the general chose someone with little experience to gather intelligence on the enemy, it must be because she had advantages that outweighed her inexperience, such as familiarity with the country.

"I'm from here, too," the officer said softly.

"Yes, sir." Her heart sped.

"I spent my youth on a farm west of here." He took a step closer. She held her ground. He wasn't close enough yet to see her clearly; she couldn't see *him* clearly. But she caught, now, the slight accent in his voice. She would have had a colonial accent, too, if her father hadn't ordered her tutors to hammer any sign of it from her voice. In Valorian, she possessed the voice of a capital courtier, polished and pure.

"I want my home back," the officer said.

"So do I." She kept her voice low, rough from coughing, but added a subtle lilt—just enough that he might think the accent had been there all along, and that he'd somehow missed it. "What are my orders?" She tried to keep the question steady. Her pulse was relentless.

"Return to your post. I'll inform the general of your report."

"Yes, sir." The words came out in a relieved rush.

"Not quite yet." The officer set the lamp down on the forest floor and backed away. "Pick up the lamp."

Dread mounted in her throat. "Sir?"

"Pick up the lamp and show me your face."

"But." She swallowed. "The infection."

"I want to see it. I'll keep my distance."

"The risk—"

"Soldier. Pick up the lamp. Show me your face."

Trust me, she'd told Arin. She remembered the strength in her voice and tried to summon that strength again. She thought, fleetingly, that this must be what memory was for: to rebuild yourself when you lose the pieces.

Slowly, Kestrel walked toward the lamp. She kept her head down, though she didn't think he could see her face yet—she'd seen nothing of his during the moment after he'd set the lamp at his feet, just before he'd backed away. She closed one eye: an old trick her father had taught her for night-fighting that involved torches or lamps. One eye adjusted to see by torchlight. One eye kept in reserve, to see in total darkness if the light went out.

"I don't want anyone to see me," she told the officer. "The disease has ruined my face."

"Show me. Now."

She grabbed the lamp and smashed it against a boulder.

He swore. Her dagger was in her hand. She heard him draw his sword.

I don't want to kill, she'd told Arin long ago. Even if she'd wanted to, she'd fail. She felt the memory of failure, of her father watching while she couldn't fight back, her arm sagging beneath the pressure of someone else's sword.

"Who are you?" He advanced, his blade probing the shadows: darting, cautious, blind. His sight hadn't yet adjusted.

But it would.

The officer would capture her and bring her to the general's camp.

There'd be questions. She'd be made to answer. Pressed, split open along her weakest lines. She thought of the prison, her twilight drug, mud and agony. She imagined her father's face as she was brought before him. She saw it in her memory. Her future. She saw it right now.

Pulse wild, stomach tight, she crouched to grasp a handful of soil. He heard her and turned. She flung the grit into his face.

A dirty trick, she heard her father say. *Dishonorable.*

But dirty tricks were her specialty.

She darted around the man, came up behind him, and slid the dagger's tip into his back, just below the ribs. "Which code do you use to communicate with the general? Tell me."

"Never."

She dug a little harder. "I'll kill you."

He hooked a leg around hers and jerked hard. She toppled. Hit the ground. She scrambled to get up, and found a sword's point at her throat.

"My turn to ask questions." The officer kicked the dagger from her hand.

A bird sang. Morning was coming. Kestrel was dimly aware of this, and of the horse she had tethered and now would never untether. She imagined Arin, who wouldn't be sleeping. He'd be watching the sky and the road. She felt the grass beneath his hand, damp with summer dew.

Half sitting, half crouching, she backed shakily away from the sword.

It followed. An axinax sword. She recognized the shorter blade, favored for fighting in forests. She shrank from it, felt a sharp rock dig into her back, and thought, oddly, of the piano. A whole passage burst into her mind, one that she hadn't played in years but had loved for its dramatic swings from high to low registers. She had liked to cross her right hand over and drive the sound down into darkness. She didn't have to stretch hard. Although Kestrel was small, she had long hands. Long arms.

Very good reach.

She groped the forest floor behind her and curled her fingers around the jagged rock that poked into her back. She swung it, smashing the man's hand where he held the sword's hilt.

He made a terrible sound. The sword fell. Its tip glanced off her thigh, slicing through her trousers. It struck the earth. Pain seared down her leg.

But she was up. Her fisted rock crunched into the man's face. His head dented. Her fingers were greasy and warm. Liquid ran under the leather of her forearm guard.

He thudded down. She dropped the rock.

The birds were mad. There was a whole chorus of them now. Her thigh was hot, sticky. There was something meaty on her fingernails. Her hand was a glove of blood.

I don't want to kill, she had told Arin. She slid into the memory and saw herself sitting in her music room across from Arin. An open window sighed on its hinges. Warm autumn air. Bite and Sting tiles, all faceup.

Her hands were shaking. She was going to come apart.

And if you do?

Her plan was already in near ruins.

Salvage the situation, then.

Look at the body. Go on. Make certain he's dead.

He was.

Now yourself. Look.

Kestrel peeled back the torn flap of cloth at her thigh. Blood seeped, it hurt, but she thought that maybe it wasn't too bad. Her leg could bear her weight.

She wiped her bloody hand in the dirt.

The tent, she told herself. Go.

She walked unsteadily to the officer's small tent and entered.

A pallet. A caged messenger hawk, hooded, sleeping. A stool, set before a table that bore papers, a pen, an inkstand, and a set of counters.

The papers.

She went for them, snatching a page. Then she dropped it, her stomach roiling when she realized that it was a letter the dead man had been writing to his mother.

Keep looking, she told herself. Forget his broken face.

She examined each page in the small pile, searching for any scrap of a coded message between the officer and her father. Since the military used several different codes, she had to find evidence of which one the officer had been using. Maybe she'd recognize it. Remember. Decode it.

But there was no evidence, only the letter to his mother and blank pages.

She limped back outside and saw, in the rising dawn, the man's crushed brow, the jelly of one eye. She swallowed hard, then searched the man and found his seal.

Relief. The seal could be useful. But there was no coded message. She had hoped to try to fake a report from the officer to her father.

An impossible thought.

A stupid one.

She didn't know the code, didn't even know the dead man's name. She wanted to bury her face in her hands.

She returned to the tent and sank down onto the stool. Blood leaked from the cut on her leg. She should bandage it. She had no bandage.

The hawk flexed its claws around its perch, shifting its weight with a scratchy, rustling sound. She glanced at it, feeling close to frustrated despair. Then her gaze fell to the counters. Beads of wood that slid along skinny steel rods in their wooden frame. Used for accounting.

Kestrel touched a bead. A memory unfolded inside her.

She unscrewed the pot of ink and found a blank sheet of paper. Glancing at the officer's letter to his mother, Kestrel got a feel for how to imitate the man's handwriting. She inked her pen and composed the first line of code.

THE HORSE TRUDGED UP THE HILL TO THE camp, its head hanging. The sun had climbed; it was near noon, and the day promised to be hot. It squeezed Kestrel's heart to hear the horse's breath. She'd ridden him too hard. But her left leg . . .

The wound had stopped bleeding. The flap of her sliced trouser leg stuck to it, hardened with clotted blood. The cut stung and the skin around it felt fiery. She was going to have to peel the fabric away to see what was underneath.

The horse slowed and sighed. Kestrel didn't have it in her to force him forward. She shifted to dismount, then winced and stopped when the movement opened the cut along its edges.

Thirsty. The sun made her queasy. At the scout's station, she'd splashed water from her canteen onto the wound. In the forest, when she'd untied the horse, she'd poured water into her palm for the animal to drink, and did it again until there was nothing left.

Now she could see the pale peaks of tents along the rise

of the hills. She was close. And really, her poor horse. She'd moved again to dismount when she heard her name.

Arin was coming down the steep hill, skidding on the grass in his haste yet keeping his balance. A breeze tore through his hair, kited his shirt. His descent became a break-neck run, and Kestrel wondered wryly whether the god of death watched over him after all, or maybe the god of grace, or heights, or goats, or whatever god might allow Arin to run like that and not trip over a hillock and come tumbling down. It seemed a little unfair.

He jogged up to her, his hair heavy with sweat. His skin had darkened on the trek south, but he seemed paler now as he looked up at her, shadows under his eyes. He hadn't slept.

He noticed her hand first. Her left side was hidden from his view. It touched her how his gaze went straight to her bloody right hand, his eyes flashing with the same thing she'd feel if her fingers were damaged, if she couldn't play, and had to hobble along the piano keys when she wanted to fly.

He stripped off her forearm guard, swearing at the straps.

"That's not my blood," she said.

"You're not hurt?"

"Left leg."

He came around the horse, saw, and went quiet. "All right," he said finally. "Come on." He helped her down. "I can carry you."

She heard the question in his tone. "No. Roshar will see. He'll tease us mercilessly about it." She smiled, because she wanted Arin to smile. She didn't like the way he looked: the drawn lines around his mouth, eyes hooded with worry.

He didn't smile. He cupped her face with both hands. An emotion tugged at his expression, a dark awe, the kind saved for a wild storm that rends the sky but doesn't ravage your existence, doesn't destroy everything you love. The one that lets you feel saved.

Nervousness rose within her. It simmered, sickened.

Unreasonable. She knew that she could lift her parched lips to his and taste the truth of his love on his tongue. Still, she couldn't say what she wasn't sure she felt.

Her thigh throbbed. "No carrying," she said lightly. "But I'll let you help me up the hill."

Leading the horse behind them, they moved slowly through the camp, Arin's arm under Kestrel's shoulders. He brought her to his tent.

"I think—" He hesitated. "Inside. You could stay outside. But." He glanced down at her bloody thigh. "The trousers need to come off. I can fetch someone else—"

"No. You."

His eyes flicked to hers, then away.

She went inside the tent. There was no canvas floor, only grass and a bedroll. She sat on the ground.

Arin glanced at her dry mouth. "You're thirsty," he said, and left.

He returned with a canteen, a bowl of water, a small pot, and clean gauze.

She drank. The water seemed to fall down a long way

inside her. She thought about the water, how amazing it felt to drink. She thought about that and not him.

Arin knelt beside her. She set the canteen aside. The cut was a dull pain: almost nothing in the wake of her heightening awareness of him, her rapid heart. Outside the tent, cicadas sang.

He unbuckled her armor and lifted it gently away. "Nowhere else?"

"Just my leg." It was a relief, at first, to be out of armor, yet once it was gone she felt exposed and too soft.

Arin didn't move. She knew what she was supposed to do next. Her fingers fumbled as she reached to unfasten the fall of her trousers.

"Wait," Arin said. "Just." He stopped, then continued, "Leave them on."

He reached into the rent in the left trouser leg and ripped it open, carefully forcing the path of the rip to circle her thigh. Soon the cloth was almost entirely detached, save for the flap still stuck to the wound. He tipped water onto it to soften the fabric. "This will hurt."

"Do it."

He peeled the flap from the wound. She sucked in air as blood ran. He pulled the cloth free, leaving her left leg almost entirely bare.

He rinsed the wound. "Ah."

"What?"

Arin lifted his dark head and smiled. "It's not so bad."

She glanced down at the blood.

"I mean," he hastened to say, "that you don't need stitches.

Which is good. Not that it's not *bad*, for you, or that it doesn't hurt, or—"

She laughed. "Arin, I'm glad, too, that it's not worse."

He began to clean it. Pinkish water ran down her leg. The ground beneath her grew damp. He blotted away blood with gauze, and it *did* hurt, yet his touch was tender and he was skilled at this, so that when he unscrewed the pot of whitish salve and began to dab it along the cut, she asked, "Did you learn this in battle?"

His head remained bowed, and he kept his gaze on what he was doing. "Some things. Others, from books. Or—" He abruptly stopped.

"Arin?"

"Under Valorian rule, we learned to do what we could for ourselves. For others. When we were hurt."

"When *they* hurt you."

He shrugged, reaching for the roll of gauze.

"I should have known. I shouldn't have asked."

"You can ask me anything."

The cream was cool and tingled. Her whole body relaxed with the absence of pain.

He placed gauze on the wound and unwound the roll, wrapping it around her thigh. Her gaze followed the gauze as it circled her skin, came up between her legs, and down again. His palm brushed her inner thigh, rough and warm. They fell into silence.

Arin came to the end of the gauze, which he threaded through its other layers and knotted to itself. He was done, yet didn't move. The heels of his hands were against her knee, palms flush against her skin, fingertips skimming the gauze's lower border. "Better?"

Her body felt lax and alive. She didn't want to answer him. If she did, his hands would slide away from her.

"Kestrel?"

"Yes," she said reluctantly. "It's better."

He stayed still. Outside, cicadas ticked and buzzed. He met her gaze, his eyes in shadow. His fingers traced a pattern that had nothing to do with healing and seemed to open her flesh in glowing lines.

Her breath caught. He heard it, and rocked back onto his heels and stood and crossed to the other side of the tent in one rapid motion before she could say anything. And then there was nothing, really, to say.

Arin sat near his bedroll. "What happened at the scouts' station?"

Kestrel sank her hands into the leftover water at the bottom of the bowl. She rubbed at the bloody grime on her right hand, concentrating on it. That glowing feeling ebbed (inconvenient, she told it. Problematic. Now, of all times. What is wrong with you, that you can't respect a friend who has asked not to be used? That everything sparks and burns at the hope of his temptation. That maybe he'll heed it, sink down into it, and it will comfort. It won't, not for him. Maybe not even for you). She washed her hand clean.

Kestrel told Arin everything from when she'd left camp last night to the moment when she drove a rock into the officer's face. "I killed him," she said, and would have said something else, yet faltered.

Arin frowned. "You feel guilty."

"He wasn't wearing armor."

Arin flicked an impatient hand. "His mistake."

"He cared about me."

"What do you mean?"

"I mean Alis, the scout. He was concerned about her."

"Are you saying that you're sorry you killed him because he was a *nice person*?"

"I'm saying that he was a person, and he's dead, and I did it."

"I'm glad you did."

"I'm not." Now she was angry, too.

"Are you aware"—Arin's voice hardened—"of what he would have done to you?"

"If he'd tried to kill me, he would have succeeded. He didn't want to. That's the only reason I was able—"

"He didn't want to kill you because he wanted to *capture* you."

"I know. I can know that and still feel sorry."

"Don't ask me to share your sentiment."

"I'm *not*."

"If he'd taken you . . ." Arin stopped, then said, "They're murderers. Slavers. Thieves. I am not sorry. I will never be sorry."

"So you've never questioned a kill."

His eyes flashed, then looked haunted. "I *won't*."

Kestrel searched his face, her anger fading with the reminder that their difficulties were different, and Arin's own damage ran deep. Whether she meant to or not, she was probing into raw places. "I've upset you."

"Yes, I'm upset. It's upsetting to hear that you feel guilty for defending yourself against someone who would have hurt you."

"There's more to it than that."

He looked down at his hands, spotted with her blood. "You can change your mind. It's all right if you do. You don't have to be part of this war."

"Yes, I do. My mind isn't changed."

"It was him or you," he said softly. "You had to choose."

Her gaze fell to the wet grass beneath her, the wrapped bandage. She thought of her past. Her whole life. "I want better choices."

"Then we must make a world that has them."

When Roshar saw her ripped, one-legged trousers and Arin at her side as they stood outside the prince's tent, his eyes glinted with mirth and Kestrel felt quite sure that the prince was going to say it was about time Arin tore her clothes off. Then Roshar might comment coyly on Arin's inability to reach a full conclusion (*Only one trouser leg?* she imagined Roshar saying. *How lazy of you, Arin*), or on the quaint quality of Arin's modesty (*What a little lamb you are*). Perhaps he'd offer condolences to Kestrel on the partial death of her trousers. He'd ask whether she'd gotten injured on purpose.

Kestrel flushed. "Things at the scout station didn't go according to plan," she said, stating the obvious in order to shunt the conversation to where it should be. Not, absolutely not, about what had happened or didn't happen in Arin's tent.

"She's wounded," said Arin—who, although he didn't look it, must have also been flustered if he, too, felt he had to state the obvious.

"Barely," Roshar said. "A mere scratch, or she wouldn't be standing."

"You could offer her a seat," Arin said.

"Ah, but I have only two chairs in my tent, little Herrani, and we are three. I suppose she could always sit on your lap."

Arin shot him a look of deep annoyance and pushed inside the tent.

"But I could have said something so much worse," Roshar protested.

"Say nothing at all," Kestrel told him.

"That would be very unlike me."

She ignored him. When the three of them were inside the prince's tent (Arin chose to stand), she explained in detail what had happened. "I wrote the letter to the general," she finished, "and launched the hawk."

"How many sets of codes do Valorian scout runners use?" Roshar asked.

Kestrel dug her thumbnail into the teak arm of her chair. "Many. I'm not sure exactly. I might not remember all of what my father taught me, or he could have chosen to teach me only some of them. New ones could have been created and put into use since then."

"So the chances that the letter you wrote is the correct code, and will be the one the general expects to see, are slim."

"Yes."

"How did you choose which code to use?" Arin asked.

"The officer had counters in his tent, which was unusual, unless he was in charge of accounting for the army's supplies, and that'd be done at the main camp where supplies are kept. I remembered a numeric code. He could have been using counters to help him write in it."

"Or," said Roshar, "your father will read the note, see one code when he expects another, and will send someone to the station, where there's a dead body."

"If so," Arin said, "then we're no worse off than we were before."

"Oh yes, we *are*. The general will know the letter's a ploy, and will do the opposite of what we want. He'll ignore the main road. He'll take back roads through the forests where our guns would be of dubious use and we wouldn't have the advantage of height. You know this."

Arin shut his mouth, glancing uneasily at Kestrel. Yes. He *had* known this, as had she. She felt worse for his effort to make her mistake seem smaller. He knew its true size.

Roshar leaned back in his creaking chair. His eyes slid from Arin to Kestrel, black as lacquer, the green lines around them fresh. "Can you tell me anything more cheerful than all this?"

"My letter mentioned nothing about a plan to use plague bodies as a defensive attack during a siege. I had to say that to the officer, to make him keep his distance. But once he was dead that lie wasn't necessary. Now the manor can seem to be an even easier and more appealing target."

"*If* your father takes the bait."

"She did what she could," Arin said.

The numbing properties of the ointment on the cut in

her thigh were wearing off. She rubbed at the bandage, studying its interleaving, and tried to swallow her sense of failure, which grew worse to hear Arin defend her.

"I know," Roshar said, "but our force is small enough as it is. We can't be in two places at once. He's going to move on Errilith. I don't want to fight a defensive battle. We can't afford it. If conflict happens here, we'd have the height of the hills, but they've got the numbers to fan out and flank us. What I liked about the plan of attacking them on the road was the chance to pen *them* in, to pin them down so that they can't move."

"Then trust her."

Kestrel glanced up at Arin.

Roshar said, "Sending that coded letter was a desperate gamble."

"It was *her* desperate gamble," Arin said. "That's why I think it will work."

They were to break camp at dawn. Kestrel watched Arin disappear among the supply wagons. She went to the river, washed the blood and sweat from her, then changed the shredded trousers, which had been the scout's, for the pair she'd worn when she'd ridden south. She did not think very much. She watched leaves bend in the wind and show their pale underbellies. There was the rushing water. The cicadas' metallic rasp.

She walked back to the center of camp.

Arin had set up a wet grinder and was, it seemed, going progressively through the spare arms stored in a wagon, inspecting each blade. He frowned at a sword and held it down at an angle to the grinder, setting its stone in motion. The sound was harsh.

Then his gaze flicked up. He saw her, and the grinder stopped.

She approached. "There are Dacran smiths in this camp. Other people can do this."

"Not well enough." He spread oil on the blade to polish it. His fingers glistened. "I like doing it." Arin held out his oiled hand. "May I?"

For a moment she didn't understand what he wanted, then she drew the dagger he'd made for her and gave it to him.

Arin looked it over—surprised, pleased. "You take good care of it."

She took it back. "Of course I do." Her voice was rough and wrong.

He peered at her. Friendly, he said, "Yes, of course. Is there a saying for it? 'A Valorian always polishes her blade.' Something like that."

"I take care of it," she said, suddenly both miserable and angry, "because you made it for me." She hadn't liked his surprise. She disliked herself for causing it, for the knitted confusion of her feelings, for the way she'd grown smaller to hear Arin defend her to Roshar, not simply because of the force of her sense of failure, but also because she'd asked Arin to trust her and now he did, unwaveringly, yet he'd asked her to love him and she offered nothing. She swung between the solid certainty of attraction and the apprehension of more.

I love you, she'd told her father. A plea, an apology, and also simply itself: eighteen years of love. Was it really nothing? So worthless?

Yes, it had been. She'd seen this when her father had lifted her clutching hands and pushed her away. She'd seen it in the dirt floor of her prison cell. Heard it in the sound of her soiled dress ripped open along its back.

She thought of the hawk, which must have winged its way to her father by now. She imagined it slewing around trees, dropping down. Talons closing around his upraised fist. Her father unrolling the coded message. The trap she'd set for him.

Walk into it, she willed.

You have a mind for strategy, he'd said once.

Come see, then.

See what I can do to you. See what you have done to me.

"Kestrel." Arin's voice was hesitant. She realized how she must look. Hand clenched on the dagger's hilt, a storm in her face. When he started to speak, she cut him off. "Do you have more of that salve?"

"Oh." He fumbled under the leather apron he wore over his clothes and pulled the small pot from his pocket. "I should have given it to you earlier. I . . . was distracted. I forgot."

She took it and left.

Usually she enjoyed her tent. It was private, which made her recall that she'd always felt watched, before the prison. In the capital, certainly. Even in Herran, when it had been a colony. Privacy was a relief. The circle of rough canvas co-cooned her. It glowed or dimmed with the passage of the sun.

Now, however, as she heard the noises of camp (people talking in two different languages; horses and birds and in-sects and the *brrr* of the grinder), she felt as she had on the first day Arin had pitched her tent: lonely.

Kestrel removed her trousers and unwrapped the ban-dage. It was damp and heavy from the river.

The cut wasn't bleeding. It didn't hurt that much. She spread ointment onto the cut anyway. When it numbed, she thought of the prison's nighttime drug. Her chest throbbed with a slow pang. She missed the drink's taste, and what it did to her.

She painted the cream down her thigh where Arin had touched her. The skin went numb.

Kestrel bandaged herself again and tried to envision the morning, when she'd break down her tent, break camp, and strike south to attack her father.

THEY SPLIT THEIR FORCES ONCE MORE. A contingent was sent to Errilith's manor to make it look ready for a siege. If Kestrel's father trusted the coded note, he'd run scouts ahead to gather information on the manor.

Roshar sent most of the supply wagons there. All of their cannons, too: a risk.

"Fast and light." He spoke as if this were an entertaining choice and not a dangerous necessity to leave their main artillery behind. But stealth was necessary (as much as a small army could be stealthy). Speed was important, too, and the terrain was bad for hauling anything. They'd need to work their way south through the forest and up to the hills overlooking the main road.

"I'm worried about the trees," Kestrel said to Roshar at the end of the first day of their move south. Irrielle birds hunted overhead, swirling into a black fingerprint against the violet sky. Kestrel flicked a playing card to the grass. A rabbit was roasting on a spit over the nearby fire, its skin a crackled brown. Arin slid a knife into it, separating the flesh. Too pink. He added sticks of resinous sirrin wood to the fire. They caught instantly, blazing blue.

"Worried, how?" Roshar glanced at his cards and groaned.

But Arin, who'd been watching their game without taking part, had already guessed what Kestrel was thinking. "We need the trees for cover," he said, "but they'll make it hard to use the guns. We won't have much hope of hitting targets on the road below."

"Better cut them down." Roshar took his turn. "The wood's undergrowth might be enough to screen us if we lie low."

Kestrel clicked her teeth; an eastern, irritated sort of sound.

"You learned that from me," the prince said, pleased. "Now tell the truth. Did you mark the cards?"

Coolly, she said, "I never cheat."

"We can't cut the trees down," Arin said.

"Concentrate," Kestrel told the prince, sweeping up the card he'd tossed down.

"To be clear, I'm *letting* you win. I let you win *all the time.*"

"Obviously we can't cut them down," she said. "My father will notice a sudden swath of felled trees. We might as well paint a sign telling him we're there."

"Or . . ." Arin said.

She glanced at him. "What are you thinking?"

"How much rope do we have?"

"Two hundred and twelve lengths."

Roshar said, "You've been going over our supplies?"

"Yes," she said.

"Could you rattle off the units by heart?"

"Yes."

"How many sacks of grain for horses?"

"Sixty-two. Play your card. You might as well. You're going to lose regardless."

"Attempts to distract her usually don't work," Arin told him.

"You play the winner, then," Roshar said, "so that I may observe your technique."

Arin checked the rabbit again, pulled it off the fire. "No."

A surprised disappointment twitched, insect-like, inside Kestrel's chest.

Roshar said, "Why not?"

Arin sliced meat off the bone onto a tin plate.

Kestrel, who wasn't entirely sure she wanted to hear Arin's answer, said, "Why do you want rope?"

"Let Arin surprise us," Roshar said. "That's how we do things. He comes up with something brilliant and I take the credit."

"Tell me," Kestrel said.

Arin set down the plate. "I won't play you because even when I win, I lose. It's never been just a game between us."

Roshar, who was stretched out on his side on the grass, elbow crooked, cheek pillowed on his palm, raised his brows at Kestrel.

"I meant about the rope," she muttered.

Roshar's gaze slid between her and Arin. "Yes, the rope. Why don't we talk about that after all, shall we?"

They were in position. Kestrel waited with the gunners behind a thin layer of trees bordering a hill that overlooked the road. A breeze flipped the leaves. Trees creaked. The gunners, mostly Herrani, nervously looked up at Arin's project.

It had taken nearly all the soldiers the better part of the day, using two-handed saws from the supply wagon. Axes, too. And, of course, the rope.

Arin had tied each tree trunk and staked the rope deep down into the forest floor. Each tree was unique, its height and width and lean calling for a different network of ropes, set at different angles. After the trees had been tied into place, soldiers sawed them at their base—though not quite all the way through.

"When the Valorians come," Arin had said, "cut the ropes."

"You want to kill me," Roshar had said. "*Embarrassingly.* A prince meets his end in battle. He doesn't get squashed by a falling tree. I bet you tied those things all wrong."

A smile tugged at the corner of Arin's mouth. The air was gritty with sawdust. "After everything," he told Kestrel, "I wouldn't let you be harmed by a *tree.*"

"Me," Roshar said pointedly. "You mean *me.*"

But Arin had already gone. Soon after, Roshar left in the opposite direction.

The plan was an ambush.

"What formation would the general use," Roshar had asked her, "for a march along a road of that width?"

Kestrel had paused, fingers on the worn map.

"She can't know for certain," Arin said.

"Here's what I would do if I were him," she said. "I'd be in the front ranks, where I'd keep most of my cavalry—the officers. New recruits would be behind the supply wagons, which I'd keep in the middle. Infantry in the back, with a few trusted officers just in case. I'd choose officers who wouldn't complain about being in the rearguard with the lower ranks. They'd be experienced. They'd be good. But there'd be few. Archers and crossbows flanking the regiment, ready to target the hills. He'll know there's a risk of a skirmish. It'd make sense, if we *were* readying for a siege at Errilith, to send small groups to harass their progress north. He'd expect the supplies to be targeted. If we destroy the wagons, we cut the legs out from under him. It's not that an attack would be a complete surprise. It's the *force* of our attack, and our ability to use a weapon he can't contend with, that give us our best advantages."

"So we give him what he expects," Arin said. "A small company of ours can attack the front lines, draw the general's attention while our larger force prepares to bucket the rearguard. The general should pull his defenses forward. We might even separate them from the center. Their officers wear metal armor. Volleys from the guns will be more effective on the center and rear. The gunners should drop as many soldiers as possible around the wagons—and, gods help us, the cannons."

"A small company attacking the Valorians' front ranks," Roshar mused. "How delightfully suicidal. Perfect for you, Arin."

"But," said Kestrel.

They both looked at her, and she could tell from the set of Arin's jaw that Roshar had said only what Arin already planned to do anyway. Arin's eyes were overcast. They had a distant, difficult regard that sent a chill down her spine. It made her wonder whether Arin's god was real after all. If he was there right now inside Arin, whispering to him.

"You command this force," Kestrel told Roshar. "It should be you. Arin can attack the rearguard."

With a smirk, Roshar said, "No, that pleasant task is mine. You, little ghost, stay with the guns."

Kestrel's fingers tightened. "You're placing me in the safest position."

"I'm placing you where you won't be seen by your father."

She thought of the general seeing her. She thought of him not seeing her. Both thoughts were paralyzing.

"You're not so different from one of those guns," Roshar said. "A secret weapon. The general must know you've escaped the work camp, must guess where you went—if you survived the tundra. But will he think you're *here*, with this army? He might, eventually. He might recognize your hand in these dealings whether he sees you or not. But I would rather—and I'm sure Arin would *very* much rather—that he have no confirmation of your presence."

She started to protest.

"You swore an oath to me," Roshar said cheerfully. "A Valorian honors her word."

Seeing that his last words made her pale with fury, he grinned and left.

"You want me with the guns, too," Kestrel told Arin.

"Roshar's not wrong."

"He's choosing according to his own best interests."

His brow furrowed. "Positioning you with the guns gains him little, personally."

"What about *your* position against the general's forward ranks?"

"Sometimes Roshar plays the selfish prince so that no one expects anything better of him. It's not who he is. He's choosing well. For me, he's chosen what I would have chosen for myself. I want the front lines."

Kestrel remembered Arin's words now as she waited in the trees with the gunners, who'd been placed under her command. She remembered how she'd wanted to explain to him that it had rattled her to try to slip into her father's mind, to know that the general's mind and her own felt upsettingly similar. She'd wanted to put her fear inside a white box and give it to Arin.

You, too, she would tell him. *I fear for you. I fear for me if I lost you.*

War is no place for fear, said the memory of her father's voice.

"Take care," she'd told Arin.

He'd smiled.

And now he was below, out of sight, beyond the curve of the empty road.

The sun poured down. The gunners had loaded their weapons. Kestrel watched the road, dagger ready.

Cicadas. The flit of birdwings.

Maybe her father had recognized that the coded letter was false.

Maybe he wouldn't take the bait.

A breath of wind. Hours passed, slow as the sweat traveling down Kestrel's back.

Her limbs ached from being in the same position. She felt a strange energy slip over her and the gunners, an elastic tension that went tight at the smallest sound, then slackened in the heat, the waiting.

Dream, wait, startle, wait, dream.

The gunners, like her, crouched among ferns and saplings. Guns angled down. Small eastern crossbows were at the ready. A sirrin tree dripped orange sap, its spindly branches low and sticky.

Kestrel watched the road.

The rapid *toc toc toc* of a bird's beak against bark. The brush of leaves. Then—faintly, stronger . . . the rhythm of thousands of boots on the paved road.

ARIN HEARD THE VALORIANS MARCHING TO-
ward him. The sound made his chest harden with anticipation.

The Valorians neared. Still hidden behind the bend in
the road, Arin turned to catch the eyes of his soldiers, no
more than fifty of them, men and women, Herrani and
Dacran both. All of them on foot, for stealth and to appear
more vulnerable to the Valorian front lines. Some of the Herrani soldiers had lined their eyes in orange and red like
Dacran warriors.

The sound of the Valorian army became deafening.
Boots and hooves and wagon wheels. Heavy armor. Metal
on metal.

His gaze on his soldiers, theirs on him. Arin lifted his
hand: *wait*.

He edged around a tree to look down the road.

The Valorian cavalry. Enormous war horses. Officers in
black and gold.

Close.

And one Valorian in particular, leading them, looking no different than he had eleven years ago. Large and armored, his insignia painted across the chest. A woven baldric over his chest, knotted at the shoulder. Helmet simple, made to show his face. That face.

Good, to have a little distance, to not quite see the general's light brown eyes—too much like his daughter's.

Better, to have this man move his horse nearer to Arin. Almost within his reach.

Do you want him? Arin's god whispered.

Do you want to crush him between your hands?

Arin glanced back at his company. "Ready," he whispered, then whispered it again in Dacran. His sword was drawn. His blood was hot.

Sweet child.

Mine own.

Go.

Kestrel saw the clash from above. Through a spyglass, she watched Valorian warhorses rear. Not the general's. He became motionless: a metal statue. His face was far away, his features a blur. Her stomach clenched.

And Arin?

Trees obscured her view. She couldn't find him. She couldn't see anything below the horses' shoulders.

Infantry against cavalry.

Kestrel, you fool.

She realized that she must have believed in Arin's god. Some unexamined part of her must resolutely trust the god of death's protection. Only that could explain why she had set Arin against the Valorian vanguard—and her father—with any hope of survival.

Dread worked its way up her throat.

In the initial crush, Arin lost sight of the general. An officer's horse nearly trampled Arin, who dodged the reared front hooves. He caught a blow from the Valorian's sword; its edge lodged harmlessly in the shoulder of Arin's hardened leather armor. As the man tugged it free, Arin snatched the reins from the man's hand and dragged the horse's head down, heard it scream. The Valorian struggled to keep his seat. Arin buried the point of his sword into the man's side above his hip, just below the low border of the metal cuirass. Arin pushed.

An inhuman sound. Blood channeled down the blade. Arin's hand was warm and wet.

The Valorian started to slide from his saddle. His foot caught in the stirrup. The greave of his leg armor raked the horse's side and the animal reared again, nearly dislocating Arin's arm from his shoulder. He released the reins. The Valorian thumped to the ground. The horse plunged, ran wild, dragging the soldier behind him.

Arin couldn't think. He knew, vaguely, that enemy archers weren't firing on his company, probably for fear of hitting the Valorian vanguard. He knew that his own soldiers were falling around him. The Valorians, instead of pulling forward to meet the attack, stood their ground and grew more compact, a wall of metal and horses.

Those stallions. The gorgeous brawn of them. High and huge.

Arin shouted in Dacran, then in his own tongue: *With me.*

He drew his dagger. A blade in each hand, he ducked into the narrow space between two Valorian warhorses and sliced open their necks.

Kestrel clenched the spyglass. The Valorian officers didn't advance, didn't separate from the middle ranks, didn't expose the supply wagons.

A warhorse stumbled. Then another.

Her father hacked his sword down. It rose up red. She saw him shout.

"Cut the ropes," Kestrel told her gunners. *"Now."*

Arin wanted to cry out. He saw an eastern woman slip past the Valorian defenses, hamstring a warhorse, and reach the general. Arin wanted to say *No*, he wanted to say *Mine.*

The general, steady on his steady horse, swung. He cut the woman's head from her neck. Blood jetted.

"Hold formation!" the man shouted.

The rest of the general's commands echoed in Arin's ears as he blocked the downswing of a horsed Valorian's blade. *Rearguard, close ranks.*

Arin's sword arm ached.

Archers, eyes on the hills. Cannons, at the ready.

He dropped the dagger from his left hand, hooked his

free fingers into the Valorian's leg armor at the upper thigh, and yanked.

Flankers, defend.

The Valorian toppled from his horse.

Sword into the fallen man's throat. A gurgling cry.

The general wasn't fooled. He'd guessed this was no little skirmish. He held his vanguard back and let Arin's company come in order to tighten ranks in defense against a larger attack.

A horse shifted. A path opened between Arin and the general.

Ah, yes, murmured Arin's god.

Then a rough, tumbling crash roared over the sounds of war. Arin almost didn't know what it meant until a crack broke the air.

The trees groaned, tipped forward, and thudded down. Most lay where they fell, but a few slid down the hill toward the road. They gathered speed, slammed into boulders or the trunks of other trees. Some speared down: leafy tops first, stopped by nothing or shunted by an obstacle into a diagonal roll that spun them off the hill and onto the Valorian army's left flank. The trees crushed men and women, cut a swath into the middle ranks.

Noise rang through the hills. Each thump and scream split the air. It sounded worse to Kestrel as the echoes died. She didn't want to hear silence.

"Ready a volley," she told the gunners. "Aim at the middle

ranks. Target archers. Drop the flankers. Drop anyone near a cannon. Cut a hole around the supply wagons."

The gunners' faces were unafraid. Their position was mostly secure, well out of range of Valorian arrows. Cannons might be a problem, but the army below was still fumbling to unhitch cannons from draft horses and unload ordnance from the wagons. Kestrel was about to disrupt that.

"Matches," she said.

They were struck.

"Light."

Short fuses burned.

"Aim."

Gunfire perforated the air. Arin heard what he couldn't see: the song of metal sailing through space. Iron balls, each no bigger than a small stone, hailed down. They punched into metal. Rang on stone. Drove into flesh.

Guttural screams. Arin saw the general's face go gray. Horse carcasses lay between Arin and the general. The shuddering wave of a stallion trying and failing to stand. The pitiable arch and flop of the horse's neck. And Valorians, two rows of them, trying to hold the front lines, confused, frightened, their eyes not where they should be.

Arin pushed forward.

Another volley of gunfire.

Far away, beyond the Valorian army, came a new sound. Hooves rattled fast up the road. There was a shrieking clash. Roshar's company must have struck the rearguard.

The general shouted something incoherent to Arin. The Valorian formation wobbled, seemed ready to dissolve.

Then a cannon boomed from the central ranks. A second cannon.

The world became too loud for Arin to understand anything he heard, too fast for him to understand more than what his body did, and did again.

Blood was in his mouth. His hands were slippery. His muscles were loose and alive.

A cannonball thudded into the hillside not far below the gunners. Kestrel felt the impact's tremor in the earth. It vibrated the soles of her boots. It trembled the thin, gummy twigs of sirrin trees.

"Again," she told the gunners.

But despite the gunfire, despite an attack on three fronts, the Valorian army didn't collapse or panic. The rearguard countered Roshar's attack. The Valorian army, thousands strong, segmented into three: front, middle, and rear ranks. But Arin's company, from what Kestrel saw, couldn't drive through the vanguard to reach the center. The rearguard's defenses were better than she'd hoped. Roshar made little headway.

Even divided, the Valorians would overcome their attacks. The only way to cripple Kestrel's enemy for the long term was to destroy the supplies. But the guns, deadly though they were, weren't precise enough in their aim. They couldn't open a path for either Arin's or Roshar's company to reach the supply wagons.

Anxiety clawed her belly. Roshar, she thought, would have the good sense to retreat if he must. She wasn't so sure about Arin. She thought that if she couldn't drag a victory out of this battle, he'd struggle against the vanguard until it overwhelmed him.

The solution is simple, her father whispered inside her. Kestrel didn't know whether it was a memory or her imagination. *If you can do it.*

She looked at the sirrin trees. Their sap oozed.

She heard the plunk of an iron ball dropped into its chamber. The dry pour of black powder. As the gunners reloaded their guns, Kestrel shakily tucked her braid into her leather helmet. She could do nothing about the obvious Valorian style of her armor. She remembered how she'd been uncertain whether she wanted her father to see her. A shudder ran through her.

No. Not seen. Never. Whatever happened, she didn't want to be recognized. She scooped a handful of forest earth and scrubbed it onto her face.

Kestrel became aware that the small sounds of reloading guns had stopped, giving way to the dull roar of the battle below. The gunners, crouched low like she was, regarded her.

She stood. "Which of you is truly brave?"

The Valorian vanguard changed tactics. They moved forward now, pressing Arin's company back.

A hand caught Arin's arm, pulled him from the path of a charging horse. He turned.

No one.

Bodies and blood. And then . . . an eerie energy in his veins. A sharp zing that made his gut tighten and his guard go up right before a tiny Valorian dagger flew into his vision, spiking through the air, straight for his throat.

As the gunners fired, Kestrel sliced her dagger through the shreds of rope left tied to the stakes in the ground. She scavenged the forest floor for smooth, dry sticks of birch. Hands wrapped in broad leaves, she broke sappy twigs from the sirrin tree. Careful to keep her skin from contact with the flammable sap, she bunched the twigs together, holding them around a birch stick and one end of the rope. With a free hand, she wound the rope around the twigs and the birch stick. Then she held the makeshift torch beneath the dripping sirrin tree, letting drops of sap coat the rope and glue it down to the twigs.

"Exactly like that," she told the four soldiers who'd agreed to join her. When they each had a torch and had taken a box of matches from the gunners, Kestrel said, "Don't hold the stick upright until you must. The sap will run. If it gets on your skin, you might burn, too." She told the gunners to fire two more volleys and then stop.

She and the four soldiers began to run down the hill.

Arin dodged the small dagger. A Needle. He knew that weapon. Needles were a set of six little knives.

He caught the next one in his arm, flung up to block the

dagger from his face. It bit into the exposed underside of his forearm where his armor buckled.

Then either his assailant had grown impatient with targeting from afar, or a new opponent had entered the game. As pain flared up Arin's arm, somebody's sword crashed into his and knocked his weapon to the ground.

Kestrel followed the scars made by the fallen trees in the forest. She skidded down the steep incline, the four soldiers following. A volley of gunfire shattered the air. A Valorian cannon boomed back. The cannonball crashed into the trees. They cracked. Broken branches hurtled through the air.

A chunk of flying wood nearly hit Kestrel. Startled, she lost her balance and stumbled, getting sap from her torch on her chest armor. But she shouted *Run*. They were nearly to the road.

The second volley hailed down. Kestrel stopped the four soldiers at the edge of the trees level with the road. Peering through the leaves, she saw that the guns had killed enough soldiers on this flank that gaps in the Valorian defenses here were wide. She spotted the wagon that must hold the black powder. A Valorian stepped out of it, lugging a cannonball in his arms. "Not that wagon," she told the four. "I'll take the one next to it. The rest of you, each choose a different wagon. Ready?"

Kestrel's fingers trembled as she opened the matchbox.

A commander never shows fear, her father said.

Her hand steadied. She lit a match.

They set their torches on fire.

Arin dodged the swing of the Valorian sword. He pulled the Needle free from his arm, felt pain spurt. Arin briefly eyed his attacker. A slender, quick form.

The Valorian lashed out again.

Just throw it and run, Kestrel told herself. *Throw and run.*

She burst from the trees. Her boots hit stone paving.

A crossbow quarrel soared over her head. Another hit a Herrani soldier running alongside her. He sagged and dropped.

One of the four, a Dacran woman, snagged his torch from the ground and lobbed it at the nearest wagon. Its canvas cover flared into flame.

Kestrel kept running. She couldn't see what the woman did with the second torch, but heard a howl of pain, a shrieking eastern curse. Kestrel understood only one word of it: *fire.* The sirrin sap, Kestrel thought. Maybe it had run down the woman's arm. Maybe the Dacran was burning alive.

Kestrel forced herself to run faster. Valorian soldiers were scattered now, disordered, cut off from the general.

She heard another wagon crackle with fire. She ran erratically toward her target. *Never a straight line if you have to run,* her father said. *Otherwise you're too easy to sight and shoot.*

She got shot anyway. An arrow hit her chest.

When the sword came at him again, Arin sidestepped it and seized the hand that held the hilt. Squeezed. Felt the knuckles pop. The sound and the scream were lost amid other sounds and other screams. With the Needle in his left hand, Arin pierced the Valorian's wrist and saw the red point emerge on the other side. Arin ripped the sword free, claimed it as his own, and stabbed.

Kestrel staggered but didn't fall. The arrow hadn't penetrated her armor.

She had almost reached her targeted wagon. Heart slamming against her rib cage, she glanced up at her torch. The sap traced a thin blue line of flame down the birch stave. Her fingers were hot. She threw the torch into the wagon's belly.

Then she spun and ran for the trees. Her legs pumped hard. She felt the old wound in her thigh split open and seep. She shouted the names of her four soldiers, cried out with ragged breath for them to run. *Run,* she called in two languages, and then a third. Even in Valorian she shouted for people to flee, because her wagon was already a bonfire, and it was right next to the wagon that held the black powder.

A breeze feathered her sweaty skin. A puff of wind.

An explosion rocked the ground. The stone road shivered under Arin's boots. Beyond the vanguard, above in the center of the Valorian army's column, flame shimmered the sunny air.

A Valorian horn blew. The sound curled—too pretty for war, Arin thought.

Stop thinking, said his god. *Fall back. Fall to the sides. The trees.*

Suddenly, there was a halo of space around Arin. "Not yet," he murmured.

They are going to charge right up this road, right over you and everyone you're responsible for. Retreat. Now.

But the general, Arin thought.

The god shrugged. *It's your life.*

Do you truly care for my life?

A laugh.

Arin called for a retreat.

From the trees on a hill, Arin and what was left of his company watched the Valorians flee. They thundered up the road—as many, at least, as could run. The rearguard, caught between the fire and Roshar's company, had nowhere to go.

LATER, ARIN LEARNED THAT ROSHAR HAD EVEN-
tually sounded a retreat of his own. The Valorian rearguard
had been trapped by the fire, but their numbers still outweighed Roshar's. Desperation and excellent training made
the Valorian rearguard difficult to overwhelm. "I have no
particular interest in dying," Roshar explained when his
forces had regrouped with Arin's on the gunners' hill. "The
loss of so handsome a man would do the world a great disser-
vice." The rearguard had fled. The road burned.

When Kestrel had staggered up through the trees, a
broken arrow shaft in her armor, her face dirty yet white
around her wide eyes, Arin caught her to him, exhaling
deeply with relief. She reeked of smoke. Her armor was sticky
with sirrin sap. He guessed what she had done, and a tremor
flickered through him even though she was safe. He pulled
away, then saw that he had printed blood on her. Traces here
and there. A faint red leaf marked her cheek. He saw her see
him. He didn't like to think about how he must look.

"Your father's alive," Arin told her, sure that it was the wrong thing to say even as he was sure that it must be said. An emotion darkened her eyes.

Later, after the fire had burned out and the road was a charred ruin littered with corpses, Roshar's soldiers had scavenged the remains, and Arin had helped catch riderless warhorses, Kestrel finally spoke. "He'll resupply." Her voice was flat. "The empire doesn't lack for black powder. He might have to return to Ithrya Island to get what he needs, but he'll hit hard when he hits next."

The stolen supplies and their wounded were loaded in wagons. The army made its way to reunite with the forces left behind at Errilith.

Outside Errilith, in the meadow near where they had first made camp in this region, Arin came to share Roshar's cooking fire. The sun had just set. The air was still heavy and warm, cast with a honeyed light.

Roshar was smoking. He'd been in a foul mood since they'd left the fire-blackened road, though Arin had reminded him that the battle was a victory. "I know," Roshar had said, yet looked nettled.

Arin helped himself to warmed flatbread toasted over the fire. Soft bread on a military campaign seemed just short of magic. He ripped off a small piece and chewed slowly. Roshar glanced at him, huffed a little, but said nothing— which was disappointing, since Arin had hoped to provoke the prince by taking his food.

A Herrani soldier passed close to their fire and moved on, though not before Arin noticed that the man's eyes were rimmed with orange like a Dacran's.

"That's nice," Arin commented to Roshar.

The prince choked on a lungful of smoke. When he stopped coughing, Arin said, "Is it disrespectful that my people wear that paint?"

"Oh, no," Roshar said, not sarcastically, yet with a bite that suggested that Arin had missed the point. "It's *nice*."

"Say what you mean."

"I am not nice."

Arin's brow furrowed. "True, but we're not talking about you."

"We should be. We should absolutely be talking about me."

Arin wished Roshar wouldn't do this, wouldn't slip on false arrogance as if it were mourning garb worn in the service of a joke. He opened his mouth to say so, then saw that Roshar looked genuinely troubled. "What's wrong?"

Roshar said, "Do you remember how you attacked me in my city, in front of the queen's guard?"

"To be fair, you *had* drugged and bound me."

"Do you remember how you were punished for that?"

"I don't see what this has to do with the paint."

"That's because you don't understand your punishment."

Uneasy, Arin said, "The queen told you to choose my punishment. You never did."

"That entire audience with my sister was in Dacran, which you didn't speak or understand at the time—or did you?"

"No."

"I was your translator. I warned you. I said that you had to hope that I wouldn't lie."

"Did you?"

"Let's say that I translated very loosely."

"Roshar."

"At the time it didn't seem important. What would you care about the finer points of Dacran law? And you didn't have anything worth taking."

"What exactly did the queen say?"

"That your life belonged to me."

Arin, whose life had already belonged to many different people, felt his lungs shrink.

"So yes," Roshar said, "I had—*have*—the right to decide your punishment, to kill you if I wish. By our law, I can also seize anything you possess."

"You're not in Dacra. Your law holds no weight here."

"My soldiers would say otherwise."

"What do you want?" Arin's voice rose. "My house?"

"This isn't entirely about what I want or don't want. But if we win this war, you'll have a prize very much worth wanting."

Arin saw what he meant. "This country wouldn't be *mine*."

"Oh, Arin. Please."

Arin fell silent. They'd let the fire go out. Shadows had grown around them.

"Puts my sister in quite an interesting position," said Roshar. "It was a public announcement. One that she clearly didn't think through, though I'll be honest and say that when you fetched up on our shores you didn't appear worth much. It cost her nothing then to offer me your life. It made for good courtly show. And now whatever is yours is mine. Despite its miserably cold weather, Herran is a pretty prize: rich, fertile. A good buffer between Dacra and the empire. My sister has a few options, depending on how this war plays out. If we win against the empire, we could seize Herran by force, which normally wouldn't cause a fuss, if it weren't for the fact that she'd be taking from *me* what our country considers legally mine. I happen to be popular with my people. Another option: she could ask me to give Herran to her."

"You wouldn't."

"Because you and I are friends? How touching. And naive. That's actually what I like about you. You're so *endearing* sometimes."

"I'd never let you. You'd have to kill me."

"Yes, little Herrani, I know." Roshar set aside his pipe. He brushed his hands as if cleaning them, then looked down at their emptiness.

Arin was no longer angry. "You wouldn't," he said again, "or you'd never have said any of this to me."

"I'd like to think that, but we're talking about the same person who deliberately let his little sister be taken hostage by his enemy. What will you say? That we all make hard choices? Do things we regret? Betray our best selves? Yes, exactly. I have wanted to tell you. I didn't. Not for months."

"What did you think would happen if we lost?"

"Usually I don't think. Usually my sister thinks, and tells me what to do. I'm quite comfortable letting other people run my life."

"You never say what you really mean."

Roshar held his eyes. "If we lose, I'll take you home."

"Your home."

"Mine, yours."

"Not possible."

Roshar sighed. "Well, lots of things are."

"Your sister . . ." Arin flushed.

"Oh, *that*."

"How does that play into this?"

"Well, *that*, as I understand, happened in my city when you were just a ragged, trespassing foreigner of little importance. Of course"—Roshar gave him a sidelong look—"you have your charms. Now you've put an end to *that*—which, I don't know, I think that if I were you I wouldn't have. Your country could always be returned to you as a wedding present."

Arin made a frustrated sound.

"It might be better for you if you didn't draw everything in such rigid lines." Roshar thumbed more tobacco into his pipe. "It might be better for me if I did."

"You know how I feel. Where I stand."

Roshar arched one brow. "Indeed."

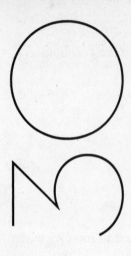

KESTREL STOPPED SHORT OF WHERE THE prince lay on his back in the grass in the midst of camp, eyes loosely closed against the sun. It was rare to see his face relaxed. The sun showed how scar tissue had thickened his upper lip and knotted where the tip of his nose had been.

She knew he wasn't sleeping. "Lazy," she accused.

"This is how I look when I conspire."

"No Valorian commander would let his soldiers see him like this."

"This is a strategy."

She snorted.

"It is." His eyes were still closed. "Aren't you going to ask me how it is?"

She toed him. He stretched like a cat and seemed to settle back into position. Then his hand lashed out, seized her ankle, and yanked her leg out from under her. She landed on her rear.

"Yes." Roshar's black eyes glinted as she spluttered. "A masterful plan. Divine."

Kestrel kicked him.

"*Tch.* Lovely lady, won't you hear my plan? It is the very best. You'll like it. Here it is: I am waiting."

"Sunbathing."

"Waiting, I say, for you to tell me what to do."

She told him *exactly* what he could do.

"Such language. Did you learn that from Arin? Stop *kicking*, little ghost. We're in full view of the camp. Weren't you just haranguing me about my honor? How can I cultivate respect in the rank and file if you kick me? Now. Truly. Look at my absolutely serious face as I say this. What would you have me do? More to the point, what will your father do?"

Kestrel went still.

"A move must be made," said the prince.

Lerralen. Kestrel had learned of the Valorians' failure to invade via the beach there. She knew how smooth the terrain would be from the beach to Herran's city.

If victory is slow, her father would say, *it becomes increasingly harder to grasp.*

He must wince from his defeat along the southern road. How could he wreak the most damage in retaliation? He could claw victory to himself by regrouping his forces to land at Lerralen with overwhelming force, with countless cannons and soldiers spread thick and wide. A costly victory. But if achieved, it'd lead to a rapid seizure of the city.

She told Roshar to garrison a contingent at Errilith to hold what they had well defended, and move the rest of his army west to reinforce the Dacrans stationed at Lerralen.

As she saddled Javelin and tightened the girth, she tried to quell the leaping worry in her belly. She should not worry.

After all, what could the general do that *she* could not do? Had she not learned war at his knee? Did his voice not haunt her? She thought about the way her memory—or imagination—of him seemed to advise her.

She didn't like the way he was right. How she listened. She wondered if there was any difference between how she listened to him and how Arin listened to his god.

Hilly terrain smoothed as the army rode west. The land grew slightly arid. The dirt was a light grit.

Kestrel saw how the Herrani soldiers lured Arin into riding with them in the middle ranks. There were requests that he consider the gait of an unruly horse. Or a story left dangling, a teasing challenge: finish it, Arin, why don't you . . . if you can. Sometimes a question: was Arin *sure* he wasn't related to the Herrani royal line? This flustered Arin, and was so likely to hold him in extended conversation and vigorous denials that it was the most common ploy used to keep him in their company.

Once, when Arin let his horse fall back to ride with the Herrani, Kestrel caught Roshar's sliding gaze. Pensive. Murky. A strange mixture of satisfaction and displeasure.

Kestrel said, "I thought you wanted them to love him."

Roshar glanced over his shoulder at Arin in the middle ranks.

They rode in silence beneath the hard blue sky. Then

Kestrel said, "On the tundra, Arin had a ring with a stone in it. Did you give it to him?"

"Never lend that boy anything. Careless. He lost it."

"It could put people to sleep."

"Yes."

"And that white salve, the numbing one—is that eastern, too? Is it made from the same thing?"

"What an observant ghost you are. Yes, Kestrel. The liquid in that ring and the salve contain different quantities of a poisonous worm from our plains. A very little bit, mixed with ointment, will numb the skin. More will send you to sleep. More still? You take the goddess's hand and live with her forever."

"Why don't you dip crossbow quarrels in it? I remember my father complaining about the poisoned arrows of the eastern plainspeople."

"Alas, we're far from the plains and my supply is limited." He squinted at the sun. "Why do you ask?"

She was quiet.

He said, "You're not thinking about crossbow quarrels."

"Sometimes I have trouble sleeping."

"In case I wasn't clear, that part about taking the goddess's hand means *dead*. As in, *you die*. In its highest concentration, you can die from simply touching the poison, even when the liquid dries."

"I'd be careful."

Roshar swiveled his horse in front of Kestrel's, blocking her path. Javelin snorted and stopped.

The prince said, "My answer is no."

He said, "You're not the only one who suffers."

He said, "You could do what the rest of us do."

Roshar spurred his horse ahead.

Kestrel looked down the open road. A lone black bird cut across the sky like a crack in blue paint. She thought about the white salve in her saddlebag, the missing ring, and how much she longed to sleep easily, without dreams. *Nothing in dreams can hurt you,* her father had said—which was another way of saying that life can. But she hadn't understood that as a child. Kestrel recalled the old comfort of her father's words, and had a sense of herself as she had been.

That night, alone in her tent, she thought about the cruel cold of the tundra. Sulfur crumbling in her grip. The panic when her memory had begun to slip. The nighttime drug: soft, dense. The fear of dying far from home. No one would have mourned her. Sorrow: like marrow in the hollow of a bone.

It had been real. It still was.

But it wasn't the whole of who she was.

Kestrel blew out the little lamp. In the dark, she recalled the road she'd traveled that day with its cloud of dirt.

You could do what the rest of us do.

She would keep going.

That night, she slept deeply. Afterward, she sometimes still wished for the nighttime drug, but it no longer held her in its power.

In this region, a variety of wheat flourished. Dull gold fields rattled softly. The grain, fully flowered, bent the stalks.

In the distance, Herrani harvested the fields. They were too old or too young for war. Other fields had been abandoned. Kestrel saw farms where chicken coops stood empty, smelling of sour straw. The animals had been slaughtered or carried away. A woven basket, left outside for months, had disintegrated into a spiky nest. When grasped, the handle came off.

The farms unnerved her. She would have preferred to say that it was because of the waste. Most of the wheat would rot on its stalks. But it wasn't that. It was the buildings. The rare Herrani villa, with a columned portico and fluted arches. The wink of an atrium's glass roof. More common: a splendid and newish Valorian manse, sprawling, flat-faced.

The slave quarters blistered in the sun. Paint peeled in long curls like an apple's skin. Kestrel noticed, with queasy misgiving, that a little house lay near the slave quarters on each farm. At first, when she went with soldiers to forage for provisions to fatten the army's supplies, she hadn't known what the little houses were for. There had been no such house on her father's property in Herran.

One day, she saw Arin see a small house. His eyes tightened. His expression went bleak.

She knew then that the houses had been for children. The memory came unwillingly, sticky and slow. She had to drag it out. When she did she understood that the knowledge had been the sort of thing she had once tried to unknow.

It had been the practice to take a baby from its enslaved mother once it was weaned and sell it to a neighboring farm. The mother would be distracted from her work, went the Valorian wisdom. Meanwhile, her master would purchase other children from other farms. These children forgot that anyone but their owners could lay claim to them, and were raised in small houses by an elderly slave. By now, such a child could be as old as ten years.

It had been commonly done in the countryside. In the city, not always. Some owners prided themselves on allowing their slaves to keep their children. Kestrel had once seen a Valorian lady coo over a Herrani child. The tiny girl had wobbled where she stood in the center of the parlor. Kestrel, who had come for tea, hadn't noticed the girl's mother at first, then had followed the toddler's gaze to see a uniformed woman waiting in a shadowed alcove.

Kestrel's father had made clear that there would be no slave children on his property. If babies were born, they were soon sold. None were purchased.

Each little house on each farm was a horror. Before—for years—she had let her mind close seamlessly, like an egg, around this wrong and other wrongs. They happened every day. It was life. But not *her* life.

Hers, an inner voice—sinister, upsetting—had sometimes disagreed.

Not hers.

Hers.

The words echoed now with the rhythm of Javelin's hooves.

Kestrel could say that she'd learned that one's life is also the lives of others. A wrong is not an egg, separate unto itself and sealed. She could say that she understood the wrong in ignoring a wrong. She could say this, but the truth was that she should have learned it long before.

The sky was frosted with stars. Kestrel found Arin seated near a fire, squinting as he retooled someone else's leather armor. A buckle had come off.

"Can you see well enough?" She remained standing.

"No." He pushed an awl through a strip of leather. "But there's no time for this by day." The army pressed as rapidly west as it could, though not as quickly as Kestrel would have liked. Roshar had warned against a forced march. Weary soldiers make for lost wars. Her father had often said the same.

Kestrel tipped her head back. The night glowed. "How do you make a mirror?"

Surprise tinged Arin's voice. "Do you want a mirror?"

"No. I just wondered how."

"You silver glass. It's not something I've done."

She turned in a half circle to look toward the western constellations. Her boots released the scent of bruised grass. "Before, people must have used polished metal."

"Probably."

"Or bowls of dark water. The sky looks like a mirror, if a mirror was a bowl of black water."

There was a silence. Kestrel took her eyes off the stars and looked at him. He'd set aside the armor and was turning the awl in his fingers. He flickered orange and red in the light of the low fire. Quietly, he said, "What are you thinking?"

She was hesitant to say.

He came to stand next to her.

"Arin, after the conquest, what was it like for you?"

"I'm not sure you want to know."

"I want to know everything about you."

So he told her.

The stars, too, seemed to listen.

They left the wheatlands. The soil became loose. Fresh water, seldom. On the fifth day out of Errilith, however, they reached a stream and replenished the water barrels stowed in the supply wagons.

Kestrel watched Roshar approach Arin as he curried his horse. "Here." The prince thrust something at him. "Do us all a favor. You're filthy." Roshar looked him over. "I think there's still dried blood behind your ears."

It was a cake of soap. Arin appeared faintly startled, as if he lived in a world where soap hadn't been invented. He broke the round between his hands and offered Kestrel half.

It crumbled a little in her grasp. Its scent was sweetly smoky. She stood there longer than necessary, inhaling the gift of a gift. It occurred to her that if she used it, and Arin used it, her skin would smell like his.

She tucked it carefully in her saddlebag, wrapping spare clothes around it so that it wouldn't be broken.

"Come with me." Arin. Eyes illuminated. "I want to show you something."

Kestrel followed without question, though the army's midday rest was nearly over. They took their horses.

She kept stealing glances at Arin as they rode toward a grassy hill. He caught her at it. "A secret," he said, and smiled.

It felt as if his smile became hers. His secret, too. The day itself: the satin sky, a speckled yellow feather that spiraled down on a breeze to catch in Javelin's mane. She held all this inside her the way a jewel holds light.

They dismounted at the foot of the hill. Kestrel noticed stone steps, overgrown with green, leading up the slope. It occurred to her that the entire hill, rare for this terrain, might have been man-made.

"What is this?" she asked. The stairs, as far as she could tell, led to nothing. The hilltop seemed bare.

Arin plucked the yellow feather from Javelin's mane and tucked it behind her ear. "A temple. At least, it used to be."

She touched the feather's ticklish plume, the slight scratch of the quill. She explored it, trying to ignore her pleasure at his unexpected gesture. "Is that your secret?"

"You wouldn't ask"—Arin's grin was mischievous—"if you didn't guess that it is not. Come see."

The steps were broken in places and wobbled beneath Kestrel's feet. When they reached the hilltop, she could see the jumble of marble that had been the temple's foundation. Perhaps it had been destroyed after the conquest; the Valorians had razed all Herrani temples to their gods. But these ruins looked ancient. The marble was bleached bone white. The carvings, polished smooth by time, were blurred and mostly indecipherable, like a dream after one has woken.

"It's greener here, isn't it?" Arin's voice was hushed. "Than the rest of this region."

"Yes."

There were birds' nests in the nooks of broken marble. A lizard darted over a fallen pillar. The place appeared at once ghostly and yet full of life. When Arin stepped into the center of the ruined temple and knelt, Kestrel thought it was to pray, but he was clearing away vegetation. "I recognize some of this." He was eager; his words tripped over each other. He seemed unaware that she wouldn't understand what he meant. "But other parts . . . I thought I knew all the stories."

Kestrel came to kneel beside him. A face glittered up at her beneath strands of ivy. Startled, she pulled the greenery away.

It was a mosaic. An entire, immense tiled floor stretched out of sight beneath the vegetation. Kestrel palmed away dirt. The face flared in the sun, its tiled features slippery and cool. The man—woman?—had wings fanned wide, a peacock's colors. Scaled skin. Carnelian claws.

Kestrel tugged more ivy free. Gorgeous, impossible creatures appeared. An enameled snake with six tails. A horse made of water. A woman whose hair appeared to be paper scrolls written in a script close to Herrani, but with so many alien elements Kestrel couldn't read it. Some of the figures looked only vaguely human. A string of eyes crowned a brow. One long, violet-skinned body had no limbs. Gold spilled in a ribbon from the lips of a god.

They were all gods. They could be nothing else.

"Maybe we should go back," Arin said, but he didn't mean it. His mouth was reluctant. He licked his thumb and rubbed a tile clean, not raising his gaze, the sun tumbling in his messy hair. A wide blade of light cut across the bridge of his nose, warming his neck and shoulders. He moved, and the sun caught his face in full.

Her limbs were light, as if with fear. Her blood seemed to float. She said, "Not yet," and saw his sudden happiness.

She helped him clear the vegetation and expose the entire mosaic to the sky.

Every chip of her being slid into place, into the image of a lost world. The boy discovering it. The girl who sees it spark and flare, and understands, now, what she feels. She realizes that she has felt this for a long time.

Lapis lazuli, kiln-fired glass, onyx and gold and shell and ivory. Jade. Aquamarine. Kestrel barely saw where each tile of the mosaic joined, the taut line of contact. Piece to piece. She pressed her palm to its surface and imagined its image imprinted on her skin.

Later, Kestrel wished she had spoken then, that no time had been lost. She wished that she'd had the courage that very moment to tell Arin what she'd finally known to be true: that she loved him with the whole of her heart.

KESTREL WAS UNUSUALLY QUIET ON THE LAST day's ride to Lerralen. At first, at the temple, Arin had thought that some new, delicate thing had grown between them. But since then she had kept her distance in a way he couldn't explain, could find no cause for. He sifted through his memories of the temple, of her, the hot green leaves, the slick tile, the hidden world of the mosaic, and how Kestrel had wanted to see it, too. He could find nothing wrong. An error lay somewhere, that was sure. Still, each moment of each memory of that day made him want to hold them all in the palm of his hand, to stash them safely and close. In a deep pocket, perhaps. On his person.

He was wary of this impulse. He suspected that he would be revealed as a child with a collection of precious things that were actually nothing valuable. A button, a river rock, a bit of string.

Or a speckled yellow feather. He wished he'd kept it. He wondered if Kestrel had kept it. Most likely it had fallen from her hair as they'd galloped from the temple's hill to rejoin the vanguard of the army.

Tawny grass rippled on the bluffs. The air was brackish. They'd soon reach the sea.

When the army stopped to water the horses from the barrels among the provisions (there'd been no fresh water in this land for two days), Arin found Kestrel brushing Javelin's coat. She glanced up at him, then away, her gaze settling on something else that Arin wanted to identify, to understand whether it was him or—what? the white-threaded sky? that gull, tipped up against the wind?—that made her seem suddenly smaller.

Her hair had reddened since coming to the south. Her skin was now the color of toasted bread. Long fingers plucked stray bits of nothing from Javelin's mane.

It was not the sky. It was not the gull.

Arin tried to set her at ease. "So, strategist. What are our chances? Or do we ride to our dooms?"

The corner of her mouth lifted—an acknowledgment both of his effort to ease her anxiety and also that what he'd asked, however lightheartedly, was an odd sort of way to do it. Yet it worked. She became more present. The skittering movements of her fingers stilled.

Not the battle, then.

Not her horse, nor the slight crunch of sand beneath their boots. Nothing, nowhere.

Him.

"There are three scenarios," she said. "We arrive late, and my father has seized the beach. Or we arrive as reinforcements for a battle that has already begun. Or we arrive before my father, and wait." She added, "Of course, there is a fourth: that I am wrong, he won't land there, and we've disastrously shifted our strengths where they shouldn't be."

"There is no fourth."

She shook her head. "I can be wrong."

"Is that what worries you?"

"Even if I'm not wrong, and we arrive before the Valorians land, it's a mixed blessing. Him landing late means he's landing with a larger force. A robust artillery. More people and more cannon take longer to mobilize. They're also harder to defeat."

Javelin knocked his nose against her shoulder. Arin saw her smile. A quiet, lost feeling stole over him like sleep or a farewell.

"I told my father I loved him." Her words were abrupt. "It was the last thing I said to him."

Arin didn't look at her. He didn't want her to see his face just then.

"I saw a basket when we were in the wheatlands," she said. "It had lost its shape entirely. You couldn't hold anything in it. You couldn't hold *it*."

"Kestrel, you are not a basket."

"I think—" She stopped.

He wondered if something can be so hard to say that it becomes hard even to say that it is hard. "You can't tell me what you think?"

"No."

"Why?"

She whispered, "I'm terrified."

"Of the battle?"

"No."

"Your father?"

Her voice was flat. "*He* should fear *me*."

Arin didn't want to relax his sinewy need for the general's death. It clenched inside him. But if it was this . . . if there'd been no error at the temple, if Arin had done nothing that he needed to undo and instead what had made her seem to try to hide from him in plain sight was dread of Arin's vengeance or her own . . . "Kestrel." He put it bluntly. He couldn't think of any other way. "Do you want his death?"

Her eyes flashed.

"I won't do it," he said, "if you don't want it."

"Kill him if you can. I don't care. He left me for dead. Worse."

Arin's hatred knotted within him. "If I did, would you forgive me?"

"You talk as if his life or death was your choice."

"It's been promised."

She squinted at him. "By your god?"

"Not in so many words, exactly."

She shook her head.

"Please answer my question."

"Maybe it will be *my* hand," she said. "My sword."

"I need to know your choice."

"Do it." Her eyes were wet. "Swear that you will."

The knot released. "Yes, of course."

"He changed us both." She seemed to struggle for words.

"I think of you, all that you lost, who you were, what you were forced to be, and might have been, and I—I have become this, this *person*, unable to—" She shut her mouth.

"Kestrel," he said softly, "I love this person."

But her slim mouth tightened. Her face shone again with fear.

Arin curled his fingers into Javelin's mane. "*I* am what troubles you."

"No, Arin." But she had hesitated.

He thought about what it meant that Kestrel's father had had her love, and had cast it aside. He wanted to tell her about the jolt of recognition that had rattled through him when he'd ripped the ivy from the face of his god, how it had been like looking into the black-water mirror Kestrel had described as they'd gazed into the clear night sky. He wanted to explain his hard joy, his relief of feeling fated for something, and how mattering to his god was akin to becoming a son again, or a brother. He wanted to warn her, to say that she couldn't know, not fully, what it was to no longer be someone's child.

Kestrel asked, "Are *you* afraid of the battle?"

This, at least, was easy to say. His smile was free. "No."

The beach was quiet.

Which wasn't true, of course, not with an entire Dacran regiment camped on its sands. But it quieted Arin to see that the Valorian ships hadn't landed, that there were no sails on the horizon, and even if Kestrel had warned that this could translate to an overwhelming onslaught, he was glad to see the empty stretch of rain-darkened sand from the tents to the shore, to see the low tide, the muck of green-plastered rocks, the gulls squabbling over crabs as they picked through tide pools. The wind was dead. The sky, a flat slate. It had stormed the night before. The briny air smelled raw.

Roshar's people were so glad to see the arrival of their prince that Arin doubted the way Roshar styled himself as someone with no political ambition. The queen had her people's fealty. Roshar, their love.

"This is a safe time of day," Kestrel said, then kneed her horse in the direction of the pale grass on higher ground, beyond which, they'd been told, was a stream that watered the army and its horses.

Arin followed, drawing his horse up alongside hers. "Yes, the Valorians will land at high tide," he said.

Kestrel looked slightly startled, not at what he'd said but that he'd spoken at all, which made him think that her words hadn't been a start of a conversation but rather just a moment in her mind that had somehow slipped out, and that she'd been deep in her own thoughts. She didn't bother to ask how he knew what she'd meant, probably because she assumed that the advantages of high tide for an invading force were obvious.

The sea will carry them swiftly to shore, murmured death. *It will froth white. Bear the weight of countless black-throated cannons.*

Arin glanced at Kestrel. This battle would be very different from the ambush along the southern road. There would be no safe place, only the open arena of the beach.

Don't look at her, Arin. Look at me. You will embrace them.

Your heart will rise, high and glad. What is an enemy? It is the stick and pull and slash of your sword. It is the clean path you cut between you and what you want. It is the path to me.

The human stench of the camp had lifted. Kestrel and Arin had ridden far enough away. There was only the swampy saline of low tide, the exposed underbelly of the sea. It smelled good.

You can wonder about her all you like, whispered death. *But I am the only one who will have you.*

Kestrel had ridden a few paces ahead. She turned, catching Arin's glance. A bead of rain fell on his cheek. The back of his neck.

You are mine. I am yours. Is it not true, Arin?

Her expression closed. He thought of a box shut so firmly that one cannot see its seams.

Yes.

That night, Arin stood with Kestrel and Roshar on the bluffs. Moonlight glazed the sea. The water sparkled black and white. The moon coated the sand with silver.

"Pretty," Roshar commented, "though it puts me in mind of pure worm poison, the way it dries to a clear sheen." He asked Kestrel, "How do you think the battle will go?"

Arin answered instead. "For them and us, it will be the kind of battle where a general puts his soldiers in such a desperate situation that the fear of death and difficulty of retreat push them to fight their utmost, because there is no other choice."

Roshar coolly lifted one brow. He looked ready to say that Arin was being needlessly dramatic.

But Kestrel nodded.

The alarm came at noon. There was a faint drizzle. The sun was somewhere, but couldn't be seen. Off to the east was a solid ridge of gray cloud. And at sea: a faint pale line of sails.

Gunners flanked the beach. The Dacran-Herrani army waited in a wedge formation, the cavalry spearheading the bristling mass of people.

Kestrel's face was taut, her hands white-knuckled on the reins. Javelin lifted and dropped one hoof. A muffled thud.

There were flat, open Valorian boats on the water, thousands of them, heavy with horses and cannon. They rowed from the anchored ships. Oars lifted and dipped in the rain.

Arin couldn't hear the Valorian command. The sound of it was lost over the sea. But he saw when Valorian soldiers began to prime the cannons. He could practically smell the black powder. For a moment, he wasn't on his horse with a sword in hand but on an unsteady boat, palms gritty with powder, hands ramming the charge home.

They'd fire even before they reached the shore.

A plea rose within him, surging hard as if unexpected, although if he'd examined himself more thoroughly earlier he would have known all along what he'd beg in this final moment, despite his promise to trust her.

Arin touched her shoulder. She startled, keyed to an extremity he knew very well.

"Change your mind," he said. "Turn back, go to the bluffs, please."

"No."

Finally, he felt the fear that infected everyone else. "Then stay close to me."

Whatever she said in reply was lost as the first explosion split and broke the world.

HE DIDN'T SEE WHERE THE FIRST CANNONBALL hit, but he heard the sick thud and felt the impact judder up from the beach into his boots. The shriek of horses, human cries. Deep into the left flank. Roshar's army returned fire, mostly missing, because it was harder to hit moving targets on the waves. Geysers sprayed where cannonballs hit the water. One speeding iron ball punched into a boat and splintered it. Horses and men slid into the sea.

Black smoke plumed across the beach.

The first Valorian boats nudged up onto the shore. Soldiers dropped into the water, knee-deep. Horses were led down ramps. Cannons would soon follow.

"Shatter them all," Roshar ordered.

His gunners riddled the first wave of Valorians. But there was a second wave, and a third, and finally a Valorian cannon was maneuvered into position to blast one flank of gunners into a bloody smoking screaming heap.

Arin's horse reared. He wrestled it down, pressing his weight into his seat. He held the horse between his tight knees, preferring that than to tug at the bit, and he was distracted, everything was loud. Even after he calmed his horse he no longer trusted it to obey him. Then came a little sound he shouldn't have been able to hear, a dry swallow.

He glanced at Kestrel. Javelin—magnificent warhorse, steady beast—was stock-still. So was she. But her skin stretched thinly across her cheekbones. Her eyes were too large and pale.

Please, Arin prayed. *Give her your mercy.*

His god was amused. *If she doesn't believe in me, how can I believe in her?*

The general had landed. Arin could see him. He saw Kestrel see him. Several columns of Valorians pushed up from the shore onto the beach.

Roshar ordered his vanguard forward.

Death bit the nape of Arin's neck, where a cat bites her kitten. *Maybe,* death murmured, *I'll show her the same kind of mercy I'll show you.*

Arin's heart thumped. His blood rushed. He put a free hand to his stinging skin and drew it away, expecting blood.

Nothing.

A push of damp wind at his back. The trembling of the horse beneath him. A cannon boomed. The animal screamed, reared again. It plunged forward, through the lines of the vanguard, right into the oncoming Valorians.

She couldn't see Arin. She couldn't see him, and it felt as if she couldn't see anything at all.

The cannons held their breath. Vanguard crashed into

vanguard. She saw the collision happen a few ranks ahead. The spurt of blood. Hideous masks of fear and hatred. An arm shorn from the shoulder. Bodies shoved from horses, crumpled into the sand beneath hooves. And the cruelty of what she couldn't see.

Where *was* he?

Javelin hadn't moved. He was stone, which made her realize that she was, too. One hand clutched a sword as if she could squeeze the hilt into nonexistence. A sword. Her, with a sword. She had no skill for it.

Terror snaked through her, slipping and winding.

The Valorians hadn't yet broken through the front lines. Artillery couldn't be used, for fear of hitting one's own. There were a few brief moments before an enemy reached her.

And maybe ahead, somewhere, was what she realized she feared most of all. Arin's emptied eyes. His blood spilling, spent.

She kneed Javelin forward and rode up through the ranks.

He was nearly thrown from his horse. A Valorian slammed into him. Arin caught a blow to his armored chest, sucked in a sharp breath. Felt the bruise, maybe a fracture. No blood, he thought. For the smallest of moments it was hard to focus, hard even to know what his hands were doing or what he saw and whom he fought. He asked his god a formless question. If he could have put it into words, he would have asked if the god's mercy was to have let him live for so long. Twenty years is better than nine. Or was the god's mercy to die *this* way, and not a different, worse way? Or simply to come home, to the haven of the gods. Mother, father, sister. A wash of loneliness, of longing, of *yes*. Yes, maybe that was it, maybe that was what the god had meant. Mercy. A promise: that the final moment before this world became the next one would be as sweet as love.

But he could not think this, or understand it. He simply felt it, this question that was many questions condensed into an iron bead, the head of a pin, a tiny hard point of dread and hope and relief.

His *horse*. His damned horse. The animal kept straining its will against Arin's. This horse was going to get him killed. Arin tried to feel worried.

His sword opened someone's belly. He wasn't sure how. His blade shouldn't have gotten past Valorian armor. But entrails probed out of a gash. A slow, wet unfolding.

Arin ended it.

To come home, mused his god, who had been able to take the iron bead of Arin's heart and make it a feather, and could separate each barb from the other, all along down the quill. The god ran a finger down the unnaturally fanned vane. *Is that what you think I meant by mercy? Is that what you want?*

Well, Arin.

Well.

Kestrel didn't understand why no one attacked her. Then she did, and felt stupid and grateful. Her armor. Her Valorian looks. Roshar's forces knew her, knew her horse. But to the Valorians, she seemed to be one of their own. Oddly positioned, if they thought about it, but no one thought. They gurgled from cut throats. They drove swords so far into bodies that their fists vanished inside someone else's flesh.

She moved Javelin among them—Valorian, Dacran, Herrani. *Little ghost.* Yes. She didn't exist. Even when someone's blood sprayed her cheek, it didn't feel real. No one touched her.

Until she saw Roshar hack a sword from someone's grip, smash his shield into the Valorian's nose, and slice in at the neck. The prince kneed his horse out of the path of the body's fall. He wheeled his horse and saw Kestrel. "Where's Arin?" he shouted.

Kestrel's voice didn't work. "I don't know," she finally said, the whisper hoarse. Roshar wouldn't have been able to hear even if he weren't several feet away.

But a nearby Valorian heard. He'd seen the look between her and the prince, had heard them speak the Dacran tongue. A cavalry officer. He shouldered his horse into hers. Reached. Grabbed her throat.

"A scout?" His dark eyes were narrow, his teeth bared. "In the vanguard? Name your regiment."

She gasped.

"Traitor." He knocked the sword from her limp hand.

"Kestrel!" Roshar.

Too far away.

She strained to breathe. She didn't break his gaze. Whispering something she knew he couldn't hear, she watched the Valorian lean forward, loosen his grip just slightly. Kestrel reached for her dagger and drove it into his armpit.

He grunted, let go. She jerked her dagger free and pierced his throat.

His weight sagged against her. He was gasping in her ear, the sound sticky and wet, blood gushing onto her as she tried to keep her seat, tried to push the armored officer away. But his horse balked. The Valorian gripped her, his brown eyes staring, vengeful, fading. With the last of his strength, he dragged her down with him. He pulled her from her horse.

Arin's horse was bad, but it'd be much worse to be without one. He cut a space around him. The frontier between army and army was dissolving. Kestrel must be several ranks behind him. The Valorians would soon reach her. *Stay close,* he'd said. His anxiety rose, making him vicious. Some part of him stared at what his hands and body did, but the larger part of him grew yet larger, and took satisfaction. There was pleasure and murder along with worry at his pleasure. Running through all of it: a sheer stream of fear. *Stay close.*

He turned his horse back.

And if he couldn't find her?

Farther back. Still farther.

The Valorians had already eaten their way into the rank where she and Javelin had been.

His lungs squeezed shut. *Where?* he demanded.

The general? his god coyly answered. *Allow me to point you the way . . .*

Arin's nerves screamed.

Open your eyes, death said.

Look, my love, and see.

Arin did. He saw, not far away, Javelin standing amid the boil of war. His rider was gone.

Kestrel's cheek was in the sand. Her mouth was full of it. She coughed and spat, her back and shoulders sinking into the beach, and pushed at the dead body heaped onto her. She tried to lever it off. Her arms gave out. She saw the misting sky. Her horse, close. She pushed again at the officer. His armor made him heavier. She was soaked with his blood. She felt it still pumping, heard the chaos around her. Panic stitched down her spine.

She shoved. The body didn't budge. She tried harder, felt the weight press her chest. Finally, she screamed.

Something slammed into Arin. He kept his seat, wheeled to see his attacker, saw the Valorian's grin—and then, too late, the serrated steel along the length of the man's boot. Arin noticed it right before the Valorian used his foot like a knife and slashed the exposed ribs of Arin's horse.

The animal's cry pierced Arin's ears. He was pitched to the ground.

In war, her father sometimes said, *you might live, you might die. But if you panic, death is the only outcome.*

She hated him for his coolness. His rules.

But.

The body crushed her.

But . . . the sand.

She tried to see if she could turn onto her belly. Wriggling, she shifted beneath the body. As she strained to turn, she waited for someone to notice her, and attack. She waited for hooves to crush her skull. But Javelin stood solidly, right where he'd been the moment she'd fallen. Cavalry maneuvered around the harmless horse. No one was looking at the ground.

Worming into the sand, she flipped onto her front and began to dig, sweeping the sand away from her as if swimming. She dug her elbows into the trough she'd made and pulled.

She slipped free.

Arin scrambled to his feet. Dodged—just in time—the kick of the serrated boot to his head. With both hands (where was his sword?), he seized the Valorian's ankle and hauled the man off his horse.

Kestrel's shaking hands sifted through the sand for her dagger. Her dagger. She must find it. She could not lose it.

When she found the ridge of it beneath a veil of red sand, tears pricked her eyes. She seized its hilt.

Javelin was steady, waiting for her. She wanted to lean against him and press her face into his hide. She wanted to become a horse so that she could thank him in a way he would understand.

She went to mount him—then saw, over the rise of her saddle, Arin.

From the beach, Arin snatched a sword—his? didn't matter—and was already swiping it down through the air toward the fallen Valorian's neck when the man surged to his feet, struck Arin's blade aside with his own, and drove its point toward Arin.

Arin countered, heard the skittering of steel against steel, and felt the vibration, the pressure. He felt the pressure give. The man's blade sank for an instant.

But it was a trick. In that moment of seeming weakness, the Valorian's other hand went for his dagger, which he stabbed into a gap where Arin's armor joined.

Kestrel was stumbling forward on the sand, her legs too sluggish; she couldn't move fast enough. The Valorian's back was to her. She could see Arin's face, the crease between his brows, the inward quality of his expression. And then something shifting: a flare, a recognition.

The Valorian stabbed. Arin cried out.

The dagger bit into his ribs. Pain laced up his side. He struck back, sword dancing harmlessly down the Valorian's armor, doing no more damage than to cut the laces of the man's right boot.

"You're mine," said the Valorian.

Which was what death always said. Arin, surprised to hear the god's words come from a human mouth, faltered. He felt strange. He thought, *Ah*. He thought, *Grateful*. He welcomed the god's warning, realized that he'd always wanted to know before it happened. He wouldn't want to blink too suddenly out of this life.

But he loved this life. He loved the girl in it.

His heart punched hard, rebelled.

Too late. The base of the Valorian's blade was coming at his head, angled for his neck.

Arin tried to duck. The hilt slammed into his temple.

Darkness bled across his vision. He couldn't feel his legs. He tried to hear his god, but he heard only silence, and then he heard nothing at all.

SHE SAW ARIN GO DOWN. SHE SKIDDED IN THE sand as she ran, her ears roaring. Her mind closed over. A shaking dread.

A few paces away. Her dagger was tight in her hand. The Valorian's back was an armored wall. The man raised his sword again. He didn't hear her come at him.

But where, *where*? She had a dagger, but there was nowhere to stab—not the back of the neck, which she couldn't reach, not the torso or even the legs. He was armored from shoulders to boots. *A dagger wants flesh,* her father would say. *Find it.*

A great pressure in her chest. Desperation as she came up behind. She didn't know what to do, couldn't think, and then it was as if someone else noticed the looseness at the top of one of the man's boots and dropped her to her knees in the sand. She seized the boot's top, yanked it back, and slashed the ropy tendon at the ankle.

He screamed. She seemed to feel him feel the excruciating pain of the cut tendon curling up into his calf. His collapse.

The pumping agony. How a girl climbed onto him—feral, foxlike. But: a girl? But: her hair, her skin, her eyes, her armor. Not the enemy. The enemy?

Then the dagger found his throat and he knew exactly what she was.

Her hand, her arm: bright red. She couldn't let go of the dagger. She made herself sheathe it. She needed her hands, she needed Arin.

The sprawl of him. She was weeping, crouched in the sand, empty fingers wild when she reached him, searched him, found the dagger in his side, his blackened brow, purple cheek, split skin. She touched his face and felt his head loll. A pulse? Or just her own pulse? Her body vibrated with it, she couldn't keep her fingers steady against the hollow under his jaw.

She made herself look again at the dagger in his side, and unbuckled the armor to see better.

Only the tip of the dagger had entered the flesh. It was stuck between the ribs. Her sudden hope was savage.

She didn't want to pull the dagger out—she had nothing to stanch a flow of blood—and returned her attention to Arin's head. This time, when her fingers went for his pulse, she found it and knew it to be his. Her tears flowed fresh.

The wound in his side was minor. Yet a blow to the head can do anything, can kill, paralyze, take away his senses, his mind. It could make him sleep forever.

"Arin, wake up."

Once the words came, they didn't stop.

"We have to move. We can't stay here."

"Please."

"Please wake up."

"I love you. Don't leave me. Wake up."

"Listen to me. Arin?"

"Listen."

Someone was weeping. Her tears fell warm on his brow, his lashes, his mouth.

Don't cry, he tried to say.

Please listen, she said.

He would, of course he would. How could she think that he wouldn't?

This felt familiar. Unreal. He had the sense that this had happened before, or *would* happen, that this was either an echo or its source. If he opened his eyes, the world would double. His skull throbbed. Stones weighted his eyes. He was covered with earth. Thick and loamy and loose. A comfort. It eased the nauseating ache.

Yet there were no stones, no earth. A part of him knew this, the same part that clung to the woman's voice.

Her voice was breaking apart. He heard it turn horrible. Soon, he realized, she would scream.

"Don't," he managed, and opened his eyes, and was sick.

He wondered at it, faintly, her expression: that mix of anguish and relief. Her hands were wholly still for a moment, then instantly busy, lifting a canteen of water to his mouth, trying to worm under his weight and lift. Too heavy. "I'm sorry," she said. "Arin, you must get up."

"I don't think I can."

"Yes. Just to Javelin. Come on." She was tugging at

him—shoulders, arms. He didn't have the heart to tell her to stop, that the ache in his head was monstrous, that every jostle hurt. He tried to focus, and saw Javelin standing nearby, saw the undulating crush of soldiers and metal. Fear entered him. This little peace that sheltered him and Kestrel couldn't last long. Impossible, that no one had noticed them, that no one had already brought a sword slicing through her neck as she knelt beside him, and pulled, and begged.

"Go," he told her.

She recoiled. "No."

"It's all right." He tried to touch her cheek, but either his vision was wrong or his hand was. He fumbled, touched her nose and lips. "I don't mind."

"Don't say that."

"Ride fast. Far."

"Don't ask me that. You wouldn't do that. You would never leave me."

But it's different, he tried to say, then became lost in what he wanted to explain, that this . . . her—what? sorrow?—was dear to him, unexpected. So hard, to heave words into his mouth. He realized his hand had fallen.

Her face screwed into an expression he couldn't read. "Get up," she said through her teeth.

"Please. Go."

She curled fingers over the rim of his leather breastplate and gripped it. "*Make* me."

This time, Arin recognized her expression. Determination. He closed his eyes so that he wouldn't see. You don't owe me anything, he would have said. You'll lose no honor if you leave. Arin wondered if she knew the way her whole being could become a vow.

He would say, *Tell me why you can't leave.* Maybe, if his head were clearer, he would know why without asking. For now, he saw only her determination and its danger.

Was this his god's version of mercy: that she would die on this beach with him?

Unbearable.

Through the thump of his head, he discovered a different pain. Traveled down it. His side. His ribs. A dagger. He pulled it out. She made an appalled cry. His side became sticky. He dug the dagger into the sand and gripped her shoulder with his other hand. Felt his head split. Arin pushed himself up, levering off the dagger.

He tried to distance himself from what he was doing, from the spasm that racked his body as he was sick again. On his knees, sky dark—rain? Kestrel's shoulder, frail-seeming in his hand. Not able to bear his weight, surely, but she did, she strained to get him to his feet. Each stumble hurt, and he dreaded how it would be to mount Javelin and ride, but he would.

He did, and she was with him. Eventually he couldn't tell if the sky was raining and dark or if his mind was. Everything was black and wet. As the horse moved beneath them, a quiet grew through the pain. A feeling floated over him like sillage from a rare perfume. He seemed to hear the tinkle of a glass stopper lifted from a tiny flacon. The release of scent. How was it possible, to smell flowers that weren't there?

Arin became aware that his thoughts were hard to hold.

They vanished into smoke. It didn't matter. He let them go. Smoke, perfume, rain. All lovely, unlasting. The same, maybe, as whatever had made Kestrel swear that she wouldn't leave him.

He wasn't sure what had made her do that. But it had been something. It had been real.

This, he wouldn't relinquish. This, he would hold and remember.

He saw Kestrel's hands on the reins. He felt his body slacken. Hoofbeats hammered his skull.

Someone—deep voice—swore. "You *tied* him to you?"

"He nearly fell," he heard Kestrel say.

Arin opened his eyes. Roshar was untying the rope that bound him to Kestrel, the prince's gaze fixed on the knots. It wasn't like Roshar not to look at him. "Well, *that* was stupid," the prince told her. "Didn't you consider that if he truly started to fall, his weight would drag you off, too?"

She was silent. She had considered this. Arin could tell from her silence.

Roshar's arm went around Arin's waist. "Come on," he said. Arin sort of slid down from the horse and was steadied and held.

"You're bleeding on me," Roshar complained.

Yes. Arin supposed that he was bleeding. But his head. The ache was worse than anything. Arin let himself sag against Roshar, dropped his brow to the man's shoulder. Then he made himself open his eyes again.

Kestrel stood to the side, arms tightly held to her chest.

Beyond her lay an army encampment, hastily thrown together. Smaller than before.

"What happened?" Arin asked.

"A bloodbath," Roshar said. "We retreated. They seized
the beach. I blame you."

Kestrel sucked in a furious breath.

"He doesn't mean that," Arin muttered.

"Are you going to make me carry you?" Roshar said.

Kestrel said something sharp. It wasn't that Arin didn't
hear the words; he was just too weary to absorb them. He
heard Roshar's slow, drawling tones, Kestrel's hiss. Arin
wanted to tell her, *He's hiding from you*. He wanted to say,
He's worried. Arin was suddenly overwhelmed by their worry,
by how everything was so unspoken. He stepped away from
Roshar's supporting arm and began to walk with no real destination in mind.

Roshar called him a filthy name. Caught him before
he fell.

"Bone and blood and breath of the goddess," Roshar said.
"What were you trying to prove?"

Arin was on his back in Roshar's bed, in his tent. The
prince stood next to his bedside, posture taut and jumpy.

A heavy warmth rested on Arin's chest. Kestrel, her head
pillowed against him as she slept, knelt on the ground, her
upper body loosely draped over the bed's edge. His armor
and tunic were gone. His ribs were bandaged. Her palm lay
on his belly.

"I would have carried you," Roshar said more quietly.

"I know."

Arin's voice woke her. She lifted her head, moved away. Her mouth was thin, her eyes smudged with shadows, braid half undone.

"The war," Arin asked.

Kestrel and Roshar exchanged a glance.

"That bad?"

"Rest, Arin," Kestrel said.

Roshar clicked his teeth. "Not too much. He keeps drifting in and out. Not good for a head injury like that. Keep him awake. Don't let him sleep." To Arin, he said, "I can't stay. I have to organize the retreat to the city."

Arin's stomach lurched. Retreat to the city was a last resort. "Don't." He scrounged for a better idea. Kestrel looked silent and grim.

Roshar said, "I *want* to stay with you. I can't."

Arin lifted his palm to his friend's cheek. This startled the prince. Arin saw him remember the Herrani gesture, yet hesitate before returning it. It made Arin sad. His hand fell. He traced a carving in the cot's frame, feeling awkward to have displaced Roshar from his bed. "Where will you sleep?"

"Have no fear. Many a bed would welcome me."

After the prince left, Arin asked Kestrel, "Why did the battle go so badly?"

The question upset her. "That's what you want to know?"

"It's important."

"More important than how you nearly died?"

"But I didn't."

Her voice was clipped. "My father has too much black powder. Too many soldiers. Too much experience."

"But how exactly did he win?"

"A full frontal attack was enough, once he eliminated the guns. I didn't see everything that happened."

Guilt pulsed with the doubled heartbeat in his head. "Because you rode away with me."

Her eyes welled.

"I'm sorry," he said. "Talk of something else. What you like."

She opened her mouth. Closed it. Her voice hushed, she said, "Do you remember the mosaic?"

"Yes."

"How everything fit. As if each tile wanted to be next to each other."

"Yes." But he was confused, he wasn't sure what the mosaic meant to her, or why she thought of it now. She talked about it as if trying to explain that left was really right, or that it was both left and right . . . which made him realize that he knew that left and right were important, but he couldn't grasp their meaning or difference. He closed his eyes.

"Arin, don't."

"Only for a little."

"No." She gripped his hand.

"Shh."

"Stories," she blurted. "The mosaic told stories, didn't it?"

"Yes, old ones."

"I'll tell them to you."

His eyes cracked open. He didn't remember closing them. "You know those tales?"

"Yes."

She didn't. This became clear as she began to tell them. She knew bits and pieces, cobbled together in ways that would have made him smile if smiling didn't hurt. "You," he breathed, "are such a faker."

"Don't interrupt."

Mostly pure invention. She remembered the images—it pleased him, how vividly she knew the temple floor's details. Which god curled around which, or how the snake's tongue forked into three. But the stories she told had little to do with his religion. Sometimes they didn't even make sense.

"Do this again," he said, "when I have strength to laugh."

"As bad as that?"

"Mmm. Maybe not. For a Valorian."

But eventually everything grew slow, unthreaded. He thought of raw cotton pulled apart, fibers trailing. Maybe Kestrel had talked for hours. He didn't know. When had she rested her cheek against his heart again? His chest rose and fell.

"Arin."

"I know. I shouldn't sleep. But I'm so tired."

She threatened him. He didn't hear the whole of it.

"Lie with me," he murmured. It bothered him to think of her kneeling on the ground.

"Promise not to sleep."

"I promise."

But he didn't mean it. He knew what would happen. She slipped in beside him. Everything became too soft, too dark, too velvet. He sank into sleep. He sighed, and let go.

WHEN SHE WOKE, HE WAS GONE.

Kestrel's heart crashed against her ribs and didn't let up, not even when she pushed her way out of the tent and found Arin making tea under the hollowed blue of a near-dawn sky. He stoked the little fire.

"What do you think you're doing?" she demanded.

"I found a box of tea in the tent." Arin saw her expression. "Roshar won't mind."

"*I* mind."

His gaze traveled between her and the pot of boiling water. "What's wrong?"

"You shouldn't have slept."

"I'm better for it."

Maybe. But it hurt her to see his face, the inky bruise that spread over his brow and cheek and into the corner of his eye. The broken skin where he'd been struck at his temple. He wore a dirty tunic, perhaps because he didn't want to soil a clean one; dried blood flaked the skin of his bare arms. An awful bubble expanded inside her chest. "*I shouldn't have slept.*"

"You needed to. The battle. The ride. It can't have been easy."

"No, it wasn't."

Arin turned the closed tea box in his hands. The dry leaves whispered. "Thank you for saving me."

"I thought you were dead. That you would die."

He considered the box. "I know how hard it is to watch someone die."

"Not 'someone.' *You*, Arin."

He nodded, but winced, set the box aside, and didn't seem to truly hear her.

She sank to sit by the fire, her crooked arm resting on a bent knee drawn to her chest. She pressed her mouth and chin against her inner arm. "You're still in pain."

"Not so much anymore, which is why you must talk to me."

"Arin, I am."

"About the war."

She looked at him.

He said, "We can't retreat to the city."

"We can't face them in open battle. Not the entire Valorian force. Lerralen proved that."

"Inviting them to lay siege to the city is no answer. I already tried once to hold the city against the general. He made short work of its defenses. He breached the wall."

"It's repaired. This time, you have the east as an ally."

"If you weren't trying to protect me right now with false optimism, what would you really say?"

The sky had lightened. She heard the camp begin to stir.

"Be honest, Kestrel."

"About the war." Her voice was flat.

His expression shifted slightly. He set his thumb against his jaw, fanning dirty fingers over his scarred cheek. "Is there something else?"

His fatigue. His bruises. The pain he was trying to hide. The way her heart had grown scales. But inside: hot as a live coal.

He said, "We both know what will happen if we retreat to the city."

So she said it. "The east might look at its losses, see a likely defeat, and leave . . . even if Roshar wants to stay."

"And then it's over." Arin's gray eyes were naked. "I can't lose. There'll be nothing left for me if I do."

"That's not true."

But he had stood. The camp was awake. His small fire had gone out. The tea, forgotten, had cooled.

She kept her head bowed. "We must retreat inland until I think of something better."

Arin stepped close to her, his footfalls hushed by the pale, sandy earth with its wisps of grass. He touched the nape of her neck, fingertips brushing down to the first bones of her back. He gently hooked the collar of her shirt.

Her skin sang so loud that she couldn't think of any words, let alone the right ones, and by the time she knew that she should, that it was *now*, that it wouldn't hurt to say what she felt, that she could give her love to someone without being broken for it, Arin had already gone.

Roshar had a litter brought to Arin, who glanced at it and the men assigned to carry it. "No," said Arin.

"Idiot," the prince sneered. "You were knocked unconscious. You look like hell. Get in the litter."

"I'll go in a cart," Arin said, referring to wagons that carried the wounded. "I don't need special treatment."

"Oh yes, you do."

Kestrel had never seen Roshar so angry.

"Why?" Arin squinted at him. "Because of your concern or because you want to send a message to the army?"

Kestrel could think of two messages: to show the Dacrans that the supposedly god-touched Herrani leader was weak, or to show the Herrani that the eastern prince valued Arin. Maybe both.

Roshar's mouth twitched into an unhappy smile.

"Then I'll ride," Arin said.

When the day ended and the army set camp on a low hill whose bushes bore thick, oily green leaves, Roshar stood near his tent as an officer set it up. The prince's fingers drummed the muscles of his crossed arms.

Kestrel didn't know where Arin was. She thought he'd gone to water his new horse at a stream near camp, but when Roshar's tent was up and the sun down, and Arin hadn't returned, an icy mist of anxiety stole over her.

"He'll be more comfortable there." Roshar jerked his chin at his tent.

"And you?" she asked.

He shrugged.

"Arin won't like it."

"I don't care." Then he added, the words coming in a rush, "The litter wasn't symbolic. No hidden message. Not everyone speaks in code. I just want him to be well."

Slowly, she said, "I think that he is." She had watched him during the day's ride, and although his face had grown drawn, it seemed more from weariness than pain. He'd easily kept his seat and met her sidelong looks with a small smile. Her concern had lessened.

Not entirely, though. Not enough to keep her from searching the camp after Roshar had left her by his pitched tent. Not enough to uncurl her fingers, squeezed into fists after the sky's humid indigo had darkened. She returned to the tent and lit a lantern. Inside, she chafed her arms as if cold, eyeing the burning wick. She meant to measure it. After it burned down to a certain mark, she'd search for him. But the wick had barely begun to sizzle before she seized the lantern's handle, hurried toward the tent's canvas door . . . and smacked into Arin as he entered.

She gasped. "Where have you been?"

He ran a hand through his wet hair, glanced down at his damp shirt. He smelled of soap. "Well."

"A *bath*?"

" 'Bath' makes a cold creek sound so glamorous."

"In the dark?"

"There's a moon."

"I was ready to make Roshar help me find you."

"Oh, I saw him. He directed me here—emphatically."

Arin lifted his brows, impressed. "The wording he used was very creative."

Kestrel became aware of how close she stood to Arin. The lifted lamp gilded his face, illuminating the peak of the tent's apex above. It radiated a small heat between him and her. She moved away.

He touched the clenched hand that held the lamp. "Little Fists, what's wrong? Both you and Roshar are angry. All I've done is get hit on the head."

"And sleep. And ride. And *bathe*."

"Well, I was disgusting."

Kestrel turned and strode to the table. She set the lamp down, practically slamming it.

Arin followed. "I don't know how to prove to you that I'm all right."

She kept her back to him. Something terrible was clawing up her throat.

"I was lucky," Arin said. "I had you. And a hard head. And the grace of my god."

"*Damn* your god."

Arin caught her arm above the elbow. She turned to face him. All trace of humor had left his face. His eyes were wide, urgent. "Don't say that."

"Why not? I can say anything. Anything except what really matters."

"Kestrel, take it back. You'll offend him."

"Your god risks you."

"He protects me."

"You're his plaything."

"You're wrong. He loves me."

Saying those words made him look so alone. He reminded her of sails curved by the wind, full and yet empty at the same time. She found that she was jealous of his god. The sudden jealousy held her so hard in its grip that she couldn't breathe.

"It's true," Arin insisted.

She saw then that she had hurt him, that his god's love was all the more precious to him because of his fear that he would find it nowhere else. Her anger rinsed away. "I'm sorry. I'm sorry. I ask your pardon. His, too."

Arin released her, his relief plain.

"I'm not really angry at a god," she said, "or you."

His brow creased.

"All right, yes, you, a little." She gently thumped his chest, then rested her palm flat and wide against his heart. He went very still. "Why is it so hard for you to take care of yourself?"

He was silent. Her thumb rested in the hollow of his collarbone. She felt his pulse jolt, and her own answered. It sped, it felt like it was slipping from her grasp, and that she'd never catch her heart, never pin it down, never keep it safe.

She did not want to keep it safe.

She said, "Why can't you see that people care for you?"

She said, "*I* care for you."

"I know that you care. But . . ." He searched her face. "Anyone would, for a friend."

"You're more than a friend."

"On the battlefield, you stayed—"

"Of course I did."

"You have a strong sense of honor. You always have. I think you think you owe me something."

"I stayed because I love you."

He flinched and looked away. "You don't mean that."

"Yes, I do."

The night outside seemed to swell against the tent. The lamp smelled like a hot stone. His face slowly opened. He touched her hand as it pressed against his heart. His caress was light, secret, almost unsure of her knuckles, the thin tendons as strong as bone. She felt him become sure.

There was no sound when he kissed her. None when she unthreaded the ties of his shirt and found his skin.

He grasped her dagger belt, flexed his fingers once around the leather, then simply held on. He whispered something into her mouth that was almost a word. It lost its shape, became something else.

He let go. She heard the brush of linen as he drew the shirt over his head, his fingertips grazing the tent's sloped ceiling as if for balance. His ribs were bound with gauze, his body marked by scars. Old ones, badly healed and raised. Others, pink and fresh. His shoulders bore pale gouges; they looked like sets of claws, almost deliberate, like tattoos. Curious, she touched them.

He bit his lip.

"That hurts?"

"No."

"What *is* this? What happened?"

"I'll tell you," he said. "Later."

His hand strayed over her shirt, which was eastern, as Arin's was, with no collar. Threadbare in places. Frayed at the neck. He worried the cloth there, rubbing it between fingers and thumb. Then he drew her shirt open, and she felt as if reality had grown larger and tremulous: a drop of water on the point of a pin.

"Kestrel . . . I've never—"

She whispered that this was new to her, too.

There was a long pause. "Are you certain you want—"

"Yes."

"Because . . ."

"Arin."

"Maybe you—"

"Arin." She laughed, and then so did he, aware that they'd already found the bed. Words had fallen away. Maybe the words lay on the earth, nestled among clothes, curled into the undone dagger belt. Maybe later, language would be recovered and pieced together. Made to make sense. But not now. Now there was touch and taste and sound.

When he eased into her, she was glad for the burning lamp, the fuzzy glow of it on his skin. The way it showed the black fall of his wet hair, the flesh and scars that made him. She didn't look away.

Later, when they were quiet, he looked down at her where she lay. Stretched out alongside her, Arin propped himself up on one elbow. "I think that I'm not awake." His fingertips floated over her: nose, eyelashes, messy braid, shoulder. "Beautiful."

She smiled. "Like you."

Arin made a skeptical cough, scrunched his face. He

found the end of her braid and paintbrushed it across her cheek.

"It's true," she told him. "You never believe me when I say it."

The lamp's wick fizzed and sparked in its oil. It would soon go out.

"I love your eyes," she said. "I have from the first."

"They're common."

"No, they're not." She traced his scarred face. "This." He shivered. "I love this." She bit him on the jaw. "And this." She continued to touch him.

"Really?"

"Yes."

"This, too." Not quite a question.

"That, too."

She felt laughter travel through him, and something else, quieter and more intense. "Your mouth," she said, "is not bad."

"Not bad?"

"Quite tolerable."

He cocked one brow. "I'll show *you*."

They stopped talking.

faces he rolled his eyes. "I want my tent back," he said.

Kestrel laughed.

She loaded Javelin's saddlebags, listening to the sounds of the army breaking camp: clatters and thumps, someone urinating against a tree, the jingle of horse tack, the sifting grate of dirt kicked over a fire. Javelin flicked his tail. Nearby, Arin was checking the hooves of his horse—a mare, one that took a moment for Kestrel to recognize. His previous horse had been left on the beach. This one's master was probably dead.

Arin adjusted the saddle's girth. As he ran his hands again over the horse, he said, "Why do you think we haven't been attacked yet?"

She slowly buckled an open saddlebag.

He said, "This isn't what I want to ask you."

He had sleepless eyes, his mouth a little swollen, the deeply tanned skin somehow burnished. Kestrel thought that she, too, must look like this: polished by desire, the way a river stone holds a luster from having been made so smooth.

"I wish . . ." He caught himself, and from the way he was looking around the busy camp, she thought that Arin had almost said that he wished there was no war, or that they could lose themselves in each other without losing everything.

But this wasn't entirely true for him or for her, and she needed to win the war as much as he did. "We haven't been attacked because my father's strengthening his foothold on the beach. Supplying his troops. Recovering, too. It was a costly victory for them. He doesn't need to eliminate us now, when his forces will be stronger later. But he'll move soon. He'll take territory along the road all the way to the city."

"Also?" Arin looked at her.

"Also," she said reluctantly, "he thinks he'll conquer the city with little trouble."

"We're herding ourselves into a trap."

"Yes, but . . ."

He waited.

"It buys us time," she said. "If we *are* retreating instead of simply *seeming* like we're retreating, and his scouts report this, then when we're able to find a way to counterattack it will catch him off guard. Sometimes it's better to *do* instead of pretend—especially if you don't intend to follow what you're doing to the conclusion your enemy expects."

"What *do* you intend?"

She stroked Javelin's nose. "I'm not sure."

"Black powder is the biggest problem. If the Valorians didn't have so much of it, we'd stand a chance against them."

"Well."

"What?"

"I could destroy it."

He rubbed the back of his neck and crinkled his brow as he listened to her explain what she had in mind.

He didn't like it.

"You know I'll go anyway."

He left his horse, dusting his hands free of the dirt from the animal's hooves. When he came close, it felt as if she'd come in out of the cold and stood next to a fire. Arin touched the dagger at her hip and ran a thumb over the symbol on its hilt: the circle within a circle.

"The god of souls," Kestrel said. "It's his symbol."

"Hers," he corrected gently.

Kestrel wasn't sure how long she'd known what the symbol meant. Maybe for a long time. Or maybe she'd only realized it last night. It was the kind of knowledge that, once it enters you, seems like it's lived there forever.

His expression was soft and entranced and puzzled. "Do you feel changed? I feel changed."

"Yes," she whispered.

He smiled. "It's strange."

And so it was.

"We could reach Lerralen by nightfall," she said, "if we press the horses. Will you come with me?"

"Ah, Kestrel, that's something you never need to ask."

The sun was gone when they reached the wind-twisted bushes that hedged the beach. Beyond were the fires of the enemy's camp; the blue-black air smelled of smoke and salt.

Kestrel cleaned her Valorian armor, strapped on a traditional-looking dagger she had taken from the arms supply wagon, and wordlessly handed Arin the one he'd made for her.

"I don't love my role in this particular mission," he said. "It's mostly watching you saunter into danger."

"You forget."

"That? That's nothing."

"You could get hurt."

He blinked. "No."

"You don't ever fear for yourself?"

"Not for something like this."

"Then what?"

He studied his hands. "Sometimes . . . I think of who I was. As a boy. I talk to him."

Slowly, she said, "Like you do to your god?"

"It's different. Or maybe I think about him like my god thinks about me. I've made promises to the child. I worry I won't be able to keep them."

"What have you promised?"

"Revenge."

"You'll have it."

Arin nodded, but more in simple acknowledgment than actual confidence.

She looked at him through the smoky night. Just light enough to see his expression, and dark enough that his body smudged into the shadows. Soon, night would truly fall. Waves folded and unfolded against the shore.

"We should wait for the moon to rise," she said, "before we go down to the camp."

"And what," he murmured, "will we do while we wait?"

She brought his fingers to her lips so that he could feel her smile.

His hand traveled the length of her braid and toyed with the leather string that bound it. He untied the knot. The sound of it coming undone was as soft as a breath. He unraveled her hair, and brought her close.

When the moon was high, Kestrel and Arin gathered what they needed and made their way down to the beach, keeping close to the ragged bushes, blending in with their darkness. They waited, crouched near the edge of camp, where they could see the supply wagons, their domed canvas covers as pale as mushrooms in the moonlight.

Finally, a sentry on his rounds walked close to their hiding spot. In one swift movement, Arin surged up, clamped a hand over the sentry's mouth, and dragged him down to the sand.

"Not a sound," Arin hissed at the sentry, the point of his dagger pricking the hollow behind the man's ear. Arin forced the sentry's face to turn up to the moon. Eyes wide. Skin strained and white. "Tell us which wagon holds the black powder."

The sentry shook his head.

"Do you remember," Arin whispered, "the punishment for runaway slaves? No? Let me remind you." He lightly drew his dagger over the man's ear, down the tip of his nose. "Which wagon?"

The Valorian shook his head again, but this time his gaze jerked in the direction of one of the larger wagons.

Arin glanced at Kestrel. Enough? his eyes asked. Yes, she mouthed, but—"Don't," she whispered, ill at the sight of the sentry pressed down in the sand, his eyes as dark as her childhood friend's, as that of any Valorian child. They were gleaming, glassy with the kind of fear a child eventually learns how to hide. But death will do that. It makes you unlearn all you know. "Don't," she told Arin again.

He hesitated, then slammed the pommel of his dagger against the man's head, knocking him unconscious.

"Be swift," Arin told her.

She cut into the small bag of black powder tied to her waist. She felt grit flow thinly from the hole. Then she straightened and walked into the camp.

She kept her head down, her tight braid trailing over one shoulder. Her face was dirty, she reminded herself as she passed campfires. She was changed. Her hair had reddened— was redder still, by firelight. No one would recognize her, surely. Not in armor. Not like this, with no trace of cosmetics, no finery, no silk or jewels or glittering gold engagement mark. She was not herself. She was simply one of them. Just another Valorian. But her throat was dry, and her stomach shrank into a stone.

The wagons weren't far off. To reassure herself, she passed her fingers through the little stream of black powder from her bag and thought about how it traced a line between Arin and her.

When she reached the wagon the sentry had glanced at, Kestrel let out a slow breath. She peered inside and saw, in the halo of moonlight through canvas, fat mounds of sacks tied with twine.

"What are you doing?" someone demanded.

Slow, very slowly, squeezing all of her sudden fear into the sound of her boot shifting in the sand, Kestrel turned.

It was a guard. The woman looked Kestrel over. "What," the woman said, "does a scout like you want with that wagon?"

The small sack at Kestrel's waist felt light. It had leaked nearly all of its black powder. Could the guard see it in the shadows? "I'm verifying inventory."

"Why?"

The words sprang to her lips before she even fully remembered them. "For the glory of Valoria."

The guard drew slightly back, startled to hear the phrase that indicated a military mission whose details couldn't be discussed. "But . . . a scout?" She stared again at Kestrel's armor, whose color and material (leather, unlike the steel for officers) indicated her low rank.

Kestrel shrugged. The empty black powder bag lay slack against her hip. "It's not for you to question the general."

"Of course," the guard said immediately, and stepped aside as Kestrel moved to walk past her . . . and tried not to walk too quickly, but *wanted* to, wanted to run all the way up into the dunes.

Then it was as if a cold, marble hand rested on her shoulder, pressing her down into her boot prints.

There was no hand, she told herself. No one touched her. *Move.*

But she couldn't, just as she couldn't help the way her

gaze lifted and saw, not fifteen paces away, her father standing in the orange light of a fire.

It cracked her open. It hatched some creature of an emotion: two-headed, lumpy, leather wings, unnumbered limbs, a thing that should never have been born. Kestrel hadn't known until she saw her father's face how much she still loved him.

Wrong, that she felt this way. Wrong, that love could live with betrayal and hurt and anger.

Hate, she corrected herself.

No, a voice whispered back, the voice of a small girl.

Her father didn't see her. He was looking at the fire. His eyes were shadowed, his mouth sad.

"Trajan," someone called from across the camp. Kestrel saw the silver-headed man approach. Soldiers fell away from him like shed water. The emperor approached his general, whose face changed, becoming full of something older than she was.

Firelight striped the emperor's cheek as he leaned to murmur in her father's ear. She saw that slight smile, and remembered the pleasure the emperor took in his games, how he could make a move and wait for months to see its final play. But there was no scheme in his expression now.

Her father answered him. She stood too far away to hear what they said to one another, yet she was close enough to see that their friendship was solid and true.

Kestrel looked away. She walked toward the dunes, careful not to retrace her steps and risk smudging the line of powder that, once lit, must burn directly from Arin to the wagon. The bushes where Arin waited were thick black scribbles. Her cheeks were wet. Valorian soldiers didn't look as she passed. She wiped her face. Sand hissed under her hurried boots. She left the camp behind.

She'd almost reached the bushes when she heard someone following her.

Pacing the sand. Right in her tracks. Coming up close.

She slowed, hand on her dagger, heart in her mouth.

She turned.

"Kestrel?"

HER HAND DROPPED FROM HER DAGGER'S HILT. "Verex."

He stood awkwardly in the moonlight: long and slopey, shoulders narrow, eyes large, his fair hair ruffled and feathery. When he met her gaze, he let out such a large breath that his chest seemed to cave in. "I was so worried for you," he said.

Kestrel crossed the sand and flung herself into his open arms.

"I tried to help," he murmured.

"I know."

"I sent a key to the prison camp."

"I got it."

"I'm ashamed of myself."

"Verex."

"I couldn't do more. I wanted to. I should have."

She pulled back, stared at him. "That key was everything to me."

"Not enough. My father—"

"Did he find out?" Her blood went cold. "Did he punish you?"

"He talked as if he knew it was me. 'Well, dear boy, have you heard? A prisoner tried to escape the north. Somehow—*how*, do you think?—she laid her filthy little hands on a key.' Never acknowledging that the prisoner was you. Never accusing me of having sent the key. Just watching and smiling. He said—he told me that the prisoner was tortured. Killed. And I—" Verex's face twisted.

"I'm all right, I'm here."

He didn't look convinced.

"What did he do to you?"

Verex flopped one hand. "Nothing."

"Tell me."

"Nothing that mattered. I think he enjoyed it: that I knew, that I tried. Failed. I have my spies in the court—I must—and when you disappeared I found out too quickly what had happened to you. He wanted me to know. All the while, he said nothing of your absence, only informed me of the story he'd tell the court, and that I'd be sailing to the southern isles. He said he'd watch over Risha while I was away." Verex thrust his hands in his pockets, slumped his shoulders. "He said, 'I know how you care for the eastern princess.'"

"Did he—?"

"No." His voice went hard. "He knows that if he did anything to her I'd kill him. She's safe in the capital."

"What are you doing here? Verex, you're no fighter."

He laughed a little. "I'd have said the same of you. Yet look at you."

"You knew it was me."

"You have this way when you walk. You stride."

"I didn't expect to see the emperor here, let alone *you*."

"I'm mostly here to be looked at. The emperor came with me in tow for the morale of the troops. There've been a few military setbacks in this campaign." He peered at her. "*Your* doing?"

She wasn't sure how to answer. For the first time, it occurred to her that it might not matter that Verex was her friend. Maybe he would seize her anyway.

Maybe he'd cry an alarm.

Maybe he couldn't be her friend when it seemed so obvious that she was his people's enemy.

She took a step back, then stopped when hurt flickered across his face.

"I think," Verex said gently, "that your father knows it's your doing."

"My father?"

"I didn't make much of it before, but after the Valorian victory on the beach, an officer mentioned the ambush along the road near Errilith. Said things about Arin. What would be done to him, if caught alive."

Kestrel's stomach twisted.

"Said something about that . . . slave with the clever tricks."

In Verex's pause, she could hear the foulness of what he didn't repeat.

"Your father made no reply at first. Then: 'Not *his* tricks. Not his alone.' And the officer smirked and said, 'You mean the no-nosed barbarian.' But I don't think, now, that the general *did* mean the eastern prince. After the battle on the beach, I saw him searching . . . he went among the prisoners taken. He turned over bodies in the sand. The way he looked . . ."

"Don't tell him you saw me."

"Maybe he should know."

"Verex, don't. Swear."

Worriedly, he scanned her face. "You have my word. But . . ." He raked a hand through his fine hair, then peered at her through narrowed eyes. He lifted the empty bag at her hip, dropped it, rubbed his fingers and thumb together, and sniffed the unmistakable odor of black powder. A slow horror stole over his face. "What exactly are you doing here?"

"Just let me walk away. Forget you saw me, please."

"I can't do that. You'd make me responsible for whatever you're going to do."

"No one will get hurt if you keep people away from the supply wagons. Make up some excuse. No one will die."

"Tonight, maybe. What about tomorrow, when we need what you plan to destroy? You're after the black powder, aren't you?"

She said nothing.

Softly, he said, "I could stop you so easily, right now."

"If you did, you'd hand your father yet another victory."

He sighed. "The awful thing is, part of me wants to please him, despite everything."

"No. Please don't. You can't."

"But I *do* want to . . . *and* I hate myself for wanting to please him, and I can't think of a way to do it without hurting you. Maybe *you* could think of a way, but would never tell me. You'd fall into my father's hands again, and your father's hands, and I'd never forgive myself."

Kestrel told him that she would miss him. She told him, quietly, as the sound of waves pushed and pulled at the night, that she wished he were her brother, that she was sorry, and grateful to know him.

There was no sound other than the waves as she walked away.

When she reached Arin, he released the parted bushes and lowered the eastern crossbow he'd held cranked at the ready.

"You wouldn't have," she stated.

Arin looked at her. He certainly would.

"Verex is my friend."

Arin unloaded the crossbow. His fingers were trembling. "You greeted him like a friend," he acknowledged. "But . . ."

They both looked back toward the camp. The slender shadow of the Valorian prince slowly retraced his steps. He dissolved into the camp's firelight, a good distance from the supply wagons.

Kestrel untied the empty sack from her waist and dusted her hands, her clothes. "Matches, now."

Arin's hands still weren't sure of themselves. He fumbled with the box. She took it, struck a match, and touched it to the trail of black powder she'd left behind. It sparked, lit, and burned down the line.

They ran.

The explosion blossomed over the beach.

They stayed off the road as they rode through the dark. Their pace was slow. Moonlight painted the land. They were silent, but Kestrel knew that it couldn't be due to the same thing, because she hadn't told Arin that she'd seen her father in the Valorian camp. The sight of him lingered with her. Her love for him closed within her like a fist. Nervous, bruised. She despised it. Wasn't it the love of a beaten animal, slinking back to its master? Yet here was the truth: she missed her father.

It seemed too awful to tell Arin.

But finally, when they stopped to sleep, not bothering with a tent, just bedding down in a hollow they'd trampled in the tall grass with their boots, Arin spoke. He slid a hand under her tunic to touch her bare back, then stopped. "Is this all right?"

She wanted to explain that she hadn't thought she'd ever bear anyone's touch on her scarred back, that it should revolt him and revolt her. Yet his touch made her feel soft and new. "Yes."

He pushed the shirt up, seeking the lash marks, tracing their length. She let herself feel it, and shivered, and thought of nothing. But a tension grew. He was still, but for his hand.

Kestrel said, "What's wrong?"

"Your life would have been easier if you had married the Valorian prince."

She drew herself up so that she could face him. The scent of black powder clung to them both. His skin smelled like a blown-out candle. "But not better," she said.

It was the next day's end when they caught up with Roshar's army, which had stopped—oddly—at a time too early to make camp, and rather late for a moment's rest. More than that, it was the uncertainty of the soldiers that gave the halt a strange feeling. They looked as if they'd had no orders at all. They held ranks, but loosely, and were murmuring among themselves, armor still buckled, horses saddled. Several remained mounted. A Herrani soldier toyed with her horse's reins. A Dacran eyed her as if he wished *his* horse had reins, so that he could do something with his empty hands. When Arin and Kestrel rode up to the vanguard, all eyes lifted. Faces turned to Arin, seeking an explanation, relieved because here, at last, was an answer. But Arin didn't even understand the question.

"What has happened?" he asked the two nearest soldiers on their horses.

"Someone came for our prince," the Dacran said.

Arin glanced at Kestrel, alert to the hesitation in the Dacran's voice. Arin wondered if he needed to translate for her.

"Someone took him away?" she asked the man in his language.

The soldier clicked his teeth. *No.* "But I heard that his face became terrible, truly. That no one could look at it. Some worry that she—"

"She?"

"Brings news of the war's end. That we're to abandon the campaign and go home." The soldier glanced sideways at Arin. "Some hope for it."

"Your queen?" Arin asked.

But it was not, in fact, the queen who had come for her brother.

ROSHAR WAS WAITING ALONE OUTSIDE HIS tent. Kestrel saw what the soldier had meant about Roshar's face. She'd grown used to the prince's mutilations; she rarely noticed them anymore. But now an emotion so scored his features that his face became pure in its damage: a mask of loss, twisted with anger and shame.

Arin went to him, eyes wide with concern. He spoke swiftly in Dacran. What was wrong? What had happened?

"My sister won't speak with me." Roshar cleared his throat. "Not without you." His gaze flicked from Arin to Kestrel. "Both of you."

Then Kestrel remembered that Roshar had more than one sister.

The three of them entered the tent, the prince last, shoulders tight, eyes roaming everywhere except to where Risha stood near the tent's center, her Valorian braids gone. Her black hair was cut close to the skull in the eastern style, her eyes rimmed with royal colors, her limbs lithe. The air in the tent was hot and dense.

"Sister," Roshar began, then faltered.

She ignored him. Her gaze went to Kestrel, who didn't understand the young woman's presence here, or the animosity toward her brother, whom Risha must not have seen since having been taken hostage by the empire as a child.

"I've come to bargain," Risha said.

Visibly hurt, her brother said, "I would give you anything."

"Not with you."

"I am so sorry. Risha, little sister—"

"I trust *you*," she said to Arin. "As for this one"—she tipped her chin at Kestrel—"Verex holds her in high regard."

Roshar said, "I regret every day since I saw you last."

"What do you regret most? *This?*" She gestured at his mutilations.

"No."

"How you let our older sister persuade you?"

"Yes."

"Or when you saw the Valorians take me."

"Yes."

"Maybe it was when you explained to a child that she wouldn't be gone long, that she must pretend to be surprised when she's taken hostage. All she has to do is kill one man."

Kestrel felt Arin's tension, the way he looked at the prince. Arin's worry was plain, his hands still at his sides yet slightly open, as if his friend might shatter and Arin needed to be ready to catch the pieces.

"Could it be so hard to kill a man?" Risha continued. "Especially when we consider her talent. Look at the little girl's grace. Her skill with a blade. A prodigy, surely. Never before seen in one so young. Yes, the assassination of the Valorian emperor should be easy for her."

Then Kestrel understood.

Roshar said, "I regret it all."

"I have wondered, over the years, whether you were weak to let my sister rule you, or simply stupid."

"I didn't think—"

"About what would happen to me *after* I killed the emperor? Brother, *I* thought about it when I walked the halls of the imperial palace. When I learned their language. Played childhood games with their prince. I thought about what the Valorians would do to the little girl who murdered their emperor."

A pressure tightened Kestrel's lungs. Her father, when he had refused to be her father anymore, had transformed into something else. A block of opaque glass, maybe. She wanted to heft the weight of his betrayal and show it to Risha, to ask if it looked and weighed the same as what the princess carried, if it ever got any lighter, or could diminish like ice.

Yet Kestrel also saw the ruined expression in Roshar's eyes. Maybe she shouldn't pity him, yet she did.

Arin said, "Name what you want."

Risha settled into a teak chair. "I will never kill Verex's father. But"—she flipped her hand at the three of them—"*you* could, with my help. Get rid of the emperor, and you can win this war without open battle."

"Wait," Kestrel said. Cautious, focused now, she said, "You're not even supposed to be here. Verex said you were safe at court."

At the sound of Verex's name, some of the anger left Risha. "Verex had left. There was nothing to hold me there. I escaped."

"And found your way here? So easily?"

The princess shrugged. "It's not hard to find safe passage if you're willing to kill for it."

In Herrani, Arin asked Kestrel, "What are you thinking?"

She noticed the switch in language and recognized that Arin believed it was safe to speak in Herrani, but she didn't risk an answer in front of Risha. She didn't say that General Trajan could have sent the embittered eastern princess with tempting bait. Kestrel feared a trap. "What kind of help are you offering?"

"I can give you a location where the emperor will be, separate from the army, with a light guard."

"How did you come by this information?"

"The court."

Kestrel didn't like this. It was too easy. "You still haven't said what you want out of this bargain."

Risha kept her eyes on Arin. "Promise that Verex won't be hurt. Protect him."

Startled, defensive, Arin said, "I don't wish the Valorian prince any harm."

But Roshar's face changed . . . and Kestrel suddenly realized why. "No," she told him, her voice rising. "You musn't. His death wouldn't serve you. You should *want* him to inherit the empire. He'd be a friend to the east."

"Doesn't matter," Roshar said. "Our queen will smash the empire to pieces if she can. Killing the emperor might win the war. Verex might become a political ally. But if he inherits Valoria, that country will always be a threat to us . . . and to you, Arin."

"Someone else would step into Verex's place," Kestrel argued. "If the prince died, the senate would elect a new emperor."

Arin's gray eyes went flat. "It'd be the Valorian general."

Roshar shrugged. "Unless we eliminate him as well. Knock down all the principal pieces in Borderlands, and what's left for your opponent? Surrender."

"You forget an important piece in this game," Risha said. "Me."

Roshar's shoulders tensed. Kestrel felt a growing disquiet.

"Verex and I would marry," said the princess.

"An alliance between east and west," Roshar said slowly.

Kestrel sought Arin's gaze. When he met her eyes she couldn't read them.

"Not so good for you, little Herrani," Roshar told Arin. "Your peninsula would get lost in the middle."

The risk had always been there, even if they won the war: that Herran would be retaken by the west, or dwindle into the east. But now Kestrel saw it as if seeing the future: how a marriage between the empire and Dacra could lead to one power ruling the entire continent. Herran would vanish.

"Decide," Risha said, "or I leave. My information for Verex's safety. Yes or no."

Arin met Kestrel's gaze. Grim mouth, hooded eyes asking whether this was worth it.

She thought about the emperor's hand on her father's shoulder.

The key Verex had sent to the northern prison.

A friend. A good heart.

But Roshar wasn't wrong.

Kestrel knew what her father would choose, in her place. She realized that she'd come to rely on his voice in her head, that it had saved her on the battlefield. Even now, the very thought of his advice was soothing . . . even as being so soothed repulsed her.

It didn't matter what her father would choose. She was not her father.

"Yes," Kestrel said. "I agree."

"Then I do, too," said Arin.

Roshar gazed at his hands. "No one can promise anyone's safety. Never. Much less in war."

"We can promise to try," Arin told him. "And you *can* shield him from the Dacran queen."

Roshar nodded, but distractedly, with a disbelieving wince, as if someone had presented him with a portrait where his features were whole, his mutilations erased, and he had no words to express how wrong this vision of him was.

"I overheard the senate leader say that if Valoria succeeded in seizing the beach, the emperor would move inland with a small contingent and take the Sythiah estate," Risha said.

"The manor there is luxurious," Arin said, "but it has nothing strategically interesting for the emperor or the army. Vineyards. The grapes won't even be ripe this time of year. There's little to be gained in terms of supplies. The estate is north of the road to the city; not convenient as a base for attack."

Kestrel, however, knew the emperor. "But the manor is beautiful?"

Arin lifted one shoulder. "The stained-glass windows were well known, before the war. There are rooms that seem to be made of colored light. Or so it was said. I wouldn't know. I've never seen it."

"The emperor enjoys beauty."

Arin's hand twitched, as if he'd meant to touch, compulsively, the scar that ran deep into his left cheek, but had stopped himself in time. It wrenched Kestrel's heart to see him remember how he'd been attacked by the emperor's minion, his face sliced open.

She hadn't been there when it happened. Still, she saw it now as if she'd been a bystander: paralyzed, robbed of sound, her throat raw. Bones like lead.

And she saw herself in her suite in the imperial palace, dressed in red, her shoulders laced with golden wire. Kestrel had forgotten this. It came to her: the tight, gorgeous bodice. Folds of crimson samite. The emperor had selected her wedding dress. He had selected *her*, had cut her from the cloth of her home, then stitched her into place beside his son. He had embroidered how she'd look and who she'd become. *I have chosen you, Kestrel, and will make you into everything my son cannot be. Someone fit to take my place.*

It was difficult for Kestrel to move, as if she had indeed become a cloth doll, the stitches drawn tight. She touched Arin's arm, felt how the muscles had hardened. "You think that he seeks only to destroy."

"Yes," he muttered.

"Beauty moves him. He destroys it only when he can't possess it."

I asked myself, the emperor whispered in her ear, *whether it was really possible that you might betray your country so easily, especially when it had been practically* given *to you.*

"He loves to shape things." A remembered helplessness shrouded her. The prince and his sister faded in her vision, were present but unimportant. She felt strange; her blood prickled as if something were growing inside her. "Every piece in place, arranged to his satisfaction. It's why he enjoys games. You know, don't you, how a game with a perfect line of play becomes beautiful?"

Yes. A growing thing. Thorny. A briar.

Arin's expression changed. She saw how he read her stillness. She wondered if she'd gone pale. Anxiety stole over his features. "Kestrel, can I have a word with you?"

Outside the tent, night had come.

He cupped her face in his hands. "You don't look right."

"I'm fine."

"No. You look like a part of you has disappeared. Like you're not really here. Like"—his hands fell away—"you do when you're plotting something."

Which was how Kestrel realized that she *was* plotting something. That growing briar inside her was an idea.

"Kestrel."

She blinked, then noticed the hurt shape of his mouth. Arin said, "Tell me." She started to speak. He cut through her first words. "No deceiving," he said.

"I wouldn't."

"Not again. After everything. Don't keep me in the dark."

"Arin, for someone who wants me to tell him something, you're doing an excellent job of not *letting me speak*."

"Oh." Rubbing a forefinger and thumb into his eyes, he gave her a rueful look. "Sorry."

"Risha could be a trap. We've no proof of her true allegiance, and while I know she cares for Verex, this might only make her firmly on Valoria's side. This story of the emperor at the Sythiah manor could be a distraction. Worse, it could lure us into an ambush. But I also believe that the emperor *would* leave the battlefield to stay in a luxurious manor known for its stained-glass windows. He's let my father fight his battles for two decades. As Verex said, the emperor is here only for show. Valoria is likely to win this war—and given our loss at Lerralen, its path to seize Herran's city is reasonably easy. Having destroyed some of their black powder helps us, but they still have the greater numbers and their tactical position is strong. Why should the emperor *not* quit the army camp for a feather bed and a view of the vineyards? It would be like him."

"Then I'll lead a small team there. Assassinate him. Death will guide me."

"No. I have a better plan for how to win this war."

She told him what she had in mind, then returned to the tent to ask Roshar for his help.

a fistful of dry grass and scattered the thin yellow blades. Again.

Kestrel, who sat near him, glanced up from what she was doing. She lifted one brow.

So he stopped, he knew it was pure anxiety, that if he didn't do something with his hands they'd tremble.

Her hands were steady. She dipped a skinny paintbrush she'd made from horsehair, a twig, and twine into the small vial resting on a wide board that had become an impromptu table. A Bite and Sting set lay spread across the board, the tiles all faceup. She flipped four of them and painted their blank backs. The liquid went on clear.

"Kestrel."

"Almost done."

"I worry the emperor won't agree."

"I think he will."

"But the stakes—"

"Will amuse him."

"He'd gamble the outcome of a war?"

"Maybe, for the pleasure of beating me." She laid the paintbrush on the board. "But he won't win." She turned a snake tile onto its face and moved it close to one that she'd painted. She studied the two blank ivory backs. They looked nearly identical, save that the painted one had a slight shine. She lightly tapped the paintbrush's wooden end against the painted tile. It left no trace. The tile had dried.

Arin's stomach was a wormy knot. "This game could go badly."

"That's why I'm cheating."

"Even *with* the marked tiles."

"It's a good plan."

"Yes, but he'll agree to play only if he believes the outcome won't matter, even if you win. *That* is what will amuse him: your expectation that he'll keep his word. He won't."

"All part of the game."

"If anything goes wrong, he'll hurt you."

Kestrel turned away from the board, saw him rake another fistful of grass. It sounded like cloth being ripped apart.

"Not this time," she said.

Arin smelled smoke from Roshar's pipe before he heard the prince approach from behind. The sun was going down. The sky looked candied.

"Pretty," the prince commented.

"Storm colors. One's coming."

"I was thinking . . ."

Arin turned to glance at the prince, alert to his quiet

tone. Roshar avoided his gaze, but his black eyes were large. Glassy. Arin was about to speak when Roshar cleared his throat and said, "Now is a good time to remind you how generous I am."

Arin refused to be distracted into a meaningless conversation where Roshar simultaneously praised and mocked himself. He knew what troubled the prince. "Give Risha time. She'll forgive you."

Roshar continued as if he hadn't heard. "The very soul of generosity. You ask for an ally in war, and lo, here I am. I dole out favors. Even to your ghost. She asks, I give. What's more, I've selected five elite fighters to accompany her and my little sister to Sythiah's manor. Truly, I'm confident that Risha would be enough to keep Kestrel safe, but I thought you'd appreciate the extra protection."

Arin realized where this conversation was going, and it was as if the storm he'd predicted had already arrived. "No. Wait—"

"A small team is best for infiltrating the manor. Silently. Efficiently. No more than seven people."

"Eight."

"Sorry, Arin. You must remain with the army."

"You can't compel me to stay."

"Am I not your commander?"

The sky deepened. Its oranges and reds were resinous. Arin's pulse leaped with anger.

But this time Roshar's voice came low. "I need you."

"What?" The air whooshed out of him.

"The emperor might be in Sythiah. He might not. What we know for *certain* is that an entire Valorian army whose forces vastly outnumber ours will be traveling up that road with a general who will probably continue to fight regardless of what happens at Sythiah. Are we to bet everything on Kestrel's game? I say, we deal with the Valorians. I say, no retreat."

"You don't need me to fight a battle."

Roshar tipped his head to one side, his shoulders shrugging, and opened his hands as if scattering seeds. The gesture—a Herrani one, used to indicate doubt—made Arin angrier. "You don't," Arin insisted. "You'd be fine without me. You're good at war."

Roshar met his gaze. The green paint around the prince's eyes was fresh, his expression sober. "You're better."

He didn't like to tell her what Roshar had asked. But he did, focused on adjusting the small lamp they'd set on the canvas tarp that covered the dirt floor of his tent. The lamp didn't burn well. Its oil was bad. It smoked. As he talked, he tinkered with the burner, the chimney. Then Arin stopped, realizing that he was close to destroying the thing between his hands.

Kestrel sat up in the bedroll, unbound hair spilling over her bare shoulders. It was the color of candlelight. She said, "Roshar's right."

Arin struggled with his unease, didn't know what to say, dreaded blurting out the wrong thing. Finally he settled on blunt truth. "You're taking a big risk. I don't want you to have to do it alone."

She sat in profile to him. Her hair had slid to curtain

most of her face, but she shoved it back, meeting his gaze with her own firm one. "It will work."

He thought of the Bite and Sting tiles carefully stowed in a velvet bag. He scrubbed the heel of his hand against his scarred cheek, saw Kestrel's quiet regard, how her expression changed the way a story does: subtle, with shifts of detail. Revealing. It calmed him a little to see her intelligence, vivid and clear.

"I believe you," he said. "I'll stay with the army. But it's strange to me that Roshar changed his mind. He was ready to retreat to the city."

"Seeing Risha changed him."

"Even so. It's hard to know what he really wants." Arin explained how Roshar could lay claim to Herran, and in the eyes of his people he'd only be taking what was legally his.

Kestrel said nothing at first. Then: "It's not like you to question someone's friendship."

With a nauseated jolt, Arin thought of Cheat, who'd been his first friend after the invasion. "Maybe I should."

"Maybe it would make you less yourself, if you did."

"And you? Do you trust Roshar?"

She considered it. "Yes."

Arin let out a resigned sigh. "I do, too . . . even if I shouldn't."

"Let the morning keep what belongs to the morning," Kestrel said, but as if she wasn't paying attention to what she said. Then she blinked. Her jaw tightened. She blew out the lamp.

He drew her to him. "What is it?" he murmured. Her heart beat against his palm.

"It just means that you shouldn't borrow tomorrow's problems. Deal with today's."

"But why does it upset you?"

"It was something my father would say." She grew smaller in Arin's arms. "I can't face him."

"You won't have to," he promised. This, he could do. Arin sensed his god listening. He felt the god's assent fall on him, light and warm, like ash.

Give him to me, said death.

As Kestrel neared sleep, it occurred to Arin that the emotion that spread through him—delicate, and unable to be named at first, because so unfamiliar—was peace.

He held the feeling close before it could be lost.

showed no signs of letting up. Mud sucked at Arin's boots as he helped Kestrel ready her horse. The rain intensified, dropping down like little stones.

Arin squinted up at it. "Terrible day to ride." He hated to see her go.

She wiped water from her face, glancing over at Risha, whose head was tipped back under the rain, eyes closed. "Not for everyone," Kestrel said, "and the rain will make it less likely a Valorian scout will notice that a small band is riding from camp."

True. The middle distance was a gray fog. Arin raked dripping hair off his brow. He tried to be all right. His nerves sparked the way a blade does against the grinder.

Kestrel touched his cheek. "The rain is good for us."

"Come here."

She tasted like the rain: cool and fresh and sweet. Her mouth warmed as he kissed her. He felt the way her clothes stuck to her skin. He forgot himself.

She murmured, "I have something for you."

"You needn't give me anything."

"It's not a gift. It's for you to keep safe until I return." She placed a speckled yellow feather on his palm.

The rain fell in a veil behind her.

The ground oozed. Mud splattered Arin's trousers as he helped load a supply wagon. He was worried, he kept thinking about the Bite and Sting set in Kestrel's saddlebag, and the mud made his work sluggish. He grew frustrated.

Oh, I don't know, said death, slightly smug. *I like the mud.*

Arin stopped what he was doing. *You do?*

There was no reply other than the rain.

Arin considered his army. He considered the general's. A strategy slowly formed, one that released an emotion close to pleasure. It was, he realized, the promise of revenge: right at the tips of his fingers.

In the prince's tent, the rain loudly percussive against the canvas, Roshar studied the map marked by Arin.

"Your people will fight better in the rain," Arin said.

"The rain might end by the time our army is in position."

"But the mud will remain. Think of that heavy Valorian armor the higher ranks wear. *We* wear leather. Most of them will flounder."

"Not on a paved road." Roshar wasn't challenging Arin's strategy, just prodding it to test its solidity. "Their cavalry is superior. The general will take into account the soggy terrain on either side of the road. Armed infantry fares worse than horses in mud. They'll try to flank us with cavalry."

"Yes." Arin tapped the map where he'd made notches on the even ground that bordered the road and ran open and smooth to the forest on either side. "Exactly."

"What is it like," Kestrel asked Risha as they rode, "to be gifted with weapons?"

Coolly, the princess said, "You've no proof that I am."

But Kestrel remembered an archery contest on the palace lawn, and how Risha aimed arrows with studied mediocrity until one final arrow punched so hard into the target's center that it drove through the canvas halfway up its shaft. "I used to wish I were talented that way. Then I didn't. Now I do again."

Risha shrugged. "It's gained me little."

"Roshar was even younger than we are when he brought you into Valorian territory. When you were captured."

"Betrayed."

"You didn't agree to go with him?"

The princess shifted in her saddle. "I was a mere child, and eager to prove myself. Children seek to please. They try so hard. My brother and sister used that against me."

"Roshar has suffered for it."

"And so?" Risha twisted in the saddle to meet Kestrel's gaze. The princess's eyes burned, her brown skin was sleek with rain, her full mouth pinched.

"You could speak with him."

Risha snorted. "You mean *forgive*. Forgiveness is so . . . squishy. Like all this mud."

Kestrel thought of her father's fire-lit face on Lerralen beach.

"It drags you down," Risha said. "You know this."

She had an uneasy feeling of not knowing what Risha would say next, but already not wanting to hear it.

"You, who seek your own father's death."

The bodies lay tumbled in a ditch not far from the Sythiah vineyards.

The rain had washed away any tracks. Still, Kestrel understood the story.

It leached into her: how the emperor's company had seized the manor and dragged the Herrani who lived there out onto the grounds. Forced them forward. A girl in the ditch had lost her shoe. Her little foot was black with mud. The shoe . . . Kestrel searched for it in the rain, feeling a growing panic and need, as if finding a lost shoe could blot away the image of ashen corpses, the way a dead woman still gripped the child's hand. The inching insects. A shoe could take away the smell, the rot of it strong in the rain. A shoe could keep down the bile that rushed up Kestrel's throat.

But when she found the shoe, stuck in the root of a tree, the inner leather sole still held the shape of the girl's foot. Kestrel could feel its imprint.

The shoe took away none of the horror. It planted it deep in the bottom of Kestrel's belly, as solid as a grown man's kick.

They crouched in the stubby vineyards with the other five Dacran soldiers. Risha eyed the manor's kitchen yard, the house's weakest entry point. Several of the house's windows glowed through the night rain.

Kestrel licked her sour lips and gripped the satchel. She imagined the game tiles rattling inside their velvet bag.

She remembered dining with the emperor. A dessert served with a disintegrating sugar fork. How encounters with him had always felt like that: as though every tool at her disposal was crumbling in her grasp. She remembered how, on the imperial palace grounds, after a hunt, she'd realized that the emperor would steal or maim her dog simply because she loved it. *My father needs for you to love him best,* Verex had said.

You need to watch yourself, he'd said.

If you play against my father, you'll lose.

A light hand touched her arm. "I don't know you well," Risha's voice was low. "But I know what Verex has told me about you, and what I see for myself. You don't need to be gifted with a blade. You are your own best weapon."

Kestrel stared back at Risha, who was almost pure shadow—a mere glint of eyes. Kestrel felt a slow, slight throb, a shimmer in the blood. She knew it well.

Her worst trait. Her best trait.

The desire to come out on top, to set her opponent under her thumb.

A streak of pride. Her mind ringed with hungry rows of foxlike teeth.

Later, at dawn, when the emperor pulled Kestrel's dagger from its sheath and touched its tip to her throat, she remembered that Sythiah's manor had always been a trap. The question had only been whether it was a trap she set for the emperor, or one that she'd fall into.

Kestrel touched Risha's hand. "Thank you."

The seven of them moved through the dark to the house.

The dawn broke bright. Clear sky. A sheen of water wavered over the road toward Lerralen, deeper in the cracks between paving stones.

Arin and Roshar had moved the army as quickly west as they could. They had reached the location Arin had chosen.

The first task: to unload the hundreds of sharpened staves Arin had ordered made.

The second: to drive them into the sodden earth bordering the road.

The third: to set their last sacks of gunpowder on the road. A snug and deadly little bundle.

And the fourth: to wait, to try not to think about Kestrel, about how she must have already reached Sythiah by now, and might have already played Bite and Sting against the emperor, and had won or lost.

The seven of them wound their way through the night-shadowed corners of Sythiah's manor. Risha moved with ethereal fluidity, and when they encountered a pair of Valorian soldiers stationed in a hallway, her knife split their skin as smoothly as if cutting through cream. The Valorians made no sound. It was quiet enough to hear the drip of blood.

They accessed the upper floors and began checking bedrooms. Kestrel knew where they'd be situated—Herrani architecture usually had bedrooms face east or west. Risha crept in alone, her posture stiffening with annoyance when the other Dacrans made as if to accompany her. She let out a low hiss. They didn't follow.

She'd return, her blade wetter than before.

"Enough of this," she whispered.

"We must go quietly," Kestrel reminded her. "We need to get to the emperor's room without waking the entire house. We can't fight them all."

Risha snorted. "*I* can."

The princess's impatience wore thin. The next time they encountered Valorian guards—again, a pair of them—she let a Dacran soldier shoot one of them with a crossbow, but pulled the other Valorian out of the quarrel's path at the same time that her other hand came down on the woman's mouth.

Risha touched her knife to the fragile skin beneath the woman's wide eye. "Stay silent," Risha whispered, "and you'll keep your eyes. Lead us to the emperor's suite."

The soldier led them to a broad door made of tiger maple, the wood smooth in the Herrani style, with little carving other than the rippled doorjamb. An oil lamp glowed in the hallway's sconce, its stained glass casting a jeweled light over the wood's natural stripes.

"Here?" Kestrel asked. Light glowed through the door's keyhole.

The woman nodded.

Risha killed her. The body slumped. Blood welled up to Kestrel's boots. She made herself remember the girl's lost shoe, the Bite and Sting set, Arin's scar, the way he heard the god of death because he believed he had no one else, the small houses in the wheatfields, the baring of her back to the cold tundra air, the way she had hoped that the night-time drug would make her forget.

"Open the door," she whispered.

One of the Dacran men, selected by Roshar for his skill at this, knelt and unfolded a leather-wrapped set of tools, then he inserted two of them—long and thin, like knitting needles—into the keyhole. He poked, then levered the tools until they heard the soft *clunk* of the lock's tumblers releasing.

He eased the door open—softly, as if his hand were no more than a small gust of wind.

Risha first, and Kestrel behind her, they entered the suite's antechamber.

They were attacked by the emperor's personal guard, who had been waiting as they'd listened to the clicking of the picked lock.

Arin set the army into formation on the western road. He made the vanguard's ranks broad, running across the road and the bordering wet earth, all the way up to the trees. Behind the vanguard, the center ranks were confined to the road.

Roshar's horse flicked its tail, shifting. The prince eyed the forest. "Those trees turn this place into something resembling a ravine. We won't have much room to maneuver."

"Neither will they."

The morning light was sheer and fresh, as pale as the flesh of a lemon. Arin imagined squeezing it down his throat. It would taste like how he felt: stingingly alive.

Kestrel couldn't count them, couldn't see how the guards carved open the bodies of the Dacran soldiers, couldn't fathom Risha's speed, the way the princess had shoved Kestrel against a wall, creating a halo of safety around her. The *snick* of Risha's knife against a windpipe. Her swivel and dance. Unerring strike. Counter. Bodies thumped to the floor.

"Hold," someone called. "I want to see."

The Valorians pulled back. Risha's knife flicked blood as it arced through the air. She had no intention of obeying the voice. Kestrel caught her arm. The princess spun, her face frustrated, as if she'd been listening to a voice whose last words had been lost in the interruption.

The emperor stood at the threshold where the antechamber flowed into the rest of the suite, his posture light and easy. For a moment, there was no sound but the rain on the roof. "You," he said wonderingly as his gaze found Risha.

Then Kestrel.

His eyes widened in delight. "And *you*."

He laughed.

The day blazed. The sun seemed to soar into the sky, all the way to its height.

Arin waited.

Nothing.

Waited.

Nothing.

He touched the hard leather shell of his armor. Hidden beneath it: his chest. His lungs. Skin. A speckled yellow feather tucked inside his tunic pocket, right above his heart.

Forget the feather, death said. *You are the road.*

The sun.

The sky.

The horse beneath you.

Comforted, Arin said, *The gods used to walk among us.*

True, said death.

Why did you leave?

Ah, sweet child, it was your people who left us.

"Lady Kestrel, you look like a dirty little savage. What *are* you doing here?"

She tried to speak.

"Did you hope to murder me in my sleep?"

Her throat was too dry.

"Maybe you've come for court gossip. Surely the barbarian princess has told you everything of interest. No?"

Kestrel swallowed. She saw her hand gripping her dagger. The knuckles were white knobs.

"You want news of your father, I imagine. Let me tell you. He doesn't mourn you."

Kestrel heard the emperor as if from far away.

Doesn't miss you.

He never did. You remember how little time he spent at

home. How awkward he became in your company. You had to beg him to stay in the capital. Oh yes, I heard. And here, a secret for you: he was relieved when you were sent north. I saw how a burden had been lifted from his shoulders.

He looked lighter.

Younger.

Free.

The emperor looked from her to Risha to the Dacran soldiers, dead on the bloody floor.

"You're resourceful, Kestrel, I'll give you that. You've survived the mines, the tundra, the war . . . thus far. You've made"—his gaze flicked again to Risha—"interesting allies. But my guard outnumbers you both, and it will take an instant for me to rouse the entire house. I don't have many regrets, but my decision to imprison rather than kill you smacks of squeamishness . . . or, shall I say, an unnecessary concern for your father's well-being. Do you know, he hasn't mentioned you once since he told me of your treason?"

"He wouldn't, no matter what he feels."

"Regardless," the emperor said softly, "I could have you killed right now and he'd never know. And if he did, why would he care? What would the life of one dishonorable would-be assassin mean to him?"

"I didn't come here to murder you."

He bit back a thin smile.

She said, "I came to challenge you."

"Oh?"

"One game of Bite and Sting. If I win, you'll end the war. Leave. Cross the sea with every last Valorian. Never return."

The emperor made a surprised half laugh of a sound.

He lightly traced the deepest line of his brow, then unfolded his hand in a flourish. "What would *I* gain, should I win?"

"What you like. Whatever I can give you."

He tapped one finger to his lips, considering. "That's not much."

"I'm sure you can think of something."

"And if I agree, and lose? You'd trust me to keep my word?"

"A Valorian honors his word."

"Yes," he said, drawing out the word. "He does."

"Risha goes free, no matter what the outcome."

"I'll wait here," said the princess. "With your guards, if you like." She gave them a disdainful look, making clear that she thought little of their chances of survival if she chose to finish what she'd started. "Until the game is done."

Kestrel said, "We play in private."

"You set quite a lot of terms," the emperor said, "but this particular one I wouldn't have any other way."

"So you agree?"

"I confess, I'm curious."

"Do you *agree*?"

"A fair warning. I'm better at this than you are."

"We shall see."

Arin heard a crash in the trees.

A Herrani scout. He ran to Arin, his face shiny with sweat.

The Valorians were coming.

The emperor led her to his bedroom. The summer hangings on the bed were gauzy, the sheets disturbed. She could see the dent left in a pillow by his head. The room smelled of his oils: powdery pepper, bitingly sweet balsam. Rain tapped the black windowpanes.

"Wash your face," he said.

There was a mirrored basin in the corner. Kestrel did as ordered, though her face wasn't particularly dirty. She was startled by the stranger in the glass and tried not to stare at herself. She caught a glimpse of shocked, light eyes, made lighter by tanned and freckled skin. A strong face.

She folded the towel and joined the emperor where he stood near an octagonal table. He had produced a bottle of wine and two glasses.

"I'll serve," she said, which made him give her a sleek look of amusement. She poured the red wine, but neither of them touched their glasses, and they both knew that the other suspected that some sleight of hand had poisoned the cup.

"Disarm," he said.

"I will if you do the same."

He unbuckled his dagger and set it gently, yet heavily, on the table. Her fingers fumbled as she undid hers.

The dagger Arin had made her looked plain next to the emperor's—but strong, like her unexpected face in the mirror.

"Interesting." The emperor stroked it where it lay. "A new acquisition? Perhaps this will be my prize when I win."

"If that's what you want."

"I haven't decided what I want."

She opened the satchel, set the velvet bag of tiles on the table, and moved to sit.

"Not yet." He held out his hand. She gave him the satchel, which he examined. Satisfied that it contained nothing else, he dropped it to the floor, then said, "You'll have no objection, I'm sure, if I make certain that you hide no weapons on your person."

Her skin prickled. "I give you my word that I don't."

"The word of a traitor is hardly to be trusted."

So she stood rigid as his hands moved over her unarmored body. They didn't linger, except when he pressed his fingers to her throat, and then pressed harder to feel her pulse jump and run.

He said, "You're welcome to do the same to me."

"No."

"Are you sure?" He seemed to dare her to admit that she didn't want to touch him.

"I trust you."

"Well then, little liar, let's play."

The approaching Valorian army shone in a silver river under the sun.

Arin looked through a spyglass. He couldn't find the general.

There was a thin, whistling whine.

Arin lowered the spyglass.

The whine stopped. ·

A cry of pain.

An arrow, studded into a Herrani soldier's throat.

More arrows sped through the air. Valorian Rangers were shooting at them from the trees on either side of the road.

They sat. Kestrel, her back to the bed, loosened the velvet bag's tie and poured the tiles onto the table.

She reached to mix the tiles, but as she had thought he might, the emperor stopped her. "Let's confirm that this set is standard, shall we?" he said.

He checked the tiles to account for their values. When he saw that the set showed the proper amount of each Bite and Sting tile, he turned them onto their faces and mixed them. His face was calm, but his gestures were eager. He touched each tile, but barely. He wanted to get to the game.

Kestrel studied his smooth expression. He didn't seem to notice that four ivory tiles were shinier than the rest. The gloom of the late hour helped. He drew his tiles.

Her stomach clenched to see the four shiny tiles left in the boneyard, from which she and the emperor would pull tiles throughout the game.

She drew her own hand. Arin had warned her that when she had a high chance of winning, her very lack of tells showed her confidence. *I don't think most people notice,* he'd said. *Your expression doesn't change. You've no tic or gesture. I just get the sense that there's an energy inside you I can't reach, and that if I did, it'd strike like lightning.*

She tried not to think about her plan, worrying that even the mere thought of it would show on her face. She felt her expression harden as clay does in a kiln.

Play, Kestrel.

She set down her first tile. The emperor did the same.

She found herself praying to Arin's god. *Please, let this be over soon.*

But she heard no answer.

"Stand your ground," Roshar shouted as arrows drove into the army. Eastern crossbows fired into the trees.

Roshar ordered Xash, his second-in-command, to lead a company into the forest to the left of the road. Roshar would take another company to the right. "We'll take care of the Rangers. You," he said to Arin, "take command of the road."

Arin snagged the prince's shoulder. "You'll get bogged down in the mud. The Rangers will shoot everyone down on the open land before you reach the trees."

"Not much choice. Continue to return fire. The Dacran archers are plainspeople. They're good."

"They're not gods."

"They *will* be, to protect their prince."

Then Roshar was gone, and Arin snapped his attention back to the road, because the enemy was upon them, thundering down the road, almost here, almost here.

Here.

As they played, the rain lessened and stopped. The glasses of wine sat untouched. The boneyard still held the four shiny tiles hidden among the others.

It was the emperor's turn. He reached for a tile, then paused, too much drama in his movements. He wasn't truly hesitant, or even pretending to be hesitant, but rather making an open mockery of hesitancy that he knew she'd recognize as such.

"Play your tile." Her voice grated.

"I'm thinking."

She said nothing.

"Don't you want to know what I'm thinking?" He leaned back in his chair, his short, silvered hair a bright bristle in the lamplight. The emperor passed his fingers over his mouth with enough pressure to pull slightly at the slack skin of his cheeks. His touch explored the grooves age had made near his mouth, and he seemed pleased.

Then she saw that his gaze had shifted to her hands.

They were trembling. She pressed them down against the table.

"I'm thinking about what I'll claim from you when I win," he said. "The particularly appealing part of the deal you struck is the *openness* of your offer. 'Whatever you like.'"

She wished she'd phrased things differently, though she didn't know what else she would have said, since part of what had made him agree to the game was his anticipation of the pleasure of what he was doing now.

"I could make you bring Arin of Herran to me," the emperor said. "He'd surrender, for you."

The world deadened.

"I never finished what I started with that boy's face." The emperor pushed the hilt of Kestrel's dagger with one finger.

The sound it made, though small, scraped down her spine.

"Or perhaps it's not *his* face that appeals to me most. We could see what might be done with yours."

Silence.

"No, Lady Kestrel?"

His gaze drifted over her shoulder. He continued to speak, voice soft as his list continued, and Kestrel's mind jumped between thinking that he chose to name the things that would torment her most, and meant none of it, or that he *did* mean it and wanted her to hope that he didn't, and that this hope was his most delicious form of brutalization.

Her heart was loud in her ears. This wasn't working. She'd made a grave mistake in coming.

"But of course," the emperor finally said, "with such an offer as you made, I could exact it *all*."

Arin ordered his vanguard to fall to the sides of the road.

The black powder sacks were lit.

The Valorian cavalry reared back from what they saw too late.

The sacks burst under their hooves. Chunks of paving stone exploded into the air.

"Do you forfeit your turn?" Kestrel asked.

"Not at all."

"You're afraid to play."

"We both know," he said, "which of us is afraid."

She reached for her wine glass and drank.

"I do admire your love for a gamble." He took her cup and drank from it as well. "I was simply thinking out loud earlier. There's no harm in thinking."

"I have my own thoughts. I am wondering why my father ever respected you."

The emperor set down the cup. "He's my friend."

"Yet you say the things that you say."

"He's not here, and if he were, he wouldn't care."

"Yes, he would."

The emperor scrutinized her. "You don't look like him. Except the eyes."

"Why?" The word burst from her lips.

His reply was gentle. "Why *what*, Kestrel?"

Her throat closed. Her eyes stung. She realized that she had forgotten the game . . . and that maybe this had been the emperor's intention. She didn't want to ask her question. Yet she couldn't help it . . . or the hurt evident in her choked voice. "Why did he choose you over me?"

"Ah." The emperor rubbed his dry palms together and templed them with a little pat. "You've provided me with an entertaining evening so far. I feel I owe you something in exchange. So: the truth. Trajan wasn't my friend—not at first. He was necessary for what I wanted. Military prowess. Imperial expansion. I, in turn, was an opportunity for what *he* wanted, which was nothing less than for his daughter to one day rule the empire. An understandable ambition. Or perhaps our friendship didn't begin there, after all. We've known each other since well before your birth. He's a man of rare intelligence. There's pleasure in finding one's equal.

Perhaps things began with that. As to how it has grown . . ." He shrugged. "Maybe it's because he knows how I am with everyone else, and knows that I'm not like that with him. I value Trajan. Ultimately, when he held your treasonous letter in his hand and saw how you had lied to him, the choice between me and you was the choice between someone who loves him and someone who didn't."

Tears spilled down her cheeks.

The emperor patted her frozen hand. "I suggest that we not discuss your father."

He played his tile.

The air reeked of sulfur and scorched horseflesh. The screams were so many and so loud that Arin couldn't really hear them. Just noise. His ears buzzed.

Valorians floundered in their blood on the broken road. Ranger arrows continued to furrow the sky. A blasted paving stone, Arin saw, had smashed into a Herrani soldier's face. Her body lay half in the mud, half where the road had been.

Arin couldn't spot the general. The Valorian army was vast. Only a few ranks of cavalry had been decimated in the blast.

Another unit of Valorian cavalry moved forward into position.

Kestrel was losing. Earlier, the emperor had delayed in order to unsettle her, to revel in it, to spear her like a worm and watch her writhe. Kestrel's tactic of delay was different. She took as much time as possible to draw the game out. Earlier, she'd wanted the game to be over quickly. Now she needed more time.

The four shiny tiles in the boneyard winked at her. She knew their values. The wolf—she could use that if it were in her hand. Or even the bee.

Her frustration rose.

The tears had dried on her cheeks, the skin tight with salt. She couldn't help returning to what the emperor had said about her father. The memory of how her father had told her that she'd broken his heart.

If he were here, she would howl at him. He had broken *her* heart, over and over, for years. He'd tried to force her into the mold of his own idea of honor. What he wanted her to be. Not what she was.

Kestrel felt her spine straighten.

Damn his devotion to honor.

When it came her turn to pull a tile, she didn't choose any of the marked ones.

"Steady," Arin called. His horse tossed its head. His vanguard still held formation: those few files of broad ranks, running across the road and up to the trees.

The Valorian cavalry nudged toward them, looking ready to tear through Arin's ranks. Arin watched the cavalry shape into a wedge. The left and right sides would pull up in the clash, and would try to flank the center ranks of Arin's army by galloping up alongside the road once Arin's vanguard had collapsed.

Yes, said death. *Good.*

The emperor pulled a shiny tile. Kestrel bit back a sound, glancing away so that he couldn't read her expression.

The windows had lightened. For the first time, she registered their intricate patterns of stained glass. In the dead of night, they'd looked black. Now they blushed with faint color. She saw what they would soon fully show. Flowers, gods, the prow of a ship. A bird's flung-open wings.

This was an eastern room. When dawn came, it would be glorious.

The armies clashed. The center of Arin's vanguard coalesced around him. But the edges—as planned—disintegrated, the soldiers appearing to retreat into the forest.

The left and right flanks of the Valorian cavalry hurtled straight into the open spaces along the road that the edges of Arin's vanguard had hidden.

Valorian horses impaled their stomachs on the sharpened staves Arin had had driven into the mud.

The emperor set down a fox. He examined the game in play. "Things don't look so good for you," he told Kestrel.

A movement amid all the others—the torque of bodies, the muddy struggle, collapse, rise, murder—caught Arin's attention. On the periphery of battle where gutted warhorses flailed, there was some rabbitlike thing. He couldn't look directly; he was too busy kneeing his horse out of the way of a rearing Valorian stallion's plunging hooves. Then grappling with the stallion's rider. Distracted, Arin seized the rider's arm.

Not a rabbit.

Much too large for a rabbit.

Still, that impression of something—*someone*—out of place. A softness. An innocence.

Arin felt the arm pop from its shoulder.

The rider screamed, but Arin wasn't paying attention. He impatiently killed the Valorian. He'd seen, now, what that strange movement far off to the side of the road was, among the bloody staves.

It was Verex. He was struggling to free his leg, trapped beneath the body of his fallen horse.

He was easy prey.

Arin saw his soldiers see the prince . . . but not see him *as* a prince, not as the one they were warned not to kill.

This, a prince?

Covered in mud, his only visible feature that straw-colored Valorian hair, Verex tugged, all thin limbs and terror. He didn't see the Dacran archer's taut bow, arrow nocked and drawn.

Arin was too far away. He shouted *No,* but the word was lost in the roar of war.

The archer aimed, and released her arrow.

"I almost wish I'd lose," the emperor mused. "It'd be a novel experience. Is it wrong for me to hope that, at least, this game will last longer? Improve, Kestrel, or this will be over too soon."

Kestrel reminded herself that there are ways to lose even if one holds the highest hand. She played her tile.

Helpless, Arin watched the arrow slice a low, true path toward Verex. It struck him, glancing off his metal armor. Undaunted, the archer nocked another arrow.

Get down, Arin willed as he tried to force his way to the edge of the road. He'd never reach Verex in time. *Use your horse as a shield.* But Verex, who now saw how the cloud of danger around him had condensed to the point of an arrow-head, froze.

Arin's gaze swiveled back to the archer, whose face underwent a curt shift of emotion just after she loosed the arrow. Her expression slackened with horror.

Arin saw what she saw: Roshar, hurtling toward the Valorian prince and into the path of the arrow.

Roshar flattened Verex into the mud. The arrow sailed over his shoulder.

Then Risha's brother raged at the stunned Valorian, dragged him out from under the horse, and hauled him toward the cover of the trees.

They were both silent now, playing in concentration. The emperor reached for a second shiny tile.

The stained-glass windows glowed, and something eased open inside Kestrel. As color seeped into the room, she felt an unexpected wish.

She wished her father were here.

You, who seek your own father's death.

But she didn't, she found that she couldn't, no matter how he had hurt her. She wished that he could see her play, and win. That he could see what she saw now.

A window is just a window. Colored glass: mere glass. But in the sun it becomes more. She would show him, and say, love should do *this*.

And you too, she would tell him, because she could no longer deny that it remained true, in spite of everything.

I love you, too.

After Roshar and Verex had vanished into the trees, Arin stopped thinking. He rarely did, in battle. It was easier to give himself over. The pressure inside was a good one. His body obeyed it.

The staves had ruined the Valorians' strategy. It was impossible to flank Arin's army, which became a solid column that thrust up the road. The edges of Arin's vanguard began to work forward, fighting to reach the unprotected, muddy sides of the road on which the Valorians stood. With a little luck, Arin would flank *them*.

When his sword cut an enemy open, Arin thought that

he would have chosen no other god to rule him, that none of the hundred could please him so well.

A gift, he thought.

This is nothing, death said. *Did I not make you a promise? Have you not kept faith with me, in hopes of this very moment? See, see what I have for you.*

Arin looked.

Just a few paces away, unhorsed, helmet gone, stood General Trajan.

This was taking too long.

It was full dawn. The stained windows were wild now, lurid with color. Kestrel had reached the end of her line of play. She held a worthy hand, yet dreaded exposing her tiles to the emperor.

It didn't matter what tiles she held. All that mattered was that the game was over, and that the emperor appeared relaxed, lids half-lowered in anticipation, his dark eyes liquid.

"Show me," he said.

Arin spurred his horse forward. The general saw him and stood tall. Arin's mind went blank, he heard nothing, not even death, and he should have been listening, because at the last possible moment, the general fell to one knee and drove his sword deep into the chest of Arin's horse.

As slowly as possible, Kestrel turned her last tile.

Four spiders.

The emperor didn't smile. She almost wished that he had. He closed his eyes once, and when he opened them their expression was even worse than his smile.

He displayed his winning hand.

Four tigers.

Arin was thrown from his shrieking horse. His head rang against the road.

And rang, and rang.

Perspiration glimmered on the emperor's upper lip. He touched it, glanced at his fingers strangely, then returned his attention to Kestrel.

She scraped her chair back.

He swept her dagger from the table and had it up to her throat in one swift movement. He pricked the skin; a tiny trickle of blood.

She'd been stupid, her plan had been stupid, a fool's gamble, yet her mind kept scrabbling for an idea, something else, anything else that could reverse her mistake or make happen what should have already happened.

"Don't take defeat too badly," he said. "If it's any consolation, I had no intention of ever fulfilling my agreement, even if you'd won. But the pleasure of the game was great. Now. Sit."

Her legs gave out beneath her.

"Let's discuss what you owe."

Arin felt the hum of metal in the air.

He rocked his body out of its path, heard the general's sword strike the road.

Arin shoved himself to his feet.

The emperor lowered back into his seat. Kestrel stared at his winning hand, light-headed with fear.

"Does the sight of this trouble you?" Her dagger still in one hand, the emperor turned his tiles facedown. Then he paused, frowning at their backs. He touched one of the two shiny ones, then flipped Kestrel's hand over, studying her tiles' backs. He found, in the boneyard, the two remaining marked tiles. "What is this?"

She made an involuntary sound.

He batted the air as if at an invisible insect. Colored light beamed into the room. The four tiles shone clearly.

"You cheated?" he muttered. "How could you cheat and still lose?"

Arin swung at the general, who cut the blow wide, deflecting it easily, holding it in a semi-bind that forced Arin's sword low. Arin's guard was open. The general was quick, his parry swift. The man's steel was so sharp that Arin didn't feel, at first, when it cut him.

The emperor licked his dry lips. He turned over the two marked tiles in the boneyard. A wolf. A snake. "These are good tiles. Why would you mark tiles and not take them for yourself?" He swallowed. The knot of cartilage in his throat bobbed.

Kestrel saw him begin to understand.

His body began to understand, too.

He lunged for her.

The sword nicked the side of Arin's neck just below the ear. It would have taken off his head if he hadn't recoiled in time.

Arin had been looking at the general's face without really seeing it. He saw it now. He saw that the man knew exactly who he was, and that he longed for Arin's death almost as much as Arin longed for his.

The emperor knocked over the wine. He seized up against the table, hand clamped around Kestrel's dagger.

She stepped back from the table as he shuddered against it. She felt a relief so deep that it didn't even feel like relief. It plunged straight into exhaustion.

"I lied," Kestrel told him.

The emperor tried to push himself upright. She thought he might be trying to do something with the dagger, but his arm had gone rigid. It thumped into the spilled red wine.

"I lied when I said I hadn't come to murder you."

His eyes were wide, stark.

"It never mattered whether I won or lost the game,"

Kestrel said. "Only how long the poison would take to kill you. It comes from a tiny eastern worm. In its purest form, the poison is clear. It dries to a shine. I painted it onto four Bite and Sting tiles. You touched them."

Foam dribbled from his locked mouth.

His breath rasped. It became glottal, the sound of bubbles popping.

Then it ended.

Arin struck back.

As they fought, viciously silent words thudded in his blood: *Mother, father, sister. Kestrel.*

Arin didn't care that the blows his sword hammered against the man's metal body were useless, that there was no art to this, that nothing would pierce the armor, that a few smashed buckles where the general's armor joined was no victory. He could see too little of the man's flesh, couldn't reach it, and he desperately wanted to make him bleed. If he couldn't carve into the general, Arin would bludgeon him. He'd beat until something broke.

The buckles, death said.

Arin shifted the path of his sword in midswipe and curved it down toward the elbow of the general's sword arm, aiming right for where the broken buckles of the general's arm guard flapped loose.

Arin sheered the man's arm off at the elbow.

Blood pumped onto Arin. If the general made a sound, Arin didn't hear it. He was warm and wet.

The general fell. He lay blinking up at the sun, at Arin,

his eyes glazed, mouth moving as if speaking, but Arin heard nothing.

For a moment, Arin faltered.

But there was nothing of her in this man, this enemy at his feet. Arin drew back his sword—more power than necessary for the death blow. He wanted to pour himself into this act.

Vengeance: wine-dark, thick. It flooded Arin's lungs.

Those light brown eyes, on him.

There was that.

That one thing that Kestrel shared with her father.

Arin heard himself speak. His voice sounded far away, as if some part of him had left this road and was as high as the sun, looking down on the half that he had left on earth.

He said, "Kestrel asked me to do this."

For she had.

Arin was a boy, a slave, a grown man, free. He was all of this at once . . . and something else, too. He realized it only now, as he plunged his sword down toward the general's throat.

He hadn't been blessed by the god of death.

Arin *was* the god.

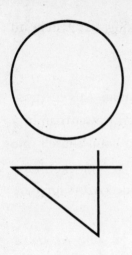

BUT HE STOPPED.

Regret wasn't the right word for what he felt later. Disbelief, maybe. Sometimes, even years after the war, he'd tear out of sleep, sweating, still trapped in the nightmare where he had butchered the father of the woman he loved.

But you didn't, she would tell him.

You didn't.

Tell me. Say it again. Tell me what you did.

Trembling, he would.

His brain had been a glass ball. Nothing in it but echoes. His mother's scent. Father's voice. How Anireh's gaze had held him from across the room, and her eyes said, *Survive.* They said, *Love,* and *I'm sorry.* They said, *Little brother.*

And then silence. It became silent in Arin's head as he stood on the road. He stopped hearing voices. He thought about how it had seemed strange that Risha would plot the emperor's death, yet refuse to kill him herself. Arin understood now. He knew how it was to have no family: like living in a house with no roof. Even if Kestrel were here, and begged him—*Let your sword fall, do it, please, now*—Arin wasn't sure that he could make her an orphan.

And he wasn't sure that she *would* beg that if she were gazing down as he did on the graying face of her dying father, the man's eyes sky-bright as he tried to speak, his remaining hand fumbling against his chest, just above his heart.

A throbbing radiance burned inside Arin; he hadn't realized the pitch revenge could reach, how murder could come this close to desire.

He felt his eyes sting, because he knew what he was going to do.

He didn't want to be here. He wondered why we can't remember when our mothers carried us inside them: the dark and steady heart, how it was the whole of the world, and no one harmed us, and we harmed no one.

Arin thought that if he didn't kill this man his memory of his mother would fade. It already had, over time. Someday she would be as far away as a star.

But he couldn't do it.

He had to do it.

Tell me what you did.

Arin dropped his sword, dropped to his knees, yanked the woven baldric from the fallen man's shoulder, and used it to make a tourniquet to save the person he hated most.

After the battle, and after Roshar had accepted the Valorians' surrender, when Arin was sick with worry because Kestrel hadn't yet returned from Sythiah, he went to the healers' tent.

The general was asleep, his cauterized arm swathed in bandages, his armor removed. A drug had been forced down him. It had been a violent scene. Even now, asleep, the man was under guard and bound in chains at the ankles, his remaining hand strapped tight to his side.

Arin tugged at his hair until his scalp hurt. If Kestrel wasn't back by noon he was going to ride to Sythiah. His brain was crawling in his skull, his stomach was a shriveled lump.

He hated seeing the general. He hated seeing even Verex (whom he halfway liked) limping around the camp, teeming with worry—for Risha, but also for Kestrel, which made Arin feel absurdly possessive, as if Verex were trying to rob him by feeling in any way similar to Arin. Arin became insufferable, he knew it, but he was constantly having to wrestle down the knowledge that if something had happened to Kestrel his heart would turn to salt.

He didn't know what to do with his hands as he looked down at the sleeping general. Arin thrust them into his pockets before they went for the throat. He reminded himself why he had come.

He ripped open the man's jacket. Arin reached for the inside breast pocket, located exactly where the man had tried to touch his chest as he had lain bleeding on the road.

Arin's fingers met paper. He pulled it out, its texture suede-soft from having been handled so much. It had been unfolded and folded many times.

It was sheet music. At first, Arin didn't understand what he looked at. Kestrel's handwriting. Herrani script. Musical notation in crisp black. His own name leaped off the page.

Dear Arin.

Then he recognized the music as the sonata Kestrel had been studying when he'd entered her music room at the imperial palace in late spring. It had been the last time he'd seen her before the tundra. He had thought it would be the last time he would ever see her.

Arin hastened from the tent. He couldn't read the letter here.

But he didn't know if he could read it anywhere, if any place would be private enough, because being alone meant he'd still be with himself, and he hated to remember how he'd left Kestrel that day, and what had befallen her after.

He was desperate to read it.

He couldn't bear to read it.

He resented that her father had kept it.

He wondered what it meant that her father had kept it.

Arin was only vaguely aware of having stumbled through the noisy camp and into the woods. The thought of reading the letter felt like a violation, like he'd be reading a letter meant for someone else.

Yet it had been addressed to him.

Dear Arin.

Arin read.

"Are you all right?"

Arin glanced up at Roshar, then returned his attention to the horse. He ran a hand down the inside of its front left leg and picked up the hoof, cupping its front. With his free hand, he cleaned the hoof with a pick, brushed it off, and used a knife to probe the outer edges of the hoof, looking for the source of the problem. Steam rose from a nearby bucket of hot, salted water. It was near noon.

"Arin."

"Just thinking." Kestrel's written words still radiated through him, making him feel larger inside than he had been before, as if he'd swallowed the sun and it somehow fit, and blazed and ached and left him dazzled: half-blind but still seeing things more clearly than before.

"Well, stop it," Roshar said. "You've been looking either dour or dreamy and neither really suits the victorious leader of his free people."

Arin snorted. The horse, feeling his knife touch a sore spot, tried to pull her hoof away. He held it fast, supporting it from below with his knee.

"You could at least make a rousing speech," Roshar said.

"Can't. I'm riding to Sythiah."

Roshar made a strangled sound.

"Not on this horse," Arin said. "She's lame."

"What are you *doing*?"

"She was limping. It hurt to look at her. An abscess, I think. She must have stepped on something sharp."

"Arin, you're not a damn farrier. Someone else can do this."

"*Tssah*," Arin hissed in sympathy when he found the abscess. The horse tried again to tug away, but he punctured the sealed wound, which instantly dribbled black pus. He worked on opening the abscess, then pressed the rest of the pus out. "Bring that bucket closer, will you?"

"Oh, certainly. I live to please."

Arin lowered the hoof into the bucket's hot water. The horse, already in pain, stamped, splashing the water as she reared her head, but Arin grabbed the halter and brought her head down, soothing her as he watched the foot to make sure it stayed in the bucket.

"Arin, why are you so transparent? Whenever you worry, you start fixing things. Draining nasty gunk from a hoof is the least of it. I don't know what's worse, watching you do that or knowing how hard it will always be for you to keep yourself to *yourself*."

Arin stroked the horse's neck. She stamped again, but began to calm.

"We won," Roshar said, "and Kestrel is fine. We've discussed this. That poison is highly toxic."

"But she's not back."

"She *will* be. You need to seize your political moment. If you don't, someone else will."

Arin squinted at him. "You call me 'transparent' as if that's a bad thing, but I don't need to make a speech for my people to see what I am."

Roshar shut his mouth. He looked ready to say something else, then didn't, because Kestrel and Risha rode into camp.

the city, some on foot, and many wounded. Kestrel stayed away from the wagons that carried them. "I can't see him," she told Arin when the army paused to rest. But part of her wanted to use this time to see her father.

"You don't have to," Arin said. In the silence that followed, as they walked away from the wagons, fragments of everything he had told her gained shape and terribly vivid color: her father's severed arm, Arin's lost vengeance, the letter that she hadn't even recognized when Arin gave it to her.

It was a moment before Kestrel realized that a jittery energy had come over Arin. He was biting his lower lip and his hands were making stunted gestures as if he were trying to speak but couldn't. Finally, he said, "You asked for his death. I didn't do it. Should I have? Did I do the wrong thing?"

A gentle feeling flowed into her. She caught his erratic hands and held them between hers. "No," she said. "You didn't."

That letter.

She read and reread it, in the high summer grasses on the sides of the road, at night by lamplight. The pen's ink had aged, gone brownish. She imagined her father reading under the sun during the campaign. Spots of the paper had a waxy transparency. The residue of oil, used to polish a weapon? Her father liked to clean his own dagger. She searched for meaning in the smudges of dirty fingerprints under certain words, but nothing, really, was evidence of anything except the urgent scrawl of her own handwriting. The bottom half of the letter was warped with rusted blood, the final sentences lost. Kestrel couldn't remember what she'd written there. Like a worn map, the letter folded instantly under the slightest pressure.

The paper looked quiet in her hand, tucked in on itself. Kestrel wanted to reach through time and comfort the girl who'd written it, even if the only comfort she could offer would be understanding. She wanted to imagine a different story, one where her father read the letter and understood it, too, and returned it to his daughter, telling her that she should never have had to write anything like that. *I love you. I'd do anything for you,* the letter said, and it was hard for Kestrel to keep from crumpling the paper in her fist when she realized that these words were what she had always wanted her father to say to her.

Three days from the city, the army had made camp for the night. Kestrel went to the healers' tent.

Her father noticed the moment she entered. He flinched, then met her gaze, and she didn't know what was right to feel—the sort of soft, heavy comfort that touched her at the sight of her father, simply because he was her father, or the rage in her chest, or how she wanted to mourn his maimed arm, and wanted to tell him that he deserved it.

"Why did you keep my letter?" she asked.

He said nothing.

She asked again.

He turned his face from her.

She kept asking until she heard her voice crumbling and thought that Risha had been wrong when she'd said that forgiveness was like mud, as if it could take whatever shape you needed.

It was hard; it was stone.

She walked away from the tent.

Verex said that he and Risha were leaving. They wanted to ride to the eastern plains, and maybe sail from Dacra's eastern coast to see what lay in the unexplored waters beyond. He had no wish to inherit the empire. He asked that rumors of his death be spread.

He saw Kestrel's fallen expression. "You think I should go back to the capital instead, and become emperor."

"Honestly, I don't want you to go anywhere. I'll miss you."

His brown eyes warmed. "I'll visit. Risha, too. She wants

to train you in your weapon of choice until you feel properly dangerous."

Kestrel opened her mouth to say that'd be a useless effort, but then it struck her that it might not be, and whether it was or wasn't didn't matter as much as the happiness the offer gave her. "I like her, too."

They were leaning against the trunk of a very broad tree near the encampment. White spores from its flowering branches floated down. She wondered if a Herrani would think this the sign of a god, and if so, which one.

"I'm sorry," she told Verex.

He knew what she meant. "I had no love for my father. He certainly had none for me."

"Still."

"I'm not sure what else you could have done. If anything . . ." He slouched against the bark. "I feel worst about being relieved." A spore landed on the tip of his boot, then floated away. In a low voice, he added, "And a bit of a coward. I worry that if I became emperor, I'd become like him."

"Not you. Never."

"And guilty, because I'm abandoning a country that might collapse on itself. It's not clear who'll rule now."

"I bet you have some ideas. I can think of a few senators who'd claw their way to power. Or the captain of the guard. I don't remember everyone at court, though, or who owes whom, or bears a grudge. You could give me a clearer picture, and I could . . . well, keep an eye on the situation in the capital."

He raised his brows. "A spy again, Kestrel?"

"Spymaster, maybe."

He picked up a thin, fallen twig and snapped it into tiny sticks.

"I think Arin needs one," she said.

"You'd be the best. I wish, however, that you didn't always risk yourself. You're too fond of a gamble."

She shrugged helplessly. "I am who I am."

Affection tinged his smile. Then he sobered and said, "I used to believe I could stomach taking my father's place. But Risha would be miserable. I would, too."

Kestrel, suddenly fierce, said, "Then be happy."

"I will," he said, "if *you* will."

Feathery white fluff came down from the tree as he described the political intricacies of the Valorian court, and then told her about how the puppy he'd given her at court had grown into an enormous, sweet-tempered dog living with a family in the foothills of the Valorian mountains. There were small children who adored her, even when she chewed their shoes. Maris—a young courtier Kestrel had intensely disliked until she found that actually, she didn't—had married well and was gleefully smug about it. As for Jess, Verex said that she had gone to the southern isles at the start of the war. "I wish I knew more," he said.

Kestrel longed to see her. She wondered if she ever would, and if they could mend the things wrong between them.

"I saw you go to the healers' tent the other day," Verex said.

"He won't talk with me."

"Try again."

When Risha and Verex left, two days before the army would reach the city, Kestrel kept her smile as she kissed their cheeks. At first it was hard to be strong in that way, and not let the farewell overwhelm her. But then she noticed Roshar, who had avoided his little sister since her return as if afraid of her, lingering nearby. Risha approached him and whispered something Kestrel couldn't hear. Roshar's expression eased. He didn't speak in reply; he simply clasped Risha's hands and kissed them.

Kestrel thought that maybe she had been wrong, and Risha had been wrong, about forgiveness, that it was neither mud nor stone, but resembled more the drifting white spores. They came loose from the trees when they were ready. Soft to the touch, but made to be let go, so that they could find a place to plant and grow.

She went to the tent again.

This time, her father spoke before she could. "Give me your dagger."

Hot tears rushed to her eyes. "Don't you dare."

"Unbind my hand. Give me your dagger."

"No."

"Just this one last thing."

"You can't ask me to help you kill yourself."

He no longer looked at her.

"Why did you keep my letter?" she asked yet again.

"You know why."

"What, regret?"

"That's not the right word."

"Then *what?*"

"There are no words."

"Find some."

"I can't."

"Now."

He swallowed. "I want to. I didn't know . . . how every-thing would become impossible. This is what happens when you destroy the thing most precious to you."

"You *chose* to do it."

"Yes."

"Why?"

He didn't say, but his eyes became clear hard shells, and she knew that it hadn't been only his code of honor that had made him tell the emperor of her treason. Her father had wanted to hurt her, because she had hurt him.

He said, "It didn't seem real when I was doing it. Like I wasn't awake."

"Do you know," she whispered, "what they did to me in the mines?"

He closed his eyes.

She described it. He let her. Water slid from beneath his eyelids.

"Kestrel," he said finally. "You know that there is only one solution. I can't be a father to you."

"But you *are.*"

"There's no place for me here. Am I to be a prisoner for the rest of my life?"

This had been discussed—loudly. Roshar was in favor of a public execution. Arin had lost his temper in a way that

Kestrel hadn't seen in a long time, had shouted back that the general's fate was Kestrel's choice alone.

"I don't know," Kestrel told her father.

There was a silence.

She said, "How can you not even ask for forgiveness?"

"Impossible."

"Ask."

For a long time, he said nothing. "I can't ask for something no one could give. I ask for mercy."

Her vision blurred, and Kestrel knew that forgiveness and mercy would take years for them both, and that she needed every single minute of that time.

She said that she still loved him, because it was true. He owed her better answers than the ones he had given, and even if he never had them, it was her right to keep asking. She would never give him her dagger. "I tried so hard to live in your world," she told him. "Now it's your turn to live in mine."

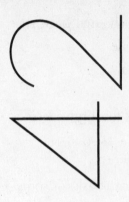

ARIN SHOULD HAVE EXPECTED IT, BUT SOME-
how didn't.

So many flowers. All the summer blooms must have been
cut from the gardens, which would be naked for weeks.
When the army came through the gate, a roar vibrated the
stone walls, and Arin flinched in surprise, hands tightening
on the reins, for the tiniest moment believing that the sound
meant danger. Then he saw the glowing faces of people
thronging the streets and thought, *Ah, happy.* Which made
him happy, and as Kestrel smiled at him from her seat on
Javelin, a pink petal clinging to her cheek, it occurred to him
that he might have to grow comfortable with happiness,
because it might not abandon him this time.

Then Kestrel's head turned, and he saw her survey the
Dacran-Herrani army unfurled behind them in Lahirrin's
main street, a tension in the line of her mouth. She said, "I'm
not sure it's wise to bring all the soldiers within the city
walls."

"This is everyone's victory. Everyone must be honored."

"I know."

"But?"

"Our eastern allies outnumber us."

He knew what she was getting at. "They always have."

"If they want this country, it'd be easy for them to take it . . . especially from within the city walls."

Arin glanced at Roshar, who'd ridden ahead to meet the queen. "I trust him."

"Yes, I know."

Arin paused his horse. Javelin stopped, too. Flowers flurried down around them. He said, "It would hurt me to suspect him."

"That's why I do it for you."

A cloth dropped onto his head from above, from a window of one of the tall, narrow homes near the market. Startled, blind, Arin tugged it from his face, his horse shying beneath him.

It was an old Herrani flag, stitched with the royal crest.

Arin said, "But the royal line is gone."

"They're looking for something to call you," Kestrel said, nudging Javelin forward.

"Not this. It's not right."

"Don't worry. They'll find the right words to describe you."

"*And* you."

"Oh, that's easy."

"It is?" It seemed impossible to name everything she was to him.

Kestrel's expression was serious, luminous. He loved to see her like this. "They'll say that I'm yours," she told him, "just as you are mine."

When Sarsine saw Kestrel, her eyes narrowed to mere cracks and Kestrel became very conscious that Sarsine was a tall woman. "For someone with a reputation for being so smart," Sarsine said, "you act like you haven't a thought in your head. Did it never occur to you that I'd worry when you disappeared from the city with no word?"

"I didn't exactly mean to leave."

"Oh, so it just *happened*."

"Yes."

"The gods made you do it."

Kestrel laughed. "Maybe they did." Then, earnestly, she said, "I'm sorry, Sarsine."

Sarsine folded her arms. "Then make it up to me."

"How?"

Sarsine's expression softened. Now there was an inquisitive gleam in her eye. "Start with the night you left. End with this very moment. And tell me *everything*."

So Kestrel did.

There was to be a city-wide feast to celebrate the military victory, with a banquet at the governor's palace, where Queen Inishanaway would preside. The cooks in Arin's house were hard at work, slaughtering every chicken in the yard, pulping erasti fruit and thumping dough against floured tables.

Arin was in the still room, trying to soothe the anxiety of a woman who was saying that she had just preserved the jams, and must *all* of them be used for the banquet, every last one? She didn't think the Dacrans appreciated ilea fruit. Why serve something they wouldn't love as much as the Herrani did? It would be best, surely, to keep at least *those* jars for winter.

Trying to explain the politics of such lavish consumption tangled Arin up in frustrated half sentences, because it didn't make much sense to him, either, to consume every edible thing in one night.

And then he heard Roshar's accented voice in Herrani drifting down the hall from the kitchens.

". . . you don't understand. The piece of meat must be the finest, cut from the loin, seasoned with *this* spice, not *that* one . . ."

Arin excused himself, told the woman he'd discuss jams later, and followed the prince's voice.

". . . and it must be well roasted on the outside, almost charred, yet bloody inside. Bright pink. Listen. This is crucial. If anything goes wrong, the banquet will be ruined."

Arin entered the main kitchen to find the prince haranguing the head cook, who slid a half-lidded look of annoyed sufferance at Arin.

"There you are." Roshar beamed. "I need your help, Arin."

"For the preparation of meat?"

"It's very important. You must impress this importance upon your cook here. The fate of political relations between my country and yours hangs in the balance."

"Because of meat."

"It's for his tiger," said the cook.

Arin palmed his face, eyes squeezed shut. "Your tiger."

"He's very particular," said Roshar.

"You can't bring the tiger to the banquet."

"Little Arin has missed me. I will not be parted from him."

"Would you consider changing his name?"

"No."

"What if I begged?"

"Not a chance."

"Roshar, the tiger has grown."

"And what a sweet big boy he is."

"You can't bring him into a dining hall filled with hundreds of people."

"He'll behave. He has the mien and manners of a prince."

"Oh, like *you*?"

"I resent your tone."

"I'm not sure you can control him."

"Has he ever been aught but the gentlest of creatures? Would you deny your namesake the chance to bear witness to our victorious celebration? And, of course, to the vision of you and Kestrel: side by side, Herrani and Valorian, a love for the ages. The stuff of songs, Arin! How you'll get *married*, and make *babies*—"

"Gods, Roshar, shut up."

Even if Arin hadn't known how much Kestrel hated to enter the palace built for the Valorian governor during the period of colonization, he would have seen it in her tense shoulders, the way she touched the dagger at her hip, and practically snarled at Roshar when the prince had suggested that surely she could forgo, this one night, the barbarism of openly bearing a weapon.

Arin gave him a warning look. The prince pretended to look innocently confused, then shrugged and moved to walk ahead of them, the half-grown tiger slinking at his heels. The tiger was eerily docile, even for a young one raised by humans. It pushed its head up under Roshar's hand like a housecat. Arin watched its solid sway, the already powerful shoulder blades rising and falling under its fur. Arin sensed but couldn't name the origin of what made people (animals, too, apparently) long to follow the prince. With an uncomfortable prickle, he suspected that if he asked and Roshar deigned to give a straight answer, the prince would say that whatever it was, Arin possessed it, too.

A strange feeling: as if filaments trailed from Arin's body. A thousand fishing lines snagging attention. Here and there. Little tugs. People caught on the lines. The way sometimes people couldn't look him in the eye, and when they did they became fish trying to breathe air.

He wished it weren't like that.

He knew it would be necessary.

Roshar and the tiger disappeared inside, leaving Kestrel and Arin alone on the path.

Kestrel was stiff, her delicate shoes planted in the walkway's gravel. She had lifted the hem of her storm-green skirts, the gesture of a lady, but he saw how she made fists of the fabric.

"I'm sorry," he said, guessing what troubled her: the memory of the Firstwinter Rebellion. Her dead friends, Arin's deception, the halls of the governor's palace choked with corpses.

She gave him a narrow look. "Part of you isn't sorry."

He couldn't deny it.

But she softened and said, "I'm not innocent either. I, too, feel sorry and not sorry about things I've done." She let her dress's hem fall to the stones and touched three fingers to the back of his hand.

Arin forgot, for a moment, where he was and what they were discussing. A marvel: that such a light touch could feel like a whole caress, that his body could ignite so easily.

Now she looked amused.

"Let's leave." He slid a hand beneath her loose hair and thumbed the slope of her neck, feeling the fluttery pulse there. Her expression changed, amusement melting into slow pleasure. He said, "Let's not go in."

"Arin." She sighed. "We *must* go in." Her slightly parted mouth closed again into a tense line.

"What else is troubling you?"

"The queen hasn't said a word to you."

"Well," Arin said, uncomfortable, thinking of various reasons for Inisha's silence.

"*All* of the Dacrans are too quiet."

"Not Roshar."

"Him, too. He just says a lot without meaning much."

Arin paused, then said, "I believe in our alliance."

"I want to, too."

He offered her his hand.

They went inside.

They sat at a table on a raised dais in the dining hall, the four of them in a line, Arin and the queen occupying the center and Kestrel and Roshar to their sides, an arrangement Roshar maneuvered without seeming to as the hundreds of people already seated watched them.

The queen gave Arin a sidelong glance, her black eyes unreadable. She said nothing, and didn't look at him again.

Roshar, the tiger curled at his feet, barely touched his food as the first courses were served, but instead drank the green Dacran liqueur he favored. Arin saw, beyond the silhouette of the queen, how Roshar clenched and released the glass. His fingers were unsteady.

"Brother." The queen spoke as if nudging him.

"Leave me alone." He refilled his cup.

When people entered bearing the main course—including, Arin noted with wry amusement, the fastidiously prepared loin for the tiger, on its very own platter—Roshar stood, swaying a little. The room hushed. He scanned the faces, Dacran and Herrani alike.

"People of the hundred," he said, using an ancient Herrani phrase Arin was surprised he knew, "who leads you?"

So many cried Arin's name that it no longer sounded like his name.

"Do you trust your country to him?"

Yes.

"Would you say that Herran is his?"

Yes.

Sudden distrust slicked down Arin's spine.

Roshar raised his hand to quiet the roaring crowd, and Arin was reminded of Cheat relishing his role as an auctioneer. A stone rose in his throat. Kestrel's hand tightened on his, but Arin no longer felt wholly there.

"Enough," said the queen . . . not so much in reprimand, but rather as if telling him to get to the point.

"I have fought for Arin, bled for him. I hold him in my heart. I have even named my tiger after him—no small honor. And yet, we have a problem. Arin of Herran was not always my friend, and once committed an offense against me that caused my queen to award me control over all he owns: his life, his belongings, and—since you say he possesses it—his country. I've been told to take from Arin what is due to me. I've been told it is mine by law. Must I? Yes. Will my people support my claim, with force if necessary? They will. Will my queen rise in admiration of me? Oh, indeed. And so I must.

"No, Arin. Sit down. Otherwise you'll make an ass out of yourself, and *that* role is mine. I see my tiger's meal is here. You, there. Yes, you. With the platter. Bear it forth."

Kestrel laughed. Arin felt rather than saw that she had relaxed beside him, aglow with mirth. He sank back into his chair, because now he too understood Roshar's game. He wanted to sag with relief. He wanted to strangle the prince.

And thank him.

"There." Roshar flourished a hand at the platter. "Arin the tiger's meal. Since I've been ordered to take from Arin what belongs to Arin, I shall." Roshar returned to his seat, platter in hand, and commenced cutting the meat. He took a bite. "Mmm. This is excellent. So well done. Now, as for what belongs to Arin the *human*, I relinquish any claim to it. Nothing of his was ever mine to take, nor will ever be. What belongs to him, I defend his right to keep, out of my love for him, and his for me." He looked directly at the queen as he ate. "This is delicious. Exactly the way I like it."

The queen forced a smile.

"Oh, and would someone bring another slice of loin? Raw, please. My tiger is hungry."

"I DON'T WANT YOU TO GO." WAVES ROCKED against the pier. The sun was too bright. Weathered boards creaked beneath Arin's feet.

"Only because you enjoy a good bully. Someone to make you behave as you ought."

"No, Roshar."

"You know well enough what to do now. You'll be fine."

"That's not why."

"Why you'll miss me? I admit that the impending absence of my keen wit would make anyone sad."

"Not exactly."

"Now *I'm* getting sad, just thinking about how it would feel to be parted from my sweet self. Lucky me: I will always have my own company."

"What you said at the banquet was true."

"*Everything* I say is true."

"That I love you."

Roshar's face went still. "I said that?"

"You know that you did."

"That was more for the drama of the moment."

"Liar."

"I am, aren't I?" Roshar said slowly. "I really am. Arin." His voice roughened. "You'll see me again."

"Soon," Arin told him, and embraced him. Then they broke away and maybe some would have thought that the sun was a little cruel, for how its brightness allowed no subterfuge in their expressions, and everything that could be seen was shown. But Arin thought that it was a kindness. He wanted to be a mirror, to reflect what Roshar was to him.

A launch waited in the water below. Arin wished him fair tides. He watched until the launch reached Roshar's ship, then watched as the ship, with the rest of the entire Dacran fleet, left his city's bay.

He glimpsed Sarsine as he walked through the city. She had a laden basket—it dragged at her arm, making its weight known even from far away. Her faintly harried expression softened at the sight of him.

Arin took the basket from her. "Coming or going?"

"I've an errand here, and won't be home until late."

"Shall I guess what brings you to town?"

"You can try."

He peeked in the basket. Bread, still warm from the oven. A bottle of liquor. Long, flat pieces of wood. Rolls of gauze. "A picnic . . . with a wounded soldier? Sarsine," he teased, "is it true love? What's the wood for? Wait, don't tell me. I'm not sure I want to know."

She swatted him. "The cartwright's oldest daughter has a broken arm."

It dropped ice to the bottom of his stomach. He thought of the ruined bodies he'd seen, including the ones he himself had ruined. He realized that he had somehow expected that he'd never have to think again about the way people damage other people.

The night of the invasion. Kestrel's back. His own. Roshar's scarred face. His own. The way a body on the battlefield could look as if it had never been human, and that was exactly what Arin had wanted to do to Kestrel's father, who was in this city, *his* city, in a prison made to be comfortable, when no comfort could return the man's arm, and no walls could imprison Arin's knowledge of what he had done and wanted to do and couldn't regret.

Yet he *did* regret.

He could not.

He did.

"Arin, are you all right?"

"How?" he managed. "How did her arm break?"

"She fell off a ladder."

He must have visibly relaxed, because his cousin raised her brows and looked ready to scold.

"I imagined something worse," he tried to explain.

She appeared to understand his relief that pain, if it had to come, came this time without malice. Just an accident. Done by no one. The luck, sometimes, of life. A bad slip that ends with bread, and someone to bind you.

It was a long walk home. But a pleasure to regain, unexpectedly, the memory of walking home as a child, secure in the knowledge that he would find everything he loved there, whole and unbroken, his certainty so absolute that he hadn't even been aware of it.

The city gave way to cypress trees. His feet were dusty. The sun made every scent stronger: his hot skin, the roasted path, a breath of lavender blown from somewhere he couldn't see.

The god of death was silent. Not gone. Inhabiting Arin, but comfortably, in a kind of kinship. Arin kept company with death, but death was not all that lived inside him.

A girl in his heart. In his home.

Waiting for him.

There were old stone steps cut into the final hill. His pace quickened.

The house rose into view, sequined with open windows. A warhorse was cropping the meadow.

Although Arin was eager to see Kestrel, he would have to wait. He caught threads of music from far away. As he came across the grass, the piano's melody strengthened. It opened within him a happiness that gathered and gleamed . . . glossy, but the way water is, with weight.

A lovely fatigue claimed him. He lay down on the grass and listened. He thought about how Kestrel had slept on the palace lawn and dreamed of him. When she had told him this, he'd wished that it had been real. He tried to imagine the dream, then found himself dreaming. Everything made sense in his dream yet he felt the tenuousness of this perfect reason.

The arch of Kestrel's bare foot. An old tale about the god of death and the seamstress. Arin would lose, upon waking, his understanding of why touching Kestrel would arouse the memory of a story he'd not thought about in a long time.

He dreamed: one stocking balled in his fist, and the stray question of how it had been made, who had sewn this? He saw his hands—though they did not look like his hands— measuring and cutting fabric, sewing invisible stitches. A dark-haired boy tumbled from a room, a god-mark upon his brow. When a guest entered and said, *Weave me the cloth of yourself*, Arin thought that he was the forbidding guest and the child and the sewing girl all at once. She said, *I'm going to miss you when I wake up.*

Don't wake up, he answered.

But he did.

Kestrel, beside him on the grass, said, "Did I wake you? I didn't mean to."

It took him a velvety moment to understand that this was real. The air was quiet. An insect beat its clear wings. She brushed hair from his brow. Now he was very awake.

"You were sleeping so sweetly," she said.

"Dreaming." He touched her tender mouth.

"About what?"

"Come closer, and I'll tell you."

But he forgot. He kissed her, and became lost in the exquisite sensation of his skin becoming too tight for his body. He murmured other things instead. A secret, a want, a promise. A story, in its own way.

She curled her fingers into the green earth.

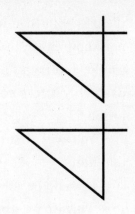

THE NIGHT WAS FRESH AND FORETOLD SUM-
mer's end. The slow, hot day gave way to a breeze as cool as
laundered sheets.

Kestrel, in the stables, fed Javelin a carrot. She promised
him apples. "Soon," she said, and wondered if horses notice
how the seasons change. Do they see apples swell on the
trees? Have they any way to mark the passage of time, or is
it always *now* for them, with no sense of *then*? Maybe *soon*
had no meaning either.

She'd meant to visit her father. She'd wanted to ask him
about her childhood. Her memory was still a tattered thing
sometimes, and Arin couldn't tell her what he himself didn't
know. She wanted to ask her father: How was it when you
gave me Javelin? What was my first word? Did you save my
milk teeth, or did my nurse plant them in the ground as the
Herrani do? What was I like, and how were you with me,
and with my mother?

She wouldn't have known some of the answers even if
her memory hadn't been damaged. Everyone loses pieces of

the past. But then it occurred to her that her father might not know either, or that he would, and say nothing. Or he would, and try to bargain his memories for the use of her dagger. Kestrel's courage failed her. She didn't go to the prison.

"You will when you can," Arin had said when she'd told him.

"I should be able to now."

"This isn't a wound in the flesh. No one can say how long it takes to heal."

Then she had noticed that Arin's fingernails were blackened, and how he kept reaching into his pocket as if to reassure himself that something was there.

She had told herself not to guess. But she could never help guessing. A smile warmed her face.

He shut his eyes in mock chagrin. "Gods, can I keep *nothing* from you?"

"I didn't mean to."

"Devious thing. I won't give it to you yet. It's for Ninarrith."

Time seemed strange; it was as if the ring were already on her smallest finger, the most vulnerable one.

"It's simple," Arin had hastened to say.

"I will love it."

"Will you wear it?"

"Yes."

"Always?"

"Yes," she had said, "if you show me how to make one for you, too."

Kestrel gave her horse a final caress. It was full night. She left the stables. Fireflies spangled the black lawn.

She thought about Arin's expression when she'd asked if he would teach her how to forge a ring for him, and the whole conversation glowed within her like one of those fireflies. Watching them, you'd almost think that a firefly winks out of existence, then comes to life, vanishes again, returns. That when it's not lit, it's not there at all.

But it is.

A night breeze ruffled a curtain. Arin's bedroom—she realized with soft surprise—had come to feel like her own. He was lazily tracing circles on her belly. It hypnotized her into a rare, pure unthinking.

He settled back on the bed, propped on one elbow. "It occurs to me that there is something we have never done."

Her thoughts rushed back. She arched one brow.

He moved to whisper in her ear.

"Yes," she laughed. "Let's."

"Now?"

"Now."

So they reached for dressing robes and the bedside lamp, and padded barefoot through his suite, rushing slightly, and then through the silent house, suppressing giddy breaths. They couldn't look each other in the face; a wild, loud joyousness threatened to break free if they did. They wound down the staircase and into the parlor.

They shut the door behind them, but still . . .

"We are going to wake the whole house," Kestrel said. "How should we do this?"

She led him to her piano. "Easy."

He placed a palm on the instrument as if already feeling it vibrate with music. He cleared his throat. "Now that I think about it, I'm a little nervous."

"You've sung for me before."

"Not the same."

"Arin. I've wanted to do this for a long time."

Her words silenced him, steadied him.

Anticipation lifted within her like the fragrance of a garden under the rain. She sat at the piano, touching the keys. "Ready?"

He smiled. "Play."

Author's Note

I'm grateful to the following books, among others, for their inspiration and guidance: Edward Said's *Orientalism*, Saidiya V. Hartman's *Scenes of Subjection: Terror, Slavery, and Self-Making in Nineteenth-Century America*, Linda Colley's *Captives: Britain, Empire, and the World, 1600–1850*, Herodotus's *The Histories*, Frederick Douglass's *Narrative of the Life of Frederick Douglass, an American Slave*, Susan Sontag's *Regarding the Pain of Others*, Elaine Scarry's *The Body in Pain: The Making and Unmaking of the World*, Sun Tzu's *The Art of War*, Arrian's *The Campaigns of Alexander*, Jacob de Gheyn's *The Renaissance Drill Book*, and Bert S. Hall's *Weapons and Warfare in Renaissance Europe*.

Thank you to friends who have read drafts or portions of drafts: Renée Ahdieh, Marianna Baer, Olivia Benowitz, Kristin Cashore, Donna Freitas, Daphne Benedis-Grab, Anne Heltzel, Mordicai Knode, Sarah Mesle, Mary E. Pearson, Jill Santopolo, and Eliot Schrefer. Many other friends, too, talked with me about various issues concerning this book, like Sarah MacLean (about amnesia); my husband Thomas Philippon (about military strategy); Robin Wasserman (about secret things); and the aforementioned Olivia, Miriam Jacobson, Nadine Knight, Sarah Wall-Randell, and Kate Moncrief (about horses). Olivia and I had several exchanges about when Arin treats a horse's hoof; her suggestions and expertise were critical. Drew Gorman-Lewis, Associate Professor of Earth and Space Sciences at the University of Washington, talked with me at length about the geology and terrain of my fictional tundra and the real-life properties of sulfur. Tony Swatton, a modern day swordsmith, gave me key advice for how Arin might transform his father's sword into a dagger. Tony can be found at his shop (and forge) The Sword and the Stone, and hosts a Web series called *Man at Arms*. Thanks to Dan Wolfe for putting me in touch with Tony, and to Becky Rosenthal, for passing the phone to Drew (and for being my very dear friend).

My publishing house, Macmillan, is the best. I trust Janine O'Malley, my editor, with my figurative life, and I applaud her and everyone else in-house, especially my publicist, Gina Gagliano, and Mary Van Akin, Simon Boughton, Molly Brouillette, Jean Feiwel, Liz Fithian, Katie Halata, Angus Killick, Kathryn Little, Karen Ninnis, Joy Peskin, Cynthia Ritter, Caitlin Sweeny, Allison Verost, Ashley Woodfolk, and Jon Yaged.

As always, I'm deeply appreciative of my agent, Charlotte Sheedy, as well as everyone at the Charlotte Sheedy Literary Agency, Joan Rosen in particular.

The close of a series is a strange place to inhabit: a kind of nimbus of sadness and excitement. It reminds me of Angela Carter's portrayal of in-between times, like the solstice, or liminal states when one is neither truly one thing or the other. As she knew well, uncertainty (and its eventual fulfillment) is the essence of fairy tales. It is a perfect fairy tale to me that I have written a book and you have read it. I'm grateful to all my readers, including librarians, booksellers, and bloggers, and want to acknowledge Stephanie Sinclair and Kat Kennedy of the blog Cuddlebuggery in particular, because they were the first people to review *The Winner's Curse*. I saw their reviews on an incredibly snowy day, and it was magic to discover that two total strangers understood my book in the way I had hoped it would be understood. I thank them, and you, too.

Photograph Stephen Grossman

MARIE RUTKOSKI is the author of the Winner's Trilogy, *The Shadow Society*, and the Kronos Chronicles, which includes *The Cabinet of Wonders*. She is also a professor of English literature at Brooklyn College, where she teaches Shakespeare, children's literature, and creative writing. She lives in New York City with her husband and two sons.

marierutkoski.com